BREAKING
THE
DARK

Praise for *Breaking the Dark* . . .

'Fresh, lively, insightful – from page one, Lisa owned Jessica, and she owned me. Astonishing. The voice and dialogue are wry with a whiff of hard-boiled. The action scenes hit like a chop. Honest, earnest, and a really cracking story.' A. J. Finn

'Exhilarating, twisty and original. Agatha Christie meets *Black Mirror*!' Claire Douglas

'Immersive, page-turning, addictive, fresh and fun – *Breaking the Dark* will go down a storm with Lisa Jewell fans, with Jessica Jones fans, and with anyone who loves a fantastic story, brilliantly told. I adored it!' Andrea Mara

'Jewell at the height of her powers: the pace doesn't let up, the characters never once slip . . . Tricksy, endlessly interesting and pure entertainment, don't miss this one.' Gillian McAllister

'A classic Lisa Jewell with an amazing supernatural twist!' Jenny Colgan

'A fun, entertaining read that really packs a punch!' Shari Lapena

'A novel that reveals the depth and complexity of one of the most fascinating and indomitable characters in the Marvel canon. Lisa Jewell has found secret reservoirs of strength and perseverance in Jessica Jones that only a writer of her skill could articulate.' S. A. Cosby

'I was hooked from the start and couldn't turn the pages fast enough. Original, clever and cinematic.' Alice Feeney

Also by Lisa Jewell

Ralph's Party
Thirtynothing
One-Hit Wonder
A Friend of the Family
Vince & Joy
31 Dream Street
The Truth About Melody Browne
After the Party
The Making of Us
Before I Met You
The House We Grew Up In
The Third Wife
The Girls
I Found You
Then She Was Gone
Watching You
The Family Upstairs
Invisible Girl
The Night She Disappeared
The Family Remains
None of This is True

MARVEL

BREAKING
THE
DARK

A JESSICA JONES MARVEL CRIME NOVEL

LISA
JEWELL

PENGUIN BOOKS

PENGUIN BOOKS

UK | USA | Canada | Ireland | Australia
India | New Zealand | South Africa

Penguin Books is part of the Penguin Random House group of companies
whose addresses can be found at global.penguinrandomhouse.com

Penguin Random House UK,
One Embassy Gardens, 8 Viaduct Gardens, London SW11 7BW

penguin.co.uk
global.penguinrandomhouse.com

First published in the US by Hyperion Avenue,
an imprint of Buena Vista Books, Inc., 2024
First published in the UK by Century 2024
Published in Penguin Books 2025
002

© 2024 MARVEL

Designed by Stephanie Sumulong

Set in 11.5/15.99 pt Times New Roman
Typeset by Jouve (UK), Milton Keynes

Printed and bound in Great Britain by Clays Ltd, Elcograf S.p.A.

The authorised representative in the EEA is Penguin Random House Ireland,
Morrison Chambers, 32 Nassau Street, Dublin D02 YH68

A CIP catalogue record for this book is available from the British Library

ISBN: 978-1-804-94790-6

Penguin Random House is committed to a sustainable future
for our business, our readers and our planet. This book is made
from Forest Stewardship Council® certified paper.

This book is dedicated to Grace O'Connor,
my brilliant friend.

PART ONE

One

Jessica turns onto her side and blinks into the darkness. The drapes are wide open, but the sky outside is so dark that they may as well be shut. It is not nighttime, but a storm is brewing over Hell's Kitchen, black and bruised and heavy.

The clock by her bed tells her that it is one minute past nine.

Her head tells her that she had her last drink about four hours ago.

She drags herself from her bed and listens to the first distant rumbles of thunder, coming from somewhere far away from the city.

Coffee. Black, strong, burned. A bowl of Cheerios with ice-cold milk from the fridge. The storm moves closer, the sky turns electric-white, and Jessica jumps—slopping milk

3

from the bowl onto the floor—as a clap of thunder splits the universe in half. For a moment she wonders about a thunderstorm this early in the day, but then she thinks, why not? The whole world has felt so dramatic lately, people seem so riled up all the time, always looking for fights and division. Things move so fast, theories come and go, superstars are born and get canceled, technology, fashions, politics all spin in dizzying, insane cycles, and meanwhile the planet is set to burn to cinders, and, yes, why not a brooding, sinister morning storm over Hell's Kitchen on a cool October morning, why not?

Her neighbor Julius just adopted a cat, then three days later had to go away to visit a sick relative. She owed Julius a favor and said she'd feed it for him. It's named Speckles.

She has a 9:45 in her calendar and it is now 9:20. She needs a shower and another coffee, but first she thinks she'll go down the hall and deal with Speckles.

She grabs the key to Julius's apartment and walks barefoot down the hall, leaving her door on the latch behind her. She wears a T-shirt that still smells of last night's chicken wings where she'd rubbed her greasy fingertips, but also smells of Luke's laundry detergent. Luke is her not-quite-boyfriend. Actually, her not-at-all-boyfriend, but boyfriend enough for her to have ended up at some point or other with one of his T-shirts in her apartment. And he really does do magic things with his laundry, she doesn't know what or how, but everything he wears smells so good.

Julius has painted the inside of his apartment into something decent: the walls are midnight blue and velvet gray. He favors mid-century furniture, teak and oak and pointy legs. He likes table lamps. They are everywhere, six in the living room alone. There is a tall, thin clock against a wall that *tick-tock*s self-importantly as Jessica walks toward the kitchen, and then there is another *flash-bang* of whiteness and she counts to twelve, and as the next thunderstrike arrives as loud as a dropped saucepan on a stone floor, she enters the kitchen to find the cat sitting terrified in a corner, all bulging eyes and flat ears. She gets closer and can see that Speckles is quivering, vibrating, that Speckles is overloaded with adrenaline.

Jessica doesn't know what to make of cats. She feels she should like them and certainly she feels bad right now for this one in its current state of mortal terror, but she doesn't know how to approach them, touch them, make them like you. She puts out a hand and says, "Listen. It's okay, all right? This is just some crazy shit that the people up there do from time to time, to remind us how small and pointless we all are. Just hang tight, kitty. Hang tight."

Speckles squeezes himself farther into the corner and Jessica reaches into the cupboard above him for the bag of cat food. Then she leans down to lift the bowl from the floor, and as she does so another thunderclap hits and the cat startles and dashes, and Jessica turns and remembers that she left Julius's front door open.

"Shit!" She drops the bowl on the kitchen counter. "Shit!" She chases the cat through the door and out into the hallway. "Speckles!" she calls out louder than she'd like to. "Speckles! Stop!"

LISA JEWELL

But he doesn't stop, he thinks he can outrun the thunder
and he helter-skelters away from her, his paws skidding over
the shiny marble flooring, and suddenly he is at the other side
of the building, the bit that Jessica never sees, where the
doors are the same as the doors on her side of the building but
are so alien to her that they may as well be in another country.
And down there is a window and it is open and who knows
where it leads. Jessica has never seen the window before and
she lets out a small husk of a scream, her hands clamped to
her face, as she sees Speckles leap six feet and disappear into
the dark, granite sky filled with clouds like rolling boulders.

Two

The cat has run down two flights of the fire escape and now sits on a narrow stone ledge that joins Jessica's building to the flat roof of the next building along. On either side of the stone ledge is oblivion. Jessica sticks her head through the window and assesses the situation. If the cat doesn't want to die, it needs to jump back onto the fire escape. But the cat is too scared to work this out for itself and sits in stasis.

Jessica sighs. It's too early for this bullshit. All she has is Cheerios and coffee to work with. But she cannot tell Julius that she let his cat die, so she allows the sickening transfusion to occur, the blood, the water, the mucus in her body to warp and distort, to become something closer to diesel and paraffin, to lighter fuel and tarmac, and she can almost smell it, taste it at the back of her throat. It makes her want to gag as she stands out on the windowsill, high above the streets below, but she swallows it down, crouches slightly, her eyes shut hard—

. . . but . . .

. . . the clouds split apart, and the rain falls hard and quick, and the cat changes its stance, sashays back toward Jessica's building, its tail a spiky brush of panic and fury, jumps onto the fire escape and then straight into Jessica's arms.

Carrying a wet, freaked-out cat through a window and down a hallway is not easy. It scratches her arms, it scratches her face. A door opens as she passes by with the cat rolling and squirming in her arms. A woman with a baby in a stroller eyes her up and down three times, a glint of disgust followed quickly by wry amusement. The baby stares at her and the cat with wide eyes. Jessica keeps walking.

As she turns the corner toward Julius's apartment, she stops.

A small girl stands by his open door. She has dark eyes, and her hair is tied in puffballs on either side of her head. She wears a metallic fur-trimmed coat and stripy tights. Jessica narrows her eyes at the girl. "You okay, little girl?"

The girl nods, her gaze held firmly on Jessica, oblivious to the angry wet cat in her arms.

"Where's your mom?"

The girl stares. She says nothing.

The sky cracks with thunder again and hard rain lands like thrown gravel against the walls of the building. The cat jumps out of her arms and runs into the apartment.

Jessica feels something burn her from the inside out. Her head rolls back, and she closes her eyes. When she opens them again, the girl is gone.

* * *

Jessica is in her grimy T-shirt and underwear, having failed to have a shower or brush her teeth, when her intercom buzzes five minutes later.

"Yeah," she says. "Come up."

She hits the button, then throws on a black jacket over her stale shirt, pulls on blue jeans and a pair of boots. She can still smell the chicken grease and the old beer on her breath, but it is too late to do anything about that now as the sound of heels clacking against marble echoes down the hallway outside her apartment.

She runs her hands over her hair and makes some kind of a smile with her face as she opens the door.

In front of her is a thin woman in an ankle-length shearling coat. Her hair is the color of butterscotch, and she has a tan that looks like it came from the sort of place that Jessica could never afford to go to.

"Hi," says the woman, visibly recoiling at the sight of Jessica, her stained clothing, her damp hair and scratched-up arms and face, the broken-down-looking room behind her. "Amber Randall." The woman looks at the door sign reading ALIAS INVESTIGATIONS, then back at her. "Are you Jessica Jones?"

Jessica nods. "Sure," she says. "Yes. Come in. Sorry."

The woman looks about forty but could be fifty. It's hard to tell with rich ladies.

Amber Randall shakes out her umbrella in the hallway and leaves it leaning against the wall. Entering, she takes off her shearling and folds it in three with the arms turned inward, hangs it neatly on the arm of Jessica's leather sofa, and sits down. She is wearing a black knitted dress with a white lace collar and black leather boots with rubber soles.

Her eyes roam around the walls of Jessica's office, searching, Jessica suspects, for one pretty thing. When her eyes fail to find anything pleasing, they come to rest on her.

"You're not what I was expecting," Amber Randall says. "I thought you'd be . . ." Her hands flutter around aimlessly for a moment before coming to rest on her lap. "Never mind. I know you have . . . I know you are . . ." Her hands flutter again. "But really, I don't need that from you. None of that. I need your . . . *contacts*. Your *insight*. You know. Because I think there's something happening, and I think it's something to do with your people."

Jessica blinks. *Your people*. She doesn't have "your people." She only has herself.

"Listen," she says. "I really don't think—"

"Hear me out," the small woman says harshly before softening. "Hear me out. Please. I need you, Jessica. I really do."

Jessica tilts her head and appraises the woman sitting in front of her. Her bones are so fine her hands are like tiny claws. The big, incongruous boots give her the air of a child, while her mouth sags at the sides where gravity—and life—has come to play.

"Try me," Jessica says.

Amber Randall smooths down her dress. "My ex-husband, Sebastian, is British. I met him when I was studying Classical Dance in London many moons ago. We got married and he came to live with me here in New York, and we had our twins sixteen years ago. A girl and a boy. Lark and Fox."

"Lark and . . . ?"

"Fox. Yes."

"Okay then."

"After we divorced Sebastian moved back to England, and every summer since then the twins have flown over to London for four weeks to stay with him. He has a mews house in Pimlico."

"Pim . . . ?"

"—lico. A posh area in London. And he has recently bought a big house in Essex." Looking at Jessica, she adds, "In the countryside. So, every year the twins fly over for a month and usually they spend time in London. They see their cousins. Sometimes Sebastian takes them to France, or to the Spanish islands. Then they come back to me and go back to school and, look—*anyway*—this year, they spent the entire time at his new house in Essex, just with him, nobody else, and I just feel very strongly that *something happened*."

"Something happened?"

"Yes. They've been home for four weeks and the thing

is—and I don't really know how to explain this—but ever since they got back, I've grown more and more convinced that it's not them. That *they* are not *them*."

Jessica feels a rush of energy spike through her, and her posture changes a degree. "How do you mean?"

"Like I say, it's hard to explain. They look basically the same, they sound the same, for all intents and purposes it is them. But"—Amber leans forward, her pale toffee hair swinging as she moves—"I don't think it is them. I think something happened over there this summer. I think someone got to them. Someone *did* something to them." She leans forward a little more. "Replaced them."

Jessica lets her eyes close for a moment. She ponders the reality of this type of woman, as observed through the media of TV shows and newspaper articles: a rich woman abandoned on the scrap heap by a rich husband, in middle age. A woman filled with resentment, possibly, of a new girlfriend or a second wife who is bound to be younger and better-looking, and of the new life in which her children have been immersed for four weeks, returning to her, no doubt, with glossy tales of experiences to which Amber Randall is not party. She imagines toxicity in every crevice of Amber Randall's life, and she sees that toxicity playing out now in this idea that her ex-husband has somehow replaced her children. She opens her eyes again and stares at Amber, openly.

"Listen," she sighs. "This sounds, I dunno, kind of messy. It sounds like maybe you and your ex—"

"No!" Amber slams her hands down against the leather

sofa. "No. This is nothing—*nothing*—nothing to do with our divorce. Our divorce was amicable. I'm very fond of Sebastian. He's a very nice man."

Jessica lifts one brow and nods. "Can you provide me with any examples of your children's behavior, or particular events that have led you to this point?"

"Yes. Yes, I can. Fox is a good-looking boy and he, well, he's just starting to know it. He's kind of vain. And particular. And he has this way of touching his hair. Like this." Amber prods at her hair with tiny fingers. "Every time he passes a mirror. And he's always taking selfies, and he always has the same smile and the same pose and the same way of looking at the camera, and since he got back, he just doesn't do it anymore. He walks straight past mirrors without acknowledging them. He doesn't use his phone for selfies anymore. He never touches his hair and, I swear, before, he had his fingers in his hair constantly. And Lark—she is a shy girl, she has some nervous habits, chews the insides of her cheeks a lot. Sometimes she pushes her finger into her cheek while she's doing it, it's just part of what it's like being Lark, it's part of her. She takes the skin off around her fingernails too, and she shreds paper. And since she got back, none of that. Her hands are just . . . *still*. Both of them seem so still."

Amber finishes talking, and Jessica hesitates before responding.

"Have they had some therapy? In the UK, maybe?" Jessica ventures. "Like some CBT or something?"

"No." Amber Randall sounds exasperated. "Nothing like

that. Trust me, I'm a therapist, I would've known. And they would have told me. And why would they, anyway? They're perfectly normal kids."

"Did something happen? A trauma?"

"No. Listen. Jessica. Please stop trying to provide rational explanations. If there were a rational explanation for it, do you think I would be sitting here now talking to you? And another thing—their skin. Both of them had the usual kind of teenage complexions before they left, and Lark, she had this tiny scar, just above her eyebrow, from chicken pox, and since they got back, their complexions are just—they're *flawless*."

Jessica winces. "Maybe the air in England is purer?"

"No, Jessica. *No.* The air in England is *not* purer. They have *not* had CBT. This is . . . *look*. Maybe this wasn't a good idea." Amber Randall stands and grabs her shearling coat. "Maybe I should just find someone who—"

"What do you want from me?"

She lets the shearling drop. "I want you to go to England and find out exactly what happened when they were there this summer."

Jessica recoils slightly. "You want me to go to England?"

"Yes."

"You should know that I don't have a passport."

Amber widens her eyes at Jessica and sighs. "Seriously?"

"Yes. Seriously. Nobody ever took me anywhere I needed to use one."

"My God. You have a birth certificate though, yes?"

14

"Yes. I have a birth certificate."

"Well, we can sort that out for you, then."

Jessica blinks. "I have a lot going on."

This isn't entirely true. Jessica just finished a case two days ago and has precisely nothing going on.

Amber nods, as if sensing the closing of a deal. "I can pay you your hourly rate and more. Plus a healthy retainer."

Jessica narrows her eyes. She has $128 in her bank account right now.

"Let me think about it."

Amber sighs. "Please don't think about it. Just do it. I can't live like this for another minute. It's killing me, this sense that I'm living with . . . *strangers*. Are they even my children? And if they're not my children, then where are they really, and what's happening to them?"

A moment passes and then Jessica feels it, the soft, sickening release of acquiescence. "Fine," she says. "Okay. I'll do it. But I'll need the retainer up front. Like now."

"How much?"

Another moment passes and Jessica says, "Five thousand."

Amber's eyes flash slightly at the realization that she is being ripped off, but she smiles and says, "It's a deal. It'll be in your account by this afternoon. Let's meet tomorrow to discuss strategy." She casts her gaze briefly around Jessica's office. "Come to my club. The Finch. East Twenty-Seventh. Ten a.m. And you might want to . . ." She gestures vaguely at Jessica's T-shirt.

"I have clean clothes, yes, thank you."

Jessica closes the door behind Amber Randall a minute later and keeps her body pressed against it until she hears the whiz and click of the elevator and the hum as it descends to street level, and then she slides down to her haunches, drops her head into her chest, and groans.

What the hell has she just agreed to?

Thirty-eight years ago
Harlem, NYC

Ophelia slides onto the stool in the near-empty bar. The golden early evening light shines through the grimy windows, adding a sense of magic to the downbeat surroundings. A thin man stands hunched over an arcade game in the corner; a less thin man sits at a table in the window, turning the pages of a newspaper without seeming to be reading it. She stares at the man behind the bar. He wears a gray T-shirt, a plaid over-shirt, jeans. His long hair is tied back, and his hand is stuffed inside a glass mug as he shines up its exterior with a cloth.

"What can I get for you?" he asks.

Ophelia feels it hard, the certainty that this man is the one she's been looking for, the one who can save her.

Finally.

She smiles and says, "Could I have a tequila sunrise? Thank you."

"Oh!" says the barman. "A Brit!"

"Yes. Yes, I am."

"Whereabouts are you from?"

"Oh, all over really. But I was born in Portsmouth. On the south coast."

"Nice."

He turns the clean glass over and stacks it on the shelf behind him, then gets to work on her cocktail. She watches him. He has a broad back, narrow hips, ears that protrude slightly from his head. He's tall and she likes the way he moves. As she watches him, she becomes aware of a song playing in the background.

She's got perfect skin . . .

She's heard it before, she thinks.

Cheekbones like geometry, eyes like sin . . .

The barman turns back to face her, and she is struck again by how exactly right he is. She'd followed his scent across an entire ocean to find him, and here he is, standing before her looking like the most normal guy in the world. No one would guess what makes him tick, she thinks, no one would ever think it of him. Only she knows the truth about him.

As if reading her thoughts, he smiles and says, "So, what brings you to New York?"

"Oh, just adventure. Fun. Never been, always wanted to."

"Well, welcome to the City That Never Sleeps," he says, tipping tequila into a highball. "It's good to have you here."

She considers him for a moment and then leans into the bar. "I've been waiting all my life for this."

"Wow." He raises an eyebrow at her. "That's a bold statement. I'd better make this a good cocktail, then."

She smiles at him. He has no idea, she thinks, just how long she has waited for this. No idea whatsoever.

He pours orange juice over the tequila and stirs them together. Then his hand reaches for the grenadine from the shelf behind him. It glows red and fresh. She watches as the grenadine hits the orange juice, watches it sink slowly to the bottom of the glass.

Her eyes go to his and she smiles. "Looks like blood, doesn't it?"

His gaze locks hard onto hers, and a flash of desire passes through his eyes. "Yes," he says to Ophelia. "I guess it does."

Three

The Finch is a narrow townhouse squeezed between two wide townhouses. It has long thin windows with frames painted taupe and a heavy bower of pink silk flowers looped over the front door. The signage describes it as an energizing, welcoming space for every woman.

A young woman sits at the front desk behind an oversized vase of green and pink hydrangeas. She wears black overalls and red lipstick and glances up through thick-framed glasses. She smiles widely at Jessica, who appears to have passed muster in a black blouse, black jeans, a black leather jacket, and a perfunctory attempt at makeup.

"Hi!" says the woman. "How can I help you today?"

"I'm meeting Amber Randall. Jessica Jones."

The woman clicks her keyboard with nails painted forest

green. "Ah, yes! She's on the second floor, in the Marsha room. Go right up."

Upstairs, Jessica finds Amber sitting on a tiny gray sofa in the corner of a tiny room. She has a teapot on a table in front of her with two cups, and a plate of warm-looking chocolate cookies. She asks Jessica to close the door behind her and then invites her to take a seat on the chair opposite.

"English breakfast?" she asks, lifting the teapot by its handle and its spout. "How do you take it?"

Jessica stares at the pot and draws a blank.

Amber goes ahead and pours it, adding milk from a small glass bottle, and passes the cup to Jessica. "You look nice," she says. "Better."

"Yeah, well, you caught me on a bad day yesterday." She lifts the cup and drinks the tea. It tastes of dirty flowers. She takes a cookie and eats it in three bites, having had no breakfast and nothing to eat since the previous lunchtime.

"Have another?" says Amber, pushing the plate toward her.

Jessica swallows down the goo of the cookie with the remains of her tea and shakes her head. "Mrs. Randall, shall we just . . . ?"

"Yes. Of course. And call me Amber, please. So . . ." Amber pulls a folder from inside a green leather briefcase on the floor by her feet and passes it to Jessica. "I can sense that you think this is all somewhat in my head. I thought that before we go any further you should see the twins for yourself."

Jessica pulls photos out of the folder and examines them. Two fine-featured children: a boy with a plume of dark blond hair, James Dean eyes, and a hard smile; a girl with a severe bob and brutal bangs, her dark brown eyes turned to the floor, a ring through her left nostril. Both look tall and rangy, unlike their small-boned mother. Both have strong noses and high foreheads. They remind Jessica of some kind of paintings by some kind of European artist from the 1920s.

"Nice-looking kids," she says.

"Thank you. But listen, Lark's been invited out after school today, starting off at a friend's and then heading to a concert over in Williamsburg. They're getting on the subway, five of them. You should follow them. Tail them, listen in, see what she talks about, how she behaves, who she talks to, what she does. These are the friends . . ."

She hands Jessica another sheaf of photos. Jessica flicks through them mindlessly, then puts them down: Two boys, two girls, rich kids, they all look the same.

"Do you have covert recording equipment?" asks Amber.

Jessica thinks of the recording app on her smartphone, the same one that Amber no doubt has on hers. Anyone could be a private eye these days. "Er, yeah, sure."

"Could you use it?"

"Sure." Jessica pushes the nasty tea away from her and reaches for another cookie. "What's the name of the band?"

Amber pulls a flyer from her folder and passes it to her.

The lettering on the flyer says AKINESIZ.

"Never heard of them."

"No," sighs Amber. "Neither have I. Singer-as-the-band-name kind of thing. Indie-emo-rock-pop something. I don't

BREAKING THE DARK

know. It's sold out, so you won't be going in. Just follow them to the venue, then you can leave."

Jessica slides the flyer into the pile with the photos, rubbing at a smudge of chocolate she's left on its corner.

"What time are they leaving?"

"Oh, Lord knows. Teenagers never leave when they say they're going to leave. But they're going from Tara's house, here." She taps the address on a list from the folder. "So just be where you can see them. Any time from six, I guess."

Jessica nods and starts to ready herself to leave.

"Did you bring your birth certificate?"

Jessica pauses and lowers herself back onto her chair. "Mrs. Randall . . . I'm not ready to hand over something like that just yet. Let's get this first report done and then we'll talk about birth certificates."

"Fine," says Amber. "Fine. So let's meet back here, tomorrow, midday?"

"Sure," says Jessica, getting to her feet. "Can we have something"—she waves her fingers over the remaining cookies—"*savory* tomorrow? All that sugar's made me feel a bit . . ." She rubs her belly.

"I'll see what I can do."

Amber throws her a small hard smile, then lowers her reading glasses onto her nose, lifts the lid of her laptop, and pours herself another cup of tea from the big white pot. Jessica closes the door behind her.

* * *

23

Jessica still feels a little nauseous as she walks back to her office. She stops to buy a bottle of water from a fancy Kips Bay grocery store and downs it in a few gulps. This helps a little, but not entirely. In truth she could happily go back to bed for an hour or two, but she has work to do.

Back at her desk in Hell's Kitchen, she's just opened the lid of her laptop when she sees movement through the glass panel of her apartment door. She can hear breathing too, and then the sound of knuckles knocking uncertainly against the wood.

"Yo. Jessica."

A small voice. A familiar voice.

She pulls open the door. It's Malcolm Powder, her very own bespectacled seventeen-year-old wannabe-private-eye-slash-stan who follows everything she does.

She sighs. "Yes."

"Whoa," he says, recoiling slightly. "What happened to your face?"

She puts her fingertips to her skin. "A cat happened. What do you want, Malcolm?"

"It's been four days."

"Four days since what?"

"Four days since you said I could come work for you."

"I did not say you could come work for me."

"You gave me your word, Jessica. You said if I found someone who knew where the Spider-Woman-Girl chick was, I could have a part-time job—and I *did* find her and literally helped you save her life, and you said—"

24

"I said if you had permission from your parents."

Malcolm turns and beckons to someone lurking to his left. A small woman appears. She looks like Malcolm, even wears the same style of glasses.

"Mom," Malcolm grunts. "Can you just tell her?"

The woman smiles. "I give Malcolm my permission to work for you."

Jessica sighs loudly. "Great," she says under her breath. She fixes the mother with a hard stare. "It can be dangerous work."

"Malcolm is a sensible boy. It will be a good experience for him, before college. Get him off the street."

Jessica turns the question around onto Malcolm. "You're going to college, huh?"

"Yeah. Next fall."

"Fine. Okay. I might have to be out of the country for a while with my current job. It could be good to have someone based here, keeping the office running."

Malcolm's face bursts open in a hundred different directions. *"Oh my God,"* he says. "Oh my God. *Seriously.* You want me to run the office?"

"No! Geez! Not run it." Jessica gestures at her desk. "Just sit in it. That is *all.*"

"Yes! Totally! I can totally sit in your office! *Absolutely!"*

"And not touch anything."

"No. Nothing. Definitely not. When can I start?"

Jessica closes her eyes and sighs again. "Not yet, okay. I'll message you."

"You don't have my number."

Jessica hands him a piece of paper and a pen. He beams at her briefly before scribbling down his number.

"Great," says Jessica, snatching back the paper. "Now goodbye."

The boy smiles at her again and turns to leave, but Jessica suddenly thinks of something. "Oh. Malcolm. Heard of this guy?"

She holds up the flyer.

"Akinesiz? Yeah. He's awesome."

"What sort of clothes do his fans wear? What do they look like?"

He looks her up and down, at the black-on-black-on-black outfit she wore to meet Amber, and shrugs. "Kind of like you, I guess," he says. "Except young."

"Get out of here," she says. "Geez."

* * *

Jessica is halfway through a premade egg salad sandwich from a fancy deli. It was superexpensive and looked amazing when she chose it but for some reason the smell is making her nauseous. She's scouting for a trash can to dispose of it in when she hears noise and movement coming from the apartment block to her left. A girl who looks like Lark Randall emerges, followed by an assortment of faux-raggedy rich kids flaunting nonconformist affectations and talking very loudly.

"Shit." She screws the half-eaten sandwich up and hurls it

toward the nearest garbage can. It lands, a perfect bull's-eye. Rubbing her hands down the sides of her jeans, she steps toward the kids.

Lark is more beautiful in the flesh than in the photo that Amber showed her this morning. She's a full four inches taller than the other girls and closer in height to the two boys. She is wearing a sheer black lace sleeveless top and a turtleneck and baggy jeans with huge construction boots and an oversized denim jacket that she's shrugged off her shoulders so it hangs from her thin milk-white arms. On her head she wears a black beanie with studded black cat's ears. Her eyes are ringed with black liner and her lips are painted pale pink. Her nose ring catches the light almost like an exclamation mark to her beauty, but nevertheless she's standing slightly apart from the others, who are all looking at a phone belonging to one of the girls and laughing.

Jessica sees Lark's eyes go to the sky, as if she's studying the rosy, dusk-tinged clouds, committing them to memory. The others start to move as one toward the subway and it takes Lark a second or two to notice she's been left behind. She picks up her pace to catch up with them and Jessica follows suit.

The group passes through the turnstile and down into the station, where the air is warm and fetid with the breath of the last of the evening rush hour. Lark dawdles behind her friends, her gaze constantly being drawn upward as if she is seeing things overhead that nobody else can see. Her hands, the hands that Amber said once used to be always in motion,

27

hang neatly by her sides. The train arrives and Lark follows her friends on board. Jessica enters by the adjacent doors and takes a seat two down from Lark, then presses record on her phone.

The conversation mainly revolves between the girl named Tara and another named Anna. The two boys sit opposite each other staring at their phones, legs akimbo. Lark gazes up at the roof of the train car and Jessica looks closely at her now that they are stationary. Her skin does look extraordinary, especially here under the harsh strip-light of the 4 train. Her gaze moves from the ceiling down to the floor and a small smile passes over her mouth.

"Lark."

Jessica squints to look. This one's Tara.

"Earth calling Lark!"

Lark breaks her trance and turns slowly to face her friend. "Yeah?" she asks, pleasantly.

"Do you have a lip balm?"

"No," she replies simply before looking away again.

Jessica observes Tara and Anna exchanging a look.

"Okay then," says Tara, a little snarky, before exchanging another look with Anna and changing the conversation.

The kids change onto the L train at Union Square and Jessica follows suit. The carriage looks like an emo party, pale kids from all four corners of New York being funneled toward Williamsburg. The carriage smells of that vanilla scent that teenage girls all smell of these days and Jessica experiences another wave of nausea.

At the recognition of the nausea, her mind turns to a night with Luke when it's possible they'd been maybe a little less than careful. How many weeks ago was it? She can't remember. But no. Even drunk she would not be that idiotic, and anyway, isn't it called *morning* sickness? Not all-day-long sickness? She shakes the idea from her head, returns her thoughts to the matter at hand, the five teenage children sitting across the aisle from her, the beautiful girl with the cat-ears beanie who does not look at her phone, does not engage with her friends, does not move her hands, who just sits, her eyes so focused and glassy, her skin so smooth and poreless, like a life-sized doll.

Jessica jolts at this realization, and for the first time since Amber Randall walked into her office yesterday morning, she starts to believe that maybe this is something more than just a wronged wife's twisted paranoia.

"Lark."

It's Tara again.

"Lark!"

Lark turns to Tara and smiles. "Yes."

"Oh my God, you're so drifty."

Tara faces Anna as she says this, and they share a pulse of laughter.

"Drifty," says one of the boys. "Is that even a word?"

"Whatever," says Tara. "You know what I mean." She turns back to Lark. "Are you okay? You're just, like, so quiet."

"Yeah. I'm good. I'm just zen."

"Zen?"

"Yeah. You don't need to worry about me. Just have fun."

"But—we want you to have fun too. You've been looking forward to tonight for months. It was all you could talk about before you left this summer."

Lark nods mechanically. "Yeah, I remember that. I remember being excited."

"But now you're not?"

"Yeah. I'm super excited. Just in a different way."

"Are you okay, Lark?"

"Never better. Truly. Don't worry about me. I'm perfect."

"If you say so."

"I do say so."

Then Tara throws her arms around Lark and squeezes her hard and the conversation moves away from Lark and on to other things, but Jessica's eyes stay on Lark.

On her hands.

Her staring eyes.

On her perfect, perfect skin.

Thirty-eight years ago
Harlem, NYC

When you've seen the most beautiful woman in the world, you know it with every single piece of you. You know it with your eyes, your head, your gut—but you also know it in your blood, and with the veins that carry that blood to all the parts of the body that need to be informed that you've just seen the most beautiful woman in the world.

The blood is the important thing. Blood contains everything, every atom of who you are: Your mother, your father, a million mothers and fathers before them. It contains your fear, your passion, your weaknesses, your strengths. It contains your future and your past. It is the most powerful essence in the world.

For some people there is more than one most beautiful woman in the world. But not for me. There is only one. She is called Ophelia.

You might say that I'm obsessed. I wouldn't blame you. She's all I think about, every second of every day. My blood pumps harder when I think of her. It touches me in places that lie dormant the rest of the time. The blood sends a rosy flush to my cheeks, sends endorphins throughout my body, sends heat to my groin.

I am all blood. I cut myself, sometimes, when she's left, just to see it, stare at it; it glows extra red, I'm sure, when it's full of her.

She agrees to join me for dinner on the night of her twentieth birthday. At thirty-six I'm considerably older than her, and I feel maybe she is being polite, but I don't show my doubt. Doubt observed is a killer.

I wear my favorite shirt; it's blue with tiny white buttons on the collar tips that hold a tie in place. I have had a haircut and a professional shave. She's only ever seen me in my plaid shirt and jeans behind the bar, and I want her to see who I really am.

At the restaurant, she orders clams in tomato sauce; I order a steak, rare, *bleu*.

She eats the clams straight out of their shells, the sauce leaving a red circle around her lips. Another rush of desire overcomes me, and I neutralize it with a nervous joke about the waiter's mustache. My steak oozes blood onto my dinner plate each time I prod it, viscous, watery. I can smell the fear in it, smell the animal's last moments of terror, picture its wide black eyes. I stifle a groan.

I invite her back to my apartment imagining that she will say no.

She says yes. Yes.

Suddenly I am poleaxed with doubts. My apartment is

clean and neat, but it might be less luxurious than someone with shiny Manhattan dreams might have been imagining.

However, she saunters in, seems pleased with how she finds it, and allows me to take her coat. She tells me it's nice and touches the spines of my books and admires a framed print of Central Park on my wall that I've always wondered about. Is it tacky? But now I am reassured that it is not, because she has told me she likes it.

The effect of her here in my private space is intoxicating.

She sits on my sofa and drinks the wine I pour for her. I put on some music, the sort of music I like, and she laughs when the first bars play and tells me that it's the sort of thing her mother used to listen to. I take the joke in good humor.

Then she says she has something to tell me.

Something about her.

About who *she* really is.

She grabs my hands. She squeezes them hard. And she whispers something in my ears no human has ever before heard.

She seems relieved that I have not recoiled. Was she too seized by doubt?

I say, "Why did you tell me?"

She says, "Because I knew you'd understand."

And then she turns my hand so that my palm is facing up. She runs her fingertips across the soft white skin, sending my blood fizzing, blasting—pumping so hard it makes my vision blur for just one second. She brings the palm up to her lips, her soft, perfect lips, and presses them against it. I feel just the suggestion of suction, of pressure, of my skin being pulled into her mouth, the tip of her tongue running up and down, gentle, fleeting as a feather, and then she brings my index finger into her mouth and sucks it before clamping down on it with hard, sharp teeth, her dark blue eyes never once leaving mine.

She releases my finger from between her bloody teeth and stares hard into my eyes.

"I know who you are," she says. "I know what you are. I know what you can do. I need you and you need me. You and I were meant to be."

Four

Jessica leaves the teens as they shuffle into the venue and takes the subway back to Fiftieth, where she heads into the sharp night, the first cold one of the year. She thinks about what she will tell Amber when she sees her tomorrow morning. She has nothing concrete to report. She has seen nothing out of the ordinary tonight, but still, she feels unsettled, she feels strange, and for some reason she feels sad. As she thinks this, she turns the corner two blocks from her apartment, and there's a small girl standing in front of her, just outside the mini-mart, and it's the same girl who was standing outside Julius's apartment the previous morning, the girl with the puffball hair, the silver parka, the stripy tights.

She smiles at Jessica as Jessica passes her.

"You again. Where's your mom?"

The girl shrugs.

Jessica looks around her, pokes her head around the door of the store, which is empty apart from the clerk, looks across the street and turns back to the little girl. "You all on your own? What's going on?"

The girl doesn't reply and Jessica sighs. What the hell is she supposed to do about this?

"Do you live in my building? Where I saw you yesterday? Is that where you live?"

The girl shakes her head.

"So, where do you live? Do you live up there?" She indicates the apartments above the mini-mart.

The girl shakes her head again.

Jessica turns in desperation, looking up and down the street, but there is no one in any direction who seems to be the parent of the child in front of her. She calls to the guy behind the counter, "Hey, any idea whose kid this is? Outside your store?"

The guy slides off his stool and slowly comes to the door. He looks down and then looks at Jessica.

"What kid?"

Jessica looks down too. The girl is nowhere to be seen.

* * *

Jessica arrives at the Finch at noon the following day and is directed to the Simone room, where she finds Amber Randall sitting with a plate of avocado maki rolls and a pot of coffee.

Amber closes her laptop when Jessica walks in, then picks up the coffee pot.

"How do you like it?"

"Black. Please."

Amber pours her a cup and passes it to her. "I got you sushi. I hope that's okay?"

Jessica nods, although she feels very strongly that she won't be eating any. "Thank you."

"So, how did it go?"

"It went fine. I mean, as in I found them, I followed them, I heard them, I recorded them. It all went according to plan. But in terms of finding anything out—not really. Just that her friends also think something's up with her . . ."

"They do?"

"Yeah. They exchanged a few looks. That kind of thing. And when they asked Lark if she was okay, she said she was 'perfect.'"

"Yes!" Amber sits up smartly. "Yes, that's what she says to me too! And Fox! Both of them have said that to me when I've asked them if they're okay. Isn't that a strange thing to say, don't you think? 'Perfect'?"

Jessica sips her coffee and nods.

"And what else?"

"Nothing really. She just seemed a little spacy. A little dis-connected. And yeah, I did see what you meant about her complexion. It's kind of freakishly immaculate."

"Yes. Like it's been airbrushed." Amber shakes her head

and sighs. "Anyway, you should probably take a look at Fox next. He's at a birthday dinner tonight, his best friend Jefferson's mother's fiftieth. I've made you a reservation at the same restaurant and I've asked for it to be close to the party table."

"How did you swing that?"

"I said you were my son's private security."

Jessica lifts an eyebrow, but she doesn't say anything.

"So, same as last night. Carry a recorder. Observe. Here's the restaurant."

Amber slides a card across the table toward her. It's mint green with tan lettering that says THE BLEEDING HEART. Underneath that it says MODERN FRENCH AND AMERICAN CUISINE.

Jessica sighs. "What do people wear there?"

"Well, it's smart casual. So you could go as you are, but maybe a blowout could be the finishing touch?"

"A blowout?"

"Yes." Amber gestures at Jessica's head. "You have pretty hair, but it's, you know, a little . . . anyway. There's a place across the street, walk-in. Here." She passes Jessica some twenties. "You could go now. Ask for mermaid waves."

"Seriously?"

"Seriously."

Jessica takes the twenties from Amber's hand and slides them into her jacket pocket. "Anything else?"

"No. That's it. Just be there at seven tonight. The booking is in the name of Jane Smith."

"Inspired." Jessica stands. "Okay then. I will go get my mermaid hair and leave you to get on with your day." Her gaze goes to Amber's laptop. "You mentioned you're a therapist."

"Oh." Amber smiles a small smile. "Yes. I am."

"What kind of therapist?"

"Post-trauma therapy mainly."

Jessica takes a breath. "That's—"

"Here." Amber waves the plate of sushi at her. "Take some, please. I won't eat them."

"Oh, yes. Sure." She grabs three and holds them inside her hand, immediately aware that this was not what Amber meant.

Amber looks askance at the handful of sushi and passes her a paper napkin. "Here," she says kindly. "Wrap them in this."

"Thank you."

Outside on the street, Jessica drops the wrapped-up maki in a trash can and scours the other side of the street, looking for the blow-dry bar, drawing in a heavy breath when she sees it. She can barely remember the last time she washed her hair, let alone the last time anybody else did. But she's on the clock and somebody else is paying for it and she has nothing else to do, so why not, she thinks. Why not?

* * *

Jessica stares at her shiny mermaid waves in the mirror in front of her. She does not look like a mermaid, but she does look a hundred times better than when she walked in an hour ago, and according to the girl—Cat—who did it for her, she won't need to wash it for at least a week now, so it's a win as far as she's concerned.

But the hair makes her feel strange once she's out of the rarefied environs of the salon and heading down West Forty-Fifth toward her apartment block. It boings and bounces and flips and flicks. She feels self-conscious and conspicuous.

She takes a woolen hat from the inside pocket of her jacket and is about to pull it down over her hair when she catches sight of her reflection in a shop window and stops. The woman she sees in the glass takes her breath away for a moment. It's her, but it's not her. It's her as if the last couple of years of her life had never happened, if that man hadn't done what he'd done to her. It's her without all the self-medicating and self-loathing. It's the *her* she used to be.

She touches the ends of her hair, lets her shoulders roll back, turns up the corners of her mouth, then tucks the woolen hat back into her pocket and heads into her apartment building, trying to hold on to the feeling. But the feeling fades with every step she takes down the dark hallways, with every sound of trashy daytime TV leaking from strangers' front doors, with every echo of crying babies, of shouting men. It fades again as she opens the door to her tragic apartment, the only place she has. And she stares at the view from her window of grimy buildings and purple-gray skies, listens to the muted soundtrack of angry traffic and, beyond that, the deathly rumble of the big rusty ships lumbering up the Hudson, and she can see no brightness, nothing anywhere that matches the sheen of her fifty-dollar mermaid blowout, nothing that makes her feel like she deserves such hair, and just then a shaft of sunlight slices suddenly through the filth of her window and catches the last five inches of dark amber in the bourbon bottle atop her filing cabinet, and she has not had a drink in two days, and there is a reason why she has not had a drink in two days, but it's not a reason she wants to dwell on for too long or in any depth, because she's not ready for it, not at all, and maybe, just maybe, she never will be.

Her hand goes to the bottle, she feels the cool of the glass beneath her fingertips, imagines the soft hit of the whiskey as it bleeds into her bloodstream from the empty pit of her stomach.

But then a cloud passes across the sun and the bottle falls back into shadow, and Jessica snatches her hand back and lets it hang by her side. No, she decides. Not now. It will still be there later if she wants it. She can wait.

And at that thought she runs to her bathroom, throws open the lid of the toilet, and is horribly and violently sick.

Thirty-four years ago
Tabasco, Mexico

Ophelia celebrates her twenty-second birthday under a bower of plum trees in a busy square next to an ornate white cathedral in the old heart of Villahermosa. They drink cold beer as the sky starts to turn red, and John makes a toast.

"Cheers," he says. "To turning twenty-*two*."

Twenty-two.

Ophelia almost can't believe she is now twenty-two.

She looks at him and smiles. "Thanks to you."

"Well," he replies, "what can I say? It was my pleasure."

They look very different from the people who met in a bar in Harlem years earlier. Her short hair has grown long. His long hair is cut short. She is now blond, he is dark. They are different people in so many ways.

Their quick New York exit turned into a multi-year road trip, and it's been amazing. Ophelia has felt herself re-forming every day, her blood settling, her nerves calming, fewer things calling to her, less noise. Just her, and him, growing older together, at last.

But now she wants more.

She wants a child.

She has wanted a child for forever and never been able to have one. All she has experienced is loss. Everyone she ever loved is dead, apart from him.

"I want to go home," Ophelia says, holding his hand in hers, tracing her thumb along the hump of his artery. "I want to go back to the UK. To have a baby."

"I know," he says softly. "It's time. I'm ready."

"You know I have no one over there? You know it's just me. Well, me and Mr. Smith." She smiles.

"Your cat. I know. But we don't need anyone. Particularly once we've had a child. We won't need anyone at all. We can just . . . freewheel. Just the three of us. I have skills, you have skills. We don't need a fancy house or fancy cars. We don't need anything, apart from each other."

Ophelia smiles, squeezes his hand hard, feels the pulse of his blood, feels the calmness of it all at long last.

Five

Jessica still feels unwell later as she gets ready for her lonely-girl dinner at the Bleeding Heart. She pairs her black jeans with a black cami and a cropped blazer and fluffs her mermaid hair out over her shoulders. She's ravenous, but the thought of rich French food makes her want to hurl.

Before she heads out, she calls in at Julius's to feed Speckles. This time she closes the door very carefully behind her and approaches the kitchen slowly, making kissy noises as she goes. The cat stares at her in that way in which he has taken to staring at her since the moment on the window ledge during the storm when she almost showed him what she could do. He could smell it on her, she knows that, the dark scent of her engines, the things that live inside her that make her able to do things that other people can't. He smelled it and now he knows it and the look he's giving her could be interpreted as respect, or even fear. *You*, he seems to say to her as his eyes narrow and he pulls his soft paws closer in toward his body, *you are not like the other ones.*

"That's right, cat, you'd better believe it," she says as she empties kibble into Speckles's bowl. "And what do you think of my hair?"

The cat says, *Eow*, before strutting toward the bowl on the floor and turning his back to her. Jessica sighs and takes a moment in Julius's pretty apartment, lets her eyes roam across the painted walls and smart kitchen tiles, the table lamps, and the framed prints on the walls. She can feel change coming in the air, a passage from here to there. She has been the same for so long now. She has become stagnant. Dull. She has not been evolving, and she needs her life to move along again, but she fears it too, the change. She fears it so badly she can taste it.

She waits with the cat while he eats and she sits on the floor with him for a while, stroking the thick fur under his chin. By the time she leaves the apartment five minutes later, her jacket is covered in cat fur, but she feels strangely happy.

* * *

The Bleeding Heart sits on the Upper East Side between Madison and Fifth. It boasts oversized Moroccan lanterns and terrace seating with heaters, and blankets draped over the backs of chairs. Jessica is taken to her table by a young woman in black and handed the wine list and the menu.

"Just water, please," she says, handing the wine list back. "Oh, and bread. Could I get some bread? Lots of bread."

The birthday party arrives a few moments later. Jefferson's mother, Susie, looks great for fifty in a fitted green silk dress, her shiny dark hair in a ponytail. The young girl with her, who Jessica has been told by Amber is Susie's niece, Matilda, is at that terrible age for girls when everything happens all at the same time—teeth, skin, puppy fat, nose. The poor thing looks petrified to find herself in the company of Fox, who is, Jessica has to concede, horribly good-looking for a sixteen-year-old boy.

Fox is taller than Jefferson's father and has the expansive, self-confident demeanor of a twenty-five-year-old. His hair is longer now than in the photograph Amber showed her and it flops onto his forehead instead of being teased backward into a boy-band pompadour. He's wearing a white shirt with green chinos rolled up at the ankle and very expensive-looking white-and-pink high-top sneakers. His wrists are circled with leather bracelets and there is a signet ring on his right-hand pinkie. And even here, in the subdued lighting of the restaurant, she can see that his skin is poreless like plastic, that his hands sit on his lap and his gaze is on the ceiling, that his face carries the same small, secret smile as his twin sister's.

Jessica sets her phone to record and then picks up the menu and stares at it. A waitress brings her a basket of bread that is warm to the touch, and when she tears it open a glorious yeasty plume of steam emerges from its heart. She stuffs it into her mouth greedily. It's the first thing she's enjoyed eating in two days and she has to stop herself from making sex noises while she chews . . . and at that thought, her mind returns again to Luke, the smell of his bed linen, the smell of his skin, the night she can't quite remember, when they may or may not have used contraception.

"Are you ready to order, madam? Or do you need a minute?"

The pretty waitress is back, and Jessica jumps slightly, swallows down the hunk of bread in her mouth. "God. Yeah. Sorry. I . . . er . . ." She stares blankly at the menu. "I have kind of an upset stomach. Do you have anything . . . *bland*, maybe?"

The waitress's face furrows. "Erm, let me see. I mean, we do have a nice potato and kale velouté. It comes with truffle oil and roasted hazelnuts on the top, but we could serve it without?"

"A veloo—?"

"Soup. It's a smooth soup."

Jessica smiles at her gratefully. "Done," she says, handing over her menu. "And can I get another basket of this amazing bread, please?"

Across from Jessica, the party guests are still consulting their menus. A waiter appears next to them and asks if they want any aperitifs, and they order champagne, plus a gin and tonic for Susie's husband and Cokes for the kids. Fox is still casting his gaze upward, which Susie notices.

"Are you okay, Fox?" Susie asks. "Is there something up there?"

The boy lowers his gaze and smiles at Susie. "No," he says smoothly. "Nothing up there. I'm good."

Susie smiles back. "How was England this summer? Did you and your sister have a good trip?"

"It was amazing. It was perfect."

"Oh, that's wonderful! I'm so pleased. What did you get up to?"

"Not much really. My dad has this new place he's renovating, out in the country, so we were there for the whole month. Just hanging out."

"And the weather. Was it good?"

"It was perfect, just perfect."

Jefferson's mother smiles at Fox playfully, sensing a backstory. "Did you meet someone, Fox?"

Fox looks at Jefferson awkwardly and Jefferson says, "Yeah, Fox, did you meet someone?"

Fox blows out his cheeks. "Yeah. Actually, I did."

Jefferson's mother rests her chin on her steepled hands and widens her eyes at him. "Spill."

"Yeah, Fox," says Jefferson. "Spill."

"Just a girl, you know."

"British?" asks Jefferson's mom.

"Uh-huh."

"What's she like?"

"She's, like, well . . . she's the perfect girl."

"Perfect how?"

"Just . . . perfect as in perfect."

"What?" says Jefferson. "Like, Margot Robbie perfect?"

"No. More perfect than her. Perfect-perfect."

Jefferson rolls his eyes. "What's her name?"

"Belle."

"Age?"

"Sixteen."

"Photos . . . ?"

"Oh, erm, yeah. Hold on." He feels his pockets for his phone and then says, "Shit, I left my phone at home."

"You left your . . . *What?* Who the hell leaves their phone at home?"

Fox tips his head back and stares into the air above his head. "Me, I guess," he says. And then he suddenly gets to his feet. "I have to go to the bathroom. Excuse me, won't you."

Fox bunches up his linen napkin and places it on the table, then heads to the left.

Jessica gets quickly to her feet and follows him.

The bathrooms are up a flight of stairs toward the side of the restaurant. Fox walks slowly, his arms by his sides, looking up as he goes. When he gets to the top of the stairs he stops. Then he holds his hands together, palms touching, and his head drops before suddenly rolling back, and as it does so a chilling cracking sound echoes around the landing, another crack, then another, like the crunch of a beetle's carapace. As Jessica absorbs the otherworldly sound, Fox's eyes rest on the ceiling a moment, and then a word comes from his mouth, barely intelligible. *Reminder? My random?* Then the boy clears his throat, lets his hands fall back by his sides, and carries on toward the bathroom door.

Jessica blinks and returns to her table, where her *veloot*-whatever is delivered to her a moment later alongside another basket of steaming hot bread.

Fox returns to the party after a few minutes, and Jessica tracks him closely. She thinks of the words he said when he thought nobody was watching. The way he crackled like tracing paper. She thinks of his flawless skin, the overuse of the word *perfect*, the way he stares upward. She thinks of the perfect girl in England named Belle.

She thinks, *Okay, Amber Randall, I hear you. I'm in.*

Twelve years ago
Portsmouth, Hampshire, UK

In a gloomy kiosk on the pier, Ophelia sits behind a small table. The table is covered by a fringed shawl, on top of which is a silk-shaded lamp whose base is shaped like an angel. A modern lamp plugged into the wall casts moving patterns of color over the red-painted walls as whooshy, nondescript music plays quietly in the background.

At the sound of a woman's voice outside her booth, Ophelia invites the visitor in.

A hand pulls back the grubby velvet curtain, and a very young woman peers uncertainly into the space.

Ophelia smiles at the girl. "Good afternoon. I am Madame Ophelia. And what can I do for you today?"

The girl pulls a handbag onto her lap as she sits down.

"Could you do me a reading, please? About my future?"

The girl is pretty but wearing too much makeup. Thick lip liner around sweet rosebud lips. Chalked-in eyebrows that don't suit her face. Thick, clumpy eyelashes. Skin caked in gunk.

Ophelia narrows her eyes. "What are you hoping to discover?"

The girl breathes in hard. "I want to know when I'm getting out of here."

"Out of . . . ?"

"*Here*. Portsmouth. I just feel . . ." She inhales again. "There's more than this. There has to be."

Ophelia keeps a steady gaze on the girl, feeling almost maternal. "There is more than this. Believe me, there's much more than this."

"Then please. Tell me how to get out of here."

Ophelia nods and holds out her hand. "Let's see."

She takes the girl's hand in hers and runs her thumb down the lines on her palm. She gasps softly at what she sees. It's very unusual.

"There," she says, pointing. "You have a fate line. Not many people have one. And it's attached, here, to your lifeline. This means that you are a self-made individual, that you are in charge of your destiny."

"Yes," says the girl, staring in awe at the line in the palm of her hand. "Yes. That's what I want. I want to be self-made."

"What do you see yourself doing?"

The girl scoffs gently. "I thought that's what you were meant to tell me?"

"I can guide you. What are your interests?"

"Makeup," she says, boldly. "I love makeup."

Ophelia appraises her and nods. "I can see that. Pretty girl like you, you don't really need all of that stuff on your face."

"It's not about being pretty." Gone is the girl's uncertainty. She's almost haughty. "It's an art form. And not only that, but it's a multibillion-pound industry."

"Feeding on women's insecurities—"

"No," says the girl. "No. It's more than that. Makeup is *powerful.*"

Ophelia raises a skeptical eyebrow. "Powerful?"

"Yes. It can make you look perfect."

"How is looking perfect powerful?"

"Because"—the girl draws in her breath—"when you look perfect, everything else falls into place. You can concentrate on other things instead."

"I don't agree," says Ophelia. "I was once perfect, and my life didn't fall into place. Before I found love, I was a victim of my own beauty."

The girl narrows her eyes at her.

"I was young once," says Ophelia. "I was young for a very long time. The only thing that matters is love. Everything else is nonsense. Just enjoy your youth."

The girl frowns. "But I can't. I can't enjoy my youth. I want *more.*"

Ophelia sighs, but on some level she understands the girl's frustration.

"I just need to know that there will be more for me than this. Can you just guide me? Please."

Ophelia picks up a pile of tarot cards and holds them gently for a moment before passing them to the girl. "Here," she says. "Ask them your questions."

The girl's well-manicured hands take the cards and shuffle them slowly. But as she shuffles, the girl's gaze goes to Ophelia, who is staring at her while humming something under her breath.

"How old are you, if you don't mind me asking?"

"Older than I look."

"You look about forty."

"I'm much older than that."

"How much older?"

"Just . . . much older."

"What skin cream do you use?" the girl asks.

Ophelia taps a fingernail against the top of the deck of tarot cards. "Please try and concentrate."

The girl takes her eyes from Ophelia's skin and focuses on the deck of cards again. But she keeps looking up, distractedly.

"Your hair," she says. "It's so shiny. What products do you use?"

Ophelia sighs. "Homemade."

Her eyes widen. "You make your own products?"

"I do, yes."

"Wow, that's amazing." The girl is suddenly very animated. "What sort of ingredients do you use?"

"Oh, nothing special. Just natural stuff. Anyway . . ."

The girl's eyes are wide and glittering, and Ophelia feels a wave of dread pass through her.

She wants this girl to go now.

"You know," says the girl, "I really think that maybe this could be kismet."

Ophelia takes the deck of cards from her hands and slides them back into their box. "I think maybe it's better if you come back another day. When your mind is more focused."

"But my mind is focused. It's *so* focused."

"I meant on your future."

"But this is my future. I've seen it. *You're* my future."

This girl has something about her, something that stirs the long-dead parts of Ophelia's psyche. "I'm nobody's future. You don't even understand the meaning of the word."

The girl casts her gaze around the grubby kiosk, the shabby velvet hangings, the splintered, peeling clapboard. "Don't you want more than this, Madame Ophelia?"

Ophelia smiles tightly. "I've had more than this. I've had *much* more than this. This"—she arcs her arm around the kiosk—"is my happy ending."

The girl sighs loudly through her nose, then picks up her cheap bag from her lap and hooks her fingers through the handles. She stands and looks around one more time, then stares imperiously at Ophelia's face.

"Your loss," she says. "Your loss."

When the girl finally leaves, a long, ragged breath escapes Ophelia's throat and she clasps her hand to her heart.

That girl contains darkness and evil. That girl, she believes, is a mortal threat to Ophelia's hard-won happiness.

Six

Back at the Finch the following morning Jessica follows the signs to the Gloria room. This one is clad with baby-pink paneling and has a huge green velvet sofa in the window scattered with pink cushions. Amber has ordered tea in a pot for her and coffee in a pot for Jessica, and there is a selection of miniature breakfast pastries on a plate in front of her. Amber's hair is tied back sharply from her face, and she looks tired. "Good morning, Jessica. How was your dinner?"

"Kind of nice, actually. They do great bread."

"Your hair looks pretty."

Jessica touches it vaguely and shrugs. Then she gets out her phone so that she can play Amber her recording.

"This was Fox when he thought nobody was there. I tuned

the audio so you can hear it through the background noise. Listen."

She presses play and watches Amber's reaction, pausing the recording just after the sound of Fox's body cracking.

"What was that?" Amber says. "Can you play that again?"

Jessica replays it.

"What was the noise?"

"I have no idea. But it came from Fox's body."

Amber shudders. "Oh my God, that's horrible." Her voice wavers as she speaks.

"Yes," Jessica agrees. "It was. You okay for me to carry on?"

Amber nods tersely and Jessica presses play again.

"Wait." Amber holds up a flat hand. "What was that? What did he just say?"

"I don't know. I've listened a dozen times and I still can't make it out. I thought you might know."

"No," she says. "I have no idea. Sounds like 'my number'?"

"Sounds like all kinds of things."

"And then what did he do? After that?"

"He went into the bathroom. I went back down. And apparently Fox met a girl?"

"Did he say what her name was?"

"Belle."

"Belle. No. I don't know of her. Did he say anything about her?"

"No, not really. Just that she was *perfect*."

"Ah, that word again."

"Yup. That word again. But Fox didn't mention this girl at all when he got home?"

"No. Nothing. I even asked him if he'd met anyone, and he said no."

"Well, he was quite happy to tell his friend's mom all about her. I mean, listen, I can follow these kids around like a freak, but sooner or later they'll notice me and wonder what the hell I'm doing. It seems to me that you need someone who can infiltrate their worlds. Someone who can be their friend."

"I know. Exactly. I was thinking of asking one of their friends, but who could I ask who wouldn't just immediately confess that I'd set them up and make my kids even more distrustful of me than they already are?"

"Why are they distrustful of you?"

"Oh God." She shrugs and turns her hand up. "I don't know. Just because. Because I'm their mother. Because I find things out about them. Because I love them, I guess. Do you have children, Jessica?"

"Oh." Jessica flinches, as though she has been shoved in the chest. "No. No, I don't."

"Do you want them?"

"Er, I . . ."

But Amber saves her from having to answer the question by cutting in over her. "It's complicated. Being a mother is complicated, and you have no idea how complicated it is until you're neck-deep in it all. But yes, I'd love to be able to infiltrate their world somehow, you know, *rent a teenager* to hang out—"

"Hold on," says Jessica, a thought leaping right to the top of her mind. "I might have just the answer. My . . ." She pauses, unsure of the correct word to describe Malcolm. "My . . . assistant," she says.

"You have an assistant?"

"Yeah, he's new. But he's super enthusiastic, and super smart. And he's only seventeen."

"Right. But where does he live?"

"I have no idea."

"How would he . . . fit in?"

"Well, for starters, he's an Akinesiz fan."

"Okay, well, that's a start. But how would he gain their trust?"

"I'm not sure yet. Leave it with me. I'll think of something. But in the meantime, I'm going to see what I can find out about this girl named Belle who lives in . . ."

"Barton Wallop."

"Barton what now?"

"Wallop. British villages have insane names. You should google them sometime, for fun. But anyway, that is the name of Sebastian's village. And his house is called Barton Manor. It has a moat."

"A, like . . . ?" Jessica draws a circle in the air.

"Yeah. That much the kids did tell me. And a drawbridge."

"Does it have a dragon?"

Amber laughs. "No. No dragons. But it should be very easy to find on Google Earth."

"Yes. I will get straight onto that. And . . ." Jessica glances down at a puddle of purplish light falling onto the cream floorboards of the room through a stained-glass fanlight. "Listen. Is there anything else I should know? About your husband? About his background? I mean . . . is there anything special about him? Or his family?"

"No," Amber replies. "Nothing like that. Just totally normal."

Jessica moves to take her leave, but Amber stops her by touching her sleeve gently.

"Jessica," she says, her sharp eyes staring at her softly. "Are you okay?"

"Yeah. Sure. I'm great."

"You seem, I don't know. Troubled."

Jessica flinches slightly at this uncannily perfect descriptor of the state she currently finds herself in.

"No. Really. I'm good."

"I would, you know, I'd want to help. If I could. If you wanted—"

"I told you. I'm good." Jessica wears a stiff smile. "But thanks. And I'll call you later about Malcolm."

"Who's Malcolm?"

"My assistant. Have a great day."

"Jessic—"

But Jessica turns abruptly and leaves, her heart lurching in her chest.

* * *

She feels the pall of the closing moments of her conversation with Amber lowering over her as she heads home. Amber has made her think of him and now she feels that always-present threat of him in the air, tastes him in the back of her throat. She wonders if she'll ever feel truly safe in this world.

Back at her desk, Jessica calls Malcolm. "I have work for you. Can you come in now?"

"I'm in class," he whispers.

Jessica groans and rolls her eyes. "When do you get out?"

"Two thirty. I can be at yours at three."

Jessica groans again. "How are you going to work for me if you're in school all day?"

"I'll find a way! Trust me! I'll see you at three. Should I pick you up a coffee?"

She sighs. "Sure. Large black. See you later."

As she ends the call, she's already glancing around her office.

She took out a long lease on this place a couple of years ago. She was desperate at the time. She hadn't noticed the cracks in the windowpanes, the smell of must and damp, the curls in the linoleum, the green stains in the washbasin, the mildew in the fridge. She'd needed a place where she was safe, where she could rest her head at night and not feel his eyes on her, not hear his voice in her head. She has not thought beyond the next moment of her life since she got here, has lived in hourly increments: wake, eat, drink, work, survive. She has left behind most of her close friends from her years as a—admittedly below par—super hero. They exist on another plane now, far above her, with their costumes and their glamour and their mystique. She is a scruffy second cousin in comparison, not thought of nor remembered from day to day. And she has felt for so long that this is where she belongs, here in this nasty apartment, doing this nasty, messy job, alone, drunk, empty inside. But surely, she wonders painfully, surely there must be more than this.

Her hand goes to her abdomen, and she cups it for a moment, tenderly, tries to imagine a baby in there, and then gasps softly, because she can't. She just can't.

She picks up her phone and scrolls down to Luke's number. She should call him. She should see him. Maybe if she saw him, then she might be able to formulate some kind of adult response to what is currently happening to her. Her thumb hovers over the call button and she sighs gently. She thinks of his voice, his skin, his smell, the way he holds her so tenderly and makes her feel normal. He is literally the only person in the world who can make her feel normal. She hits the call button and holds her breath.

The call rings out to his voicemail. She stays on the line for just a moment or two before hanging up.

* * *

"Wow, your hair looks . . . different."

Malcolm, fresh from school, his bag slung across his chest and clutching two paper cups of coffee, hovers in the doorway.

Jessica steps aside and touches her hair absentmindedly. She'd forgotten about it. "Yeah . . . I went to a salon."

"What the hell."

"It was for the undercover thing."

"It looks pretty."

"Whatever. Right." She walks behind her desk and gestures to him to take a seat. "I need to know a few things about you."

Malcolm slides her coffee across her desk and then unloops his bag from his torso and sits down. "Fire away."

"You're seventeen, right?"

"Yup."

"Where do you live?"

"A few blocks up from here." He takes four packets of sugar out of his jacket pocket, rips their corners off in one go, then tips them into his coffee.

"And who do you live with?"

"My mom."

"Just the two of you?"

"Yeah. Why are you asking all these questions?"

"I'm trying to get a handle on you for some undercover work. Trying to work out how adaptable you are."

"Oh my God. I am super, *super* adaptable." His brown eyes are gleaming with excitement now. "Seriously. I have so many different types of friends, you know, and I just fit right in with all of them. I'm like a freakin' social chameleon. I can—"

Jessica stops him by putting her hand between them. "Fine," she says. "I get the picture. But are any of your friends unbelievably wealthy and living in Upper East Side penthouses?"

"Well, no—but I still think I could fit in. I mean, look, you went to a salon and got flicky hair to go undercover, I'm pretty sure I can find a Ralph Lauren polo shirt in a thrift shop and slick my hair back. What's the job? I *swear*, whatever it is, I can do it."

Jessica leans back in her chair and appraises Malcolm. He has a nice face; it's one of those faces that looks like it comes from everywhere. But he is so very intensely himself, so very Malcolm in every movement of his face and intonation of his voice, she cannot possibly imagine him in the Bleeding Heart eating steak with the right cutlery, or on the subway with Lark's pretentious friends and their talk of Hamptons houses and therapy.

She leans forward again and says, "The job is sixteen-year-old twins, went to the UK for the summer, came back as different people, mother wants to know what's going on but everyone's acting like everything's normal. I've shadowed them both and there's definitely something not right with them. They came home with freakishly perfect skin, they go out without their phones, the boy's skin crackles, and he talks to the sky when he thinks no one's looking. But these kids, Malcolm, they're rarefied as hell. They live a life that's so far above and beyond anything you and I could possibly imagine. Getting close to them would be hard enough in the most normal of circumstances, let alone these circumstances." She pauses, suddenly doubting herself. Is this in fact a terrible idea? But seeing Malcolm's face gleaming with excitement, she relents. "I need someone to get really close to them, close enough for them to share their secrets, and you are literally the only teenager I know, and you are far from perfect, but I am willing to take a chance on you, if you think you can do it."

His eyes light up again. "I can so do this, Jessica. I mean, I feel like I was *born* to do this. You know, I was always the lead in the school plays at elementary and middle school. Always, ask my mom. And I'm the one my friends always sent into any situation they felt uncomfortable about, you know, like getting balls out of backyards, asking parents if their kids can come out, it was always me because I'm good at talking to people."

She puts up her hand again. "Okay," she says. "I hear you. How would you go about this?"

"Well, is there anything they do after school? Like an extracurricular thing I could join to be around them?"

Jessica scribbles this down. "I'll find out."

"And what do they do socially? Where do they hang out?"

"Well, the girl, she's an Akinesiz fan, that's why I was asking after him the other day. She's a bit of an emo."

"I can do emo. I can totally do emo. I'm kind of already half emo, I just hide it."

Jessica sighs. "Great. Good. Well. Let me find out more."

"So, what now? Do I need to fix my hair? What next?"

She drops her eyes to her notepad, wanting to think. "I'll be in touch."

A moment later, she still sees him loitering in her peripheral vision. "We're done here."

He nods, then holds his thumb and pinkie up to his face. "Call me."

"I will."

"Soon."

"I will."

And then finally, Malcolm leaves.

Twelve years ago
Portsmouth, Hampshire, UK

The girl waits and watches from the other side of the pier until Madame Ophelia emerges from her booth at the end of the day. The older woman pulls the door closed behind her, locks it up with a padlock, and tucks the key into her canvas shoulder bag.

Ophelia walks very slowly, which the girl finds frustrating as she herself is a fast walker. The woman and her shadow thread lugubriously through the backstreets of town, toward the shopping center, the evening light growing dark gold as the sun sets. The girl sees a friend she recognizes across the street and turns her head away before the other girl catches sight of her and tries to waylay her for a chat.

Ophelia stops outside an old-fashioned shoe shop on the high street. A young man is outside the shop locking up the doors. He turns when he sees Ophelia and smiles. She smiles too and gives him a brief embrace, then waits while he rolls down the electric shutters, clips the keys to a ring that hangs from his belt loop.

"What do you want for your dinner?" she hears Ophelia ask.

She stares at the young man afresh. *Ophelia's son.*

He's tall and lanky; his hair is long and hangs greasily on both sides of a pale, slightly beaky face. And then it hits her. She recognizes him. His name is Arthur. She went to school with him, he was two years above her, and he was the weirdest kid in the whole world. Had a brain the size of a planet, knew everything. It was said that he had the highest IQ in the county. Everyone expected him to leave school and go to Oxford or Cambridge and invent things and change the world. But clearly that wasn't the case. She feels a stab of sadness for him. He looks as stuck as she is, managing a cheap shoe shop in Portsmouth, living at home with his mum, all the crazy, untapped potential going to waste.

Ophelia and Arthur walk together without hurry. They stop at a Premier corner shop and come out with two blue plastic bags of shopping. They trundle on.

After a few minutes they come to a halt outside a small redbrick terraced house just off the main road, and Ophelia opens the front door with a key from her handbag. A cat sits in the doorway. Ophelia says hello to it.

The door closes behind them and the girl exhales.

Arthur looks lonely.

Arthur looks lost.

Arthur looks in need of a girlfriend.

Seven

According to Amber, Lark has guitar lessons on Tuesdays at five and Fox plays rugby on Wednesdays. On Fridays they both go to boxing classes at their local gym. Jessica relays this information over the phone to Malcolm, who says, "Boxing. Send me to boxing. And I thought of a name. I will be Sly McNeil. What do you think?"

Jessica ponders whether perhaps she made a mistake. "What's wrong with Malcolm Powder?"

"They'll google me, won't they? And I can't have them coming across my real online being. I've made a Snap account and everything. Insta. The works. And I'm bleaching my hair."

"What? Why?"

"Because it transcends class. Y'know? You can be anyone with bleached hair. You're just the kid with bleached hair."

"Great. Whatever."

"And I'm going to say I'm new in the city, just come in from Saint Louis."

"How are they going to believe that with your accent?"

Malcolm pauses and then responds in a perfect flyover state accent. "I will talk like this, Jessica. That is how."

Jessica can't help but laugh. "Well, Malcolm, you are a surprising boy."

"I told you, didn't I? I told you."

* * *

The following morning is the day of Julius's return and the last time that Jessica needs to feed Speckles. She is fond of the cat now and finds reassurance in the fact that the brainless fur ball inspires soft feelings within her, almost, she might say, maternal feelings. She sits for the last time on the floor of Julius's apartment and strokes the cat, listening to the hum of his purr, until the hum of his purr merges with the hum of her phone in her jeans pocket.

She pulls it out and sees Luke's name on her screen.

She gathers herself and swipes reply.

"Hi."

"Hi." He sounds slightly nervous. "How you doin'?"

"I'm good."

"I saw your missed call yesterday."

"Yeah. Sorry. Nothing important. Just wanted to say hi."

There's a weird silence on the line and Jessica's mind finds ways to explain it, most of which involve the presence of another woman. "You okay?" she asks.

"Yeah. All good. Just getting ready for another day protecting Matt 'maybe I'm Daredevil, maybe I ain't' Murdock. What are you up to?"

She laughs. "I'm at my neighbor's place. Feeding his cat."

"A cat?" He issues a small laugh. "Can't picture it."

"Hold on." She moves the phone from her ear, then angles the camera at her and the cat, takes a snap, and texts it to Luke. "Check it out."

She waits a beat for him to open it and then enjoys the sounds of his laughter. "That's a *big* cat."

"Yeah. He's big. I almost lost him a few days ago. He jumped out the window, I almost had to . . ."

"Fly?"

"Yeah. I almost had to fly." She breathes out heavily. It feels good to talk to someone who gets it.

"And how was that?"

"It was not great. I was pretty relieved when he jumped back into my arms."

"Maybe he sensed it?"

"Ha!" Jessica smiles widely. "Yes. That's what I thought. He's been different around me ever since. I wondered if maybe, you know, animals, maybe they can smell it."

"I'm sure they can. They can smell tumors and low blood sugar and seizures. I'm sure they can smell us."

The conversation halts again for a moment. Jessica closes her eyes and listens to Luke's breathing.

"You okay, Jessica?" he asks after a moment.

"I'm—I'm okay. Got a big job going."

"Oh yeah?"

"Yeah. Kind of out of my depth. But that's okay. I'm on top of it."

"Wanna tell me about it?"

"It's a strange one. Some teenagers acting like androids or some such. And I have to go to the UK."

"Whoa."

"Yeah, I know. Straight out of my comfort zone. I've never even left the country before."

"Hey, y'know, you should check in with my friend Danny. Danny Rand. He travels a lot, spends a lot of time in the UK. He might be able to give you some tips?"

"Oh," she says softly. She worked alongside Danny back in her active super hero days, and as with everyone from that era of her life, the thought of seeing him again makes her feel edgy. "Cool. Good idea. Thank you. Send me his number and I'll message him."

"I sure will. He's my buddy—he'll love seeing you again. Anything else I can do?"

She swallows down a wry smile. My God. How about *rescue me*, she wants to shout. How about help me pack a bag and get me out of here. How about somehow telepathically know that I am in love with you without me giving you any single suggestion that that might be the case. How about ask me if I might be pregnant and tell me that you'd be fine with it if I was. How about *everything*? Every damn thing?

"No," she says. "Nothing else. We're good."

She waits for him to say something, anything that might make her feel that there's more to them than friends with benefits. But he doesn't.

"Well," she says, an edge of slight coldness to her voice. "Thanks for calling. I appreciate it."

"Jessica," says Luke. "Anytime. Seriously. Anytime."

"Well, not anytime," she says, thinking of the time she turned up drunk in the middle of the night and found him with another woman. "Obviously."

Luke sighs. "That was . . ."

"It doesn't matter what it was. It's your life, Luke. You're a free man. Anyway. I'd better go. You take care now."

And then she hangs up, before she starts crying.

* * *

Jessica never feels comfortable contacting people from her former community. For a while she had had a costume. And a name. Jewel. Yeah. A shit name. She'd been young and perky back then, though never really confident enough in her own pretty base-level powers to feel truly part of the gang. But she'd showed up, pretended she belonged, played her small part. And then a few years ago she'd been kidnapped by a psychopath who'd exerted mind control over her to make her do unspeakable things on his behalf.

And then one dreadful day he told her to kill Daredevil—and

off she went, in a stupid, dumbass mind-controlled haze—and accidentally picked a fight with the Avengers of all people. *Shit.* "Her people" beat her so badly she was in a coma for weeks until one of them cared enough about her to break into her addled mind and shake it awake.

Afterward it had felt like her reputation, what little of one she'd had, remained in tatters, even once there was an explanation for her actions. The others made a good show of forgiving her and accepting her—they even offered her a job of sorts. But it will always be there, this thin wall of reserve.

She feels almost as if she should crawl toward them now, prostrate on her stomach. It doesn't matter how many times they tell her they've forgiven her, that what she did wasn't her fault, she doesn't quite believe it. The power that sick man held over her had waned even as she left him to hunt Daredevil, but, still, she hadn't been strong enough to seize her own will until it was almost too late.

She can never truly forgive herself for that and so now, as she tries to word her message to Danny Rand, she feels shame at burrowing into his precious time for help on a case that might be nothing more than two spoiled kids who had a glorified glow-up in the UK.

But then she recalls the weird sounds that emanated from Fox's body at the Bleeding Heart, and curiosity makes her brave again.

She texts: Hi. It's Jessica. Luke suggested I drop you a line. I'm working a case in the UK. Looks like it might involve someone with malign powers, and I don't know anything about the

UK. Luke says you go a lot. Could you give me some pointers?
No need to go to any trouble. Only reply if you can. Sorry to
bother you.

She rereads the message and deletes the final four words.
Too pathetic. Too weak.

She presses send and waits. The cat waits with her.

Eight

Malcolm is in her office again.

It's six o'clock and Jessica was just about to shut her laptop for the day. In some ways his unexpected arrival is a blessing, as she has nowhere to be and nothing to do, she can't drink because she might be pregnant, and she doesn't even need to cross the landing to feed Speckles because Julius is back.

She blinks as she takes in his appearance.

"What do you think?" He runs his hands over his white-blond hair.

"I think—wow."

"Do you like it?"

"Yeah. Uh-huh." She nods and smiles tightly. "What did your mom say?"

"She hasn't seen it yet. But she'll love it. She loves everything I do."

Jessica nods again. She's starting to make sense of Malcolm. "So, what can I do for you, Malcolm?"

"I've been doing some thinking, about like how everyone these days presents themselves to the world as, like . . . perfect. I mean, it's not like it was when you were young."

"Holy crap, Malcolm, I'm not that old."

"Yeah, but you know what I mean. Like back when you were young it was okay to look rough."

"What the—?"

"But it kind of was. And now there are all these expectations for kids to look flawless. At least on-screen, you know? All these filters and shit. Just got me thinking . . ."

As he talks, Jessica switches on her phone and hits her camera roll. There's the photo she took earlier to send to Luke of her and Speckles and there is, yes, some kind of filter on the shot even though she has never knowingly activated it. She zooms in on the image, closer and closer, and it doesn't matter how far in she goes, there is not a hint of a pore or a line or a blemish.

She glances up at Malcolm as he continues. "It's gotta be just a matter of time before someone works out how to filter people in the real world. Don't you think? And imagine the power of that? Imagine a world where everyone is perfect."

* * *

Shortly after Malcolm leaves, Jessica's phone buzzes. She picks it up and sees a message from Luke's friend, Danny Rand.

I'm in the city. Come meet me?

She sees that he is still typing and bites her lip as she waits for his next message. It's a link to a noodle bar in Chinatown, followed by the suggestion: 7:30?

She replies: Great. See you there.

This meeting is strictly informal but still feels weirdly like a combo date/job interview, and she decides to shower and change and put on some halfway decent clothes. She eyes herself in the bathroom mirror before she leaves and pulls the last fading curls of her mermaid hair over her shoulders. She doesn't know what Luke might have said to Danny about the two of them, if he talked to Danny about her at all, but in any event, he's Luke's friend and she wants to look nice for him.

Danny is halfway through a giant bowl of ramen when she walks into the noodle bar an hour later. He sees her walk in and wipes his chin with a paper napkin before getting to his feet. "Hey!" he says. "Jessica!"

He's tall and blond, as stupidly good-looking as ever.

"Danny, good to see you." She shakes his hand and then slides onto the banquette opposite him.

"Here." He hands her a large, laminated menu. "I'm sorry I didn't wait for you. I missed lunch. But they're fast here."

Her eyes skim the photographic menu, and she notices that her nausea has subsided. She wonders then if maybe she's not pregnant after all, and at the thought of that possibility she feels a confounding bolt of both sadness and relief. She hasn't eaten a proper meal in days, and she orders a Singapore laksa with a side of crystal shrimp rolls.

"So," says, Danny, eyeing her with interest. "Jessica Jones. Luke told me you've been hanging out."

"He did?"

"Uh-huh. He said a lot of nice things." He smiles reassuringly. He has impossibly white teeth and crazy-blue eyes. "You look good."

"No, I really do not. But thank you."

"How've you been holding up?"

He's talking, of course, about what they all talk about when they think of her. Not that they know what *really* happened.

"Good days, bad days."

"You deserve better, you know."

Jessica startles at this statement. "Better than what?"

"Better than . . ." He sighs. "Sorry. I know you're a pretty private person. But I just always thought . . ." He visibly struggles with his words.

"Oh my God," she says impatiently. *"What?"*

"Nothing. Forget I said anything. I just don't think we should let the past define us, is all."

Jessica bristles. "It does not define me. I have a lot of other stuff going on. Seriously. I'm all good."

Danny laughs. *"What!"*

"Nothing," says Jessica, drawing her ire back. "Seriously."

Danny sighs and holds back a smile. Then he looks up at her again and says, "So, tell me, this case in the UK . . . ?"

She runs the basic bullet points past him: the perfect skin, the talking to the sky, the crackling skin, even the house with the damn moat, which makes him smirk.

"Well," he says, pushing away his empty ramen bowl and balling up his napkin. "I know London very well. The countryside, not so much. Will your client fund the trip?"

"Yeah. She's very wealthy."

"Well then. Five star all the way." Danny smiles. "Sounds like a gas. And you think there might be something, you know, unorthodox at play?"

Jessica's food arrives, heady with the scent of coconut and lime. She waits for the nausea to hit, but it doesn't, so she unwraps her chopsticks from the paper. "It's possible. I'm pretty sure that's why my client booked me."

"Is there like a place where you can do some research into British superfolk, like, a secret intranet that only certain very special people know about?"

Jessica laughs wryly. "Well, if there is one, I don't know anything about it." She digs her chopsticks into the noodle soup and twirls them around.

"Whereabouts in England did you say these weird twins had been?"

"Village called—I kid you not—Barton Wallop in Essex."

"Whoa!" He laughs. "I must say I'm kinda jealous."

"Jealous?"

"Yeah! I'd love to be jetting off to an old-world English village to uncover secret plots."

"Ha, yeah, when you put it like that . . . !"

"But listen, Jessica, if you need anything, any advice. I'm a seasoned traveler. I know people—my connections might come in handy. And Luke told me to look out for you, so, y'know."

"Thank you."

"What's the real deal with you and Luke?" He raises a pale eyebrow. "Are you, like, seeing each other?"

Jessica throws him a dry smile. "I'm not seeing Luke. Me and Luke are not a thing. Never were . . ."

He raises a brow. "Never will be?"

"Never will be."

"That's a shame."

"Why is it a shame?"

"I don't know. I think you'd make a cute couple, that's all. Anyway, I'm going to get another beer. How about you?"

"No," she says. "No thank you. I'll just have a . . ." She picks up the drinks list and scans it quickly. "A mango-kale smoothie."

"Ew. Sounds gross. Don't you want a real drink?"

"A smoothie *is* a real fricking drink."

"Fine." He smiles. "Sorry. That was out of line."

He throws her a full-hearted smile and Jessica can't resist returning it.

Nine

There's a pharmacy open two blocks down from the noodle bar. It rings with the brisk sound of spoken Mandarin and gunfire from the arcade machine in the corner being commandeered by three teenage boys with shaved heads. She steps inside.

She knows what she's looking for but meanders a while up and down the aisles, enjoying the bleaching harshness of the fluorescent lighting after the soft lantern red of the noodle bar. She picks things up and puts them down. A young man stacking shelves stares at her.

"What?" she asks.

"Nothing," he replies.

She shakes her head slightly at him and carries on toward the family planning section of the aisle, where she gazes numbly at the pregnancy testing kits.

Her head spins with the weirdness of everything. Noodles with Danny Rand. Going to the UK. And this . . . this gigantic freaking six-foot flashing-light question mark hanging over absolutely everything. She turns her head suddenly at this thought, and through the window of the pharmacy she sees a cab idling at a set of lights and there in the back of the taxi she sees a child turn to catch her eye, and she gasps. It's her again, the little girl in the silver coat. The girl raises her hand to her, and Jessica raises hers back. The girl kisses the palm of her hand and throws it to her, and Jessica breathes in softly, not sure how to respond. She suspects she's meant to catch the kiss and hold it next to her heart, but that sort of thing is not really in her DNA. She notices that the girl is alone in the back of the taxi and also, strangely, that the driver has not switched off his duty light. She lets her hand drop, the girl turns away, and a second later the taxi drives off.

Jessica drops the packet of pregnancy testing sticks she'd been holding on to a shelf and leaves the pharmacy. She is four miles from home. What was that child doing alone in the back of a taxi? Why was the for-hire light still showing? And does the girl even exist, or is she a figment of Jessica's imagination—a signifier, maybe, that Jessica is in fact going full-blown, stone-cold nuts?

* * *

"Malcolm *who*?" asks Amber the following morning. She's called using FaceTime and consequently Jessica has a jumpy view of her scowling face from under her chin as she walks down a busy street somewhere.

Jessica adjusts her phone so only half of her own face is showing. It's too early for this shit. "Powder. Malcolm Powder. I told you. But he's going to use the name Sly McNeil."

Jessica sees Amber push open a heavy chrome door, disappear, and then reappear a second later in an opulent foyer. The background noise recedes and is replaced by the babble of people as Amber moves through them.

"And you trust this boy, do you?"

Jessica bites her lip. "Yeah. Totally," she says. "He's super trustworthy." She has no idea, of course. She barely knows him, but he's her only option right now and she will have to trust her gut.

"And he's not going to blow our game?"

"No. He is not." Jessica shakes her head decisively, but in reality this is her biggest fear, that he will do something or say something stupid, and Lark and Fox will somehow divine that they are under surveillance.

Amber nods. "Good. And I got notification today that your passport will be ready to collect Monday morning. So I'm looking at London flights for you for Tuesday. Are you good with that?"

Jessica's stomach turns a little and a shiver of nerves runs through her. "Yes. I'm good with that."

"Excellent. And maybe we can get together again over the weekend. Talk through the plan for your trip. Are you free?"

Jessica nods and smiles wryly. "No plans at all."

She hears the ping of an elevator arriving and then an automated voice telling Amber to stand clear of the doors. "Listen," Amber says. "I have to go. I'll send over the details for the boxing class tonight for this Malcolm boy. He'll need to sign up on their website for the six p.m. class. I'll send a link. Okay, Jessica, I'll speak to you later. Bye."

And then the screen goes blank.

* * *

Julius invites Jessica over for takeout that night, to thank her for feeding Speckles.

"Don't bring anything," he says. "It's all on me."

But she heads to the bodega down the block beforehand anyway and picks up a bottle of something called Psycho Ghost Chili Hot Sauce and a bag of Herr's Smokin' Hot Ghost Pepper Potato Chips; if nothing else they will give her and Julius something to talk about for a moment or two.

She passes them to him at his door at six thirty and he eyes them curiously. "You like spice?" he asks, one perfectly micro-bladed eyebrow tipping up slightly.

"Yeah. Doesn't everyone?"

She follows him into his living room, which looks plush and glowing with the light from every last one of his numerous table lamps. Speckles appears from the kitchen and moves purposefully toward Jessica. She leans down to greet him, and he meows loudly.

"Well, look at that," Julius observes. "Besties now, I see."

"Yeah. We bonded," says Jessica. "He thinks I'm cool."

"Well, Jessica, you kind of are."

"That," she says, "is not true. But thank you. How was your trip?"

"Oh, it was every bit how you'd imagine a week in Toledo in the middle of October waiting for your mother's favorite sister to die would be."

"I'm sorry for your loss."

He pooh-poohs her condolences with a wave of his hand. "Yeah. It was sad. She was a nice lady. But at least now I have no reason to ever go to Toledo again. Anyway, what can I get you? Wine? Whiskey? Beer?"

"Oh, yeah. I kind of stopped drinking."

"Oh, now there's a curveball. What's brought that on? You're not pregnant, are you?" He asks this in humor, and she responds in kind. Even if she is pregnant, Julius is not the first person she would be telling.

"Nope," she says. "Nothing growing in this dried-up old husk of a uterus."

The words sound harsh as she says them, almost, she ponders, a betrayal of some sort, but not one she can quite define. "No. I just felt it was time to clean up my act, you know. I have a reputation, and nobody wants to have a reputation."

"*I'd* like to have a reputation," Julius replies.

"A reputation for being a boozer is . . . not good."

"So what can I get you instead? A soda? Tea? Juice?"

"Juice, please, whatever you have."

He heads to the kitchen and Jessica leans down again to

stroke Speckles, who is still sitting by her feet. She thinks of what Luke said about animals being able to smell the essence of other creatures—their weaknesses and illnesses, their tumors and their auras—and she wonders if Speckles can smell pregnancy—assuming there even is one—and maybe it is this that the cat has been drawn to, rather than the scent of her latent powers.

"Oh," she calls into the kitchen, "by the way, there was a kid waiting outside your apartment a few days back. A little girl. Do you know anything about her?"

"What kind of little girl?"

"Well, short. Obviously. Wears her hair in puffballs. Really pretty."

"No," he says, appearing in the kitchen doorway with a glass in one hand and a carton of juice in the other. "No idea."

"You haven't seen her in the building before?"

"Well, God, that's another question entirely. I mean, there's gotta be a hundred people living in this building. Maybe more. What did she want?"

"She didn't say. I tried to get her to talk to me, but she wouldn't. And I've seen her again since, out on the street, and last night I . . ." She pauses, not sure if she trusts Julius with what might in fact be evidence of her own imminent descent into madness. "I saw her in a taxi, down in Chinatown. On her own, and it's . . ." She pauses again, to see if he's listening enough to be concerned about her, but she senses not. "It's all kind of strange."

"Yeah. It sounds like it." Julius passes her a glass of juice, then holds out his own glass of red wine to her and says, "Cheers, Jessica. To you, from me and from Speckles, thank you so much for coming to the rescue and saving the day. We're very, very grateful."

She smiles and touches her glass to his. "It was actually fun. I discovered that I like cats."

"Well then, you should get one. Keep you company."

She smiles. "Mad cat lady. That's me."

Julius gives a look of faux concern. "Then what does that make *me*?!"

"You have a boyfriend at least."

"Well, yeah. But one who refuses to live with me."

Jessica watches as Julius brings his wine glass to his mouth. She sees the glistening red of the wine tip toward the rim and the meniscus breaking as it slips between his lips. She shudders lightly with combined feelings of revulsion and compulsion. She wants a drink so badly. She craves the heat of alcohol, the warm amber of the dregs of whiskey in her apartment, the sultry ruby of Julius's Merlot. She wants to feel her mind closing over with the soft drapes of drunkenness. She has not gone this long without a drink since ... no, she can't remember. But as Julius takes the glass from his lips, and she sees the brown stain of it on his teeth, smells the slightly meaty, bloody odor of it, she thinks suddenly, I'm good. I can do this.

She lifts her juice to her lips and drinks, enjoying the sharp clean tang of it.

* * *

Malcolm FaceTimes her a few minutes after she walks back into her own apartment laden with Thai leftovers from Julius's feast. She drops the boxes on the kitchen counter, swipes reply on her phone, and is taken aback afresh by the nuclear glow of Malcolm's hair.

"Malcolm. Hey."

"Hey, Jessica. I just got through with boxing class. You free to talk?"

She glances at the time on the kitchen wall clock. Ten fifteen.

"Sure," she says, moving to her office chair and popping her feet up on her desk. "How'd it go?"

"Going," says Malcolm, with barely repressed excitement. "It's still going. I'm at their place."

"What!" Jessica pulls her feet down and sits upright in her chair.

"For real! I'm in their bathroom, right now. Look!" He pans his screen around a full marble bathroom with double walk-in showers and two washbasins with fat golden faucets.

"Oh my God. How come?"

"I charmed my way in!"

Jessica shakes her head slightly. "In what way?"

"In the way of being charming. And telling a lot of lies."

"Who do they think you are, Malcolm?"

"Well . . . they kind of think that I know Akinesiz personally. They also think I have family in the UK. Oh, and that my dad's a top sports agent and I live on Park Avenue."

"Seriously?" Jessica replies. "They believed all of that?"

"Yeah, they totally did. And now we're going to do some gaming."

"Just the three of you?"

"No, there's this other guy. He's named Jefferson. And Mrs. Randall is ordering us in some sushi. But listen. I gotta go now or they're gonna think I've got like IBS or something. Although, yeah, actually, that could be a good detail for Sly. IBS. Yeah. I like that. I'll message you when I'm home. Later!"

The screen of her phone empties and Jessica blinks slowly at it for a moment before putting it down. She feels slightly stunned and doesn't know what to do with herself. Her eyes go again to the five inches of whiskey on her filing cabinet. With that inside her she could drift slowly and softly from here to a deep numb sleep. Without it she is slightly lost. She wishes she was gaming with Malcolm at Amber Randall's apartment. She wishes she was in a bar somewhere. She wishes she had somewhere to be and someone to be with. Ten thirty on a Friday night never felt so lonely.

She picks up her phone again and scrolls through her recent contacts. Luke's number sits near the top and she stares at it, hard, as if the power of her own emotions might spontaneously trigger a call to him. And then she presses the message button and types fast, before her nerve deserts her: Hey. I'm sober and bored. Can I come over?

She sees Luke typing immediately, and her heart races.

I'm here and waiting.

Ten

The sensation of waking the next morning in Luke's bed with a clear head and an unsullied memory of the night before is novel. She turns toward Luke and props her head on her hand. He's lying on his back, looking at his phone, and his face opens up at the sight of her. He puts the phone down and turns so that he is facing her fully.

"Good morning, Jessica Jones."

"Good morning, Luke Cage."

"So this is what you look like in the mornings when you don't have a stinking hangover."

"Yeah. Pretty, huh?" She pulls a cheesy smile.

"Yeah," says Luke, moving his face closer to hers. "So pretty."

She pushes his face away from hers playfully. "What are you doing today?"

"Oh, you know, putting up shelves."

"Putting up shelves? Seriously?"

"Yeah. Seriously. You might have noticed that I do not have any shelves. And I also have things that need to go on shelves. So I am putting up shelves."

"And where are you going to get the shelves from?"

"I already have the shelves. I got them last weekend from IKEA."

"You went to IKEA?"

"Er, yeah. Where else do you think I'd get shelves from?"

"I really can't say I've ever thought about it. Maybe I just thought you'd hack down a tree and carve it into slices with your bare hands."

"Really?" He laughs. "You think that?"

"No. I don't think that. But you know, self-assembly hell, even you might need some help with that. Would you like my assistance? I could use one of those things with the thing in it?"

"One of those things with the thing in it?"

"Yeah. For straight lines. It has like a little blob of oil in the middle? I think?"

"A spirit level?"

"Yeah! A spirit level! I can do that if you need me to?"

Luke smiles lazily at her and finds her hands. He picks them up and squeezes them gently. "Jessica Jones. I would *love* to put up shelves with you today. Thank you."

"No. Thank you. It's nice to have someone to spend time with. I've just been feeling . . . since I gave up drinking . . . just so . . ."

"Bored?"

"Yeah. Bored. Time goes slowly, doesn't it?"

Luke laughs. "It can."

"Just so slowly. And rooms feel so . . . hollow. And my mind. It goes places. And plays tricks on me. And I keep seeing this girl . . ."

She pauses, unsure for a moment, but then she glances up and sees Luke's soft gaze on her, so she continues. "A little girl. She looks about five. And at first, I thought she was real? But now I'm not sure. And it feels like maybe my brain made her up? I can't . . . I can't explain it."

"What makes you think she's not real?"

"I don't know. Because she sure as hell looks real to me. But whenever I see her, she is always alone, and what sort of five-year-old is always alone? Like no five-year-old, that's who. I dunno. Maybe I'm losing my mind a little."

"We're all losing our minds a little."

"Are you losing your mind, Luke?"

"Of course I am. Every minute of every day."

"Like, right now?"

"No, not right now. But the rest of the time."

"Why not right now?"

Luke rolls his eyes. *"Duh,"* he says. "Because you're here."

Jessica's stomach reacts to this with a sickly sweet lurch. "Ha," she says. "Interesting."

"In what way interesting?"

"In the way that it sounds like you're saying something nice to me."

"And why wouldn't I be saying something nice to you?"

"Because . . ."

She stops. She wants to say *Because I'm a loser*. But she feels for a moment like maybe she isn't a loser, especially here, in Luke's fragrant bed, with a clear head and a shaft of golden morning sun cutting through a gap in his drapes, with his eyes on her like that, like she is a good thing, not a bad thing, and the soft, shocking secret that may be growing inside her right now.

"No," she says instead. "You're right. I'm freaking amazing."

"Well, I did not say that precisely," he replies with a twinkle and Jessica rolls her eyes and play-pushes him before sighing and leaning back into the pillows. "Do you ever think about the next ten years, Luke?"

"What aspect of the next ten years?"

"I don't know, I guess the substance of it? What they're going to be for? I mean, did you ever think about, I don't know, having kids? With any of your exes?"

"Kids?" Luke lets out a small dry laugh. "No. No, I never did think about kids. I mean, what sort of a world is this to bring new life into? This shitty, disgusting world. No. It was never on the agenda."

Jessica feels the playful mood dip and she stifles a sigh. "And now?"

"Well, I don't see the world getting any better, do you?"

"So you don't think a child's world is what you make it?"

"Hey, I know I have super-powers, but I'm not sure they extend to ending poverty, racism, war, and disease."

"But you can protect your children, can't you? Surely?"

"I'm not sure you can. Especially a child of mine, whose skin would be the wrong color for this world. Maybe it would be unbreakable like mine, but damn sure everyone would try to test that. Every day would be an uphill battle. And I'm tired enough fighting for myself, let alone for a child that didn't ask to be born."

Jessica nods, mutely.

"What about you?" he asks. "You ever think about having a child?"

She smiles tightly. "Yeah, I mean sometimes, I guess. But then I think, what sort of mother would I be? You know. With all my *issues*."

"Well, yeah, there's that too. Not just the world that can mess up a kid. Moms and dads can do a pretty good job of that too."

Jessica reels slightly at his words, not the words she expected, not what she was looking for—instead, confirmation of every doubt she's ever had about herself and her place in this world. She feels tears spring hard behind her eyes and pushes them back down and then, thank God, her phone buzzes and Malcolm's name appears on her screen.

"Sorry," she says. "I have to take this. It's work. Yes?" she says abruptly as she answers.

"Yo. How are you?"

"Please don't make small talk, Malcolm."

"Yeah. Sorry. But listen up, I have news. I have in-for-ma-tion."

Jessica rolls her eyes at his division of the word into four precise syllables and mutters, "Shoot."

"I can't do this on the phone. I think we should meet up. I can be at your office in ten minutes. Maybe seven?"

"I'm not at my office."

"Oh. Where are you?"

"None of your business. It's Saturday morning."

"Yeah. I guess. But—"

"Look. I'll meet you there later, okay. But in the meantime, maybe you could write me a report."

"A report?"

"Yeah. With words in it."

"Sure. Yes. Absolutely. I will have a full report for you by . . . ? When can I come?"

Jessica sits on the side of the bed and looks at the solid, beautiful expanse of Luke's naked back as he stares at his phone. She feels, somehow, that if she were just to stay here now she might never have to leave again, that she might drift seamlessly into the next chapter of her life, the good bit, the soft bit, that the gloomy Hell's Kitchen apartment would somehow pixelate and evaporate, that the bad thing would evolve backward to a point of nonexistence, that every dark moment of her life would collapse in on itself until there was nothing left to remember, and that she would wake up every morning in a state of fresh, untainted, dewy-eyed neutrality with Luke by her side telling her he wanted her to have his baby.

She takes her eyes from Luke's back, and sighs. "I'm busy today," she says to Malcolm, "but come by at five. I'll be there."

Twelve years ago
Portsmouth, Hampshire, UK

The strappy sandals are the least nasty pair of shoes in the shop but are still quite revolting. Trying not to sneer, the girl lets one hang from her manicured fingertip as she crosses the shop floor to the man standing with his arms behind his back staring into the middle distance.

"Hi," she says, breaking into a fresh smile. "Do you have this in a five and a half?"

The young man snaps out of his reverie and glances down at the sandal. "Oh," he says softly, "no, we don't do these in half sizes. I'm really sorry."

"A six will be fine, then!" she says. The five and a half she always asks for is something of an affectation anyway.

The young man nods and takes the sandal. "Let me just check . . ."

She watches him as he heads towards the stockroom. He is skinny, but tall, probably just over six foot, and could definitely fill out with a bit of time at the gym. His hair is terrible, but clean and thick and easily fixable with a trip to a decent barber. He pairs a sweatshirt with some kind of logo on it with suit trousers. Dreadful, just dreadful. But again, a simple fix. And the slightly beaky face? It's fine. She's seen worse.

She can do this, she thinks. She can seduce Weird Arthur from School. No big deal. She fixes the smile on her face for his return.

"We have them," he says, holding a cardboard shoebox triumphantly, and gestures for her to take a seat on the nasty threadbare chair.

"Thank you." She sits and, holding his gaze, slowly slips off her zip-up boots.

She sees him still for a second, like a cornered animal, his breath held.

"Could I?" she asks, pointing towards the shoebox in his hands.

"Oh, yes, sorry. Of course."

A pale flush passes across his face; how easy this is going to be. She slides on the sandal and fastens the side buckle.

"What do you think?" she says.

"It looks nice. Here. Try the other." He hands it to her.

She models the shoes around the empty shop, giving him ample opportunity to absorb her form-fitting skinny jeans, tight polo neck sweater, the way she's piled her long blond hair atop her head to reveal the curve of her neck. She stands in mirrors and appraises herself, pushes out her chest, turns this way and that.

"I'll take them," she says.

His face brightens. "Great. Let me get them wrapped up for you."

"You know," she says, as she stands at the shop counter and watches him place the sandals back in their box, "I feel like I know you from somewhere."

He glances at her askance. "Really?"

"Yes. Where did you go to school?"

He produces the name of her old school, and she smiles. "I knew it," she says. "Me too. When did you leave?"

"Four years ago."

"Yeah! Me too!"

"That was after my A levels."

"Oh," she says. "Right. I left after my GCSEs. So you're two years older than me?"

"I'm twenty-two."

"I'm twenty. Well, almost twenty. Next week. What have you been up to since you left school? Did you go to uni?"

"No. My parents needed me to work."

"Seriously? God, that's surprising. You were so clever at school. I remember. You were like an actual genius."

He flushes at her words, stands a bit straighter. "This is just temporary," he says, gesturing at the shop. "I still want to go. One day."

"What would you want to study?"

"Quantum physics."

"Quantum physics? What's that?"

He shrugs. "It's the science of matter. Of energy. Of what makes everything exist."

".Wow," she says, exploding her fingers outwards at her head, to suggest her mind being blown. "You really are a genius!"

"Well, not really, I just like . . . you know, understanding how the world works. And seeing how much further it could be taken." He smiles and tucks the tissue paper back around the sandals before replacing the lid. "The world is full of untapped potential."

"A bit like you," she says, deliberately allowing her fingertips to brush against his skin as she passes him a ten and a twenty for the shoes.

He presses the penny change into her hand and she feels it, the electric tang of his interest, his excitement.

He laughs nervously. "Yes. I suppose so."

She touches her lips with the tip of her tongue and cocks her head. "You know, my head, it's so full of ideas. Full of plans. My brain, it never stops, it's like a whirring machine, all day long. But I can never quite find the key to it all. What it is I'm searching for. I feel like I need to talk to someone who can help me make sense of everything. Someone with a big brain and big ideas. Someone like you . . ."

She watches his face react to this announcement, the pale flush grow deeper.

"Maybe I could take you for a cocktail tonight and pick your brain a bit."

"I mean, er . . ."

"What time do you get off work?"

"Five. But then I have to go home and help my mum with dinner."

She throws him a look of disappointment.

"It's just . . . it's what we do."

"Every night?" She folds her arms across her chest. "Really?"

"Yeah. Every night."

She sighs and leans closer towards him across the counter. "Meet me after dinner. I'll be at the Claremont, in the lounge bar, eight p.m. Cocktails on me."

"But I—"

"See you there."

"Er—er . . . But what's your name?"

"It's Polly."

She smiles as she lets the shop door bang shut behind her.

Eleven

After Luke's harsh words, Jessica finds it hard to return to the soft place in which she'd woken up. The emotional connection that they'd experienced the night before feels diminished, foolish almost. Instead, she and Luke proceed in a companionable and workmanlike fashion, constructing and installing bookshelves, breaking off for burgers and fries, messing about, throwing around playful insults, sexless teasing, brother-and-sister stuff. And then it is time for Jessica to leave, and when she closes Luke's door behind her and heads into the dank October afternoon she wonders if she just blew her life down the wrong road.

Malcolm is waiting on the street outside her building when she gets there at ten past five. He has his hood up and is bouncing from foot to foot, holding a manila folder in his hand. He springs toward her when he sees her approach and waves the folder wildly. "My report! Here!"

He tries to force it into her hand, and she backs away from him. "Stand down, dude. We'll look at it upstairs."

In her office the heating has been off all day, and she can virtually see her breath in the air. "Shit," she says, twisting the thermostat up to seventy. "Shit."

She throws some coffee into her machine, leaves it to brew, then returns to her desk. "So," she says, rubbing her hands together to warm them up. "What you got?"

He passes her the folder, and she slides it away. "Just tell me."

Malcolm's face falls. "I worked on that all day."

"Yeah. I'll add it to the dossier. Great work. So, what did you get?"

"Well, it was kind of a weird night and, yeah, I totally get what Mrs. Randall is worried about. Those twins, they're sort of amazing, you know. I mean, they're kind of beautiful, obviously. But they're really . . . *out there*? Like on another planet. And I think, even if I hadn't been looking for it, I'd have seen it? So, anyway, we did our boxing class, and they were freaking incredible. The boxing instructor kept praising them, saying, 'I don't know what you kids have been doing this summer, but keep doing it.' And this girl turned to me and hissed, 'Steroids,' in my ear and I said, 'What, really?' and she said, 'I dunno, but they're doing something, they both sucked last year.'

"So I went up to them after the class and I told them how

freaking awesome they both were, and then I just kind of finagled the whole Akinesiz thing into the conversation, and then I mentioned my grandmother's house in London and how my dad represented all these famous footballers—and I could tell that they were warming to me, you know, but I genuinely was not expecting them to just say, 'Come back to our place.' I mean, I know I'm good, but I did not know I was that good. So out of the gym and into an Uber, penthouse apartment, elevator doors open out straight into this colossal hallway. This dude Jefferson came over too. We ate sushi— you ever had sushi? I mean, I have, but this stuff was next level, seriously like nothing I've ever eaten before. And so we were talking at the table, and the upshot is that when they were in the UK, they were hanging out with this kid named Belle whose parents live abroad somewhere. They said she lived with, like, a caretaker, goes to boarding school, is sixteen years old, that was it. I tried to push for more, but that was as much as they gave me.

"I said, 'You guys have the most incredible complexions, what's your secret?' and they both just kinda smiled at each other and said, 'Soap and sunscreen,' like it was some kind of inside joke. And I said, 'Seriously though, I've never seen skin like that before. Can I touch it?' And, Jessica, they let me touch their skin and it felt like . . . glass? And I said, 'Whoa, it doesn't even feel like skin—are you sure you guys are real?' And they looked at each other again and said, 'We're perfectly real.' And they both said it *at the same time*. It was so weird."

Jessica realizes that Malcolm is not going to pause to catch a breath, so she leans back and lets him do his thing.

". . . and the dude, Fox's friend Jefferson, he threw me a look as if to say, 'Back off,' you know. And then when the twins left the room he said to me, 'What do you think of them?' I said that I thought they seemed cool. He sort of shrugged and said, 'I guess,' but then he said, 'You don't think they're kind of weird?' I said yeah, they seemed a little unusual. He said, 'Ever since they got back from England, they've been like this.' So I said, 'Oh, what do you think happened in England?' to which he answered, 'No idea, they won't talk about it. But something went down out there, that's for sure.' He started telling me how Fox's gotten taller since summer, and how his grades have gone through the roof, like he was never a straight-A student before, but now he's acing everything. Then he said how he and Fox used to game all the time, but now all Fox wants to do is watch old movies from the eighties. And listen to old music. He kept playing this on a loop . . ."

Malcolm presses play on a phone video and beneath the chatter of teenage conversation Jessica can hear the outline of a song.

"Listen to the lyrics," Malcolm urges.

Jessica listens. Something about eyes reaching out in vain and then there, she hears . . . *She's got perfect skin . . . she's got perfect skin.*

"I googled it," says Malcolm, "and it's a song from the eighties by some British band called . . ." He reads from his phone: "Lloyd Cole and the Commotions? I dunno. So I asked this Jefferson dude, 'Have you asked them what's going on?' and dude says, 'Tried, but he won't talk to me. Just keeps saying everything's *perfect*, *zen*.' And then the twins walked back in the room together, kind of in sync, you know. Marching, like crazy giant Aryan soldiers or such."

Malcolm shakes his head in wonder.

Jessica blinks at him. *"And?"*

"Well, that is kind of it really. Except, oh, I snuck into their bedrooms, took a load of photos. Things on their walls and whatnot. I can text that to you, see what you can find. And check this out . . ."

He swipes on his phone then and turns it toward Jessica. It's a selfie of him and the twins, Fox on the left, Lark on the right. They're all smiling.

"Okay?" Jessica peers at the picture on the screen, then notices something and zooms hard into the image, toward the kids' eyes. "Look," she says, pointing at his screen. "Look at their eyes. And look at yours. See how you can see the lights reflected in your eyes, but not in theirs?"

"I know, right?" says Malcolm, taking his phone back. "It's weird, and I think there's something there. I've been doing some research, into, like, the latest filter technology. Specifically, AI technology. Deepfakes. Lensa. All of that. I wrote it all up for you." He jabs at the file folder on the desk, impatiently. "It's all. In. There."

Jessica sighs. "Explain it to me like I'm five."

"Well, I mean, it's hard to explain really. There's a lot going on in the world right now, and every day the tech is getting crazier and crazier. I didn't find anything definitive, but I did look into the area where the twins were. You said Essex, right?"

"Yeah."

"So at like four in the morning—I swear I was up all night doing this—I found an Instagram account for a girl who describes herself as an 'AI witch and facialist.' Her page is set to private, but I used an app to track her IP address and get this: It's in Essex."

"Show me this girl, this AI witch."

Malcolm fiddles with his phone and then passes it to her.

There on the screen is a tiny profile photo of a girl with such a strong filter used on her face that she barely looks human. Her profile name is Perfect Peach and her bio details underneath say *AI witch, facialist, follow me for perfect skin and much much more*, followed by a sequence of emoji including hypodermic needles, peaches, and UFOs.

"Could be her, huh? Could be Belle?"

Jessica grimaces. This stuff, it's beyond befuddling. What does any of it mean? She sighs loudly and leans back into her office chair. Then she sits up straight again and slaps her hand down on the folder. "Right, well, looks like I've got some reading to do. Good work, Malcolm. Really good work. Any plans to see the twins again?"

"Yeah. Fox asked me to hang out after his rugby thing on Wednesday."

"Where did you tell him you were at school?"

"Oh, I told them a public school where I knew they wouldn't have any friends."

"But didn't you tell them you were wealthy?"

"Yeah. But I said my dad sends me to a public school because he wants me to be grounded in reality."

Jessica nods. The kid is some kind of evil genius. "Great," she says. "Good job. And from Tuesday I'll be in England. So, you know, you can use my office as a base. It would be great if you could come in once a day, keep it warm, answer the phone. You can do that?"

"Yeah, shit, I can do that. *Of course!* I'm done at school at two thirty most days. I'll come straight here, do my homework, keep it all nice for you. But how do I get in?"

Jessica opens a drawer in her desk and riffles around with her hands for a moment, dislodging all manner of random and unidentifiable objects before alighting upon the spare key she put in there the day she moved in.

"Here." She passes it to him. "Do not fricking lose this, okay? And do *not* let anybody else in here with you under any circumstances."

Malcolm holds his hands together in a praying gesture. "I swear on my mother's life."

"Good. Now go and do whatever you do on a Saturday night."

After Malcolm is gone, Jessica feels it all closing in on her again, all the boredom, all the dark. She pours herself a coffee from the machine, ignores the furious compulsion to tip whiskey into it, then takes her phone, her laptop, and Malcolm's report to her cold bed, where she stays until the following morning.

Twelve

Amber is in an ankle-length fake fur and wearing a baseball cap and sunglasses when Jessica meets her in the park at ten o'clock. One thin hand holds coffee in a metal reusable cup and the other the leash for a small black dog that is sitting very still at her feet.

"Good morning, Jessica," she says brightly. "How are you today?"

Jessica grunts. "Who knew that going to bed so early could make you so tired?"

"Come," says Amber. "We'll do a half loop around the reservoir. It'll help blow out the cobwebs."

The park is Sunday-morning busy. The paths are ornately patterned with the first of the fall leaves, and there are dogs, so many dogs. In particular, so many dogs wearing *clothing*.

Amber walks fast for a small person in big boots and Jessica has to hustle to keep up with her.

"What's the dog's name?"

"Charlie."

Jessica nods. Amber gives her children animal names and her dog a human name. Rich people are weird.

"So," says Amber, "your little friend came around on Friday night."

"Yeah. I know. And he's not my friend. He's my . . ." She's still not sure what to call Malcolm. "My *intern*."

"Sorry. Yes. Quite a character."

"He is that."

"Did he get anything?"

"Well, yeah, a little. He found a pretty girl on Instagram who lives in Essex and looks to be some kind of freaky-filter-using beauty influencer with a fondness for the word 'perfect.' He thinks she might be Fox's Belle, so he's sent her a follow request. But more importantly, he's got plans already to see Fox again, Wednesday night."

Amber's eyes widen slightly, and she nods. "Wow," she says. "That is impressive. Both my kids are pretty friendly, but letting someone in from left field like that, very unusual. He clearly has a knack. The sort of knack that could be used for very bad ends if he so chose."

"Yeah," says Jessica. "I know what you mean. But he is a good kid. I promise."

"I hope you're right. Anyway." Amber reaches into her shoulder bag and pulls out a plastic envelope. "Here's everything you need to collect your passport tomorrow. And all your travel details. You'll need to check in online the minute you have your passport details. Your flight leaves at ten past ten Tuesday morning, gets into Heathrow ten o'clock that same night. I've booked a car to take you to a hotel in Kensington since you're getting in late, and then Wednesday, first thing, another car to drive you to Essex. Your booking is at the Manston Oak Inn, seven nights, but can be extended. I haven't booked you a return yet. We'll see how you go. But stay in touch. We can FaceTime anytime. Talk on the phone. Whatever. Keep track of expenses. And more than anything, stay safe."

She hands Jessica the package and Jessica smiles. "Thank you," she says, feeling oddly touched by Amber's concern.

"As far as I'm aware, Sebastian is still at the Essex house overseeing the renovations, and I need you to find a way to talk to him without him knowing that I sent you. You'll need a cover story. Sebastian is something of a frustrated novelist, so I was thinking that you could say you were researching a novel?"

"A novel? You think I could pass as a novelist?" Jessica points her fingers at herself.

"Yeah. Of course. Why not? What does a novelist look like anyway?"

"I don't know. Not like me though, I'm pretty sure."

The dog has squatted to take a shit. Amber sighs and pulls a green plastic bag from a tube attached to the dog's leash and flaps it open. "Just say you're writing a crime novel," she says, crouching to collect the pile of poop inside the bag. She eases herself back to standing and smiles at Jessica, the bag hanging from her fingertips. "Listen," she says. "You're a private investigator. You don't need me to tell you what to do. But Jessica, before you go, I wanted to reiterate what I said to you the last time I saw you. I would be happy to have you in for a session, when you're ready. You seem like . . . and please don't take this the wrong way, but you seem as though you're letting trauma hold you back and I can feel"—she pushes her fist gently into Jessica's collarbone—"the pain in there. It's almost tangible, Jessica. And I like you. I don't know you. But I like you. And I would really, really like to help you. A girl like you shouldn't be living alone in that apartment. A girl like you should—"

And there's something in the tone of Amber's voice, and something about the wholesomeness of this, a sunny fall Sunday morning in Central Park, surrounded by the sort of people who take walks in Central Park on sunny fall Sunday mornings, that makes Jessica feel like she could just come right out and say it, and she opens her mouth and she says, "You know, I think I might be . . ." But a cloud passes across the sun, the moment dies, and she stops.

Amber tilts her head at her. "You think you might be what?"

Jessica smiles, tightly. "Nothing. Just, I think I'm tired. That's all. Just tired."

"Well, they say that a change is as good as rest. Maybe this trip is going to be exactly what you need. But seriously, once you're back, please come and talk to me. I'd love to help you."

Jessica smiles. "Sure," she says. "When I'm back."

PART TWO

Thirteen

Jessica peers through the windows of her limo as her driver takes her through the ugly outskirts of West London. She stares at the big mud-colored night sky and the high-rise buildings and feels strangely small and alone. It's ten p.m. here, which makes it five p.m. in New York, and Jessica pulls out her phone and sends Malcolm a message:

All OK?

Immediately she sees that Malcolm is typing a reply:

Yeah

She's about to reply when she sees he is still typing, then:

Your place is musty dude.

Plus your fridge is moldy.

I could clean.

Underneath is a praying hands emoji. Jessica sighs.

Don't touch ANYTHING

Seriously

She switches off her phone and shakes her head. What was she thinking, she asks herself, letting that kid into her private space, handing him her door keys?

The car slides in front of a small hotel down a glitzy backstreet somewhere in Kensington. The driver opens her door for her and passes her battered backpack to her as if it were a thousand-dollar piece of Mulberry leather. The hotel is shiny and fancy and pale and everything that Jessica would have expected it to be, given that Amber had chosen it for her. Once inside, she finds she has a small double room overlooking a dank back alley, but the bathroom is dove-gray-veined marble from floor to ceiling with a rainfall shower head, the bed is fat with pillows, and there is a small mini-bar and a big TV screen. After a full day of travel she does not need a nice view, she just needs a hot shower and a good bed.

Jessica puts her hand on the metal cap of a miniature bottle of whiskey and is about twist it off but stops. She shuts her eyes and sighs loudly, then glances down at her belly. She remembers Luke's words on Saturday and thinks, whatever's in there, if there is anything in there, it's not real. It's just fairy dust and goo. It won't be a baby unless she wants it to be a baby. She puts the miniature down and picks up the remote, kicks off her boots, and immerses herself in the soft density of the hotel bed and a soothingly narrated documentary about Madagascan wildlife.

Five minutes later, and still fully dressed, she is asleep.

* * *

There is a message from Amber on Jessica's phone when she wakes up suddenly and horribly the next morning.

Car coming at 9am to take you to Essex. It's a two-hour drive.

The time is currently four forty-five a.m. and she is half delirious with jet lag. She makes herself black coffee from the little Nespresso machine and glugs lukewarm mineral water from the bottle. Through the gap in the curtains, she sees specks of rain on the windowpane, the dark sky beyond. Everyone in America is getting ready for bed, everyone here is still fast asleep, and for a minute she feels like the only person in the world. She pulls on her boots and her leather jacket, locates her key card, and heads downstairs.

The woman at the front desk smiles at her and says, "Good morning."

"Hi," says Jessica. "Is there anywhere near here that's open all hours? For something to eat?"

"Not really," she replies. "There's a Tesco Express round the corner, that's open twenty-four hours."

"What's a Tesco Express?"

"It's a supermarket. Or there's an all-night diner, but it's about a twenty-minute walk."

"Yeah. That's fine. Which direction?"

The receptionist tells her where to go and Jessica heads out into the damp early morning, her heavy boots splashing up the dirty water of shallow puddles as she walks. Her head spins with everything, with tiredness, with hunger, with loneliness, with fear.

Her whole life has been a slow-motion multiple pileup. She lives on the edges of everything, at the sharp pointy corner of existence between normality and extraordinariness where she is neither one thing nor, truly, the other. She can do extraordinary things, but she doesn't like doing them. But she can't be normal either, she's too broken, too other. As she walks, she tries to imagine her hands gripping the handlebar of a stroller, a baby wrapped in soft layers of clothing held together with tiny buttons fastened by her own loving fingers. But the pictures in her head soon warp and twist, those same hands lifting the stroller and hurling it a hundred feet, two hundred feet through the air, those hands picking up grown men and throwing them against walls, those same hands lifting hunks of solid metal, upending cars, smashing through walls as the filthy engines inside her push her on.

She shakes her head. No. She's no mother, and there is surely no baby.

Even with that thought, she sees that London looks pretty as a Christmas card in the predawn gloom. The streetlights here glow a soft golden white through rusty trees, the houses are white and sit in neat rows around tiny garden squares framed with wrought iron railings. And then the diner emerges mirage-like from the sodium gloom of a wide dual-lane road, all chrome and gray velvet, and it comes alive as she opens the door to the hiss and splutter of a gigantic coffee machine behind the bar and to the chatter of rich-looking studenty types at banquettes and some older folk talking fast in languages that Jessica doesn't understand. She stares at a huge basket of oranges behind the bar until someone seats her. She peruses the paper menu, ponders something called "bubble and squeak" for a long moment before ordering steak and eggs and a large Americano. Then she turns to stare through the window, feeling the oddness of everything, the dull ache of emptiness, until suddenly her attention is diverted to a figure reflected in the glass, standing right next to her.

She swivels her head and it's her. The girl in the silver puffer coat.

The girl slides into the next booth along and stares at Jessica.

"Hi," she says. It's the first time she's spoken.

"What the . . . ?" Jessica looks around from left to right and behind to see if anyone can see this child. "What the heck is this? What are you doing here?"

"I'm on vacation."

"What? That's—don't be crazy. Where's your mom?"

"I'm just waiting for her."

Jessica looks around again, then narrows her eyes at the small girl. "How old are you?"

"I'm five."

"That's very young to be sitting on your own in a diner, don't you think?"

"I'm not on my own. I'm with you."

"Yeah, but . . ." Jessica pinches the bridge of her nose. "Why are you here? What's going on? Are you even . . . *real*?"

"Of course I'm real. Here, you can pinch me."

She pulls up the sleeve of her silver coat and offers out her arm.

Jessica closes her eyes. "No. For God's sake, no, I don't want to pinch you. I just want to know what the hell is going on. I think maybe I'm going crazy. I probably am."

The group of foreign men is preparing to leave. Jessica turns and watches them pulling on jackets and coats and once they are close enough to her, she calls over to them and says, "Hey, do you see that child?"

They glance over at the girl and then back at her. The oldest one nods and then they move on.

Jessica shakes her head hard, sure that there is something lodged in her brain that she could get free if she tried hard enough. She squeezes her eyes shut and when she opens them the child is gone. Jessica sees her outside, walking alone through the dark morning gloom, the shiny fabric of her coat gleaming iridescent under the streetlights and the pale moonbeams.

Twelve years ago
Portsmouth, Hampshire, UK

Arthur looks thrown at the prospect of ordering a drink in the glitzy bar where he and Polly have met for drinks.

"Er," he says, his eyes frantically trawling the cocktail list. "Er."

Polly smiles at the handsome barman, who glances from shabby Arthur to shiny Polly and clearly wonders what the pair are doing together.

"Tequila sunrise," Arthur says decisively a moment later.

"Really?" asks Polly, laughing a little and exchanging another conspiratorial look with the barman.

"Yes," says Arthur. "It's my mum's favorite. I remember her telling me that once."

Polly sparks with delight at Arthur inadvertently taking the conversation exactly where she wants it. "Tell me about your mum and dad."

"Oh. Nothing much to tell. My dad is American. He followed my mum over here for *lurve*." He blushes as the inane word leaves his mouth. "And my mum is a clairvoyant. She works on the pier, doing tarot and whatnot. That's it really. How about you?"

"Oh, right. Well, my mum is a lazy slag, and my dad is dead. And I have a seventeen-year-old brother who never leaves his room apart from to score weed."

"Oh." Arthur looks momentarily frozen with surprise. "That's . . ."

Polly shrugs nonchalantly, as though she is used to carrying the world's weight on her back. "It is what it is. I'm moving on. I'm an entrepreneur. At least, I want to be an entrepreneur."

"Oh," says Arthur. "Wow. That's great. What sort of business are you thinking of going into?"

"Beauty," she says, decisively. "I'm doing nails at the moment. But I want more. Much more. I'm looking into new products. New ways of making people look perfect." She leaves a moment of silence to let her words sing.

"Perfect?"

"Yes, perfect . . . You know, Arthur, you should go to uni. Get a proper job. Get out of here. Then you could really help support your family. Much more than just working in a shitty shoe shop."

Arthur flinches at the slight. "I'm the manager. I don't just work there."

"Yeah. But still. You're clever. You could do more. I can see it in you . . ."

She sees a flush of pride pass across his face and she knows that she's bringing him round. "It's . . . just . . . my parents. I can't leave them."

"Why?" she says plainly. "Is there something wrong with them?"

"No. Not quite. They're just . . . we're close-knit. We always have been. Really, really tight-knit. I'm their only kid. My mum—she waited a long time to have me. A really, really long time. And my dad. He has some mental health issues. They sacrificed a lot to have me and if I wasn't here, I sometimes feel like they'd fall apart."

Polly resists the urge to tut and sigh. The patheticness of it! Grown people who can't live without their child! Instead she puts on a sympathetic smile and nods gravely, as if she fully understands. "So where did you tell them you were going tonight?"

"I told them I was seeing friends from school."

"Do you think they believed you?"

Arthur shrugs. "Probably not, seeing as I didn't have any friends at school." The barman passes him his tacky cocktail, and he picks it up and takes a sip. Polly regards his hands, notes that they are elegant, that his fingernails are clean and neat. She feels a sudden and bizarre compulsion to touch them.

"You could go to college here?" she suggests. "You don't have to move away?"

He glances at her. "It's not just about being at home. We need the money too."

She sighs. "Well, for what it's worth, unless you have

ambitions to one day be the CEO of Shoe Fayre, I think you're wasting your life."

He shrugs. "Yeah," he says. "I guess."

"You're letting yourself be trapped."

"Yeah. I know. But—"

"I can help you."

"How?"

Polly bites her lip and moves her face closer to his. She sees him blink, notices the rise and fall of his Adam's apple. She lowers her voice so that it is breathy and raw. "I'm getting out of here," she says, her eyes fixed on his, "and I think you should come with me. Are you in, or are you out?"

Fourteen

The car arrives at Jessica's hotel at nine a.m. She hands her backpack to the driver and slides into the back seat. She pulls out the paperwork from the folder that Amber gave her about her ex-husband. In the photos that she gave Jessica, Sebastian Randall has a large head that houses small features. He wears trendy tortoiseshell glasses and has thick dark hair that recedes at the temple, making his head look even bigger. He has the satisfied air of a man who was told by his mother that he was the most handsome boy in the world and has believed it all his life.

Sebastian Randall is a trust fund millionaire via Janet and David Randall, who own a global casualwear company. Over the course of his fifty years, he has variously been an actor, a dancer, an art dealer, an antiques dealer, a novelist, and a public speaker. And is of course currently overseeing the restoration of a seven-bedroom Jacobean manor house in the middle of Barton Wallop called Barton Manor.

Jessica is booked into the hotel in the village, where the rooms, according to their website, start at £225 a night. It has a topiary garden and a champagne bar.

"Won't I be kind of conspicuous?" she'd asked Amber.

"I want you to be conspicuous," the birdlike woman replied. "I want Sebastian to notice you. He loves America, he loves good-looking women, and he loves writers. He'll be all over you. And that's what we want. To get you into his inner sanctum."

The car pulls up on a small carriage driveway in front of a pretty hotel. On the other side of the narrow street is a pub, a clothes shop, a deli, a pharmacy, and a veterinarian.

Everything in the hotel is tiny—tiny windows, narrow doorways, low ceilings. An inscription etched into the stonework says it was built in 1687, when people, Jessica assumes, were very small. She checks in and takes her bag to her room—it's housed in a new addition at the back of the hotel with a normal-sized door—and then she heads out into the village.

Mild for October, the sky is clear and blue. In the deli she gets herself a black coffee and a ham salad baguette and takes them to a bench at the end of the main road overlooking Sebastian Randall's house, which does indeed have a moat, around which ducks float in a clockwise direction.

Jessica eats the sandwich and drinks the coffee and

practices her spiel in her mind. She is Jessica Allan, a writer from New York doing research for a detective novel about a murder in an English village. It's her first novel, she hasn't had anything published, and before this she was an administrator for the NYPD for ten years, which is what turned her on to the idea of writing about crime. She's recently divorced and here for a week. A simple, virtually foolproof cover story. Less is always more when it comes to a backstory. And men always think a divorced woman is eager for company.

After fifteen minutes there is no sign of life at the Randall mansion and Jessica stuffs her empty coffee cup and paper bag into a garbage can and heads back into the village proper. Outside the tiny wobbly pub, with windows so low down the frontage they almost touch the sidewalk, a chalkboard says that there is live music tonight: THE MIKE MILLER BAND + GUESTS. It kicks off at seven p.m. Which gives Jessica just over six hours to sleep and make herself look like an aspiring novelist.

She is about to turn back toward her hotel when her eye is caught by the next shop along, the pharmacy. Going over, she pauses for a moment at the threshold and then pulls in her breath and opens the door. Like everything else here, the shop is tiny, two aisles wide. At the far end is a tall mahogany counter, behind which sits a very young boy, surely not much older than seventeen. He stares at a textbook open in front of him and then looks up and smiles lazily when he sees Jessica. "Good morning," he says.

"Er, hi." Jessica throws him a sideways smile and heads

down the first aisle. Here, between the birth control and the deodorants, is what she needs. Pregnancy testing kits. She picks one up and turns it around in her hands.

"Need any help?"

She drops the box and quickly scans around for something else to pick up. A can of Dove deodorant.

"No," she calls back. "I'm good. Thank you."

She takes the deodorant to the counter and pays for it.

"Are you American?" asks the boy.

"Yup."

"Whereabouts are you from?"

"I'm from New York."

"Oh," he says, scanning the code on the deodorant. "Are you anything to do with the twins?"

She flinches slightly. "Twins?"

"Yes, the twins from the big house at the end of the village? They're from New York, I think."

"I don't know anyone here at all. Pure coincidence. Are they here now?"

"No. I don't think so. They were just here for a few weeks this summer."

"What're their names? Maybe I know them?"

"Ha, that's like saying that just because you're from New York you'd know, like, *the Daredevil*."

Jessica holds back a burst of facetious laughter. "Yeah . . . I suppose it is. But try me."

"Randall. That's their surname. Don't know what their first names are. They're not exactly friendly."

"Nope. Don't know any Randalls. But I do know quite a lot of unfriendly New Yorkers." She hands him a five-pound note and waits for her change. "Thank you."

He hands her the deodorant in a small bag and the change and smiles.

On the way out she passes the pregnancy testing kits again and sighs. Two more days, she tells herself. Two more days and if her period hasn't come by then, she'll take a test.

* * *

The pub is stupidly small. Way too small for normal people. The ceiling beams all have signs on them that say MIND YOUR HEAD, and the whole place is just a series of tiny rooms connected by tiny doorways. Jessica heads to the bar and waits for the woman to notice her.

When she does, she smiles widely and says, "What can I get you, lovey?"

"Oh," she says, surprised at being referred to as a *lovey*. "Yes. Can I get a . . . erm . . . a Diet Coke?"

She takes the soda to an empty table in one of the rooms toward the back of the pub. Her phone vibrates with a message. It's Amber.

Amber: How are things going?

Jessica: I'm in the pub. Looking conspicuous af. Anything happening at your end?

Amber: No. Kids still pretending to be normal

Jessica: OK. My assistant is seeing Fox tonight. Hopefully he'll have something back for us tomorrow.

She finishes typing and looks up to find a man staring at her. He's about her age, maybe older. He has a short beard and is clutching what looks like a glass of pond water inside a rough-knuckled hand.

"How are you?" he says.

Jessica narrows her eyes at him. All her instincts want her to tell him to back off. She did not fly halfway across the world to get hit on by men with beards and glassy eyes. If she wanted to get hit on by drunk guys in bars she could have stayed right at home. But, reminding herself that this is why Amber Randall has spent thousands of dollars to send her here, she manages a small smile and says, "I'm good, thank you."

"American?"

"Yes. Yes I am."

"New Yorker?"

"New Yorker," she says, the smile starting to strain a little.

"Oh. Right. I've never been, always wanted to. I've got family in Florida though, you can't really do both in the same trip, can you?"

"No. I don't suppose you can."

"Do you mind if I . . . ?" He indicates the stool opposite her.

She shrugs. "Sure."

"I'm Gavin, by the way."

"Jessica." She gives him her hand to shake.

"So, what brings you here? You something to do with that Randall guy?"

"Randall? No. And that's the second time today that someone's asked me about him. Who is he?"

"Oh, some rich bloke, bought the big manor house last year."

"Oh, so you know him?"

"No. Not really. Only inasmuch as everyone knows him, because he's got the big house." He peers into his murky drink and then up at Jessica. "So, what is it that you're doing here, then?"

"A bit of research. For a book."

"Oh yes? What kind of book?"

"Historical detective novel."

"Set *here*?"

"No. Set in a fictional village, a bit like this, but not this one."

Gavin looks at her skeptically, but then appears to decide that this is acceptable, and nods. They fall silent for a moment before Gavin looks up at her and says, "You married?"

"Oh, no. No, I'm not."

"Boyfriend?"

"No. Not that I'm aware of."

"I'm not chatting you up by the way. Happily married man." He shows her his ring. "Just don't like to see a beautiful woman sitting all alone."

"Oh, that's so kind of you."

"Yes, well, we're like that round here. We're good people. Here. The music's about to start up in the front bar. Fancy it? I can introduce you to a few locals. Some of them might be

131

able to help you with your"—he waggles his fingers dismissively—"detective novel."

Jessica makes a long, silent inward sigh before collecting her drink and saying, "Sounds good!" as brightly as she can.

She follows Gavin back through to the main bar and he sits her down at a table with a group of men and women of varying ages and says, "This here is Jessica from New York. She's writing a book."

As they all stare at her, Jessica lifts her glass. "Cheers," she says, wishing suddenly and painfully to be alone in her hotel room staring at a wall.

"Wow," says a woman with pink streaks in her hair. "What's your book about?"

"Well, I haven't started writing it yet. But it's going to be a historical detective novel, set in the 1800s."

"Oh," the woman replies. "I love historical crime. Have you read any S. J. Parris?"

Jessica laughs nervously. "Oh God, probably, I'm terrible at remembering what I've read."

"Have you had anything published?"

"No. Not yet. I haven't started writing yet. Just doing some research."

"Ooh." Another woman joins in. "You know who you should talk to?" She turns to her friend. "What's his name? The guy in the big house?"

The friend furrows her brow and then says, "Sebastian Randall?"

The woman nods. "Yes. Him. He's had a novel published.

It wasn't historical, I don't think, but it was set in an Essex village. I bet he'd have loads of great advice for you?"

"Randall?" says Jessica, turning back to Gavin. "Isn't that the guy you were telling me about?"

"Yes! I didn't know he'd published a novel."

"Yes, a few years back," says the woman. "Don't think it sold anything though. Probably more of a vanity project . . . I wouldn't be surprised."

A disparaging rumble goes through the group and Jessica clocks it as a sign that Sebastian Randall is not held in high regard in the village of Barton Wallop.

"What's the deal with him? Not liked?"

"Well," says the pink-haired woman, "I wouldn't say that. But just, you know, these out-of-towners turn up and then don't try to fit in. And his girlfriend is a bit of a stuck-up bitch."

Jessica hides her surprise. "Girlfriend?"

"Yeah. She's much younger than him, dresses like a Barbie doll, carries her dogs around in bags. I think she thinks she's a celebrity."

"Oh," says Jessica, processing the fact that Sebastian has a girlfriend that he clearly hasn't told anyone about. "What's her name?"

"No idea. We just call her Barbie."

"Wait. She's not named Belle, is she?"

"Belle? No. I don't think so. Why?"

"Oh, no reason." She picks up her Diet Coke and takes a long sip, aware that she's just potentially outed herself as having more of an interest in Barton Wallop than merely a location for a detective novel.

"And what's he like, this Sebastian guy?" she asks, trying to move past the subject briskly.

"He's just a bit of a dick, really. But harmless, you know."

"Well," Jessica says, "it sounds like he'd be good to talk to, and maybe get a sneaky look inside his house for research too. Does anyone have a number for him?"

"Can do better than that," says the woman with the pink streaks. "My husband does the moat."

"Does the moat?" Jessica repeats. "What does he do to the moat?"

"The upkeep. He's going in tomorrow. I'll get him to mention you to Sebastian. Where are you staying?"

"I'm at the hotel across the street."

"Oh, my daughter works there! I can get her to get a message to you. Jessica, is it?"

"Yes. Jessica Allan."

"Watch this space," says the woman. "But while you're waiting, there's a little historical society with a library just above the chemist's. It's only open in the mornings. Might be worth having a little dig around in there. This village has some very strange stories to tell."

"It does?"

"Oh yes. Stranger than any fiction. Way, way stranger."

Twelve years ago
Portsmouth, Hampshire, UK

Arthur appears at the door of the small, terraced house looking apprehensive and vaguely terrified. He glances up and
down the street and then back at Polly before hissing at her,
"Come in. Quick!"

Arthur's father has a hospital appointment. His mother is
at work on the pier. Arthur has taken the afternoon off work.
They have exactly two and a half hours before Arthur's father
returns, and Arthur is clearly not comfortable with this plan.

"Calm down," says Polly. "I am allowed to come into your
house. There's no law against it."

"I know," says Arthur, running his hands anxiously through
his lank hair. "I just don't want anyone to see though. In case
they say anything."

Polly rolls her eyes and steps into the house. She glances
around. It's basic, early eighties: pine-clad walls, watercolor
landscapes, a patterned carpet running up the stairs, an arched
entrance into a brown kitchen down three steps at the back of

the house, dimpled glass windows onto a garden. A cat sits on the bottom step and stares at her.

"Who's this?"

"That's Mr. Smith."

He's a raggedy-looking cat, bony and scrawny.

"He looks very old."

"He *is* very old. My mother's had him for a long time."

Polly's gaze falls upon a framed family photograph on the anaglypta-clad wall. A tall man with black hair and thick-framed glasses, a small woman with a blond pixie cut and chunky jewelry, and three small girls in brightly colored clothes. She throws Arthur a questioning look.

"It's not our house," he says, awkwardly. "The people who own it are living abroad for a year and they have two guinea pigs that they didn't want to take with them. So we're house-sitting for them. Just until Christmas. Then we have to go."

"Go? Where are you going to go?"

Arthur shrugs. "I don't know. Back to the chalet park, I guess."

And as he says this she remembers. "Which chalet park?"

"Spring Dene?"

A shiver passes through her. "Spring Dene?" she repeats. "The one up on Eastney Beach?"

"Yes. We lived there for about three years. Do you know it?"

She does know it. A gone-to-seed holiday park, the small wooden houses now turned over to long-term renters. "Yes. I had a boyfriend who used to score weed there. I think I might have even seen you there, a few times."

"I don't remember," he replies, nervously, as though it was a test.

"No. But I do."

The chill sits in the base of her spine. She remembers the dealers' chalet. She remembers them talking about the guy next door—not Arthur, but his dad. They said he was a nonce. They said he was a weirdo. They said people went into that chalet and never came out. Strange noises. Comings and goings. A bad vibe.

She smiles brightly to dislodge the uncomfortable thoughts from her consciousness. "Will you show me around?"

"Er, yeah. Sure. But can I . . . get you a drink? I have champagne. Or not actually champagne, some kind of fizzy thing, I put it in the freezer about an hour ago, it should be nice and—"

She touches his face gently with her hand. "Show me around first, then we can have the fizzy thing."

"Right. Yes. Come through."

He leads her into the living room: tired and frumpy, saggy chintz sofas, shiny mahogany coffee table, a milky-white-and-gold overhead light fitting, beige carpeting, fake flowers, a dining table covered with a tablecloth printed with country scenes.

"And here's the conservatory . . ."

He slides a door at the back of the house onto a tiny

stuck-on plasticky sunroom with floral upholstered bamboo furniture in it. It overlooks a small, graveled garden featuring a birdbath in the middle. On one side of the room is a large pet cage filled with tunnels and terraces and toys.

"Hobnob and Gingernut," says Arthur. "The guinea pigs. Look."

He lifts the lid of the cage and leans into it, emerges with a handful of red fluff. "This one's Gingernut," he says, passing it to her.

She takes it from his hand and coos at it. "Nice," she says. "Cute."

But she's not here to look at guinea pigs and interiors, she's here to work out who these people really are.

She follows Arthur up the steep staircase to the next floor, a tiny landing, two small bedrooms, a carpeted bathroom that makes her stomach churn. She goes to push open the door to one of the bedrooms and Arthur stops her.

"No," he says. "Don't go in there."

"Why not?"

"It's my parents' room. It's private."

"Okay," she says, pressing her hand to her chest. "I hear you." Behind his back she rolls her eyes, then pushes open the door to the other room.

Arthur clears his throat. "It's very small," he says, apologetically. "I mean, it's fine, but you know . . ."

A single bed made up with a burgundy striped duvet and navy-blue pillows, posters of various super heroes and action figures pinned to the walls and displayed on shelves, a large computer screen on a desk, a scruffy gaming chair in bright red and black. The bedroom of a sixteen-year-old boy, not a twenty-two-year-old man.

She hears him clear his throat again. "Anyway . . . let's go down. I'll open the champagne."

"Okay," she says, stroking his waist absentmindedly. "I'll be right down. I'll just use your bathroom first."

She sees uncertainty pass across his face, a flash of distrust. "I'll wait here."

"No, no," she says, shooing him away. "It's rude to wait outside a bathroom when there's a lady in it. Go down. I'll see you in a minute."

His face softens with surrender. She squeezes his waist again, feels him melt at her touch. He turns to head downstairs.

She stands in the bathroom for a count of twenty, her breath held against the damp smell of the old carpet, at the thought of thirty years of misdirected pee, then she turns the tap on and off again and very quietly tiptoes across the landing to the main bedroom.

She feels it the moment she opens the door, a raw energy that she cannot define. It rocks through her: something dark, yet something at the same time tender. And there is a smell, dense and metallic, like stale pennies. She scans the room, quickly. She opens jars and pots and sniffs the contents. They have that same old-penny smell that pervades the room. She rubs some cream into the freckles on the back of her hand and watches them for a moment. Nothing happens.

There's a dull drone in the room, a deep rumble, and she traces it to the built-in wardrobes that run down the back wall of the room. Inside one wardrobe is a small, padlocked fridge.

Polly recoils, sucking her breath in dryly. She reaches out to touch the padlock, weighing it with her outstretched hand.

"Polly?"

She hears Arthur calling her from downstairs and lets the padlock drop.

"Polly? Are you okay?"

Her heart is racing. "Yes!" she says, stepping quickly onto the landing. "Just coming."

She closes the door quietly behind her and heads back down, to Arthur, to his fizzy stuff, to closing her eyes tight while he kisses her with his amateurish lips and his amateurish tongue, to his boy's hands over her woman's body.

She will close her eyes and pretend that he is someone else entirely.

She glances at her hand on the banister as she readies herself to step down the stairs.

Where she spread Ophelia's skin cream, her freckles have faded to nothing.

Fifteen

When Jessica gets back to her hotel room two and a half hours later, she is absentmindedly humming yacht rock classics under her breath and feeling strangely happy. She liked Mike Miller and his band of long-haired old men with cheeky faces, including the little skinny one with dyed black hair who kept winking at her. She liked all the people she met tonight in the pub. Jessica thinks of the lonely echo in her Hell's Kitchen apartment, the empty bed, the long days and longer nights. Maybe, she thinks, as she strips off her clothes and turns the dial on the shower, maybe she should move out of the city, find a little place on the coast, a cutesy village with a cozy bar and a pharmacy and a local history society. She could open a pizzeria. Or maybe even write that damn novel.

Jessica loses herself in ridiculous small-town fantasies as

the hot water rains down on her head and she runs soap all over her skin until her hand comes to the rectangle of skin above her groin and her brain floods with some kind of sped-up film footage that she must have seen on TV at some point in her life: a sperm infiltrating an egg to fertilize it, the egg splitting and doubling and splitting and doubling, limbs and eyes and hands and feet and fingers and toes appearing—and Jessica presses her eyes shut hard at the very moment that the thing in her head starts to look like a real baby and she quickly turns off the water and grabs the towel from the handrail, rubs herself hard, expunging and exfoliating and growling to herself under her breath because how can she make pizzas in a small town when she can't even make herself a hot meal in her own kitchen? How can she make friends with strangers if she doesn't know who she is? And how can she be a mother when she can't even be a human?

* * *

The same boy who served her in the pharmacy the day before lets her in through the door with the plaque on it that says BARTON WALLOP AND BARTON WALDEN HISTORICAL SOCIETY AND MUSEUM.

"Oh," she says. "It's you again."

"It is. Good morning."

She follows him up a narrow set of gray-carpeted stairs. "So you own this place too?"

"We own the whole building, yes."

"And who runs the society?"

"My mum. She's a historian. But I help her out with it."

"In between running the shop?"

"Yes. And studying for A levels."

"You're a busy boy."

"I am. Yes."

"Where are your parents?"

"They're on holiday. Turkey." He slips a key into a door at the top of the staircase and pushes it open. "They'll be back next week. Here." He turns on some lights. "Sorry, it's a bit chilly in here. No point heating it when nobody ever uses it. But I can plug a heater in for you, so you don't freeze to death."

"Sure," says Jessica, looking around the room. "Thank you."

It's a beautiful room, high ceilings decorated with ornate plaster moldings. All around are mahogany filing cabinets and display boxes full of ancient paperwork and objects, a silken embroidered banner decorated with medieval-looking figures attached to one wall, the walls filled with framed letters and maps and sepia-toned photographs.

"Where would I find out stuff about the house at the other end of the street, the one with the moat?"

"Barton Manor? That's where the Randalls live. The family I was telling you about with the American kids. It's one of the oldest houses in the village, so there's loads about it, here." He pulls open a drawer and tugs out a huge book with a fabric cover. "Press cuttings, accounts, plans, all sorts in here."

"Thanks," Jessica says, taking the book to a small desk in the window and pulling out a chair.

"Anyway. Just shout if you need anything else. We close at one p.m., so you've got plenty of time."

"Great stuff," she murmurs over her shoulder, and then she hears the door close and footsteps back down the stairs and she is alone in this strange room in this strange village in this strange country.

"Right," she says to herself. "Let's get this thing started."

An hour later she finds something in a book called *The Bartons Through the Ages* by a Miss Anne Satchel, who appears in a photo on the backflap as an elderly lady with a small white poodle perched on her lap, in front of a bush of pale pink roses. The book was published in 1978, and Jessica strongly suspects that neither the author nor her dog is still with us.

Very little is known about the village of Barton Wallop in the 1400s, it begins, *but a small plaque in the local chapel, St. John and St. Peter, commemorates a terrible tragedy that blighted the village for dozens of years.*

In 1436, Barton Wallop had a population of just over three hundred people. It was farming land, mostly owned by Lord Thomas of Walden, who resided with his large family in the sprawling estate of Walden Manor, which was demolished in the 1800s and is now home to the market town of Barton Walden, five miles from Barton Wallop.

In September of 1436, the harvests had been gathered. It had been a remarkable year for crops and local farmers ran out of space to store them and dug underground for extra capacity. In late September there were three days of torrential rain that turned a freshly dug-out grain store into a mud bath. Twelve local children ran to the mud bath after church one Sunday to play and were buried alive when it collapsed on top of them. The children were aged from nine to eighteen and accounted for over 30 percent of the village's young. The entire village went into a prolonged period of mourning that lasted for well over five years.

For many centuries, this ground was said to be both cursed and blessed, and rituals took place to prevent anyone from using the ground for building on. The land lay empty for three more centuries, until eventually all the ancestors and memories of the lost children were long gone. In 1789, the land was bought by a London merchant for a country retreat, and a large home built upon the very spot where the children had perished. The house was built in a trapezoidal plot, surrounded by a moat, and to this day is known as Barton Manor.

Barton Manor? thinks Jessica, an icy chill running through her. That's Sebastian Randall's house. And it appears, according to Miss Satchel, to have been built on cursed and hallowed land, on top of the bodies of twelve dead children.

She has no idea what this has to do with the Randall twins coming home with perfect skin and cracking bones, but she is more desperate than ever now to get inside that house.

* * *

"Miss Allan!"

Jessica does not turn at the call of the receptionist as she walks across the foyer toward her room, because she is not Miss Allan, but when the name is called a second time, she remembers.

"Sorry!" she says, turning to the front desk. "Yes!"

"I have a note for you!"

"Oh, thank you."

She takes the note into the lounge at the back of the building and opens it next to a lit fire in a soft armchair. It's a stiff card with the words *S. J. Randall, Barton Manor* printed at the top in a swirly cursive. Underneath in scruffy handwriting it says:

Hi Jessica. My name is Sebastian Randall. I hear you're in town researching a novel and I'd love to have a chat about that as I am a budding novelist also! Could you come for drinks tonight at 6 p.m.?

Jessica exhales forcefully and swallows back a wide smile of triumph.

Only twenty-four hours in Barton Wallop and she's already crossing the drawbridge.

Sixteen

Five minutes after she gets back to her hotel room, Jessica's phone rings.

"Yo! Jessica!"

Jessica closes her eyes and breathes in against the onslaught of Malcolm Powder energy swooping down the phone line from New York.

"Yo yourself. What's happening?"

"Last night is what's happening."

"So tell me?"

"Do you have coffee?"

"I have coffee, Malcolm. Talk to me."

"Okay, so, we meet up outside Fox's building. He wants me to take him to my place, I'm like, 'Nah, my dad's there, I don't want to see him.' He didn't ask questions. He says,

'Let's take a walk.' He says he doesn't want to be in the house, because his mom is on his case. I ask him what about. He says his mom's been 'acting weird' ever since they got back from the UK. I'm like, 'Weird, in what way?' He says she's always looking at him funny and asking him if he's okay. I say, 'And are you? Are you okay?' and he says, 'Sure, I'm perfect.' And I went in. *BAM!*"

Jessica jumps slightly and recoils from her phone.

Malcolm continues, oblivious. "I say, 'You use that word a lot. You and your sister.' I say, 'What's the deal with *"perfect"*?' He says, 'I dunno. I guess it's just another way of saying *"good,"* y'know? But better. Like, anyone can be good, but being perfect, isn't that the goal?' So I say, 'I guess. What's your secret?' He's like, 'My secret?' I say, 'Yeah. You're, like, sixteen. Yet you're so slick, so suave, so manly.'"

Jessica grimaces. "You told him he was manly?"

"Yeah. Why not? Sly's secure. And he says, 'Good genes, I guess.' And then he stops, right there on the sidewalk, got people cussing at him, he stops and stares up into the sky, just stares and stares, and I say, 'What's up there?' And he says, 'Just . . . Miranda.'"

"Wait, *what*? Who's Miranda?"

"I have *no clue*. I ask him, he says, 'Oh, nothing. Nobody. Just thinking about someone.' 'Your girl?' I ask, and he laughs and says, 'No. Not my girl.' I say, 'Oh, yeah, your girl is named Belle. Unless you got two girls.' He laughs. 'No,' he says. 'No. Miranda is not a girl. Miranda is not anyone.' And then he changes the subject, and we start walking again and we're walking and walking and walking and it's starting to get dark, and I say, 'Where are we going?' But he says, 'Nowhere,' so I say, 'I'm cold, man. Let's get inside somewhere.' So we go into this Starbucks, I get us some coffees—hey, I kept the receipt, I can put these through on expenses, right?"

"Right," Jessica replies.

"Anyway, I sit down and he's staring again, through the window, up at the sky. I'm wondering what the hell is this. Why did he want to meet up? Why am I here? What does he want with me? I say, 'You *sure* you're okay?' and he says, 'Listen. You wanna see something cool?' and I say, 'Sure.' He gets us an Uber and we end up in Harlem, down this shitty dead-end street around the back of Broadway, and he takes us into this, like, abandoned bar, all boarded up, all dead and empty. He opens the door *with a key*, so I'm like, 'Where'd you get a key from for this place, bro?' He touches his nose. I say, 'Okay then, sure, whatever. What even *is* this place?' He says, 'It belongs to Belle's family.' I'm all, 'Belle in the UK?' and he says, 'Yeah,' so I say, 'How come?' He says, 'I don't know. But she told me there's a secret basement here. I keep coming back to find it, but I can't see it. Wanna help me find it?'

"So we spent like half an hour just searching this bar, the backyard, the front sidewalk. We're looking for hidden entrances, secret trapdoors, like, where is this secret basement. I say, 'Listen, dude, there is no basement here, I think Belle was playing you.' He says, 'I swear, it's here. She wasn't lying. And it's meant to—' and then he kind of cuts off, y'know? Just stops talking. Then he says, 'Let's get out of here.'

"He gets a car. I get the subway. I'm in bed an hour later thinking, *What the hell just happened?* I tell you, it was the weirdest night of my life, Jessica. Something is not right with that kid, and whatever it is, that freaky abandoned bar has got something to do with it."

Twelve years ago
Portsmouth, Hampshire, UK

It takes four long hours for Arthur's dad to leave his house on Thursday, four long hours, while Polly stands under an umbrella in the rain. He does not leave until after lunch in the end, just as the rain finally dries up. She watches him from across the street: a tired-looking man, sixty or so, in worn-out jeans, a green fisherman's sweater, a scarf, a waxed jacket, and a flat cap. He has a scraggly beard, and there are reading glasses perched on top of his cap. Builder's boots. Gnarly hands. He's handsome-ish. A GILF even. He does not look like a nonce or a weirdo. He slings a bag around his torso and finally he heads off to the allotment that Arthur told her about a few days ago after some gentle probing.

She waits another moment or two before going to the door of the house. The key is stiff at first—she only had it cut just yesterday, copied from Arthur's, which she'd pocketed during their lunch and then returned to him at the end of the day pretending he'd left it on the table. But the lock yields a moment later and she is in.

The cat appears from nowhere and stares at her, harshly.

"Hello, Mr. Smith," she says, crouching slightly to greet him. But he backs away, his hackles rising, and issues a piercing hiss. "Okay then," she says, straightening up. "Whatever."

She heads upstairs.

Halfway up, the cat blocks her path.

"Shoo, cat."

He hisses at her again.

She stares into his eyes and for a moment her head spins and her stomach rolls. Melon pip pupils. Golden irises. But as she stares, she sees that the irises swirl, kaleidoscopic, like oil on water. She blinks, hard, once, twice. When she opens her eyes, the cat has turned away from her. She exhales and steps onto the landing. Quickly, she goes into the bedroom, unloads her bag, the sample pots and jars she brought with her, the tiny spoons and scoops and baggies, and the selection of objects she brought with which she will attempt to unlock the fridge in the wardrobe.

She peers from the front window just to check that Arthur's father hasn't forgotten something and returned. The coast clear, she turns back to the room, opening Ophelia's pots and jars, taking scrapings and samples, sealing them into plastic sandwich bags. She rubs a little cream onto her nose, feels a tingle, a heat.

Then she turns to the fridge in the wardrobe. It's a small padlock, one that opens with a tiny key, like the one she had on her *High School Musical* diary as a teenager. She's even brought the key with her, in the vain hope that it might be the same one, but of course it doesn't come close. She takes out hairpins and tiny screwdrivers and keeps fiddling until she can feel a clammy sweat breaking out all over her body.

"Shit," she hisses to herself, rocking back on her heels.

She catches her breath and then starts again, this time with tiny pliers. There's a small crunch inside the lock mechanism and then a click and the hook goes flaccid. She pops it out, lifts back the flap and grabs the handle, the door creaks open, and . . . She gasps, almost slamming it shut again.

What? she thinks. What the hell is she looking at? Rows of tiny glass bottles, all labeled and filled with what looks like . . . *blood*?

She pulls one off the shelf and looks at the label. Gobble-degook. Letters, numbers, symbols, nothing that means anything. She puts it back and picks up another one. The same. On the next shelf down are more vials and test tubes, these filled with clear viscous liquids. In the door are larger bottles, what look like recycled water bottles with the labels peeled off, filled with the same dark, blood-colored substance as the smaller containers. She turns one around to properly read the six-digit inscription on the sticker. They are dates, ascending chronologically. Most are from this year. Whatever is in these bottles, and it really does look a lot like blood, is fresh. But whose is it? And why? Is Arthur's father diabetic or something? Surely Arthur would have mentioned it if that were the case. And is that what people do, when they have diabetes? Do they collect blood? In empty water bottles?

She thinks of the drug dealers in their thickly curtained chalet next to Arthur's in the park, their dark talk of missing people and strange noises. She thinks of how closed off Arthur's family are from the world. She thinks of the old-penny smell of the cream in Ophelia's pots, that tangy, metallic undertone. She goes to the mirror on the chest of drawers and looks at her nose, sees the blemishes gone, the tiny blackheads now invisible, airbrushed out. She leans in closer, turns her face this way and that. Whichever way she looks, the patch of skin remains perfect, flawless.

She inhales sharply and feels a giant pulse of adrenaline surge through her at the sound of a key in the door down-stairs. She looks out of the window and sees that it is raining again. How long has it been raining? Long enough for Arthur's father to have abandoned his trip?

"Shit," she whispers.

The fridge is still open, her collection of bags and instru-ments still spread all over the floor. The front door slams shut, and the cat mewls loudly, and she hears a man's voice saying "What's up with you, buddy? Something rattle your cage?"

It's an American accent, deep and solid.

"Something up there?" he asks the cat. "What's up there?"

"Shit," Polly hisses under her breath, falling to her knees to collect all her stuff together, hurling it into her rucksack. She shuts the fridge, but not before plucking just one small vial of blood from the very back and tossing it into her bag too. She snaps the padlock shut and quietly closes the wardrobe door. And then she rolls herself under the bed and holds her breath, listening to the creak of someone standing on the landing outside the room, the deep breathing, the squeak of the bedroom door, and then a sigh.

"Nope," she hears him say as he lowers himself onto the bed, inches from her face. "Nobody up here, Mr. Smith."

The cat yowls and the man *tsk-tsk*s him. "Enough now. Leave me be."

She hears the man sorting through a bunch of keys, then getting up heavily, his breathing crackly and hard. "Okey dokey," he mumbles to himself. "Okey dokey."

She sees him open the wardrobe and lean down into it, hears the click of the padlock, the clink of the glass vials as they bump up against each other, and then she sees him pluck one of the big bottles from the door of the fridge.

"Just a drop now," he says to himself. "Just to take the edges off. The cold got into me. Right into my bones. Just a drop."

Polly hears the twist of the plastic lid, then a sound that turns her gut, of liquid glugging. Smacked lips. *"Mm-mm."* The lid fastening back onto the bottle, the bottle going back into the fridge, the door closing, the padlock snapping closed.

She controls the urge to throw up, holding tight against the convulsions building throughout her body.

Seventeen

Sebastiàn himself greets Jessica at the door to his house that evening. He's wearing a Nirvana T-shirt and jeans, and Jessica is taken aback by the fact that he is a full inch shorter than her. She thinks of the twins' fine-boned mother with her tiny dolly feet, and she cannot fathom where those children got their height from.

"Good evening, Jessica!" he says, taking her hand into his and pumping it up and down twice. "Please excuse the chaos." He leads her into a huge living room with four sofas in it and a fire burning behind a grate the size of a small car. "We're renovating."

Jessica glances around at her opulent surroundings and says, "Truly, I would happily swap you my entire apartment for the worst room in this house."

"Oh, thank you. But it's a huge job and I'm struggling to keep on top of it all. There's always wind whistling through a window or rain pouring down the walls or something threatening to collapse in the night." He smiles and heads toward a drink tray on a cabinet. "What can I get you? I have all the usual"—he waves his hand across a row of sparkling decanters—"or I can whip you up a spicy margarita?"

Jessica grimaces and Sebastian misreads her face and says, "Or wine? Beer? Tea?"

"Tea! Yes, tea. Thank you."

Jessica hopes that she might finally get proper English tea and half expects Sebastian to ring a bell and for an old man to appear with a big silver tray, but instead he nods and says, "I'll be back in a tick," and disappears through a door.

He reappears a moment later with no tray, no teapot, just a big white mug, which he places in front of her. "Oh," says Jessica, staring down into the circle of milky brown liquid. "Thank you."

"So, you're writing a novel," Sebastian says, pouring himself a large scotch and bringing it to the sofa with him. "That's very exciting. Tell me all about it."

Sebastian is disarmingly pleasant, and Jessica feels strangely guilty to be playing him like this. But needs must, and she fixes him with a sincere look. "Well, there's not a lot to tell yet. I'm calling this a research trip, but really, it's more of an inspiration trip. I'm just taking a lot of photos and soaking up the feelings."

"And why Essex? I mean, you're a New Yorker, I hear?"

"Yes. I am."

"So what on earth makes a former cop—?"

"Well, not a former cop, just a number cruncher."

"But still, you worked in that environment, which must be a very particular environment, and then you chose to set a novel here." He arcs his arm around the room, suggesting his living room, but meaning the village of Barton Wallop.

"What can I tell you. I had a dream."

"You dreamed of Barton Wallop?"

"Yeah. Kind of. Or somewhere just like it. And I was reading about this house earlier, up at the historical place in the village? It's got quite a colorful history, got me feeling super inspired, and then, like, ten minutes later, I get your invite to come visit. Perfect timing. Thank you so much." She raises her mug of brown tea toward Sebastian, who raises his scotch back in return.

"You're quite welcome," he says. "I'm always keen to meet fellow writers."

"So is it true, what they told me in the pub last night, that you published a novel yourself?"

"Yes! Yes, indeed I did! It was . . . well, let us say it did not bother the bestsellers in any way, shape, or form. But it was a great experience, and I'm always fantasizing about writing another one. But that will have to wait until I've got this money pit under control." He smiles and Jessica smiles back.

"I hear you have children in New York," she says.

"Yes, I do. Lark and Fox. Twins. Apples of my eye."

"You must miss them?"

"Well, yes. I don't see nearly enough of them, it's true. But they were both here for the summer. Four weeks."

"That must have been fun," says Jessica. "How old are they?"

"Sixteen."

"What kind of kids are they?"

"Oh, they're great kids. Very cool. Too cool for school. But fun as well. Here . . ."

He pulls out his phone and swipes the screen a few times before showing his camera roll to Jessica. "These are from the summer."

Jessica has become so familiar with the faces on the screen that she has to pretend to be taken aback by their beauty afresh.

"Wow," she says. "Gorgeous kids."

"Yes. They are quite striking. They take after my mother."

"Oh, not their mother, then?" Jessica asks, feeling strangely defensive about this man stealing his children's superior genetic makeup from Amber's side of the family.

"Their mother is a very attractive woman. But these kids are in another league."

She ignores the backhanded slight against her client as best she can. "So sixteen-year-olds who are used to the bright lights of the city, they must have found it challenging out here in the sticks. How did you entertain them?"

"Oh, they found ways to entertain themselves. It was a glorious summer, warm and dry every day. And they made local friends."

"In the village?"

"Well, not really in the village, the village is, er . . ."

She waits for him to find words that won't cause offense.

"Not really their kind of people, you know. And there's probably only about ten kids here. But luckily there was a friend down the lane, a short walk away, and they hung out with her most days."

"Oh yes? Who was that?"

"A girl called Belle."

Bam! There it is.

"She lives in a place up the lane called the Old Farmhouse."

"What was she like?"

"Oh, I didn't get to meet her. The kids told me she was, er, agoraphobic, you know, never leaves the house. Kids these days and all their neuroses. Mad. Why can't they just enjoy being young, like we did?"

"Ha," Jessica says dryly, thinking of her own horribly fractured childhood. "Yeah."

"Anyway." He hits her with one of his charming idiot smiles. "How do you fancy a tour of the place? For your research?"

"Really?"

"Oh, yes. I'd love to show you around. But you will have to forgive the state of parts of it. It really is still very much a work in progress. Here"—he holds out his hand for her still-full mug, and she passes it to him—"follow me."

Jessica has been inside some remarkable houses in her

time, but she quickly realizes never one quite so sprawling and ornate as this. She is awed by the existence of not one but two libraries, one of which is lined with linenfold carved mahogany panels and contains a secret door into the other, which, Sebastian tells her, was built simply to home the original owner's first editions. There's a huge kitchen overlooking the gardens that Sebastian tells her is about to be ripped out and replaced because the units are brown, and brown kitchens are a thing of the past.

"Teal," he says thoughtfully, as they stand at the doorway. "Or perhaps a vivid sage."

"You're kinda nifty with color," she says playfully.

"Oh, no," he says, slightly apologetically. "Not me. My girlfriend. She's into interiors."

The secret girlfriend! Jessica hides her excitement. "Ah," says Jessica. "I see. The woman's touch. I thought I spotted it. Have you been together long?"

"Oh, no, just a few months. I mean, to be honest, I haven't even told my ex about her yet. It feels a bit early, you know? Still quite fresh. Don't want to, er . . . upset any applecarts."

Jessica spies a set of spiral stairs leading down from a corner of the kitchen. "What's down there?"

"A cellar, so I've been told," he says, "but I'm too scared to go down."

She eyes him, questioningly.

"Spiders," he says, with a slightly camp shiver. "Everywhere. I've got a phobia."

She nods. "You know, when I was at the historical place

today, in the village, I read in a book that this house was built on cursed land."

Sebastian sighs, heavily. "Yes . . . so I've been told. Although not until *after* I'd paid full price for the place." He snorts, derisively. "Well, I can't say it surprises me much. This house does feel cursed sometimes."

"In what way?"

"Oh, you know, everything that can go wrong does go wrong, and the electrics are insane."

Jessica gestures to the stairway. "Can I—Is it okay if I take a look?"

"Yeah, be my guest. For what it's worth. There's not a lot down there. Well, according to my girlfriend, at least."

"*She's* not scared of spiders, then?"

"No. I can't say she's scared of anything, to be honest. She's quite formidable."

He smiles at her encouragingly and Jessica descends the narrow stairs, circling her way down into the cellar. She uses the flashlight on her phone to light up the interior.

As Sebastian said, nothing down here. A smooth concrete floor, water pipes, a blank canvas.

But then she catches something else. Something dark, something electric in the air. It fizzes in her veins, it makes her hairs stand on end. Looking down at the concrete base, she sees holes drilled through it. She crouches and puts her hands to the holes, feels inside them with her fingers; they're smooth inside, not too dirty, so newly drilled. Must be something to do with controlling the damp, she surmises, before getting back to standing.

"What did you say this space was for?" she calls up to Sebastian.

"I have no idea. I mean, I suppose it must have been used for storage at one time. But now it's just a place to keep water pipes. If I wasn't so scared to go down there, I could use it for wine storage. Or a gym. Maybe even put in a home cinema."

Jessica arcs the flashlight one more time around the empty space, shudders, and then heads back up to the kitchen.

"See any ghosts?" Sebastian asks as she reappears.

"No," she says. "No spiders either. Looks immaculate. Have you had some work done down there?"

"Just some plumbing. A water pump for the fancy rainfall showers my girlfriend told me to get installed upstairs. Apparently we *have* to have rainfall showers, otherwise we're basically Neanderthals." He shrugs, then leads her back into the hallway and up a sweeping flight of stairs to what he refers to as a minstrels' gallery above. It's built from barley twists of ebonized wood, and all around the gallery are ornately carved black doors.

"Seven bedrooms," he says, gesturing at the many doors. "Only three renovated so far. Mine, and of course . . ." He opens a door to a pair of adjoining rooms with bowed leaded windows overlooking the manicured lawns at the back of the house. "The precious offspring."

"Nice," says Jessica, caressing the footboard of an over-sized rose-pink padded velvet bed.

"Yes. I had to get these rooms ready first, of course. No way would those kids countenance staying in subpar accommodation."

"Well, you have great taste, I have to say."

"Ah," he says, "that'll be my girlfriend again. Although my daughter, Lark, did keep referring to this bed as her 'big butt cheek' bed, so I'm not sure it was *entirely* to her taste."

Jessica lets out a burst of laughter and then asks to use the bathroom. Sebastian opens a door to reveal a shared en suite between the kids' rooms, which he refers to as a Jack and Jill bathroom. "I'll leave you to it," he says. "See you downstairs."

Jessica waits by the bathroom door until she hears the creak of Sebastian's footsteps on the staircase and then she opens Lark's wardrobe—a couple of hoodies hanging lonesome, a pair of scuffed-up sneakers on the floor, on one shelf a half-used bottle of cheap perfume called Brazilian Crush alongside scrunched-up T-shirts, and on another a bra with unfeasibly tiny cups. She falls to her hands and knees and peers under the huge velvet bed. Socks. A phone charging cable. Hair ties. She opens and closes several drawers, then peers behind the curtains and pulls up the cushion on the window seat there, finds nothing but fluff and hair and a bobby pin.

She goes through the bathroom and into Fox's room and carries out another search. Finding similar teenage detritus, she is about to give up and return downstairs when she notices something on the floor under a desk. It's a sketch on a scrap of paper of what looks like a small child bursting through the earth with arms raised up toward the beams of the sun. Underneath the sketch is the word *Miranda*.

Her head explodes with the memory of Fox on the landing outside the bathroom at the Bleeding Heart talking up to the ceiling and then Malcolm's report earlier about Fox's strange oration on the streets of New York.

Miranda? she thinks. Who the hell is Miranda?

She tucks the sketch into her jacket pocket and heads back down to Sebastian.

Eighteen

When Jessica gets back to her room later that night, it's nearly nine o'clock, so four p.m. in New York and the perfect time to speak to Malcolm, who should be fresh out of school and sitting in her office. She loads up Google Earth while she waits for Malcolm to pick up her call. It rings and rings and just as she thinks it's going to go to voicemail, he answers.

"Hi, Jessica."

His voice is quiet, so quiet.

"Malcolm. Are you okay?"

"Yeah." He's whispering.

"Why are you whispering? Where are you?"

"I'm on Old Broadway. Back at the Upside Down."

"The what?"

"The bar. You know. The one Fox brought me to last night."

"But how'd you get in? Shit, Malcolm. I promised your mom you wouldn't be doing anything dangerous!"

"I'm not doing anything dangerous. I literally just got in through a back window. I unlocked it last night when Fox wasn't looking."

"Well, illegal, then. If you get caught that'll be Harvard off the list."

"Well, I'm flattered, obviously, but Harvard isn't really—"

"That'll be *all* the colleges off the list, Malcolm! Get out of there, *now*!"

"Yeah yeah yeah, I am, just give me a minute. I just want to find this basement . . ."

Malcolm switches to video, and Jessica lowers her phone so that she can see the screen. It's the interior of a shabby, disused bar, dusty shelves attached to the wall, tables and chairs pushed up around the edges of the room, a huge window overlooking a scruffy backyard, old posters peeling from the walls.

"I mean, I've even been pushing, you know, on this solid wall, thinking maybe it was a secret door. But nothing doing."

"Look. Whatever. Get out of there now, for the love of God. Get back on the street." Jessica's heart is racing.

"Okay. Okay. I just want to take some photos. I'll call you right back."

"I'll be waiting."

She ends the call and sighs heavily, questioning her choices yet again. Mental footage of Malcolm being hauled out of the empty bar by a pair of cops and thrown into the back of a car,

Malcolm's tiny bespectacled mother signing in at the front desk of a Harlem precinct, her stricken face as she sees her perfect boy in cuffs, his future in tatters—it all runs through her head in a sickening rush.

"Come on, come on," she mutters under her breath. And then finally, her phone buzzes and Malcolm's name appears on the screen.

"You out?" she barks.

"Yeah. I'm out."

"Good, now listen." She pauses to calm herself. "Earlier on, when you were telling me about Fox, you said he mentioned a woman's name when he was staring up into the sky. Tell me again what it was?"

"It was Miranda."

"Yeah. That's what I thought. Miranda. It's the same name that was written on a drawing I found in Fox's bedroom here in the UK. And I just replayed the audio from my surveillance of Fox at the restaurant last week, and that was definitely what he was saying: Miranda."

"Seriously?"

"Yeah. Seriously. And I spent this evening with the twins' dad. He said he never met Belle because she was—get this—*agoraphobic*."

"Ha," says Malcolm. "Convenient."

"Yeah. Really convenient. But now I know where she lives, so tomorrow I'm going to head over there, to Belle's place, first thing, see what I can see. It looks pretty secure, from what I can see online. Tall walls, you know. But I'm sure I can find a way in."

"Hey, you should get a drone."

"Ha!" She laughs a staccato laugh. "A drone. And from where precisely am I to get a drone here in the actual butt crack of nowhere?"

"Amazon?"

Jessica sighs. "Yeah. Maybe. Why don't you order me one? I'll send you my account details."

"Sure," says Malcolm. "I'm on it."

"And listen. You're seeing Fox and Lark tomorrow, right? Boxing?"

"Uh-huh."

"Find out who the hell Miranda is, will you?"

"Yeah. Yeah. Totally. I will totally, I—"

Another call is coming through. It's Amber Randall and Jessica switches the call without saying goodbye. She rearranges the fat hotel pillows behind her back so that she is sitting straighter. It makes her feel more professional.

"Hi."

"Hi, Jessica, how did it go?"

"It went okay. I mean, Sebastian, he doesn't appear to know anything."

Amber sighs. "Yup," she says. "Sounds like him. How did he seem?"

"Oh," says Jessica, not sure what Amber wants to hear. "He seemed, you know, fine, I guess. Seems like a nice guy."

"He is. He is a nice guy. And that's why I got so agitated back in your office when you were suggesting some kind of friction between us. You know, it's just not like that. He's just a kind of a benign idiot, you know? How's his place looking?"

Jessica blinks, and nods slowly. "It's, er, yeah. Kind of amazing, but kind of a mess."

"Don't know what he was thinking, buying that place. Such a money pit, and what for? I mean, seven bedrooms. Who the hell needs seven bedrooms? It's—"

"Listen," she cuts in, not wanting to get involved in a marital dispute, "how are the twins?" She brings her legs off the bed and sits on the edge.

Amber sighs. "They're okay. Still acting weird. I hear your intern was out with Fox last night. Did he have anything to report back?"

"Well, yeah."

Jessica gives a streamlined retelling of Malcolm's rant and Amber breathes sharply when she gets to the bit about Fox letting himself into an abandoned bar in Harlem, with a key.

"Are you *serious*?"

"Yeah, well, that's what Malcolm told me. Said that Fox's Belle had given them the key when they were in England. Told them there was a secret basement in there. They tried looking for it, couldn't find it, and when Malcolm pushed Fox for more details, he dried up. Stopped talking."

"But—I mean—a bar in Harlem? I don't understand. What on earth could that have to do with the twins?"

"I really don't know, Amber. I mean, maybe you could ask?"

"No. I'm not going to ask. They'll want to know how I know, and how would I explain that?"

"You could say you followed them yourself?"

"No," Amber responds forcefully. "I have to maintain their trust. If they think I'm sneaking around after them, who knows what they'll do. And anyway, there's no point asking them anything, they're simply not talking to me. They're closed down. They're empty."

Jessica sighs. "Have the twins mentioned someone named Miranda at all?"

"Oh!" she exclaims. "Yes! I heard Lark the other day, talking to someone named Miranda when she was in her room. I thought she was on her phone, but when I walked in, her phone was charging on the other side of her room. I said, 'Who were you just talking to?' She said no one. I didn't push it, because, well, you know. Who do you think she is, this Miranda woman?"

"As of yet I have no clue, but I strongly believe that they met her here, in the UK. And that she has something to do with Belle. So tomorrow that is going to be my primary goal. I'm going hunting for Miranda."

* * *

When Jessica wakes the next morning there is a message on her phone from Malcolm that says READ ME and comes with a link, which Jessica quickly clicks.

171

On an amateur-looking website in maroon text on a background meant to evoke yellowing paper, she reads:

No. 14 Old Broadway was built in 1877. The bottom floor was originally a baker's shop, but by the early 1980s the lower floors had been converted into a bar and nightclub called the Upside Down. The club closed for good in 1994, and in 1998 the building was briefly infamous after the discovery during gas line maintenance of the remains of three young homeless men beneath the dance floor in the basement. Their bodies were mummified and had been drained of blood, leading to the unknown killer being dubbed the Harlem Vampire. The basement to the club was bricked up and the building now sits empty.

Jessica—Malcolm continues underneath—WHAT THE HELL IS GOING ON?????

Twelve years ago
Portsmouth, Hampshire, UK

Polly hears the bed creak as Arthur's father gets to his feet, then his heavy footsteps across the landing, his voice from downstairs a moment later talking to the cat.

"Let's get you fed, then, shall we."

It's hard to believe that it's the voice of the same man who only two minutes ago was sitting on the edge of this bed *drinking blood*. Polly holds her rucksack hard against her stomach, sees it rising and falling in rhythm with her breath. Adrenaline is pumping through her body and her flesh feels chilled. She tries to make sense of what has just happened, but she can't.

Arthur's father keeps blood in a fridge in his bedroom, which he drinks to give him a "lift." Is he a vampire? Is Ophelia a vampire? What about Arthur? She shudders with distaste at the thought that she might have been having sex with a blood-drinking killer all these weeks.

LISA JEWELL

Who the hell are these people? she thinks. Who the hell are they?

Maybe she should abandon this whole thing. She has her samples of Ophelia's creams now. If she can just get out of here alive, she can get them home and try to re-create them. She doesn't need Arthur anymore. She doesn't need any of these freaks.

But then ... she thinks ... what if the blood has something to do with the magic cream? What if it's all part of the same thing? What if it's the blood that makes the cream work? She needs to find out. She needs to *know*.

She tiptoes halfway down the stairs and, seeing Arthur's father in the kitchen leaning away from her to tip biscuits into the cat's bowl, she quietly exits the house, her mind spinning out of control.

* * *

The next day, Polly follows Arthur's dad to his allotment. It's a bright day, soft clouds scudding across a clean blue sky. The first of the season's Christmas lights are starting to appear in shop windows, but it still feels like early autumn.

The allotments are at the end of a dead-end street three roads away from Arthur's house. There's a metal gate set between two tall walls, and Arthur's dad takes a key from the large set he carries on his belt and unlocks it. It closes slowly enough for Polly to grab it and squeeze through just before it locks again.

The plot of allotments is small at the front, but beyond, it stretches out towards the open horizon. She sees Arthur's father heading to the left and follows behind. His allotment is about halfway across, a scruffy square of land with a small ramshackle shed, a Formica-topped table, and two broken-down wooden chairs. It's shaded from the sun by a large tree, and tucked away, out of view. Arthur's dad sits himself at the table and pours himself tea from a thermos flask. He eats a sandwich that he unpeels from cling film. Then he eats three biscuits from a packet, which he tucks back into his shoulder bag. He takes off his hat, smooths back his hair, replaces his hat, and gets to work.

Polly quietly backs out of the allotment plot and waits outside for an hour or so until she hears the clank of the metal gate, sees Arthur's father leaving with his bag slung over his shoulder, and then she makes her way back inside. The shed in his allotment is padlocked twice, once at the top, once on the middle. She pulls on a pair of fitted suedette gloves, unscrews the padlocks from the cheap wood, and puts them in her pocket.

Then she pulls the door open.

She goes to step in, then immediately jumps back when she sees what's inside. Gardening equipment, yes: secateurs, shovels, a rake, a strimmer, trowels, pots, and trays. But other things that bear no relation to gardening: metal kidney trays, boxes of test tubes, belts, rope, a jar of plastic ties, muslins, bandages, metal hypodermics, plastic hypodermics, clamps, wires, scalpels, packages of PVC gloves, a heart monitor. Behind a waxed waterproof coat, she finds a white plastic apron.

A globule of vomit appears at the back of her throat, and she swallows it down, determined to maintain her resolve.

What, she thinks. What is this? Who are these people?

She wants to run helter-skelter out of here so fast that she can't breathe. But she also, more overwhelmingly, wants to *know*, wants to understand. The fridge full of blood, the shed full of surgical apparatus, the weird, insular family, the dark rumors, the cat with spinning eyes, that noise that Arthur's father made as he tipped blood down his throat, a noise that has haunted Polly ever since.

She takes photographs of everything, then carefully rescrews the padlocks into place and leaves.

Nineteen

Jessica bumps into Gavin from the pub as she turns out of the hotel later that day. He's wearing a tracksuit and carrying a mop and bucket.

"Oh, hi, Jessica! Lovely morning, isn't it?"

Jessica looks upward into the sky, which is a soft, creamy blue. "Yeah," she agrees. "It is."

"Where are you off to?"

"Oh, just going to do some research."

He nods dismissively and says, "Listen, I don't suppose you're free tonight, are you? Me and the wife, we're, well . . . in all honesty, we're going through a bit of a rough patch, and she's gone to stay at her mum's and I'm not very good with my own company. You know. It'd be nice to have someone to share the evening with."

He has the grace to flush slightly as he speaks, and Jessica considers him through narrowed eyes. "You literally just told me two nights ago that you were happily married. What happened?"

"Well, I'd only just met you, I wasn't going to come straight out and tell you all my personal problems, was I?"

Jessica pushes out her bottom lip and concedes his point with a nod. "I guess," she says, still nodding, trying to play nice. "But yeah, listen, I'm not really here for that kind of a thing, you know? There's a lot going on in my life right now and I need to keep my decks well and truly . . ." She describes a straight line with the edge of her hand. "But thank you, Gavin. I'll see you around."

She throws him what she really hopes is a kind smile, but she is also aware that kind smiles aren't a part of her physical repertoire, and sure enough Gavin's face drops, and he says, "You didn't have to be so patronizing. I was only trying to be friendly."

Jessica breathes in hard, holding back the urge to really show him patronizing, acutely aware of Gavin's slumped shoulders, his mop, his bucket, his scruffy tracksuit, his tiny, punctured ego deflating on the sidewalk behind her as she walks away from him.

Fifteen minutes out of the village, just a short walk from Sebastian's house, Jessica finds the tall rusty gate and the sign naming THE OLD FARMHOUSE that she'd seen on Street View earlier. There's a button next to the gate and she considers for a moment that she could just press it, see what sort of welcome she gets as an unexpected visitor, but her instincts tell her that the welcome would not be warm, so she follows the wall of the grounds for a while as it turns a corner into a tiny lane. About a quarter mile up this stretch of the perimeter she sees a section of the wall built lower to accommodate a bowed-over tree. It's low enough for her to clear it in a way that would get the locals talking if anybody saw her doing it, and she is about to gear herself up for the maneuver, to engage the engines, pull on the invisible throttle that lives inside her, when she remembers what else may currently be living inside her and her hand instinctively goes to her stomach.

Should she, she wonders, not be doing this anymore? Is it up there with drinking alcohol and going on roller coasters as a thing that a newly pregnant lady should not be doing?

It is not advisable to engage your super-powers in the first trimester.

She feels quite sure that Google does not have an answer to this particular conundrum, and so she again has to trust her instincts, and her instincts tell her that this wall is not that high and that a really fit person could probably manage it without super-powers, and thus so can she. She hooks the toe of her boot into a nick in the surface, pushes up to where she can grab the top of the wall with both hands, and then pulls herself up until she's crouching like a large raptor ready to take flight. A second later she lands, soft, limber, strong, on the grass on the other side. And that is when she hears it. The terrible sound of a pack of dogs approaching.

They appear through the overgrown grass as a blur of fur and flesh and teeth and gums and she turns and grabs hold of the branches of the nearest tree, pulls herself as high as she can get, and stares down into their open jaws, adrenaline ripping through her veins, pumping through her head till her eyeballs throb.

"Oh my God, *shit*," she says to herself, her hand held to her thumping heart. "Down, boys. Just back the hell *off*."

But the more she talks to them the louder they bark, the higher their lips creep up their gums, the more their gigantic bat ears lie flat against their gigantic heads. And then suddenly, as quickly as the noise began, it stops, and a girl appears behind the dogs, making strange clicky sounds with her tongue against her teeth. The six dogs swarm around her, panting loudly, wet tongues lolling from frothy lips.

The girl is wearing an oversized military-style coat with metal buttons, and a red knitted hat with a bobble on it. She peers up into the branches of the tree and smiles widely at Jessica.

"Hi!" she says. "Who are you?"

Jessica peers down at her. "My name's Jessica. What the hell are those things?"

"They're dogs."

"No, I mean what *breed*? They look like wolves."

"No. They are Belgian Malinois."

"Fancy," says Jessica. "Am I safe to come down now?"

"Of course. Here." She moves toward her. "Do you need a hand?"

"No," says Jessica, navigating the branches until she is low enough to jump. "I'm good."

The girl stares at her, a small smile playing on her mouth, then puts out a hand. "Belle. Nice to meet you."

Jessica's heart jumps. This is her. This is perfect Belle. Except she doesn't look perfect, she just looks . . . *normal*.

Jessica takes her hand. "Nice to meet you too."

The girl smiles coolly at her. "*So* . . . what brings you over my wall?"

"I, er . . . well, it's kind of crazy, but I'm researching a novel and I saw this place on a map and thought it looked kind of cool. Sorry. I didn't know anyone lived here."

"Please don't be sorry. I'm always happy to see a new face. It's lonely being stuck out here."

"Don't you live with someone? A family?"

"Well, sort of. I have an in loco parentis type of arrangement. My parents live abroad. I'm at boarding school, I come back for holidays."

"Is it a holiday now?"

Belle looks momentarily nonplussed. "No," she says, finally. "No, it's not."

"So how come you're here?"

Her nose wrinkles slightly. "I suppose it must be exeat."

"Exe—?"

"It's like a mini-holiday. I don't usually come back, but I must have been missing the dogs. And now I'm sort of wishing I was back at school? It's always just like . . . there's never a place I really want to be."

Jessica eyes her gently. There is a blankness about the girl. A sadness. Jessica looks beyond the girl, her gaze scanning the grounds.

"Is there anyone else here?" she asks.

"No, just me and Debra. My guardian."

Debra, Jessica clocks. Not Miranda. "Is she here?"

"Yes, she is. She's in the house. Making lunch."

Jessica nods. "I don't suppose . . ." she begins. "I mean, tell me to take a hike, obviously, but since I'm here, maybe I could just take a look at the grounds, for my novel?"

Belle's eyes narrow, she turns to look over her shoulder, and then she shrugs. "I guess. Why not?"

The dogs, now placid as poodles, follow them eagerly as they walk, panting and sniffing at the grass.

"How'd you do that?" Jessica asks Belle. "How'd you get them to calm down like that?"

Belle throws her a sweet smile. "Tricks of the trade," she says. "Debra taught me. Clicks. And treats." As she says this Jessica notices her pass one of them a tiny scrap of dried meat from her coat pocket. "You always have to have something they want," she says, and then she turns away again.

Slowly as they walk, a house begins to reveal itself through the unkempt landscape. It's a brick farmhouse. Scruffy. Rambling. It has a moss-laden glass lean-to attached to one side, a tumbledown garage attached to the other, a rusty car in the driveway. A large barn slouches on the other side of the driveway, two metal storage containers covered with ivy nearby.

Everything is overgrown and wild, with an air of slight abandonment.

"How long have you lived in this place, Belle?"

"Not sure really. All my life, I suppose. Want to come in?"

"Er, yeah. Sure. Thank you."

"Great!"

She follows the girl through a mud-splattered back door and directly into a terra-cotta-floored kitchen with peeling mint-green cabinetry. A middle-aged woman stands in the kitchen prodding at a piece of cooked meat in a baking tin.

"Oh!" she says when she looks up and sees Jessica. "Hello!"

"Jessica, this is Debra. Debra is the custodian of the Old Farmhouse."

Jessica sees a look of alarm pass across Debra's face, which she quickly covers with a warm and welcoming smile.

"Custodian," she says, disparagingly, wiping down her hands on a tea towel. "Makes me sound like a hundred-year-old man with a limp. I prefer housekeeper. Nice to meet you, Jessica."

Jessica takes the proffered hand and notices dry skin and a firm grip. "Nice to meet you too."

"Cup of tea?"

"Yeah, thanks, that would be great."

"Belle, make our guest a cup of tea. Good girl."

Debra is a tall woman, somewhere between midforties and early fifties. She has dark hair held back in a scrunchie, and shiny bangs that overhang sad-looking eyes framed with funky red plastic reading glasses. She's wearing a baggy black turtleneck and black leggings, with thick socks and green fingerless gloves.

"So, what brings you to the wilds of Essex?" Debra asks, pouring a jug of stock over the piece of meat and re-covering it with foil. "That sounds like a New York accent to me."

"Yeah," says Jessica. "Born and bred. And in fact, I was talking to the guy at the pharmacy—"

"Elliot," says Debra.

"Right. Elliot." Jessica turns back to Belle. "He told me there were some other New Yorkers here this summer. A pair of twins about your age. Did you meet them?"

Belle shakes her head. "No," she says. "I was away all summer, with my parents."

Jessica pauses for a beat, absorbing this unexpected lie. "Oh, you weren't here this summer?"

"No," she says vaguely. "I don't think so."

"I saw them," Debra cuts in. "In July, I think it was. A boy and a girl. I saw them around."

"Oh. Did you get to talk to them?"

Debra scoffs. "Er, no. They were not exactly what you'd call friendly."

"Yeah. So I hear." The woman is lying, and Jessica needs to know why. "So, how long have you been the housekeeper here?"

"Oh, a few years. Just since Belle's parents moved abroad."

"Where do they live?" asks Jessica.

"Spain," says Belle.

"Just outside Barcelona," Debra finishes. "They run a hotel."

"You'll get to see them soon, I hope?"

Belle throws a quick glance at Debra, a tight smile on her lips.

"Christmas," Debra says and straightens. "Belle will go out to see them at Christmas."

"They don't come back here? To see you?"

Belle again looks at Debra.

"They really can't leave the hotel," says Debra. "It's all-consuming."

"Yeah." Jessica nods back and forth at both of them. "Yeah, I guess it would be."

What is going on here? Jessica wonders. Is this child being held here against her will? Is she being brainwashed? And if so, why? Who is this woman, Debra, and what is her game?

"You know," Jessica says. "I've been out all morning, and I could really do with using a bathroom. Would that be okay?"

Debra's posture stiffens slightly, but she smiles. "Yes, of course. It's right at the back of the house, just beyond the stairs. The light cord is broken, you'll have to pull it a few times before the light comes on. And there's probably an elderly cat in there. Just ignore him."

As she exits the kitchen and walks down the hallway Jessica sees frayed dirty-red carpeting coming away from stair treads, faded wallpaper hanging in strips, corners festooned with ancient dusty cobwebs. While Jessica can imagine that this was once a handsome home for handsome people, what it does *not* look like is a home belonging to a pair of cool Gen X parents who own a hotel in Barcelona. Something is off about absolutely every last element of this setup, but she has no idea what it is.

She pushes open the door into the bathroom. Curled into a gnarly ball on a threadbare bath mat is the very elderly cat. He looks up at Jessica with rheumy eyes and then attempts to uncurl himself from his ball to come and greet her.

As a newly ordained cat person, Jessica is pleased to meet him, and gives the poor creature a few scratches, then turns the faucet on and off, flushes the toilet, and creeps away from the bathroom and farther down the back hallway. Here there is a small brass handle embedded into the rose-print wallpaper and Jessica tiptoes slowly, ancient floorboards creaking gently underfoot, until at the far end of the hallway her hand goes out toward the brass knob. She touches it but is startled by the sound of a throat clearing behind her. She jumps, her hand on her chest, turns to see Debra.

"Everything okay?"

"Oh, yeah, sorry. I was, er, these old houses, they kind of fascinate me, and I saw this secret door thing. I was just being really nosy."

Debra smiles. "I understand. It's tantalizing, isn't it. Do you want me to show you?"

Jessica throws her an uncertain look. "What, is there like a hobbit in there?"

Debra laughs before turning the handle and pulling open the secret door, to reveal a brick wall.

"Oh," says Jessica, her eyes searching the solid surface for some clue as to why it is there.

"Yeah. I know. Weird, isn't it? Think maybe there must have been something there, once upon a time, and they knocked it down. But who knows with a house as old as this one. It'll be full of secrets." She waves toward the brick wall. "You going to put that in your novel?"

Jessica looks at her curiously.

"Belle told me."

Jessica nods. "Yeah, you know, I might. That and the ancient cat that lives in the bathroom."

"Ah, yes. Mr. Smith. He has been on this Earth for a very, very long time."

"How old is he?"

"Nobody really knows. He was old when I adopted him, and I've had him for fifteen years. He must be at least twenty."

"Wow."

"Yes. Every day's a gift. Anyway, since you're here, why don't you stay for lunch? Lamb's nearly ready."

The smell of roasting meat is wafting down the hall toward them and Jessica has not eaten today. "That would be great, thank you so much."

* * *

The dogs sit and watch them eat. They pant heavily. One of them has a slick of drool hanging from its jowls. Jessica sees Belle feed them shreds of lamb from her plate when Debra isn't looking.

"So . . ." says Debra. "What brought you here to Barton Wallop for this novel you're writing?"

"I had a dream."

"Seriously?"

"For real. Crazy, huh?"

"And was there something in your dream that led you to this house in particular?"

Jessica folds her napkin neatly and puts it back on her lap. "Well, no. Not as such. It was actually the house in the village that I had a dream about, the one with the moat?"

"Oh." One of Debra's eyebrows shoots up. "Ha."

"Do you know it?"

"Well, yes, of course. It's the fanciest house in the village. Obviously I know it."

"The guy who lives there invited me over for a tour yesterday. Sebastian Randall?"

"Oh yes, I've heard the name."

"He's the father of the twins I mentioned earlier. That's where they were staying apparently. This summer."

There's a strange silence, which Jessica leaves to play out deliberately.

"Well," says Debra, "that was nice of him, to let you have a tour. What's it like, his house?"

"Yeah. Kinda quirky. Kinda grand. Kinda spooky. He thinks it's haunted."

"Oh, does he?"

"Uh-huh."

"Well," says Debra crisply. "I don't believe in ghosts. Do you?"

"No," says Jessica. "I believe in a hell of a lot of things. But not in ghosts."

"When you're dead, you're dead," says Debra. "Don't you think?"

"Yup. I certainly do. At least, I hope so!" She laughs dryly at her own attempt at humor, but then glances at Belle and notices a strange look on her face, as if she wants to say something, but cannot find the words. The atmosphere has become taut and slightly edgy. Something's changed and Jessica's not sure what.

Then Debra pushes back her chair and says, "I must say, it's been very nice having some company, even if it was somewhat unexpected, but Belle and I should probably be getting on with things now."

"You've been very hospitable," says Jessica, mirroring Debra's action and pushing back her own chair. "Thank you so much for the delicious food. It's been a while since I had a home-cooked meal like that."

"Well, you're not being looked after properly, are you?"

Jessica stops and looks at Debra. "I'm sorry?"

"Sorry," says Debra. "I get notions about people. And I just feel like someone should be looking after a nice girl like you, and they're not." She smiles and it's oddly warm, almost unnervingly maternal.

Jessica feels a swoop in the pit of her belly and returns a

stiff smile. She grabs her jacket and points toward the front door. "How do I get to the front entrance? I kind of came in the side way."

"Oh yes, just follow the path from the driveway to the left, then you'll reach a small copse. Cut through it, veer right over the bridge, and rejoin the driveway there. Then it's about another two minutes."

"Great! Thanks. And good to meet you both. I'm in town for a few more days, so maybe I'll bump into you in the village?"

"Oh, I doubt it. We don't get out much." Debra says this with another warm smile, but, still, her words leave Jessica with a chill in her gut.

Jessica leaves the ramshackle house and sets off through the overgrown grounds. A moment later she hears footsteps behind her, and turns at the sight of Belle, running to catch up.

"Hi!" she says. "Thought I should guide you, make sure you don't get lost." She casts a small glance in the direction of the house as she says this. And then they walk in silence for a while, a sharp breeze whipping at their hair, the only sound that of the dogs sniffing and panting behind them.

Suddenly Belle turns to Jessica, her hands deep in the pockets of her military-style coat, her cheeks flushed with color. She stares hard into Jessica's eyes.

"Please," she says, "tell me—am I *real*?"

Twelve years ago
Portsmouth, Hampshire, UK

After work the next day, Polly catches the bus to the chalet park at the other end of Eastney Beach. Her memories of the layout of the park are vague. She hasn't been here since she was sixteen, but she remembers a central area, like a small roundabout with a stone sundial at the center, and gravel tracks that radiate out from there in various directions. She remembers that she and her ex would go straight across this roundabout in his car and that the dealers' chalet was halfway up, with a sharply obscured view of the sea, just before a curve in the road.

And then there it is, right in front of her, just as she remembers it. Heavily curtained, unkempt. Could it be possible, she wonders, that those feckless boys who once supplied half of Portsmouth's year 10s with weed still live here?

She knocks on the familiar door and hears a gruff voice. "Yo. Who's that?"

"It's Polly, I used to go out with Jordan Brown?"

"Polly?"

"Yes. Jordan's ex, four years ago."

"Calm."

She hears locks turning and then the door opens, and a man she remembers vaguely is standing in front of her. As she recalls, he was the nicer of the two who lived here.

"Oh, yeah," he says, his eyes roaming up and down her body. "Polly. Yeah. I remember you. Sweet. You coming in?"

"Yeah. Please."

He gestures for her to come indoors; it smells as she remembers, pungent with the combined aromas of skunk, of men, of unwashed T-shirts. She perches herself gingerly on a foldout chair.

"So," says the guy, whose name she cannot recollect. "Polly. You good?"

She nods. "I'm good."

He puts his hand on a cheap plastic kettle. "Tea?"

"No. Thanks."

He takes his hand off the kettle and sits opposite her. "You see Jordan anymore?"

She shakes her head. "No. He moved away."

The guy nods, then appraises her. "You buying?"

"No. No, I'm not. I'm . . ." She rearranges herself on the uncomfortable chair and sighs. "Listen. Remember the family that lived next door to you, back then?"

The guy wrinkles his brow. "You mean that, like, *serial killer*?"

Polly startles slightly.

He smiles, revealing a missing tooth. "I'm kidding ya. Obviously. It was just, like, a running gag, y'know."

"But what was the deal with him? I remember you saying weird stuff used to happen there."

"Yeah. There was a woman here one time, banging down their door, screaming for her son."

"What was she screaming?"

"Oh, yeah, just kind of, 'I know he was here! I know he was here! Where is he?' That sort of thing. And that man, the dad, like, he was always making friendly with my customers. Out there"—he jerks his head—"fiddling with cars, in his boilersuit, making small talk. Asking weird questions."

"What sort of weird questions?"

"Just about their families, like. About their health. That sort of thing. I'd say to him, what are you, like, an effing doctor?" He laughs.

Polly smiles, to keep things moving. "And what would he say?"

"Nothing. Rude bastard. Never talked to us. All three of them were the same."

"The mum, and the son?"

"Yeah. Acted like they were the only people in the world. The mum, you know. She's like a psychic or something? We used to . . . *feel* stuff? Coming from there."

"Stuff?"

"Yeah. Vibrations. Or like . . . like"—his hands dart around as he searches for the right word—"waves, more like. We used to call it *the wiggles*." He wriggles his fingers. "You

193

know, like, when someone opens the back window of the car when you're driving fast? And these mad noises. Thought maybe she was, like, doing a séance or summink. Inviting, like, evil spirits in. You know? And that kid. What was his name?"

"Arthur?"

"Yeah." He clicks both pairs of fingers and thumbs. "Arfur. That's it. Used to hear him crying all the time. And then there was this one time . . ." He sucks his breath in through his teeth. "He brought a mate home? Heard all sorts that night, banging, shouting. The kid crying. Shit." He sucks his breath in again.

"So did you call the police?"

He looks at her in amazement, and then around his drug den. "Are you actually kidding me?"

"Oh, yes," she says, realizing the stupidness of her question. She glances through the window at the other chalet. "Who lives there now?"

"Nobody. Empty. Has been since they left."

"Seriously?"

"Yeah. Seriously. Think it needed too much work, management decided it would be cheaper to leave it. Plus, hard to rent out given the, er, next-door neighbors, y'know." He grins sheepishly. "So why all the questions?"

"No reason. Just bumped into the son in town the other day. Seemed nice, but remembered you'd said stuff about them."

"Yeah. I wouldn't touch them lot with a barge pole, to be honest. Wouldn't go anywhere near 'em. Bunch of freaks."

Polly nods, stifles a smile.

He doesn't know the half of it, she thinks. He does not know the half.

* * *

Polly gets to her feet, dusts down the knees of her jeans, tucks her hair behind her ears, and looks around. The inside of the old chalet is as bleak and unhomely as the house Arthur's family is looking after in the town, colder inside than it is out, and wall-to-wall grubby carpets and a smell of meat and mildew. The place has been stripped bare: just mattresses in each of the two bedrooms, scuffed-up hippie rugs on the laminated wooden floors, a dreamcatcher, a cardboard box full of old school textbooks, an old cat food bowl.

But even through the emptiness, Polly can feel something—something alive, something demanding, an energy that seeps through her, unpleasantly. She pulls the box of textbooks towards her and leafs through them. As she would expect, it's mainly computer studies stuff, plus maths, science, a few word puzzles, comic books, a few magazines about UFOs. But there, towards the bottom of the pile, she finds something unexpected and unsettling. She slowly pulls it towards her.

It's a sketchbook, small in size, with a black cover. On the inside page is *Ophelia Simms Age 13*, written in old-fashioned cursive ink pen, and there, on the first page, under a sketch of two children playing with a ball on a beach, are the words *Magnus and I, Eastney Beach, 27 Oct 1812*.

Polly shakes her head slightly, then starts to make sense of it. Ophelia must have been named after a relative. But on the next page there is a photograph; it's a tiny portrait in black and white, printed on thick card, and it's of a beautiful young girl with black hair, a knowing smile, a lace-collared jacket, and it's her. It's Ophelia. Except it can't be Ophelia, because Ophelia is only about fifty and this photograph is dated 1822. Polly pockets the photograph and keeps turning the pages. More sketches of family scenes, scraps of poetry, shreds of news from yellowing newspapers. And then there's a strip of passport photographs from an old-fashioned booth, and it's the same girl, the young Ophelia, but this time with black eyeliner and a flicked-out bob, and underneath it says *Me, 1963*. But in 1963, Ophelia should barely have been born. She slips the strip into her bag alongside the black-and-white photo and carries on looking through the book.

About halfway through, the tone of the book changes; the images are of pop stars, faces that Polly recognizes vaguely. There's one that looks like Morrissey, another that looks like the lead singer from the Cure. There are articles taken from old music magazines, one dated *12 January 1983*, another dated *20 July 1984*. And then—Polly's breath catches—an article photo torn from the *NME*. It's about a British band called the Diagonal, which was touring the US for the first time, and there's a review of their first gig, at a venue in New York called the Upside Down. And there, underneath the review, is a photograph of the band after their performance, posing with sweaty hair and beers in their hands next to the manager of the bar, a man called John Warshaw.

Polly pulls the article closer to her and tilts it towards the windowlight.

She peers closely at the photograph and then gasps softly when she realizes that the man in the photograph, the manager of the Upside Down bar, photographed many years ago as a young man, is none other than Arthur's father.

Twenty

Jessica stops at the gates of the Old Farmhouse and blinks at Belle. "I'm sorry?"

"Am I definitely real? Do I look real?"

Jessica pauses. Here it is, she thinks. Here is the weird stuff that she'd come all this way for. This is it.

"Well, yeah. You look real. Extremely real. Why do you ask?"

"I dunno. It's just sometimes, when I'm here, in this place, everything feels a bit . . . hazy? Like it's not real? Then when I get back to school it feels like I was never actually here. But then I start getting this feeling that I want to come back here. All the time. And that doesn't feel real either."

Jessica considers Belle for a moment, her thoughts spinning wildly, aware that she needs to tread so carefully right now, that this moment is as delicate as blown glass. "Back in there," she begins. "Just now, when we were talking about Sebastian Randall's house. About ghosts. You looked like you wanted to say something. What was it?"

Belle smiles sadly. "I don't know," she says. "That's the thing. I keep losing myself. It's like there are two stories running through my mind all the time, they keep overlapping, winding and twisting. I can never get them straight. And when you mentioned Sebastian's house, it made me think of something. Ghosts. Dead people. But now I can't remember what it was."

"Belle. Do you know someone named Miranda?"

Belle furrows her brow. "Miranda? No, I don't think so. But then, maybe I do. I don't know. I just really don't know."

"Do you feel safe, Belle? With Debra?"

"Yes. Always. Debra takes care of me. Debra loves me. I feel really safe with her."

Jessica sighs and casts her gaze around. She needs a way to find out who this girl really is. She says, "What school are you at?"

"Oh, just a tiny place, near the coast in Suffolk."

"What's it called?"

"Truscott House."

Jessica nods. "Shall I call them?"

"What for?"

"Ask to speak to you. See what they say. Then you'd know if you're real or not. Yes?"

Belle's eyes grow wide. "Oh," she says. "Yes. Why not?"

"What's the number?"

"No idea."

"Oh, okay, let me google it."

She goes to take her phone from her pocket, but then Belle says, "There's literally no service out here at all."

Jessica sighs. "I'll have to do it when I get back to the village. You could come with me if you want? Apparently, they serve a cream tea at my hotel from two. I've been wanting to have one. I mean, what even is a cream tea?" She hits Belle with what she hopes is an agenda-free smile.

Belle returns the smile. "It's just tea from a pot, with some cakes and sandwiches on the side."

"Tea from a pot! I've been here for three days and not one damn person has given me tea from a pot. I must say I'm a little disappointed."

"Life's too short for teapots," says Belle with a smile. Then she looks behind her in the direction of the house. "I mean, it sounds nice, but I kind of don't really go into the village."

"Why not?"

"I don't really know. It's just, I get to the gate and then . . . something always happens. Or sometimes I don't even get to the gate at all. I think maybe I might be a bit agoraphobic?"

Jessica frowns at hearing that word again. "Really? But what about when you leave for school?"

"I'm not really sure. I suppose I just get in a car and go. But when it comes to me just, you know, leaving, it never quite happens."

"Well, let's test that, shall we?" She gestures to Belle with a nod of her head.

Belle nods back and guides her toward the driveway and the pair of rusty gates.

"How do they open?"

"There's a button," Belle replies. "Just under that little bush."

Jessica locates it and presses it. The rusty gates begin slowly to come apart. Belle instructs the dogs to stay, with the strange tongue clicks, and then starts to walk toward the gap. Jessica stands and watches. All seems normal, all seems fine. And then suddenly the blue sky turns black with storm clouds and rain begins to fall, so hard and so immediate that they are both soaked to the skin within seconds.

"Oh my God," says Belle, turning up the collar of her coat and dashing back in the direction of the house.

"Hold on!" Jessica calls out. "Just wait! It's only rain!"

"I hate the rain!" Belle calls back. "We'll go another time."

"No!" Jessica yells and then she feels it coming, the diesel and the grossness and she knows she should resist it, but she also knows that she wants to go home, and she can't go home until she's made progress on this case, and she knows that this here now, this crazy rain-drenched moment, this is her chance to make progress on the case, and so she allows herself to fill up with the sensation and then she races back to Belle. It takes her a second to scoop her up, she feels light as air in her arms, and then another second to swoop through the air, through the hard, lashing rain and through the tall rusty gates and then come to a halt on the soft grassy verge across the lane, where she gently unhooks her arm from around Belle and lowers her to the ground.

Belle stares up at her breathlessly. "What *was* that?" she asks in awe.

They both look up into the blue, blue sky, and then down again in unison at the dry, dry grass, at the layer of dust that sits atop the dull surface of the road, and then across to the slick puddles of rain on the driveway of Belle's house as the gates slowly come back together with a menacing metallic smash.

Jessica looks at Belle and shrugs.

"Did you just fly?" asks Belle, staring up at her with wide eyes.

"I would not refer to that as flying. Just very adept jumping."

Belle makes a scoffing noise. "Oh my God," she says. "What are you? Are you a super hero?"

"No. I'm just sporty. But hey, talk to me about *that*." She points at the blue sky now hanging over Belle's property. "What just happened there?"

"I don't know. It . . ." Belle looks lost for words, her hands upturned at her sides. "I don't know," she says again and lets her hands drop.

"You think that was normal, what just happened? Has it happened before?"

Belle nods. "Yes. It often happens. I think it's a microclimate?"

Jessica groans. "A *microclimate*? God help me. No, that was not a microclimate. That was some crazy voodoo shit. That was—" She cuts herself off when she sees the girl's rather blank expression. *What's the point?* "How are you feeling?"

"I feel fine."

"You feel fine?"

"Yes."

"So, no agoraphobia?"

"No."

"You up for a walk?"

"Yes! But I should probably tell Debra where I'm going first."

"Can you just message her?"

"She doesn't have a phone."

"She doesn't have a—?"

"Yes. I know. It's weird. She's anti-tech. In this time-warp kind of thing. Forever stuck in the 1980s when everything was *'perfect'* apparently. Hates modern stuff."

"Wait," says Jessica. "What did you just say? Perfect? Debra likes things to be perfect?"

But as she says this and before Belle can reply, there is a loud metallic clank, and the rusted gates begin to swing open again slowly. Debra appears between them, her arms folded across her chest, the dogs standing panting behind her. She looks different somehow, less unassuming, more threatening, and Jessica feels a thrum of energy pass between them, something dark and solid. She wonders, for just a brief moment, if maybe Debra has super-powers, but stores the thought away.

"What's going on?" says Debra, looking from Jessica to Belle and back again.

Jessica takes hold of Belle's arm, gently. "I'm taking Belle for a cream tea at my hotel. Want to come?"

Debra narrows her eyes. "Belle is not really meant to . . ."

"What? Go out?"

"Her parents prefer her to remain at home, so they know where she is."

Jessica glances at Belle. "How old are you?" she asks her.

"Sixteen."

Jessica looks back at Debra. "I think, probably, it's safe for Belle to wander into the village for some tea and cakes at two o'clock in the afternoon with a responsible adult."

"I'm sorry, Jessica, but whatever you say, I am fully in loco parentis and my instructions are very clear. Belle must stay in the grounds at all times."

Jessica looks at Belle. "What do *you* want to do?"

"I want to go for tea," she says, quietly.

Debra pulls herself tall and says, "I'm sorry, but if you take Belle another step further from these gates, I will have no choice but to call the police and tell them that she's been abducted."

The fire leaves Jessica's belly. She cannot have the police involved, not at this stage of a delicate private investigation.

"Fine." She turns to Belle. "I'm sorry. We'll do it another time. I'm here for a few more days. And here, take my number. Call me if you need me, at all."

She passes her a scrap of paper with her number quickly

scrawled on it and then stands and watches as Belle slips back through the rusty gates, Debra's hand on the small of her back leading her away as the gates slowly close behind her. Her heart aches painfully, not just because of the blow to her investigation but because of the girl. Belle. The vulnerability of her. The sadness. She's not safe and Jessica wants to save her.

* * *

Back at her hotel, Jessica goes straight to her room, ignoring the conservatory full of people enjoying their cream teas, the quiet murmur and tinkle of teaspoons against porcelain. She makes an espresso from her little machine—*sue me, unborn child*—opens up her laptop and googles the name of the boarding school that Belle mentioned. She calls the number and a moment later a woman says, "Good afternoon. Truscott House."

"Oh, hi. Good afternoon. I was hoping to speak with one of your students. She's named Belle."

"Hold the line for just one moment, thank you."

The woman returns and says, "I'm sorry, but there is nobody called Belle at this school."

"Oh." Jessica is both surprised and entirely unsurprised. "Are you . . . are you sure? This is Truscott House, yes, in Suffolk? Near the sea?"

"Yes, that's correct. And yes, I'm sure. I'm sorry I couldn't be more helpful."

"No," says Jessica. "No, really, you have been more than helpful. Thank you so much."

Jessica ends the call and then her eye is caught by something on the screen of her laptop. In the search results for Truscott House, to the left of the Google feature box where she found the phone number, there is a result with the headline:

TRUSCOTT HOUSE: STUDENTS STILL MISSING AFTER SCHOOL TRIP

Her breath catches and she clicks on it. It's dated July of two years before, twenty-seven months ago.

Parents of three pupils missing from the girls' boarding school Truscott House in Aldeburgh, Suffolk, are tonight still waiting in agony for news of their daughters' whereabouts. It's been three days since Grace Partridge, Audrey Hill-Lock, and Amina Sultanov, all age fifteen, failed to return to their coach after a school trip to Saffron Walden. The three missing girls were last seen taking part in a "treasure trail" of the picturesque Essex town, where students were given a series of clues that would lead them through the town discovering historical facts. The girls were divided into groups of three and CCTV shows the last sighting of Grace's group at four forty-five p.m., leaving a sweet shop and turning off Museum Street in the direction of St. Mary's Church, a five-minute walk from the car park where they were due to meet their coach. The girls never returned. Fellow students at the £8,500-a-term school claim that the trio had been "obsessed" with an Instagram account run by a beauty influencer and would spend hours talking about the unidentified account holder. One girl said that the missing students had talked about wanting to go and see her to have a face-to-face beauty consultation. "It felt almost like they were being groomed into a cult," said one student, who shared a bedroom with a missing student. "Like the influencer was brainwashing them. It was weird."

Alongside the article are photographs of the three missing girls. Audrey is shown on what looks like the terrace of a hotel somewhere hot, her blond hair tied back, tanned arms, a white tank top, her soft smile making a dimple in her left cheek. Amina is shown sitting on a sofa alongside her younger brother, her arms wrapped tight around his shoulders, grinning widely at the camera. Grace is shown in an official school photo, wearing her school uniform. She's a slight girl, very pretty but with dark shadows under her eyes, and fine brown hair tied back into a ponytail. She's smiling in the photograph, but still looks sad.

Jessica leans closer to her screen and zooms into the photo and then gasps as it suddenly hits her that the sad girl in the photograph looks just like Belle.

Twenty-One

Jessica is ten miles deep in the internet researching the disappearance of the three Truscott House schoolgirls when her phone buzzes.

It's Amber. She drags herself out of the rabbit hole and sighs, before taking the call.

"Hi."

"Listen. There's been a development. I got a call from the twins' school this morning and am just leaving the principal's office now. He's worried about the twins. Says that he's heard things on the grapevine about some kind of *cult*?"

"A what?"

"Yeah. I know. He was vague on details. But word has got to him that the twins are supposedly brainwashing their friends? I mean, yeah, I dunno, it sounds insane. Quite clearly, they're not brainwashing their friends. But it is possible that they're involved in some kind of sinister online thing or organization. And that their friends want in on it? You know, because of the *perfect skin* and what have you." Amber sighs heavily down the line. "The principal is launching an investigation, internally. So yeah, shit is getting real and, seriously, whatever you have from over there, I need it ASAP. If this ends with my kids being thrown out of school, I want to be ahead of the game. I want to know. So what have you got, Jessica? Please."

Amber sounds desperate and drained, and Jessica feels a pang of empathy for her. "I sort of don't know where to start," she says. "This whole thing, Amber. It's kind of crazy." She tells her about meeting Belle and Debra, about the missing schoolgirls, Belle's inability to leave the property, her resemblance to Grace Partridge. "And this Debra woman," she adds. "I dunno, there's something off about her. Alternately unassuming and quite fearsome. I'm pretty sure she's behind the kidnapping of the three schoolgirls, I'm pretty sure Belle is Grace Partridge, and I'm also pretty sure that Debra is using some kind of mind control or drugs to keep her there against her will. I need to get back into that house, get her out of there, but it's guarded by these, like, wolf-dogs, they'd tear me limb from limb."

"But surely you could just . . ." Amber trails off.

"Just what?"

"Well, you have, I mean, I hope this isn't personal, Jessica, but you have your super-powers, don't you? You could . . . outrun them? They couldn't really hurt you . . . ?"

"Okay," Jessica says. "I mean, yes, technically I could, and no they couldn't. But the dogs would still go nuts and make my presence known. And also . . ." She inhales tightly and then exhales again. She doesn't want to tell anyone this, but equally, she cannot keep this to herself for a moment longer and for some reason Amber is the person she feels most drawn toward telling. "There's a very slight chance," she says, tautly, "that I might be pregnant."

Pregnant.

The word sounds wild, crazy, surreal, ridiculous coming from her mouth. Amber will surely laugh at the very notion.

But Amber does not laugh and in fact the notion seems to switch her mood entirely and she responds in a brighter voice than Jessica has ever heard her use before. "Oh! Congratulations! I did wonder, I have to say, during those meetings with you in my club. The way you were with food. The pallor. It did occur to me. How far along are you?"

"Eight weeks, I think. But I don't even know if I am. I was going to take a test, tomorrow."

"Jessica, why wait?"

"I . . ." She pauses. It's too complicated a question to give a simple answer to. "No reason really. I suppose I'm just not quite ready for it. The father doesn't know. I'm not sure he's going to want to know. And, well, I'm, *as you know*, I'm *different*. There are things I don't understand about my body. About how it works. And the thought of making another body inside this body, it's kind of overwhelming. Scary. And my life—that place I live, you've seen it. What kind of a place is that for a kid? And me really, just *me*. I'm not . . ."

"Not what?"

"I'm not good enough."

"Not good enough, how?"

"I'm a mess. I sleep around. I drink too much. I don't change my bedsheets, like, *ever* . . ."

She hears Amber sighing loudly. "Jessica. Listen. The powers stuff, I don't know. You'll maybe have to find a specialist OB-GYN to put your fears to rest. 'Assemble the Avengers' for help, if need be. And the father—give him a chance. He doesn't know how he's going to feel about it any more than you. But the other stuff? Seriously, you think mothers come off an assembly line, all shrink-wrapped and cookie-cut? Without histories? Without regrets? No mother does. No woman becomes a mother without some sense of fear and even some . . . *distaste* at the idea of themselves in that role. We all had mothers and those mothers left their own imprints on us, some good, some not so good. That's a lot of baggage to bring to the check-in desk, y'know? So just be kind to yourself, Jessica. If I can be a mother, believe me, *anyone* can be a mother."

Jessica makes a scoffing sound down the line.

"No," says Amber. "It's true. Bulimia, self-harm, sexual, ah, abuse. You know. Been there, done that, still here. So.

Yeah. Get that test done, Jessica. Get your answer. Then move forward."

* * *

Elliot looks up in surprise when Jessica walks into the pharmacy a few moments later.

"Hello again."

She says, "Hi," and then sidles away from him toward the aisle where all the baby stuff lives. She picks out a packet quickly and brings it to the counter. The boy doesn't look at it, just scans it, heedlessly, while asking her about how her research is going. She puts her card through the machine and watches as he slides the packet into a paper bag. She smiles grimly as he passes it to her, relieved that he didn't register the purchase. Or maybe he did and he's too young to give a crap . . .

She slips the paper bag into her jacket pocket. "Oh, Elliot—?"

He frowns at her. "How do you know my name?"

"Er, I had lunch earlier with this woman. Named Debra? You know her?"

"The Old Farmhouse?" he says. "Loads of dogs?"

"That's the one."

"You had lunch *there*?"

"Uh-huh."

"Wow. That's surprising."

"Is it?"

"Yeah. The woman who lives there, Debra. She's basically

a recluse, completely keeps to herself, gets all her food and provisions delivered. No one's seen her for years."

"That sounds about right. And what do you know about the girl who lives there. Belle?"

"Girl?" He grimaces and shakes his head. "I've never seen a girl there."

"Yeah, apparently she's agoraphobic." Jessica sighs. "You don't happen to know Debra's surname, do you?"

"No. 'Fraid not. But it's probably online, you know, land registry or something?"

"Sure." She taps the counter a couple of times with her fist, throws him a tense smile, and then turns and leaves.

Twelve years ago
Portsmouth, Hampshire, UK

Polly has finally persuaded Arthur to arrange a meeting with his parents. It didn't take much in the end, not once she'd done a light internet search for "John Warshaw" and discovered that Arthur's father was wanted for the torture and murder of three homeless men in Harlem in the 1980s.

They meet on a Saturday morning outside a seafront café. The cold air is biting, filled with sharp pins of rain. Polly sees a flash of recognition pass through Ophelia's gaze as Arthur introduces them. Arthur's father seems distracted, looking out at the ocean.

"I think we've met," says Ophelia.

"We have," Polly replies. "You work on the pier."

"That's right."

"I came to see you, a couple of months ago. I was asking you about your beautiful skin."

"I remember. You were talking about your . . . ambitions."

"You have an excellent memory."

"I certainly do."

Ophelia fixes Polly with a gimlet gaze. Polly can tell that she thinks she can freeze this unwanted interloper out of her life, but she has no idea, thinks Polly, no idea who she is dealing with.

Polly holds the café door open for her. "After you," she says.

Age before beauty, says her internal monologue.

The café is loud and clattering. The windows are steamed up with condensation from overloud conversations. A waitress brings them plastic-covered menus, which they peruse in awkward silence. Polly glances up at Arthur's father, who sits opposite her. He looks benign. Looks so like a man who potters around an allotment and feeds kibble to a cat, not a man who tortures people and drinks blood out of bottles.

"Nice to meet you, Mr. Simms."

"Not Simms," he says bluntly. "That's my wife's name. And my son's. My name is John Jackson. You can call me John."

Polly dampens down her thrill at catching his blatant lie. "Well, nice to meet you, John."

"Likewise," he says, eyeing her intensely. "Likewise."

Once they've ordered and their menus have been collected, Polly smiles at Ophelia. "I'm really grateful to you for agreeing to meet up," she begins carefully. "I know you don't really want Arthur to have a girlfriend—"

Ophelia cuts in. "Of course we want Arthur to have a girlfriend."

"Well, you've definitely given him the impression that you'd prefer it if he didn't."

Ophelia bridles. "Arthur can do what he wants. He's a grown man."

Polly smiles and squeezes Arthur's hand atop the table. "I keep telling him that. Don't I, Arthur?"

Arthur shrugs.

Polly sighs. "Man of few words."

"Arthur is cerebral. It's all in there." Ophelia points at her son's head. "But doesn't often make it out here." She gestures at the space around them.

"Yes. I get that. It's one of the things I love about him."

"What else do you love about him?" John asks skeptically, making it sound like a trick question.

Polly moves her hand below the table, onto Arthur's leg, and fixes John's gaze squarely with hers. "I love his brain. I love his gentle soul. I love his hands. But mainly, I love how much he loves you two."

Ophelia tips her head back slightly, then nods. "We're very close-knit."

"Yes. And I admire that. It's very much not what I've had."

"What's your family like?"

Polly blinks slowly. "My mum suffers from long-term chronic pain and depression and spends her whole life on the sofa getting stoned with my brother, who only leaves the house to score more weed. My father is dead. My mother's family don't want to know us. We're kind of a shit family really. Which is why I so appreciate what Arthur's told me about you all."

She can see a softening of Ophelia's features. "Family is everything," the woman says, with a faint nod.

"I agree." Polly turns her gaze toward John. He is staring into the middle distance, unengaged. He has that black look in his eyes that Polly sometimes notices in Arthur. A void.

Suddenly the man turns to look at Polly and says, "I'm sorry. I don't mean to sound skeptical, but what does a girl like you see in a boy like Arthur? Aside from a big brain, a good heart, and nice hands?"

"What more should I want?"

"A girl like you, all"—he flutters his fingers—"all dressed up to the nines, all spruced and polished, your fingernails just so, your hair just so, the way you hold your mouth . . ."

"The way I—?"

"Like this." He puckers up his lips. "Like someone is about to take your photo."

"Dad," says Arthur.

"No, Arthur," says Polly. "It's fine. I can take care of myself. And I think it's a reasonable question. I can see we maybe make a bit of an odd couple. But actually, we comple-ment each other. We're both looking for the same things."

"Like what, exactly?"

"Like a chance to use our skills. Break free."

"Break free of what?"

She gestures around the scruffy café and out towards the frothy brown sea. "Of *this*."

"What's wrong with this?" Ophelia asks.

She sees a muscle in the corner of John's mouth twitch,

and she knows that he knows *exactly* what's wrong with this. He's trapped here because of what he is, because of what he's done. There's no escape for him.

"It's fine," she says, appeasingly. "But it's just not enough. And with my business acumen and Arthur's brains, we could really get something going. Have you seen the website he made for me?"

She pulls her phone out of her bag and pulls up her website, turns the phone to Ophelia. The product displayed is called Beauty X. It's not launched yet, but it looks polished and exciting. The webpage has large open spaces where text and photos will go when she's got a full range of items to put on sale. Up top it says *Do you want perfect skin? Well, you've come to the right place!* and the logo is an *X* with a kiss mark behind it.

"You know," she says, "like a kiss, and a kiss."

Ophelia turns the screen of Polly's phone to John. He nods neutrally.

"And then there's this new social media platform called Instagram. It was just launched a couple of years ago. I've got an account on there. Only have a few followers at the moment, but once my product is ready to launch, I'll do most of my marketing from there. And Arthur is going to help me with that too. He's so good at all those kinds of things."

She pauses as she takes the phone from Ophelia and slides it back into her handbag. "Just need to perfect the product really. Which is where you come in."

She leaves the statement there, leaves it hanging between

them. John looks at her, then out the window, where the endless ocean gray moves only slightly.

Arthur bends forward slightly, looks hard at the tabletop.

"I don't know what you're talking about," says Ophelia at last.

"Yes," Polly replies simply. "Yes, you do. You know exactly what I'm talking about." She dips her hand into her handbag and pulls out the photographs she took of the sketchbook she'd found in the old chalet and the news clipping about the bar in Harlem, the police report about the bodies found under the dance floor. She spreads them out in front of Ophelia and her husband and watches them react. "I know all this about you, and yet I still want to be a part of your family. So all I'm asking, Ophelia, is for you to let me in."

She stops and lets the ringing silence that follows this speech play out, revels in the dreadfulness and profundity of it. But she's not worried. She has all the power right now.

She has Ophelia's son; she has Ophelia's secrets.

It won't take long, she thinks, until Ophelia gives Polly everything she wants.

Twenty-Two

The plastic stick sits on the edge of the sink. Jessica sits on the closed lid of the toilet. The time on her phone ticks down the seconds.

Five minutes later, the beep tells her the result is ready. But she is not. She really is not.

She pulls her hair away from her face in her fist and blows out her breath.

Then she picks up the stick.

There sits the word *pregnant*.

She sighs heavily. She knows now. She knows with a clarity that nearly blows her teeth out of her head.

She doesn't want it.

She can't want it.

It can't happen.

She dumps the stick in the trash, lets the lid shut with a loud bang, and drops heavily onto the edge of the bed, where she sits for a long time.

* * *

The pub is quiet at four o'clock in the afternoon. Three solitary men sit at the bar, spaced a few seats apart from one another. Two are scrolling through their phones; the third stares into the middle distance.

The bartender greets Jessica with a smile of recognition. "Good afternoon, lovey. And how are you today?"

"I'm good, thank you. How are you?"

"Oh, you know . . ."

Jessica doesn't but nods anyway.

"What can I get for you?"

"A scotch, please. Whatever you've got. A double."

"Ice with that, lovey?"

"No. Thanks."

The bartender pours it and passes it to her. Jessica pays for it and takes it to a table in a side room far from the ponderous air of the silent men at the bar. She places it in front of her on a small table overlooking a dank backyard with a mildewed marquee tent in it. She stares at the drink, turns it around and around. Her heart pounds in her chest. She picks it up and brings it to her nose. The smell catapults her back, Proust-style, through most of the worst times of her life. It takes her back to her grim apartment in Hell's Kitchen. It takes her back to dimly lit bars and rough men and mornings that felt like sick jokes. It smells like purple.

She puts the glass back on the table.

She thinks of the word *pregnant* on the plastic stick in the trash.

She thinks of Luke.

She thinks of the future.

She picks up the glass.

She puts down the glass.

And then she notices a figure appear in her periphery.

A small figure.

A child.

She turns.

"Oh no." Jessica groans. "Oh nononono. What the actual . . . ?"

It's the small girl. The girl she first saw standing outside Julius's apartment nearly two weeks ago and last saw in a diner in South Kensington on Wednesday morning. And now she is here, in Essex, in a deathly quiet pub full of dust motes and boozers, wearing the same silver parka, the same stripy tights, her hair arranged in the same puffballs on either side of her face, and she is real. She is as real as real can be. There is a loose thread hanging from one of the buttons on her coat, a scuff on her left sneaker. She cocks her head to one side and looks at Jessica thoughtfully. "Are you okay?"

The sound of an American accent is strangely comforting, and Jessica feels herself soften a little. "Er, yeah. Or at least I would be if I could think of one single explanation for what you are doing here."

"I'm here with my mom."

"Where is she?"

"I don't know. I'm waiting for her. I'm sure she won't be long."

"Listen, kid, I keep seeing you around and you keep telling me about this *mom* of yours, but I have never seen her. And I'm starting to wonder if she even exists."

"Oh yeah. She exists, all right."

"Well, she seems a little neglectful, if you don't mind me saying."

"Yeah. She can be. But that's okay. Because I'm really, really independent. I can pretty much do anything I need to do."

"Really? Give me an example."

The girl shrugs and says, "Well, okay then." Then suddenly she is across the room and lifting a table by one leg. She holds it aloft, high above her head, as though it were made of card. It is solid wood, with metal legs, and most children would have trouble lifting it off the ground even a foot, but this child, she stands like that for a full ten seconds before gently placing it down on the floor again.

She rubs her hands together and looks at Jessica. "You don't need to worry about me, see? I am really strong. I can take a *lot*."

"Hang on. Are you . . . ? I mean, your powers, are they . . . ?"

"I don't know. I guess I'll have to find out."

"What's your name?" Jessica asks her.

"What do you want it to be?"

"What do *I* want it to be?" Jessica puts her hand to her chest.

But the girl doesn't reply. Her eyes go silently to the glass on Jessica's table. She stares at it deeply, darkly, for many moments and then turns her gaze back to Jessica, shaking her head at her, admonishingly.

"You need to get out of here—you have a job to do, lady." she says. "You need to find out what happened to those girls, what happened to Grace and Audrey and Amina. They *need* you."

She walks away and Jessica leaps to her feet to follow her, but the child is nowhere to be seen.

"Little girl!" she calls out.

The bartender and the three drinkers at the bar all turn and stare at her.

"The girl," says Jessica. "The kid. Where did she go?"

"What kid?" says the bartender.

"The—" Jessica stops. "Nothing. Never mind."

She turns to look back at the glass of scotch, still sitting on the table in the side bar. She thinks of the child holding the heavy table aloft. And suddenly she knows. She absolutely knows.

The girl is not real. But she does exist. She *has* to exist.

Jessica walks back out onto the street, and then, with a start and a shock, she opens her eyes, her voice catching on a forgotten word, and finds that she is on her hotel bed, tangled up in sheets, awaking from a dream.

Twenty-Three

Jessica leaves the hotel for a walk around the village a short while after waking from her vivid dream. While she walks, she listens to a podcast called *Is There a Vampire in the House?*

"It was once a lively bar and music venue," it begins, "beloved by locals for many years, but by the 1980s the Upside Down bar, like Harlem itself, was run-down and neglected by the powers that be, crime-ridden, blighted by the drug problems prevalent all across New York at the time. But while drug deals and fights were breaking out on the first floor, underground, unimaginable things were happening. In 1998, city workers made a disturbing discovery underneath the disco lights of the dance floor in the basement—the remains of three young men, wrapped in layers of cloth, their corpses drained of blood and partially mummified. Two of the victims were identified by their teeth. One, who disappeared from the streets of Harlem in 1986, when he was twenty-two years old, was a local man named Diep Davis, known by all as DD. The second, Jean Michel Diavolo, had been reported missing by his brother in 1988 after losing touch with him when he moved to the city four years earlier. Diavolo was twenty when he left his hometown of Detroit. The third victim has never been identified.

"In 1988, the bar's manager, a man named John Warshaw, had been brought in by detectives from the NYPD for questioning after he was seen letting a young man into the premises in the early hours of the morning, a man who was later reported missing by his wife. The premises were searched and when no evidence of the missing individual was found, Warshaw was released without charge. Warshaw left his job at the Upside Down soon afterward and the bar closed for good in 1994. When gas line workers gained access to the lower floors of the building in 1998, it had been empty for years. After the discovery of the men's remains, a nationwide police search was undertaken for John Warshaw, but his whereabouts to this day are still unknown.

"In this episode I will be recording my journey as I attempt to track down Warshaw and find out what really happened under the bright lights and in the darkest shadows of Harlem's Upside Down bar."

By the end of the final episode though, the podcaster isn't any closer to tracking down the elusive vampire bartender and the narrative trails off into rambling theorizing, as these things so often do. Still, there is a witness whose anecdote jumps out at Jessica, a man named Judd Winter, who had employed John Warshaw to run his bar during the eighties.

"A nice guy," Judd tells the interviewer. "Genuinely, just a nice guy. But had . . . issues. Childhood trauma, that kind of thing. He flunked med school, then just bummed around the world as far as I know. Turned up here fresh-faced and desperate for cash. I gave him a room above. And he worked for me for, yeah, round about six years in the end. He liked it here. He was regular and hardworking, the customers liked him, he could talk, but he also knew when to stop. Most importantly, I could trust him. I could trust him with my life. And so when the police came to my door back in '98, telling what they'd found under the dance floor, telling me they were looking for John. I mean, *no way* was all I could think. *No way*."

The interviewer asks him, "Where do you think he might be now?"

Judd Winter sighs. "Honestly? I have no idea. He had no roots. He had, well, he had no one. I mean, there was a girl, she used to come in a lot. A British girl. A real looker. She'd sit at the bar, and they'd flirt, but to be honest, I thought she was wasting her time because he never seemed like that kind of guy. She was really young, you know. He was in his thirties by then, a bit of a loner. But he seemed taken with her. I don't know what happened to her, but I figure if you could find her, you might be able to find him."

"What was her name?"

"Her name—and I remember this because it was so beautiful—was Ophelia."

* * *

Back in her room, as she waits for the night to fall, Jessica spends some time googling *first symptoms of pregnancy*. It's not the first time she's asked the internet about her predicament, but it is the first time she's lasted longer than five minutes before slamming down the lid of her laptop in horror. Apparently, she is not meant to be drinking more than two hundred milligrams of caffeine a day and that, frankly, is beyond a joke.

The world on the other side of her positive pregnancy test alarms her still. It is illustrated on the internet by fresh-faced women cupping neat bumps and sitting in airy rooms in white clothing with handsome husbands. It is peopled by women who are not like her in any way whatsoever, living lives that bear no resemblance to hers. And what of her powers? And Luke's? Will their abilities automatically guarantee a child with powers? Will the baby grow faster? Bigger? Will it burst from her womb hard enough to break her in half? Will it fly across the birthing unit and smack its head on the wall? She remembers what Luke said last week, about life being hard enough in this world for a normal kid, let alone a kid with super-powers. Should she even be considering this?

She clicks on a link to a "due date calculator" and puts in the date of the first day of her last period.

You are 8 weeks pregnant.

Jessica slams down the lid of her laptop and picks up her phone.

The time is 11:30 a.m. in New York. Malcolm will still be in class, so she messages him instead:

I'm heading back to the farmhouse soon. I'm going to get Belle out of there. If you haven't heard from me by the time you wake up tomorrow morning, I want you to call this guy Elliot at the pharmacy in Barton Wallop. He knows where I am. OK?

And do not do anything dangerous tonight. Message me the minute you are through. And stay the hell SAFE.

She pastes in the number for the village pharmacy and presses send.

Twenty-Four

Night has fallen as dark as night can get as Jessica arrives outside Belle's house. The perimeter wall looms above her, ten feet high. She looks from left to right and back again, and then hurls herself upward. She perches on the wall for a second and she waits for the noise of the dogs. Sure enough, it comes. Like a tornado in the night, the pack appears below, and with a lurch in the pit of her stomach that almost makes her puke, Jessica throws out a handful of cubed ham, then jumps, legs ablur, arms pumping the cold night air like engine parts, heart swelling in her chest. As she lands, one dog manages to get close enough to take her heel in its mouth. It's the same dog that Belle was feeding morsels of lamb to earlier, who'd taken them from Belle's fingers as daintily as a high-born lady. Now that same soft mouth is embedded in her flesh and Jessica kicks her leg hard enough to boot the dog a few feet across the grass, where it lands with a whimper. Jessica knows she has a very short opportunity to make it across the grounds to the house before Debra and Belle are alerted, so she overrides the pain and runs.

The house is in darkness when she reaches it. Jessica has a few seconds to get into the house before the dogs arrive and wake everyone up. She shimmies up a water pipe toward the middle floor, where Belle will be sleeping, but is halfway up when she hears the dogs. She pulls in her breath and peers around the corner, where she sees Debra in a towel robe and sheepskin slippers, standing just outside the front door with a huge flashlight in her hand. She looks like someone's mother, waiting to greet their late-returning child. She does not look like a child abductor or a killer, with the soft slippers, the glasses on top of her head, the moonlight shining off the night cream on her cheeks.

"Hello?" she hears Debra call out. "Someone there?"

Jessica hears the skitter of dogs' claws across the graveled parking area, the clamor of barking nearby. They can smell her. They know she's here.

"What?" she hears Debra say to the dogs. "Is there someone up there? What is it?"

Jessica sees the beam from the flashlight arc across the top of the house and she tucks herself tight in away from it. The dogs are coming for her, and she knows that she needs to either get out of here, or get into the house, so she breathes in hard and pulls herself up the drainpipe to the second floor, where she pushes open an unlocked window and climbs onto the landing. She opens and closes three doors before she finds Belle's bedroom. And there is Belle, asleep, curled into herself on a narrow single bed under a thin quilt. Her room is cold and damp.

"Belle!"

The girl stirs.

"Belle! Wake up!" She touches Belle's shoulder gently, and the small figure wakes slowly from a very deep sleep.

"Oh," she says. "What's happening?"

"I don't have time to explain. I just need you to come with me, right now."

"What?"

"Listen to me. This is not really your house. You were kidnapped and are being held here against your will. You're not really Belle. Your real name is Grace."

"Grace?"

"Yes. Grace Partridge. That's your real name. Look." Jessica switches on her phone, which she's already preloaded with the photo from the news article.

Belle looks at the photo and then looks up at Jessica with wide eyes. "I don't understand . . ."

But there's no time for her to understand. Jessica can hear Debra moving through the house, the urgent creaks of footsteps on the stairs. She regards the window over the small bed. It's small too, with a metal frame, but it looks big enough for them both to get through. She looks at Belle, in her tiny floral-print pajama set, then hurls open her closet doors and pulls out a hoodie and a pair of track pants.

"Put these on," she says. "Quickly."

Belle stares at her with blank eyes.

Jessica growls and wraps the clothes around the girl roughly, picks Belle up in a bear hug, climbs onto the bed, blasts the window out with one hard kick that snaps the metal frames and splinters the glass into a thousand shards, and then, with a slick of bitter bile hitting the back of her throat, grips the girl's body hard and jumps.

Nine years ago
Farnham, Surrey, UK

Polly poses, her phone on a stand on the kitchen counter in front of her. She looks at her face on the screen of her phone and sees shadows cast from her brow bone that darken her eyes, so she strides across the room and turns off the halogens, redirects the table lamps so they shine more directly upon her, and returns to her spot.

But now there's something not right about the corners of her mouth.

They look slightly mean, slightly downcast. And her eyebrows are wrong. She goes back to her mirror, digs into her makeup bag, smudges off her lip liner and reapplies it. Then she combs through her eyebrows, making sure each hair is exactly in place. She throws a tea towel over one of the lamps and takes her spot again. Still not quite right, but at this time of year with no decent light to work with, it's the best she can do. She leans forward and presses record.

"Hi, guys," she begins, holding aloft a tube of her latest product, Beauty X Pore Magic. "Look at this! I have just this minute got it back from the lab, and I am too excited to show you how this works."

She holds the packaging up to the camera, the distinctive mint-green box with the hot-pink lettering. She opens it and pulls out the golden tube.

"Look," she says, showing it to the camera. "Isn't it beautiful? But just you wait until you see what this stuff can do. Remember how much you all loved the Visage Magic Serum, well, this goes one step further. One application, over your serum, leave it for just a minute or two, and I swear you will see your pores simply disappear. Let me show you."

She brings her face closer to the screen and spreads the serum over the right side of her face.

"So, all I've got on this side of my face is the serum, nothing else, and look, you can see how patchy my skin still is in places—even the Visage Magic couldn't completely smooth over those areas. But watch this."

She adds the serum to the left side of her face, layers the Beauty X Pore Magic on top of it, and then steps back again. "Right, I'm seeing a difference already. Look at that . . . can you see?"

Polly always feels a little silly talking to the camera like it's going to answer. But in the end, that's a small price to pay for her goals. She knows these products are incredible. And so they should be. They come at quite a price. But all the effort is worth it when she gets the comments under her posts from the women who've been empowered by her products, by her words, by *her*.

She has nearly two and a half thousand followers now. She'd have more, but she has to set her page to private, so it's more like a members' club than an Instagram account. She markets it that way, uses the exclusivity factor to ramp up the value of her brand and to allow her to charge one hundred pounds for a tube of cream. But the truth, of course, is that she needs to vet her followers the same way she needs to vet everyone who buys her products, because of the very particular nature of those products. Because they are untested and unlicensed. Because the smart mint-green-and-hot-pink packaging is printed with nonsense ingredients and nonsense declarations of authenticity and nonsense assurance of adherence to organic standards. She can't exactly market the truth about her products, that they are unethical to the nth degree. What her customers need to know is that these products work.

Her customers are addicted to them, but still there's only so far Polly can go before she gets caught out. She's constantly watching her back, living in a state of adrenaline-fueled paranoia. Panic every time someone DMs her with too many technical questions. Panic every time the phone rings with an unknown number, or the doorbell goes. She hadn't thought about any of this when she started out three years ago. All she'd wanted to do was get her hands on Ophelia's recipe, get her to show her how to make that magic cream, and then give it to people, watch their faces when they see how beautiful they look.

Now Polly has money. She and Arthur rent a small house in Farnham, a newbuild on a pretty estate within walking distance to town. She has designer things. She has two Havanese dogs. She has influence. She has Arthur. She is looking at a pony. She hasn't decided about the pony yet, it's a lot of time and she doesn't have much time, her life is busy and buzzy. Her inboxes are full. People talk to her as if she's powerful, important. Followers get overexcited when she replies to their messages. They tell her she's beautiful. They are invested in her. They notice when she buys new things. They love her.

She's poised, Polly knows, poised for great things.

But there's this obstacle in her way.

The product itself is the obstacle.

She manages to forget about that sometimes, when John and Ophelia turn up in their little van with the boxes of pretty stock. For whole hours at a time she can believe it's just face cream and that she is just a normal businesswoman. When she's smiling into the camera for her followers, she can believe that she is just a bright-eyed girl from Portsmouth with big dreams, living her best life. In those moments, she forgets entirely about the things that are in these little pots of cream, about all of the darkness that is the backdrop to the whole operation.

She cannot rely on John and Ophelia forever, cannot forever keep them hostage to her whims. John is getting old; his bloodlust is diminishing. Ophelia is getting even older; her life force is evaporating. Polly has their son, but her hold over them grows weaker every day. Perhaps worse, her market is self-limiting because of the nature of the product. She will never take over the world by selling from behind secretive, closed doors. Polly needs to find the next thing, the thing that will take her out of the shadows and propel her into the spotlight. She just has to work out what it's going to be.

Polly beams into the camera, her professionally whitened teeth gleaming on the screen in front of her. "There," she says to her followers. "Look. Can you see that? My skin is perfect now. Literally perfect."

Twenty-Five

Jessica awakens on a sofa. She sits up and stares around the room, which feels both strange and familiar. She's in some kind of cottage, or, like, a farmhouse maybe. Shabby but kind of charming. Rose-print wallpaper. Twee watercolors. A view through a window of trees and rolling grounds. Then she jumps slightly at the sound of a voice coming from across the room. She turns and sees a woman. She has shiny dark hair with bangs, and wears an oversized turtleneck sweater over leggings and sheepskin slippers. In her hand is a big mug.

Debra, she thinks. She knows her. But who is she?

"Good morning, Jessica," she says. "How are you feeling?"

Jessica considers the question for a moment and then

realizes that she feels absolutely magnificent. "I feel great," she says. "I feel . . ."

"Perfect?"

"Yeah," says Jessica. "Yeah. *Perfect*. What . . . what time is it?"

"It's nearly eleven o'clock. On Saturday."

"Saturday? And yesterday was . . ."

"Friday. Yes, that's correct."

Jessica feels something about Friday slipping and sliding around her consciousness. Wasn't something supposed to be happening? Wasn't she supposed to be talking to someone? She feels the strange, faint outline of another place: a cozy room with a bed in it, another room across a courtyard filled with ladies drinking tea from pots and eating cakes off stands. It's her hotel. But she feels like she was there a very, very long time ago; it's like a distant memory. "Is it still October?"

"Yes. It's still October. You got here last night."

"It feels like longer."

"Yes. It will feel like longer."

"How do I know you?"

"You're a friend of Belle's."

Belle, thinks Jessica. Belle. She knows who Belle is. She's the pretty girl. The one in bed upstairs. She feels a warm feeling when she thinks of Belle. But then something dark flashes through her mind and she shudders. The sound of breaking glass. A woman's voice in her ear. A hand, hard over her mouth. Blackness. Darkness. But as quickly as the shadow falls, it passes and she is back, right here in the moment, basking in the glow of a perfect, sunny Saturday.

Jessica sees Debra glance down at the hem of her jeans, which are mud and blood encrusted and ripped on one leg. Another image flashes through her mind: a sky full of stars, a dog at her heel, the pain of torn flesh, a ramshackle farmhouse.

"What happened?" she asks.

"Oh, just a misunderstanding with one of the pups. But you've healed amazingly quickly. Almost miraculous really, almost as if there never was any damage at all. Apart from your lovely jeans. But not to worry, I can get you a change of clothes."

Jessica smiles at Debra. "That would be *amazing*."

Debra passes her the big mug. "Here," she says. "A nice cup of tea."

Jessica looks into the mug. It's a vivid shade of tan, milky and rich. It looks great. She takes a big sip and smacks her lips. "Thanks," she says, "that's delicious."

Debra returns a moment later with a pair of leggings and a cropped T-shirt. Jessica takes the clothes and goes into the bathroom to change, gasping as her eye catches her reflection in the mirror.

My God. She turns this way and that, eyeing every inch of herself, her tight, high backside, her endless, flawless legs, her toned thighs, her feet, so elegant and fine-boned, and her breasts—*good God*, the most perfect breasts she has ever seen—she stares at them in awe. And then her eyes go to her face, and she gasps again. Her skin is . . . perfect. Her eyes are clear and shining. Her eyebrows look like she's one of those women who pay someone to do things to them every two weeks. And her teeth—she pulls her top lip up and examines them in detail—they are pearl-white, perfectly straight. Her lips are plumper, her eyelashes are longer.

She is freaking exquisite.

She showers and puts on the fresh clothes, then admires her reflection in the mirror again: the way her butt fills out the leggings, her flat stomach beneath the crop top.

Her gaze pauses, her hand stops moving. She looks at her stomach and feels a small pulse of disquiet pass through her, but then bats it away.

Debra speaks through the door. "Come to the kitchen when you're done. Come and eat. I'm just going to check in on Belle. Make yourself comfortable."

In the kitchen there is a huge spread of delicious-looking food on the table, fresh fruit, pastries, bagels. Jessica loads a plate and makes herself a coffee and takes them out to the front of the house, where she sits on a bench to eat, admiring the perfect view: the rolling, manicured grounds, the Titian blue sky, the air cool, but the sun warm enough to cut through it. She swings her long shiny hair from one shoulder to the other—*it's so slinky!*—and sighs with pleasure. She could stay here forever. Everything is just so perfect.

She sits like that for a while. Eventually, the dogs come to greet her, tails wagging. The one who bit her heel last night stares up at her with chocolate-drop eyes, and she feeds him a slice of banana before going back to watching the landscape.

And then, through the silence, she hears a strange, high-pitched humming noise.

She looks up and sees a drone hovering about twelve feet overhead. It stops when it sees her looking at it, then slowly lands on the bench next to her. The dogs all surround it, ears pricked. She makes a soft clicking noise at the dogs that makes them back off and she picks up the small machine.

There is a piece of paper taped to its underbelly.

Jessica tugs it off and unfolds it. Scrawled on it are the words:

IT'S ELLIOT THE CHEMIST. MALCOLM HAS BEEN MESSAGING YOU ALL NIGHT AND DAY. ARE YOU OK? PLEASE GIVE THE DRONE THE THUMBS-UP IF YOU'RE OK? THUMBS-DOWN IF YOU'RE NOT. AND IF THERE'S ANYTHING YOU WANT TO SAY, WRITE IT ON HERE AND SEND IT BACK UP.

Jessica stares at the drone, then stares up into the sky. She doesn't have a pen, but even if she had a pen, what could she possibly want to say? Everything is perfect.

The name Malcolm reminds her of something. A place far away, another life of hers, away from this one. She feels warm when she thinks of him, but she cannot bring his face into her mind. She tucks the paper back into the drone and watches as it rises back into the sky. As it hovers above her, she remembers the written instructions and she gets to her feet and waves at it. She swings her hair and beams with her big white teeth and throws both her thumbs aloft and shouts out as loud as she can, mouthing the words widely and clearly:

"I'm FINE!" she yells at the drone. "I am PERFECT!"

The drone hovers for a moment more and then floats back across the sky, over the treetops and out of sight.

* * *

Jessica spends the day drifting. She plays with the dogs, she watches movies, she eats the food that Debra keeps making for her. Debra is pleasant company, easy to talk to. She tells Jessica a little about her childhood, about how she always felt on the edges of things, never felt like she fit anywhere, until she was twenty, when it all fell into place for her. She has a playful energy about her, but also a sadness that makes Jessica ask her if she's really okay.

"Oh," says Debra, her pale eyes sparkling, light glinting from the gold chains around her neck. "Yes, I'm okay. Just getting a bit tired. You know." She squeezes Jessica's hand in hers, then heads to the back of the kitchen with the words "Hot chocolate?"

Jessica nods. She feels good, she feels unburdened, like the spiky bits of her psyche have been planed down, as if other bits of her have been cast away in a thorough spring clean. Her body feels new, like she just pulled it out of its packaging. Her thoughts are filled with songs she barely remembers, films she hasn't seen for years, but whenever she reaches for a memory, it slithers away from her and then she is distracted again.

Lunch appears. Arancini and olives and ciabatta. She eats it on the sofa in the cute living room. "Nice arancini," she says to Debra. "Where'd it come from?"

"The deli in the village. They deliver."

Jessica nods. Deli? she thinks. Village?

And then she remembers the village, that strange little street of higgledy-piggledy houses, a hotel, a pub, a pharmacy with a boy in it. The boy. What was his name? Elliot. Yes. Elliot the Chemist. He was the one who sent the drone. Malcolm asked him to. Who's Malcolm? For some reason she feels a sharp spike of concern when she thinks of Malcolm. Is he her child, she wonders. Her boyfriend? Her phone, she thinks. Malcolm will be on her phone.

"Debra," she calls out. "Where's my phone?"

"It's over there," says Debra, "by the front door. It's charging."

"I need to check it."

"Of course. Feel free. But remember, there's not really a signal out here. And no Wi-Fi."

"Okay."

She gets to her feet and locates her phone. She turns it on, but the screen stays black.

"Oh," she says to herself. And then she can't remember why she needed her phone anyway.

"How are you feeling, Jessica?" asks Debra.

"Great, yeah. Perfect."

"Excellent. I'm so pleased. Do help yourself to more food."

"Yes. Yes, I will. Debra. Do you have any old movies?"

"Yes! Of course! What did you fancy?"

"Do you have *Pretty in Pink*?"

"*Pretty in Pink*? Coming right up. Why don't you go and get yourself another hot chocolate. And there's popcorn in the cupboard too. Stick some in the microwave."

Jessica smiles. "Yes," she says. "Good idea. Sounds perfect."

"I'm glad you picked *Pretty in Pink*. It's one of my favorites. The eighties, Jessica, really were the best decade. People talk about the nineties, don't they? And the sixties. But I disagree. And I should know."

Eight years ago
Farnham, Surrey, UK

Hi begins the DM that will destroy Polly's life. I've just received two of your products, Pore Magic, and Visage Magic. I'm amazed by how effective they are, seriously. I don't know why they're not famous! We should be seeing this stuff everywhere! I have over 250k followers and would love to feature your products in my page. But out of a duty of care to my followers I can only feature licensed products and I can't find anything about Beauty X online. Anyway, I passed on the serums to my father-in-law, who works in pharmaceuticals. He's had both products tested and he just called me to say that he's found some troubling components? I don't know if you're aware of this? But he said the products contain like traces of human DNA from multiple people? I mean, I know that sounds crazy! And I don't know if you're aware! I'm kind of keen to follow this up, to know more about how you make these products. I'm slightly worried TBH. And seriously, I don't want you to take this as a threat, but I might have to take this to the authorities if you don't want to talk with me. So listen, here's my number, give me a call. I want to help you monetize this incredible product, but only if it's legit. So let's talk! Love, Clara.

Arthur, who has been reading the message over Polly's shoulder, takes a sharp breath and says, "That's it. We have to shut down the account. Cancel all the orders and shut it all down. Now."

Polly shakes her head, but then nods, because she knows he's right. "Yes," she says. "Yes."

Arthur is already opening his own laptop and tapping buttons. "You need to reply to her. Tell her you're shocked, tell her you're taking the product off the market while you investigate. Thank her for informing you, et cetera, et cetera. Then we need to take all the stock to Dad's allotment and burn every last bit of it."

"Yes," says Polly. "Right." And even as she knows she has to do this, her heart is breaking. Her stock. Her beautiful stock. All those gorgeous mint-green and hot-pink boxes piled neatly in their garage. All those golden Jiffy bags, the names and addresses on mint-green labels, all ready to go. Her followers! She holds back a sob as she thinks of her followers! They love her so much! What are they going to do? They'll be devastated. She'll have to issue refunds for all her pending orders. Her life will be . . . What will her life be? For three years it's been Beauty X. It's been all she's thought about from the moment she awakes to the moment she falls asleep. Filming content, heading to the lockup in Portsmouth where Ophelia and John make the serums, then sitting here in the living room packaging it all up, slipping in little treats (lollipops, miniature tubes of Love Hearts), taking the Jiffy bags to the post office every day at four o'clock, filming more content, replying to comments and messages, liaising with the packaging manufacturers, testing new products.

It's her whole entire life, and now it's coming to a grinding halt.

But what about this girl, she thinks to herself, clicking on her profile, this Clara? What is she going to do about her?

Clara posts several times a day, and unlike Polly, she doesn't only produce content from inside her own home. She reports back from girls' weekends and holidays and trips to the playground with her two-year-old daughter, Mai. She has left a breadcrumb trail beyond belief, and it doesn't take Polly more than ten minutes online to establish that Little Miss Ethics lives in a suburb of Birmingham called Topsville in a tiny pink cottage with puffball fig trees in pots outside and a wreath on the door made out of dried hydrangeas. On the door is the number 2. The playground where Clara takes Mai for photoshoots is just across the street. Ten more minutes scanning Google Maps Street View takes Polly to her house. And now she has Clara's address.

She shows it to Arthur. "That's where the bitch lives."

A shadow passes across Arthur's eyes.

"What?" she says.

He turns slightly to look at her and goes back to his screen. "Nothing," he says. "Nothing."

"Well, what else are we meant to do?"

"She's got a kid."

"Yes, I know. I have eyes. But what's our alternative?"

"She's high-profile, Pols. People will notice. It would be headline news every day for a month. A beauty influencer with a *quarter of a million followers and a cute kid*. We can't, okay? We have to find another way."

Polly sighs. She knows he's right, but how are they going to keep this bitch quiet? What's the answer? As Arthur turns away she takes a photo of the details of Clara's home on her computer screen with her phone.

Arthur turns back to her. "You need to deal with the stock, Pol. Get it in the car."

She nods and gets her car key out of her bag. She goes into the garage, pings open the boot of her Audi Q3, and then fills it with the boxes. She puts the dogs on the back seat, throws on her Barbour, pulls on her Hunters. She sounds the horn for Arthur, who appears after a few seconds. He adds some boxes of paperwork to the pile in the boot, and then he straps himself into the passenger seat.

"Ready?" he says.

Polly nods and puts the car into gear, lifts the garage door with the remote, and then, just before they drive away, she selects the photograph of Clara's little pink house that she captured a minute ago and sends it to Clara with the words *Leave me alone, if you want me to leave you alone.*

Twenty-Six

Jessica tips the uneaten popcorn down the waste disposal unit in the kitchen. Through the grimy windows, she sees the day growing dark and bruised. She thinks it must surely be near dinnertime. Shreds of things keep wafting through her thoughts, a sense of other places. She has a hotel room in the village, she knows that, but when she thinks of the hotel room she associates it with bad things, with feeling unhappy, with loneliness and dissatisfaction. She also knows that she has a home in New York, and a boyfriend named Luke who is the most beautiful man in the world. She knows all of these things, and yet they don't feel real to her anymore. Nothing feels real apart from here and now, the moment. And the moment is just one long unending sensation of perfection and wonder. This house, her perfect body, her perfect face, Debra, food, pleasure, movies, joy. *What more is there? What else matters?*

Music plays in the background. It's something Jessica vaguely remembers from her childhood, maybe from the soundtrack of a movie, she's not sure. A harmonica, an uncertain smile. She dances as she makes herself a smoothie. She stares upward into the sparkles of the night and all she can think is Miranda. Miranda. Miranda.

At first, she wonders who Miranda is. Then she forgets to wonder.

A moment later something crashes through the music and the peace and the harmony. A doorbell chimes, loudly, insistently. The dogs on the grounds start barking crazily, and Debra peers into the kitchen and says, "Don't worry, Jessica, we have some visitors at the front gate. You just relax."

But Jessica can't relax. The song she was singing has gone from her head, she can't pick it up again. The atmosphere feels wrong. The wonder has gone. Why are the dogs barking? A memory pierces her consciousness, the dogs barking as she perches on a wall, worrying. What was she worrying about up there on the wall? A little girl? A little girl with stripy tights and a silver coat.

Her eyes drop to her belly, and she gasps.

The little girl in there.

Her baby?

Is she pregnant?

Her eyes go to the stairs and then an image of another girl is blasted like a rocket into her mind's eye. This girl has wide eyes and lies in a small bed under a comforter. And where is she now? The feel of a window giving way under the power of Jessica's foot, the taste of oily bile at the back of her throat, the weight of a person in her arms. And then—what?

They were on the ground. And the girl . . . Where is the girl?

Jessica can hear a conversation on an intercom between Debra and whoever is at the front gates. A woman's voice: ". . . an anonymous call. Could we come in, please? We just need a minute of your time."

"What's this regarding?" Debra says stiffly.

"It's regarding a missing person case. We've received an anonymous call which gives us reason to believe there may be a child being held here against her will."

"What nonsense."

"Well, that's as may be, Miss Phipps, but we really do need to come in."

"I'm sorry, that's not going to be possible."

"Miss Phipps, we have a warrant. I'm afraid you have no choice in the matter."

There is a moment of silence, and then Jessica hears Debra sigh and say, "On what grounds did you get this warrant?"

"On the grounds that new information has shown us that the IP address associated with the Instagram account that Grace Partridge was in contact with before her disappearance was in this location. Now we will require you to allow us access immediately. And you will need to bring your dogs under control."

Jessica hears the sigh of Debra's breath on the intercom. "Fine," she says, "but you'll have to give me a minute or two to put the dogs away."

Jessica gets to her feet and peers around the kitchen door into the entrance hall. She sees Debra pull on rubber boots and a big coat and head out into the grounds, and the sound of the door slamming closed behind her jolts the final shards of confusion from Jessica's mind, and suddenly she is free. Her mind reshapes, her body hardens, and she feels her blood quicken, her senses awaken.

The girl is upstairs. She's named Grace Partridge, and Debra is keeping her prisoner here under some kind of mind or drug control. Jessica has already tried to rescue her and been stopped somehow, she cannot remember how. And now the police are here, and Debra seems unperturbed, as if she has nothing to hide, and at this thought, Jessica's heart lurches and she takes the steps three at a time up to Grace's room, hurtles around the corner, and is about to fling open the bedroom door when the cat appears directly at her feet.

The ancient feline stares at her, dispassionately, with his swirling golden eyes. She tries to step over him, but he keeps putting himself in her path.

"Come on, dude," she says. "I have something I need to do."

He hisses at her as she leans down to try to pick him up.

"Geez," she says and backs away. "Let me in, dude," she says, but he hisses again.

From outside comes the sound of feet crunching over gravel, and Jessica peers down the stairs just as the door opens, and Debra comes in followed by two police officers in uniform, who look up at her, curiously.

"This is my friend, Jessica," Debra says to the officers. "She was just about to leave. I don't really think she needs to be here for this."

The female officer looks Jessica up and down.

Jessica fixes her with a direct gaze and says in a voice filled with certainty and strength, "My name is Jessica Jones. I'm not Debra's friend. I'm actually a private investigator working on behalf of a client in New York to find out what happened to her children when they were here in the UK over the summer. My client has good reason to believe that something bad happened to them and that it was something to do with a young girl named Belle. I have spent time here with Belle and Debra, and I believe that Belle and Grace Partridge are the same person, that Debra has exercised some kind of control over Belle to keep her here, and that Debra has something to do with her abduction, and the abductions of Audrey Hill-Lock and Amina Sultanov, using an Instagram account as a grooming platform. I don't know where the other girls are, but I have a very strong feeling that Debra will be able to tell you."

The officers stare at her, and then at each other. Then both of them run up the stairs, taking them two at a time, and Jessica stands and waits until a moment later she sees them return with Belle, who is wrapped in her comforter, startled and small. The female officer has her arm around her while the male officer calls for an ambulance on his walkie-talkie.

Jessica exhales with relief at the sight of the girl. "I'm at the Manston Oak Inn if you want to come and talk to me later, but I'm leaving this place now. I've been here long enough."

She gives Debra one last look before she grabs her coat off the peg by the door, unplugs her phone from the wall, pulls on her boots, and strides out across the overgrown grounds. At the rusty gates, she presses the button beneath the foliage and waits for them to swing open. For a moment she worries that something will happen and that she will be forever trapped, like Belle.

But then she remembers she's not as malleable as normal folk, that she has freed herself from whatever spell Debra cast upon her and now, unlike poor Grace Partridge, she is free to walk out of here. She puts one foot across the threshold, and then another, and then another, and soon she is striding through the narrow country lanes, the purple moon just starting its placid ascent through the grimy night sky. With shaking hands, she pulls her phone out of her pocket and sees that she has full charge and enough signal to make a call. She brings up Malcolm's number.

"Jessica. Shit. Are you okay?"

"Yeah. I'm okay. I'm out. The police came. Was it you? Did you call them?"

"Yeah, well, I asked Elliot to, because my mom would complain about the international charge. But when I saw you on the drone footage, I knew something was seriously wrong. I mean, shit, Jessica, you were wearing a *crop top*."

Jessica glances down and realizes that she is indeed

wearing a crop top. She subconsciously pulls at it with her free hand as she walks.

"I sent Elliot a link to that weird Insta account, so he could send it to the cops over there. See if the IP address was a match. Was that okay?" says Malcolm. "Did I do okay?"

"Yeah. You did good. Like, really good, Malcolm. The IP address was a match and the cops have got this now. They'll take over the case, find the girls. I'm done here. I need to get back. This isn't good for me, I shouldn't be here. I want to be home . . . I don't know what happened to me in there. I don't know what she's done to me. I could have died. I could have . . . It was like . . ."

Suddenly she is holding back tears as confusion and guilt flood her system. Malcolm says, "Jessica, do you want me to call someone? Are you okay?"

"No, no, I'm not okay. I'm really not. And no, don't call anyone. I just need . . . I need to come home. The police have this now. I'm going to call Amber, ask her to arrange my flights. So just, you know, stay tuned. And seriously, Malcolm, just back off this whole thing, okay? I don't want you involved anymore. It's too dangerous. I think I only managed to get away because I have some kind of built-in defenses, you know. But you don't have them. So please, just stay home tonight. Keep away from the twins. I'll tell Amber you're off the case too. Promise me, Malcolm. Just promise."

"Er, sure," he replies.

Jessica stops walking. *"Seriously."*

"Yeah. Seriously. But Jessica, what was it? What was the

LISA JEWELL

deal? I saw you, on the drone footage. You were, like, so weird, you were like the twins. You said you were perfect."

"Crap. Did I?"

"Yeah, I can send you the footage, I have it in my phone."

"Yeah, that'd be good. Thank you. Because listen, Malcolm, I can't remember anything. I mean, I remember shreds, snatches. I remember kind of floating around, eating popcorn, watching movies. I remember the drone, kinda. But basically, the last day is like a blur."

"Do you have any idea what happened to you?"

"*No*, Malcolm. I seriously don't have a freaking clue. I just need to get home. Get my head back together. Now stay safe. Okay?"

"Okay."

"And keep away from the twins."

"Yeah."

"Promise me."

"I promise you."

The call ends and Jessica stares at her phone for a few moments. Then she turns her gaze up to the sky, looking for the special light, the wonder, the soft, golden maternal glow named Miranda that had enveloped her for so many hours. But it's not there.

It's gone.

Seven years ago
Bristol, UK

Life without a following is untenable. Every day Polly scrolls through Instagram, her eyes systematically homing in on the number of followers each profile has, running down the adoring comments under each post. She cannot bear that she is irrelevant, that nobody cares where she is or what she's doing. She cannot bear that she has no influence.

Polly lives in a caravan now, with Arthur and the two dogs. The caravan is modern and clean, but it is still a caravan, and is far from ideal. They needed to go into hiding after they moved out of the Farnham house a few months ago; they needed to start afresh in case there was any comeback from the Clara episode.

Polly works in a nail bar, where she doesn't even do nails, just answers the phones: "Hello, Crystal Nails, Nails and Spa! How can I help you!"

They think her name is Rebecca. Everyone calls her Becky. They see her sitting behind that tiny front desk in her crisply ironed shirts, her fitted tops and slicked-back hair, her lips just so, her mascara-coated eyelashes separated with a pin, teeth so shiny and white, rail-thin legs crossed in tight jeans, her perfect, perfect skin, and they think, *There's Becky*. They think, *She's pretty*. They think, *She's the pretty girl called Becky, who takes my money once I've had my nails done*. And that is all they think. And that's how it needs to be, as much as Polly wants to shine, wants to shine so bright that it blinds the universe. But she has to lie low. It's been nearly eighteen months since Clara discovered human DNA in Polly's beauty products, and it appears that Clara took Polly's threat seriously, as Polly never heard from her again.

Surely it's been long enough now, she thinks.

Surely it's time to get back out there and start to make her mark.

Then one afternoon at the tail end of May, when the nights are getting lighter and lighter and Polly's boredom and frustration are rising like the sap in the trees, she sees her future. And her future sits in the palm of her hand, shining out at her from the black glass of her smartphone. She scrolls and toggles through the buttons at the bottom of the screen and stares at her face as it changes, depending on which lens the app is using. It's a relatively new platform called Snapchat. All the kids are using it. It was developed to make sending photos less permanent, users can only see a photo once, and then the universe swallows it up forever. Who knows where it goes! It's like surgery, somehow, a memory excised before it's had a chance to take root.

Polly downloaded the app to her phone a few weeks ago and has just discovered the filters. The girls at the salon use the filters all the time and make themselves die laughing. Polly uses them to see what she'd look like if she had red hair or a round face or blond eyebrows.

There are new ones added every day by creators and she wonders how easy it would be for her to make one. Could she get famous that way? she wonders. If hers were better than anyone else's?

But she's not tech-savvy. She wouldn't know where to start. She glances across the caravan at Arthur, who sits at the tiny dining table, staring at his laptop.

"What do you know about AR?"

"*A* what?"

"AR? Augmented reality? It's the tech they use to make filters on apps."

She shows him her phone and he smiles slightly as his face changes from screen to screen.

"Ha!" he calls out with delight as rabbit ears appear on top of his head. "Look!"

"Do you think you could make one of these?"

Arthur closes the lid of his laptop, a sign that he is engaged with something that exists in the real world. He scrolls through the app with his nice fingers. Polly perches next to him and watches as he navigates the app. Those dreamy eyes light up. He's on. She feels the swell of attraction she always feels in the moments when she remembers how clever he is. Possibly the cleverest person she's ever known. An IQ of 168, Ophelia

LISA JEWELL

once bragged. *Highly gifted.* Polly can forget how clever her boyfriend is sometimes, as it gets swallowed up by the otherwise idiocy of him, his vagueness and nonsense and strange obsessions, his total and utter lack of common sense. But when it comes to crises, his brain explodes into action.

And when it comes to tech, he cuts right into it all like a freshly sharpened knife.

Twenty-Seven

Back at the hotel, the receptionist looks at Jessica with concerned eyes as she unhooks her key from the board and hands it over to her. "Are you okay, Miss Allan?"

"Yeah. Big day. Need to sleep now," Jessica says and turns to go.

"Are you sure you wouldn't like to have a bite of something to eat before you head up? The dining room just opened."

Jessica smiles wearily. "No, thank you. I've had plenty to eat today. But I might get a visit at some point from two police officers? Please send them up to my room. Whatever the time."

"*Oh,*" says the receptionist, her eyes shining with scandal. "Yes. Of course. And actually, I hope this is okay, but Elliot

Redd came in earlier. From the chemist's? He said you'd asked him to collect the Amazon package that came for you this morning, and I did give it to him. I really hope that was okay?"

"Oh," says Jessica, remembering telling Malcolm to order her a drone the other day. "Yeah, that was totally okay. Thank you."

The woman smiles with relief and says, "Can I do anything else for you, Miss Allan?"

"No, thank you, that's all for now."

Jessica walks to her room and flops heavily onto her bed. She stares around herself in numb surprise. Where has she been? What has happened to her? She fingers the hem of the crop top she's wearing. She tugs it down, but it won't cover her flesh. She gets to her feet again and strips off the clothes, sees herself in the mirror, and recoils slightly at the normality of her reflected self. Dark circles under her eyes, limp hair, dry lips, cellulite at the tops of her thighs, a three-day stubble on her shins. She pulls on jeans and a T-shirt and tries to repel the feelings of disgust that an image of her normal self now evokes. She forces herself to stare at her real image, stare and stare until she likes what she sees, until it feels like her again. What, she wonders, did that woman do to her? What trick did she play? Has she left something in her? Is she implanted with something? A chip?

She opens up her phone and goes to the video that Malcolm has forwarded to her. She sees herself standing outside the farmhouse in the stupid clothes, her hair gleaming and shining, her skin dewy, her eyes wide and bright, teeth madly white, beaming up at the lens of the drone, thumbs in the air, like a sick, twisted doll. It grosses her out, makes her stomach churn.

Jessica shivers and shudders, climbs into bed, and pulls the covers tight around her. She wonders what's happening at the house. She wonders how Grace Partridge is doing. And the other two, Audrey and Amina? Have they found them? Are they arresting Debra, at this very moment?

They will come to her soon, and what will she tell them when she can't remember anything except watching *Pretty in Pink* in a crop top?

She closes her eyes, and she waits for them to come.

* * *

The police knock on the door to her room an hour later, their arrival breaking into a weirdly liminal, half-formed dream from which Jessica awakens with a start. She kicks off the covers, jumps to her feet, and straightens her hair in the mirror. Then she opens the door. She recognizes the female officer from Debra's house. The other officer, a young Asian man, is new.

"Miss Jones," says the female officer. "I'm DC Rowena Lord. This is PC Robert Zhang. Could we take a few minutes just to go over your story again?"

"Sure." She opens the door to allow them in. "How is she?" Jessica asks. "Is she okay?"

"Yes," says the woman. "She's okay. She's been formally

identified as Grace Partridge and is on her way to the hospital."

Jessica feels a swell of relief pass through her. "Was she okay about it?"

The police officers exchange a look. "I can't say that she was," says the woman. "She seemed very confused. She'll be undergoing medical tests to see what's happened to her. We think there might have been some kind of mind control, maybe drug dependence. We're not sure."

"What about the other two? Audrey and Amina?"

"No sign of them as yet," says the man.

"And Debra. Where is she?"

"She's been taken in for questioning. We're just waiting for her to get a lawyer and then we are going to begin our interview."

"Did she go easy?"

"Yes," says the woman. "She did, actually. Surprisingly so. Almost as if she was relieved. What were your observations in her home?"

Jessica knows she should tell the cops about her experiences at Debra's house, but she can't risk being held here and made to undergo a medical examination. She has given them all she is going to give them. She needs to sleep. And then she needs to get the hell home. So she tells them all about her experiences with Belle: her weird hazy memories, asking Jessica if she was real, her claims of agoraphobia, and the tight control she saw Debra exert over her. Then she tells them about the twins displaying similar behavior back in

New York and she gives the officers Amber's details and one of her business cards and then finally the officers thank her for her time and leave.

After they've gone, Jessica collapses against the door and sinks to her haunches. She came so close to being broken at Debra's house, and maybe she is. Maybe, like a virus, she won't really know what damage has been done to her until a long time from now. What did that woman leave inside her? Inside her unborn child? What did she take from her? What did she do to her?

She has one last thing she needs to do before she can finally slide into sleep. She picks up her phone and calls Amber.

"Hi, Jessica. How's it going?"

"Oh, yeah, kinda crazy. How are the kids?"

"You know, amazing as it sounds, they seem to be getting better. It seems like whatever it was is wearing off."

"It is?"

"Yeah. Uh-huh. They've picked up their old habits. Their skin looks more natural. They use their phones more."

Jessica feels a flicker of surprise. Is it possible, she wonders, that Debra's current state of incarceration has somehow diminished her powers? Weakened her hold over the children? "That sounds great," she says, not sharing her thoughts with Amber.

"Yes. It is. Although I still want to know what happened out there. Are you any closer?"

"In some ways, yes. But listen, I need you to get me back home now. Like literally, the first feasible flight. Please."

"Jessica, are you okay?"

"I actually don't know. I just know that I am done here. The local police have taken over the case from this end, and I have work I need to do back home."

"Jessica. What's happened? Have you been hurt? Just tell me."

"I'll tell you everything when I'm back. But I have to sleep now. More than anything."

"Well, okay. I'll let you go. But just call me if you need anything. You've got me really worried over here. And with your current condition, you know, I . . ."

"It's fine. I'm fine. Just message me the flight details. I'll see you back in New York."

She ends the call and then finally crawls into bed and into an immediate sleep.

Twenty-Eight

Jessica awakes a few hours later at the sound of her phone buzzing numerous times in a row. She turns on her screen and sees that it is 5:30 a.m. and that the notifications are messages from Amber, outlining the details for her return journey. A car collecting her from the hotel at nine, a flight from Gatwick Airport at two, arrival at JFK at five in the afternoon.

The final message says:

I'd love for you to talk to the twins about what you saw in Essex, about what happened when you were there. It might help them to frame their own experiences and finally start to talk about them.

Jessica sighs. How the hell is she supposed to talk to anyone about her experiences when her experiences have been wiped from her mind? She downloads some guided

269

meditations to her phone to listen to during the flight back. She needs to find a way into her own head, to unpick and uncover the mysteries of the past twenty-four hours. But first she needs to shower and pack and get out of this place.

* * *

At eight thirty a.m., she's sitting in the hotel reception area, watching the village through dark glasses, tapping her passport on her thigh. An automated message to her phone tells her that her car is due in thirty-two minutes, and, feeling restless, she decides to go for one last walk.

There's a cobbled lane just behind the main street that she's noticed earlier in the week, with the tip of a church spire just visible at its crown. According to Miss Anne Satchel's book, this is the church that contains a plaque memorializing the children who died in the 1400s beneath Sebastian Randall's house.

The church is nestled in front of a small green space with three benches facing toward it. It's tiny, around twenty feet wide. Jessica steps inside, where the air is cold and cloying. Small honey-colored pews sit in rows on either side of a narrow aisle. Red velvet kneepads hang from brass hooks. At the top end of the chapel, a small altar bears a pedestal draped in an embroidered cloth, and behind that a semicircle of stained-glass windows set high up the back wall casts colored light across the floor. There's a small wooden pipe organ to the left and a door to the right that Jessica assumes leads to the room where the priest puts on his priest outfit.

The *vestry*. The word finds her from nowhere, and she is surprised by it.

All along the internal walls of the church are engraved plaques and memorials. Jessica sets off in a clockwise direction to read them. A quarter way around, she sees it:

In

the year of our Lord 1436

the souls of twelve of the blessed children of this parish

all gone

hearts rent

joy paused

life blighted

pain no more

in the arms of the Lord

for all their perfect eternity

The words are strangely beautiful in their simplicity, and in the way in which they vaguely form the shape of a cross, but it is an etching just beneath the words that startles Jessica. It depicts a small child, their arms outstretched from a pile of earth, reaching up toward a ray of light. It's the same image from the sketch Jessica had found in Fox's bedroom. She takes out her phone and photographs the image and the engraving. Below the inscription there are more words engraved in a circle around the image, in what she assumes to be Latin:

o adolescentia admiranda semper bella sitis

Ad*miranda*.

Bella.

Jessica takes a picture of that as well and stumbles from the chapel. She needs Wi-Fi so that she can translate the Latin. She needs to get back to the hotel. As she hurtles down the cobbled pathway toward the high street, she almost collides head-on with Elliot, the boy from the pharmacy.

"Sorry," says Elliot.

"No. My bad. Listen. Malcolm told me what you did yesterday. Sending the drone. Calling the cops. I wanted to thank you."

He shrugs. "You're welcome, I'm glad you're okay. What happened to you over there?"

"Can't discuss it, I'm afraid, it's an ongoing case."

"Oh," he says, looking disappointed for a moment. Then he perks up. "Oh, hey, your drone! Do you want it back?"

Jessica smiles. "No, Elliot. Please keep it. As a gift. I think you might actually have saved my life."

He peers at her, curiously. "You okay?"

"Yeah. Just about. Heading home soon. But listen, what do you know about this? I just saw it in the little church up there." She shows him the pictures. "Know anything about these dead kids?"

"Er, no. Can't say I'm familiar with this one. My mum would probably be able to help you, but obviously she's—"

"In Turkey. Yeah."

"But I can tell you what that means," he says, pointing at the Latin words engraved around the image.

"You can speak Latin?"

"Well, sort of, I got an 8 in my GCSE."

"Er, okay." She passes him her phone. "*Admiranda?* What does that mean?"

"It means, like, 'in wonder'? Wonderful? Something like that. And *adolescentia* is 'adolescents' or 'children,' and then *semper* means 'always' and *bella* is 'pretty, beautiful'?"

He beams at her, then looks back at the screen. "My guess is that it says, 'Oh wonderful children, be forever beautiful.'"

PART THREE

Twenty-Nine

The sight of the Manhattan skyline from the back of a cab soothes Jessica's soul.

The sun has just set, the sky is a faded denim blue with streaks of gold, and the lights of the buildings across the river glimmer through the damp night air like armies of fireflies. She is home, but she feels alien. Everything hurts. Even her eyeballs ache. She touches them with a fingertip and flinches.

Her time in Essex feels frayed at the edges. Random images scroll through her head, shreds of disconnected thoughts. Somewhere in her fractured mind lives the answer to what is happening in the Old Farmhouse, who Debra is, what she's done to Grace, and maybe even what she's done to Amina and Audrey. The lost hours at Debra's house have blown out all the proportions of her life; the missing chunk of consciousness has distorted everything. More than anything in the world she wants to know what happened to her between the moment she jumped from the window with Belle and the moment the police arrived, when she finally managed to break the spell. There is only one person who can help her now, and it's one of the last people in the world she wants to see.

The cab pulls up outside an imposing forty-plus-story apartment block overlooking the Hudson River. Jessica pays the driver and hits the intercom by the front door. "Hey. It's Jessica Jones. I need to see her now."

Through the intercom, an officious voice: "I'm sorry. It's Sunday. Madame Web doesn't—"

"I'm sure she doesn't. But this is an emergency. I need her *now*. She's psychic, she must've known I was coming."

After a moment the intercom buzzes and the latch of the door clicks. Jessica takes the elevator up to the thirtieth floor and bangs the door of 30-D with a heavy fist. The door cracks open slightly and a woman eyes Jessica superciliously.

"No need to thump like that," she says, widening the gap so that Jessica can walk in. "Madame will be with you shortly."

The apartment gives her chills; dark and gloomy, lit by candles and dirty bulbs, the ceilings loom twelve feet high, the windows are covered with shutters painted the color of old blood. There's a smell in here, a smell of soil and abandoned places. A sharp chill cuts through the stagnant air, and there, sitting dead center of the biggest room in the apartment, surrounded by teetering candelabra and dozens of overgrown plants, is Cassandra Webb, stiff in her wheelchair.

The woman turns Jessica's stomach—the yellow pallor of her skin, black-shaded eyes, the sharp point of her chin, the look of sour resentment that warps her face.

"Jessica," a voice with an ancient crack in it says. "I wasn't expecting to see you here again."

"Yeah, I can assure you that I was not expecting to be back. Not after what you did to me last time."

"Jessica, sweetheart," Webb says flatly. "You know I was only trying to help. I was a little heavy-handed in my encounter with you, but it was out of my control. Your thoughts just came to me, so strong, so violent. Still, please, accept my apologies."

Jessica shrugs. "Thanks."

"So, what brings you back here? You feel troubled. You feel . . . Hold on." Her head tips down slightly and Jessica sees her blank gaze fall to her abdomen. "Are you *pregnant*?"

Jessica gulps, dryly. She should have guessed that Webb would pick up on that first thing. "Yes. I'm pregnant."

"Is that why you're here?"

"No, that's not why I'm here. I'm here because . . ." Jessica wrestles with possible words.

The woman straightens slightly. "Someone broke you again?"

Jessica's shoulders slump. "Yeah. I think so. And they took some memories, and the memories contain the key to the case I'm working on. It's all in there, but it's gone. Can you . . . ?"

Webb breathes out loudly through her nose. "Who did this to you?"

"I don't know. I was trying to rescue this kid, she'd been abducted, brainwashed, something like that, and I got her out of her bed and through her window . . . and then I wake up and become a different person for a whole day. Like, I was me, but I wasn't me. I was me without all the . . ."

"Darkness."

"Well, yeah. I guess. Darkness. Doubt. Awareness. Context."

"Stripped of your humanity."

"Stripped of my humanity . . ."

"And then?"

"An event broke through her hold. The police arrived and it broke the spell. I could suddenly see exactly what was happening and walk away from it."

"And now?"

"Now I feel like someone took a huge handful out of my guts. Like there's a hole inside me."

The old psychic stares at Jessica, and it seems like she's staring right through her.

"Yes. That's what I suspect. I will need you to hand yourself over to me completely. Are you prepared to do that?"

Jessica stares at her. Webb violated her the last time she saw her, but now she is her only hope. Jessica wants to walk straight out of here, but she knows she can't. Not while part of her is still missing.

"Yes," she says, heavily. "Yes. I trust you."

"Good," says Cassandra. "Then we begin."

* * *

Jessica sits on a chaise longue next to a tall window over-looking the Hudson. It's so close to the part of Hell's Kitchen she inhabits, but this high up, the drone of traffic disappears, and a soft atmospheric drumming takes hold. It's an entirely different world from hers. In an apartment across the street, she sees a couple eating a late dinner, the glitter of wine being poured into glasses. When all this is over, she tells herself, that will be her. She will sit in a pleasant apartment drinking wine with a pleasant man, with a pleasant child tucked up in bed at the end of a pleasant day. She just needs to get through this. And then: no more. No more danger. No more fingers inside her head. She closes her eyes and concentrates on the old woman's words.

"Jessica, try to keep your thoughts still for me. Imagine your thoughts as limbs and my mind as a knife doing very delicate work. Think, if you can, of the center of a flower. Or maybe the eyes of a cat."

At the mention of the word *cat*, Jessica is immediately sent reeling back in her thoughts to Mr. Smith staring at her from outside Grace's bedroom door, and she sets her thoughts now firmly on the image of Mr. Smith's eyes, the ancient, rheumy whites, the melon pip pupils, the irises of green and gold.

"Good, Jessica . . . that is good. Now . . . I will tell you what I see." She is silent for a moment and then sucks her breath in loudly between her discolored teeth.

"What? What can you see?" Jessica wriggles with impatience.

"Stay still, Jessica. Stay still. Okay . . . I am finding pieces of your lost memories, they are divided and scattered. These things will come to me in no order, please just stay with me . . . You've been in a place that has a long history. Another country . . . England?"

"Yes. Well, that I could have told—"

"Small houses . . . An old church. A . . . small flying machine?"

Jessica wriggles slightly at the discomfiting sense of a stranger rifling through her private memories.

"Please . . . try to recenter your thoughts to the eyes of the cat."

Jessica does as she is told.

"And now I see a house on a piece of land shaped like a—"

"Trapezoid."

"Yes. And I see dogs. Many dogs. A girl, with empty eyes. And a woman." Webb closes her eyes tight, throws her head back slightly, and exhales. "This woman. She is timeless, infinite."

"What? What do you mean?"

"I don't know." Jessica keeps her eyes closed, flinches slightly at the sensation of the woman's bony fingers touching her temple. "The age of her soul . . . as if she has lived for many centuries. She has learned many things. She has powers."

"Super-powers?"

"Maybe. Maybe not . . . skills learned over centuries. The ability to manipulate and control. To control people, to control animals, to control the weather even. And she has controlled the girl, I see it. And you were controlled too. You were with the girl and your mind was entered and a voice said . . ." Webb draws in her breath and looks hard into Jessica's eyes. "It said, 'Do you want to be perfect?'"

"She said what?"

"'Do you want to be perfect?' And you became immediately enchanted, brought under. You said, 'Yes, I do want to be perfect . . .' And you let go of the girl."

The image plows head-on into Jessica's consciousness. Yes. There it is. The fingers tight around her thoughts, her arms loosening around the girl, her mind softening, the girl going to Debra, Debra holding the girl in her arms.

The old woman continues. "The woman led you both back into the house, meek as pet lambs. Then—*oh!*—there is black light from a black screen. And this black light . . . It is like blood, being pumped through veins, Jessica, veins that run beneath the house, rivers of it. The light is black and it's in the earth, it's in the woman's hands . . . But the hands. They are young. The hands of a young woman. Not the old woman. There is another woman. She is a crook, this woman, please believe me. A grifter . . . And this light, in her hands . . . It's hot—Jessica, it burns. And now it's in your eyes, Jessica. It's shining in your eyes—it looks like blood—your eyes are black—and you are . . ." She gasps. "You are perfect."

Jessica feels it then, hot and dark, the shock of the flash from the screen of a phone. A pair of eyes on hers. Staring, with glee. Debra's eyes? But no, not Debra's. Somebody else's. Who was it? And then a second later a sense of everything lifting away from her: her self-doubt, her trauma, her sharp edges, her fear of the future.

"I see the black light enter you . . ."

Jessica sees it too, a pulse, from a phone, the shock of hot blackness in her eyes.

"And now you think you are perfect."

"I *think* I'm perfect?"

"Yes."

"But I'm not?"

Webb tilts her head as if considering this and says, "Nobody is perfect, Jessica," but quickly looks up at the ceiling in concentration. "And I see another picture in your head. A child . . . up from the earth . . . arms outstretched toward the light. An etching, yes? This image. It is in your past, but I see it also in the future. This . . . it's coming soon. The child. The rays of light. It will be with you so soon."

"I don't understand." Jessica feels a rush of cold dread pass through her and sits up.

"No reason to understand." Webb closes her eyes. "Just remember that I told you this. This image. It's in the future, and you must beware. Because it is dangerous. Children could get hurt, Jessica. Children could get hurt."

Thirty

Jessica gulps in the cold October air when she emerges from the building a few moments later. It's entirely dark now, and a light drizzle has formed and is dropping softly from low clouds. The pictures thrown at her by the old psychic make a sort of dizzying collage in her head. She needs to get to Amber's apartment and talk to the twins.

She calls Amber as she walks.

"I need to talk to the twins right now. Can I come over?"

"Oh God, Jessica. I'm so sorry, I don't know what to say to you. But they're not here. I mean, I specifically told them they were grounded until further notice. I specifically told them to stay in their rooms until you got here. I told them and they promised. And somehow, I mean I *really* don't know how, they snuck out, and it's Sunday so the doorman isn't

285

here, and I don't know what to tell you, Jessica, I don't know what to say."

But Jessica is only half listening to Amber because as she walks, she has remembered something. The image that she'd seen on the sketch in Fox's bedroom and also on the plaque in the church, she's seen it somewhere else, and now she thinks she can remember where. She ends the call with Amber and stops on the sidewalk to find the photo Malcolm sent her of the interior of Lark's bedroom. She zooms in and there— there it is. On a piece of paper pinned to Lark's corkboard. She opens it up as big as she can get it and homes in on the detail.

It's Fox's drawing of the child, the outstretched arms, the rays of light. There are words on the paper too, but they are too blurred to read. She sighs, feeling the crush of tiredness in every atom of her being, but she still has work to do. The Grace Partridge story has broken overnight in the UK. It's two in the morning over there and all the headlines carry news of the rescue of Grace Partridge and Debra Phipps's arrest, the intensive police search for Amina Sultanov and Audrey Hill-Lock.

She's not far from home, but, too exhausted to walk, she catches a cab and as she rides, she reads every article she can find. The word *brainwash* is used numerous times by the journalists. It's a word that always fills Jessica with dread. The true meaning of the word is so unbearable to Jessica that it can take her breath away. The washing of the brain. Some-one with a virtual sponge, rubbing away at parts of another person's very essence, obliterating free thought, erasing precious memories, implanting falsehoods and warped truth. All without a knife, without hands even. Just with words. Is there anything more sinister than that, she ponders, the ability of one human being to access another human being's very essence and do with it as they please? Debra Phipps, for all her unassumingness, is a dangerous woman. She used her ability to control another person effortlessly and brilliantly on Jessica, who has at least some psionic defenses. She can only imagine how she could use that power to control a vulnerable young girl without Jessica's super-powers. But if Debra Phipps is so powerful, then what is she doing holed up in a scruffy house in the middle of nowhere making roast lamb for Grace Partridge? Why has she kept her there under her control for over a year? What has she done with the other girls? And how does it all fit with what happened to the twins that summer?

She thinks of poor Grace, her pale skin and haunted look, staring up at Jessica and asking her, "Am I real?"

It strikes her that while "Belle" was not real, Grace Partridge *is*, and so is Debra Phipps. Which means that there are people out there who know both of them in the real world. And some of them must now be reading these news stories and heading onto social media to share their take on the story with the world. She finds something on a UK news site from a "local woman" who says that she is shocked to hear that Debra Phipps who has lived reclusively in her village for so many years could have been hiding such terrible secrets.

"We never saw her, she lived out there with those dogs and had all her food delivered. But by all accounts, she was a harmless old woman. I can't believe she was capable of such a thing."

The words "old woman" jar Jessica as she reads the account. Debra is not young, but neither is she old, with her shiny hair and trendy reading glasses. She thinks of Madame Web's words just now: *She is timeless, infinite . . .*

Jessica messages Elliot in the UK: What does Debra Phipps look like? then switches off her phone as the cab pulls up outside her building.

She stares upward through the window as she waits for her change back from the driver.

The windows of her block glow in all the different colors of people's lives.

Her windows on the fifth floor sit like dead eyes in between.

Jessica slings her backpack over her shoulder and finally goes home.

* * *

She wakes up early the next day, a Monday morning, the city outside loud and urgent. Her eyes take a moment to adjust to her surroundings and when they do, she grimaces. After nearly a week in five-star hotels, her bedroom looks particularly unappealing.

She switches on her phone and sees that Elliot has replied to her question of the day before about Debra Phipps:

My mum used to drop her prescriptions off for her. She said

she just looks like a regular old lady with gray hair. She said she's very small. Wears dentures. Shouts when she talks.

She searches the overnight news reports from the UK about Grace's rescue, but none of them have a photograph of "Debra Phipps."

If the woman at the Old Farmhouse claiming to be Debra Phipps is not in fact Debra Phipps, then who is she? And where is the real Debra Phipps?

She sighs and climbs out of bed. In the bathroom she stares at her reflection for a few moments. She did the same thing last night, searching for what had been done to her, her mind full of Webb's words about the "black light" that someone had shone into her eyes. There is still a dry ache behind her eyeballs, a vague feeling of residual pain. She can't see anything unusual, but as she stares at herself, deep into the dark centers of her eyes, she remembers looking at the photo that Malcolm showed her of him and the twins, remembers saying how their eyes didn't reflect the light. She immediately heads back to her bedroom, grabs her phone, stands in the window, and takes a selfie.

She zooms in on the selfie.

She looks hard for the reflection of the bright New York morning in her pupils, the window-shaped squares of light that should be there.

But they are not.

Thirty-One

The doorman calls up to Amber's apartment. "I have a Jessica Jones here for you, Mrs. Randall."

Jessica hears a pause and then Amber's disembodied voice replying, "It's very early. Can you tell her to come back later?"

Jessica sighs and tucks her hair behind her ear. "Please tell Mrs. Randall that I have news about her kids. Urgent news."

The doorman nods, knowingly, and relays the message.

A second later, Jessica is riding the elevator to the top floor.

Amber greets her at the door to her apartment, her eyes wide with concern.

"It's seven a.m., Jessica. What's going on?"

"Are they here?"

"Er, yeah. They're getting ready for school. You'll have to be quick—"

Jessica follows Amber into the kitchen. Fox and Lark are sitting at the breakfast counter in a long narrow room with three tall windows overlooking Central Park. They glance up at Jessica with tired eyes when she walks in.

"Kids," says Amber defeatedly. "This is Jessica, the lady I was telling you about yesterday. Jessica just got back from the UK. She spent some time in Barton Wallop and got kind of involved in a big news story over there. And apparently it has some connection to you?"

Jessica sees their eyes widen and their body language shift uncomfortably as they absorb their mother's words. She also notices that they both look normal. Shadows under their eyes, a scabbed-over pimple by Fox's nose, dry skin around Lark's mouth. Both were gazing at their phones when Jessica walked in, and both have slouched postures and frown lines.

"Why do I recognize you?" asks Fox.

"I have no idea, but listen, while I was in Barton Wallop, I met a woman named Debra and she was living with a young girl named Belle, and Belle told me she'd met you, when you were on vacation this summer?" An expedient lie.

The twins exchange a look and shrug in unison.

"She said she'd spent a fair amount of time with you both, that you'd been to her house, hung out?"

"I guess," says Lark, her voice a little husky.

"Right." Jessica feels a blaze of frustration at the two recalcitrant children. "Well, I don't know if you're both aware, but

Belle is not Belle at all. Her real name is Grace Partridge, and she went missing from a school excursion over a year ago with two of her best friends, Audrey and Amina. The woman who calls herself Debra Phipps is now in police custody about to be charged with her abduction, and the British police are searching the grounds for the two other missing girls as I speak. At some point they will want to be speaking to you both, I'm sure. So listen: Is there anything you want to tell me about what happened when you were in the UK this summer?"

The silence that passes after Jessica's speech is profound. Nobody is breathing, apart from the small black dog who sits on the floor staring expectantly at Fox's empty cereal bowl and panting lightly.

Amber's eyes dart sharply from twin to twin. "Well," she says. "Kids? Is there?"

The siblings glance at each other and then both shake their heads.

"What—*nothing*?" Jessica prods.

They look at each other again and then Fox speaks up. "I mean, we knew that Belle was, like, kind of weird. I think we thought she was, like, you know, maybe on the spectrum? Or like, borderline personality disorder, you know, she kept changing her stories. One minute her parents were abroad. The next minute they weren't. One minute she was at school in Suffolk, the next minute she'd left years ago. And there was the agoraphobia? Like, she never wanted to leave the house? So yeah, she was kind of strange. But I would never have thought that there was anything like that going on."

"And Debra was just nice, you know?" says Lark. "She cooked good food and took such great care of Belle, and of us. I would never have thought she was doing anything bad."

"Well, your nice Debra put me under her control for a while, using some kind of hypnosis or mind control. Does that mean anything to you?"

"No way," says Fox. "No. She never did anything like that. The whole thing, the setup, the house, all of it, was just wholesome, y'know. Like the kind of place you'd want to be."

"Really?"

"Yeah, really."

Jessica stares at Fox, notices his defensive body language, the hard set of his jaw. Lark, in contrast, looks uneasy, haunted almost, picking obsessively at the skin around her fingernails.

"How did you meet them? Belle and Debra. What's the backstory here?" She directs this at Lark, more interested in her take on this situation than her brother's, as he seems to have an agenda.

She sees the twins exchange another look, and then, interestingly, both turn to glance at their mother.

"What?" says Amber, picking up on the mood.

The twins look at each other again and then Lark says, "Well, Dad has kind of this *girlfriend*. I mean, she's not like a technical girlfriend. It's not *serious*. She's helping with the house. I think they hang out sometimes. That's all it is. And this one time she was there, and she said if we were bored we could walk up the lane, that there was a girl there, in the house? She said to drop by, say hi. So we did."

"Did you know about her?" Amber asks Jessica.

Jessica nods, apologetically. "Yeah. The locals I met in the pub mentioned that Sebastian had a girlfriend. And then Sebastian backed it up when I asked. He kinda didn't want you to know about it. Said he thought it might be a sensitive issue."

"Oh, for Pete's sake," says Amber. "How ridiculous. As if I'd care." But even as she says it, Jessica can hear from the brittle tone of her voice that she does in fact care, very deeply.

"Okay, so this woman, she says you could meet up with this girl, Belle. And what was her connection to them?"

"She said she'd done some work on the house there, for the owner."

"Seriously?" says Jessica. "I mean, you and I have both been inside the Old Farmhouse, so we can all agree that no work has been done on that house since at least 1936."

"Yeah," says Lark. "I did kind of think that."

"And did you ever see her again? This woman?"

"No. Just that one time."

Jessica pauses for a moment, giving herself time to work out how to follow this thread without letting the twins know that they have been under surveillance.

"After spending time there, with Belle and Debra, did either of you ever feel anything, like a discomfort in your eyeballs?"

The twins look at each other again. "No," says Fox, with a dismissive tone that suggests the question is bizarre.

Lark shakes her head. "No," she says, but she sounds less convincing.

"Why are you asking them that, Jessica?" asks Amber with concern.

"Because I had a very strange experience when I was there. Someone flashed a light in my eyes and I came away with partial memory loss, and very sore eyes. And I think you might have had the same strange experience. Did you?"

The air crackles with unspoken truths.

"No," says Fox.

"No," says Lark.

Jessica sighs. These kids are not going to crack, not here in front of each other, in front of their mother. "Did you ever meet anyone else when you were at Debra's house?" she says, changing tack. "An older woman maybe?"

"Nope," says Fox. "Just Debra and Belle."

"Nobody else ever came to the house?"

"No, apart from food deliveries."

"Did you ever see anything strange there? Anything that didn't make sense?"

"Seriously," says Fox, blowing out his cheeks slightly. "We made friends with this crazy girl named Belle, who was being looked after by a regular-seeming woman named Debra and we spent a lot of time with her. We played with her dogs, we rode her quad bikes, we watched old movies with her . . ."

"Wait, what kind of movies?"

"Like, I dunno, ones from the eighties? Belle really liked the eighties. The films, the music, the fashion, all of it."

"Right. Okay. Yeah." Jessica nods along with Fox's words as pieces of the puzzle jostle in her head, trying to find ways to fit together. "And you and Belle, have you been in touch much since you left the UK?"

"No, not really," says Fox quickly. "She doesn't really do phones, you know. The reception there is terrible. She said we could write each other letters, but that sort of hasn't happened. And I'm not really a letter-writing kind of person anyway."

"I wrote her," says Lark. "Like a month ago. But I never heard back." Her eyes go to the clock on the wall. "You know, we really gotta—"

"Yes. Sure. Sorry. But seriously, this is a major case now in the UK. Your dad will be hearing about it, he'll want to talk to you, the police will likely want to talk to you, so you know, if there's anything, anything at all . . . ?"

"There really isn't," says Fox, firmly.

Lark echoes his words with a small shake of her head, then slips from her stool and disappears into the hallway. Fox slides off his stool too and puts his empty bowl into the dishwasher, watched with eagle eyes by the small black dog, before grabbing a water bottle from the fridge and leaving the room.

Jessica exchanges a look with Amber, who has her arms clasped tight around her waist. She shrugs and plucks at the sleeve of her blouse. A moment later the children call out goodbye to their mother, who absentmindedly tells them to have a good day, followed by the bang of the door and the click of the elevator.

Amber sighs. "I don't know what to say."

Jessica glances around the apartment. "I'd like to take a look in their rooms."

She sighs again. "I have been through both their rooms forensically, and there is nothing, literally nothing."

"But anyway . . . I'd like to."

"Of course," says Amber. "Go ahead. But don't move anything, they're like hawks, they'll know in a nanosecond."

"I won't leave a trace."

* * *

Lark's bedroom is first. It's at the rear of the apartment, tucked away in a corner. The drapes are closed, the air is still and heavy with the smell of vanilla and musk. Jessica pulls open the drapes and peers down into the roof garden of a lower apartment. Her dressing table is littered with beauty products, scrunched-up tissues, and overturned cans of sprays and deodorants. Her walls are papered with unsettling posters and dark art, and her bed—unmade and scattered with discarded items of clothing—is a futon on the floor with piles of dark gray bedding, a far cry from the airy sugar-pink room that her father's girlfriend designed for her in Essex. Jessica's eyes scan the details, looking for the paper she saw in Malcolm's photo.

She finds it pinned to a board:

MEET MIRANDA
NYC
* *

7pm October 24th
SCAN THE CODE for details

She pulls out her phone and scans the QR code. Her phone goes black briefly and she bangs at the screen, but a few seconds later it comes back to life and some text appears over the top of the familiar graphic of the child with outstretched arms.

**You're all signed up! . . .
Location details will be sent direct to this
device at 6pm 10/24 . . .
Be ready! . . .**

The text fades away and Jessica's phone vibrates gently, just once, followed by a small burst of heat against the palm of her hand, and then it is gone, and she is looking once more at her home screen. She searches her phone for an app to correlate with what she was just seeing, but there's nothing. No new icons on the home page. No sign that the page was ever there. She feels a prickle of discomfort run through her as she continues her search of Lark's room.

It's not until a few minutes later that she notices the small mint-green pot on Lark's dressing table. There is a label on the lid that says BEAUTY X in swirly hot-pink cursive. Jessica's mind scrambles at the sight of it. She takes it and stares at it. It looks weirdly familiar. She's seen it before, she's sure she has.

Carefully, she unscrews the lid from the pot. It's empty, just a sleek residue clinging to the inside of the container. She brings it to her nose and sniffs. The smell hurtles her back to the Old Farmhouse, the sweet metallic smell that sat under the damp and the dust.

She screws the lid back onto the pot and tucks it into her jacket pocket.

Jessica had thought it was detergent, or surface cleaner.

But no, it was the smell of Debra herself.

Four Years Ago
Bristol, UK

Polly has a new Instagram account. At last!

Her new persona, Perfect Peach, is entirely anonymous. *Peach* never shows her real face on her Insta account, only one distorted by filters. She doesn't display a name, or a location. She talks about the beauty products that she gets sent for free because her account has nearly a hundred and fifty thousand followers, which makes her, officially, an influencer. And all it took was for Polly to wipe every trace of her authentic self from the account.

Peach reviews creams and potions, smoothies and lasers. She even reviews dog products and cleaning products. Every day Polly goes to the cash converter shop in town where she has a locker and collects the things that have been sent to her. The account is her full-time job; she replies to every comment, to every message in her inbox. She tests products vigilantly and thoroughly and writes up her reviews to the very best of her English GCSE abilities. She makes stories and spends ages splicing reels together, finding the perfect pieces of music. Her followers use words like *exquisite* and *magical* and *stunning* about her posts, and about her.

The filters are all Arthur. He is one of the most prolific filter designers across all the social media platforms now and has started playing around with AI. It's not there yet, but he reckons it won't be long before filtered images look totally natural and nobody will be able to see the difference.

None of this is making them any money though. Polly still works at the nail bar, and they still live in a caravan. But she has plans. Soon she'll take Perfect Peach to YouTube, when she gets better video equipment. She'll get subscribers by offering bonus content and private one-on-one tutorials. She and Arthur have their next steps in place.

But then, one sunny August afternoon, a message appears in Polly's inbox.

Hi there! My name is Jodie, and I hope you don't mind me asking this, but are you the same lady who used to sell Beauty X on here? I know you're anonymous but there's something about your face that reminds me of her! And your dogs are the same as hers! If it is you, I just really wondered what happened to your brand? It was so so so amazing, especially the Visage Magic and I ran out years ago and nothing else has come close. If it is you, do you still sell it? I'd be happy to pay for it, just name a price! ANY PRICE! I just want to have perfect skin again!

This is followed by three heart-eye emoji in a row, followed by three praying hands emoji.

Polly clicks on Jodie's profile. Her page is public and shows a life of endless beach holidays and nights in London rooftop restaurants. She has a husband and a baby and a small dog and long blond hair and wide eyes and white teeth and tons of friends and a shiny car and lives in a house with windows on both sides. She looks like the happiest woman in the world, a woman with everything. But still, it's not enough. She wants more. She wants to be *perfect*.

She shows the message to Arthur and he grunts, dismissively.

"Isn't there something we could do for her? She's willing to pay?"

Arthur continues poking at his laptop. "Well, we could give her a recipe for vampire face cream that could get us and my whole family thrown in prison. Beyond that, I have no suggestions."

"But, babe, there must be a way," she says. "Surely? It doesn't have to be cream. It could be something better than cream. Something like what you're doing with the filters. I mean, surely"—she feels her heart begin to race with excitement—"with all this new technology, with AI and everything, there must be a way to bring filters into the real world? Like some kind of special lenses, or a special light or something?"

At the introduction of a technical challenge, Arthur looks up, nods, and strokes his jaw. "I don't know about lenses . . .

but the laws of quantum physics allow for the transfer of one reality onto another."

"What do you mean?"

"I mean that if someone could find a way to transfer, let's say, physical defects from one person to some other kind of entity that doesn't care what it looks like, some kind of receptive vessel . . ."

"Yes, go on!" Polly feels it, that burning physical desire she feels whenever Arthur displays his brilliance.

"Well, in theory, you could create the impression of physical perfection. The defects would still be there, but they would just exist in another dimension."

Polly moves closer to Arthur, feeds her fingers through his hair. "And that's, like, a thing that's possible?"

"Well, I have no idea. It's all highly theoretical slash technically impossible. I'd have to know a hell of a lot more about quantum physics than I do currently."

"But you think if you studied it, you could find a way?"

"In theory. Yes."

He says this with a small firm nod, and with confidence. His voice sounds deeper, his jaw sits squarer when he talks like this. He looks more handsome, more manly. She runs her fingers down the back of his T-shirt and then under and along the smooth flesh on his back. She feels him shudder pleasurably.

"I think," she says, her mouth just millimeters away from his, her other hand pressed against the waistband of his trousers, "it's time for you to finally get your big brain to college, Arthur."

Thirty-Two

After her visit to Amber's apartment, Jessica heads home, stopping en route at a high-end market, where she fills a cart with the things she feels a pregnant woman should be eating: nuts and fruit and fresh pasta and avocados. She buys protein balls and ginger shots, and even plucks a packet of decaffeinated coffee from the shelf.

Her head buzzes as she passes through the store. She thinks about the twins, the innocuousness of them just now. Two normal kids who had a normal summer hanging out with a cute, quirky girl in the English countryside. Are they hiding something, she wonders, or have they been entirely brainwashed, rinsed clean of every memory of every bad thing that happened to them in Essex? Are they lying, or are they merely devoid of the truth?

She pays for her groceries, wincing at the final total, observing how much more expensive healthy food is than shitty food. It's nearly eight a.m. and it occurs to her that she hasn't heard from Malcolm since she got back last night. She sends him a quick text:

Hey. How you doing? I'm back in town. Maybe come by after school?

She watches the message for a moment, but no reply comes, and she assumes he must already be in class.

The clerk watches as Jessica piles her groceries haphazardly into two large bags.

"You got a long way to walk with all that?" she asks. "We have a free delivery service, save you carrying it."

Jessica smiles dryly as she lifts the two bags with obvious ease. "I can manage," she says, "but thanks."

* * *

The sun comes out as she walks up her street with the two bags of groceries. She can feel the burn of it against her tender eyeballs and pulls sunglasses from her jacket pocket and puts them on. Julius, her neighbor, is just leaving his apartment when she gets back to hers.

"Whoa, early bird," he says. "Already out for groceries!"

"Yeah, well, jet lag, I guess," she says. "It's lunchtime in the UK so I'm kinda halfway through my day already."

"Yeah," says Julius. "Of course. How was your trip?"

"My trip was . . . eventful."

"Solve your case?"

"Not quite. Upended some applecarts though." A thought occurs to her. "Hey, listen, Julius. Tell me again what your boyfriend does? I mean, his job?"

"He's a pharmaceutical engineer."

"Oh yeah. I thought it was something like that. What is that, exactly?"

Julius gives a small dry laugh. "I swear I don't even know. Something to do with pharmaceuticals and engineering, I guess."

"Do you think he might be able to do me a huge favor. For my case?"

"Er, maybe." He grimaces. "That depends. What is it?"

"It's this . . ." She puts her groceries down on the hall floor and pulls the small green plastic pot out of her pocket. "These kids I'm investigating, for my case. Found this in the girl's bedroom. The smell of it. The look of it. I dunno. I feel like it might be something . . ."

"Sinister?"

"Yeah. Right. Is that the sort of thing he might be able to test for me, do you think?"

"Hell knows. But I can ask. I'm meeting him for lunch later. Want me to give it to him?"

Jessica eyes the plastic pot and then glances up at Julius. "I dunno. What if you lose it?"

He rolls his eyes. "Whatever."

"No, but . . . tell you what, where are you meeting him? I'll bring it myself."

Julius shrugs. "Sure," he says, before giving her an address for a bistro in Soho. "One p.m.," he says. "See you then."

Jessica waves at him as he heads toward the elevator and then she turns and lets herself into her apartment. She takes the shopping into the kitchen and starts to unload it. She pulls open her fridge and is ready for that smell to hit her, the stale smell that always hits her when she opens her refrigerator. But it's clean and white and shiny and smells of spray. All her sad, half-empty jars of pasta sauce and mayonnaise have been polished and lined up neatly in the door shelves. The arrangement of ancient vegetables swimming in brown juices in the crisper has been removed, and the drawers shined and polished. There's even a gallon of fresh milk and a four-pack of green apples.

"Malcolm," she says under her breath, affectionately. "You bad, bad boy."

She makes herself a decaf coffee and sits with it at her desk, her laptop open in front of her. She takes a bite out of the protein ball and immediately spits it across the desk.

"Urgh."

She sorts through her travel backpack to find the card for the female police officer in the UK and calls the number.

It goes to voicemail, and Jessica sighs. "Hey," she says after the tone. "Jessica Jones. Have you checked Debra Phipps's ID? Sounds like the woman you have in custody might not actually be the same woman who lives there under that name. Apparently the real Debra Phipps is quite elderly. Give me a call when you get a minute."

LISA JEWELL

For the next hour she reads everything she can find on the internet about the Grace Partridge case, about Debra Phipps, about John Warshaw, trying to find the connection. She pins notes to her corkboard as she goes, and printouts of all the attachments from Malcolm's messages: the photo of the twins' reflectionless eyeballs, the shots from inside their bedrooms, the inside of the Upside Down bar and its Wiki page, articles about the Harlem Vampire, pictures of the plaque in the church in Barton Wallop, the photo of the sketch in Fox Randall's Essex bedroom, a screenshot of the Google Earth image of Debra Phipps's farmhouse, the news article about the Truscott House disappearances, and the news of Grace's discovery.

She steps back from the corkboard and stares. And stares. And stares.

What? she thinks. What is this?

She finds herself wishing that Malcolm was here; she needs someone to bounce off, because none of this makes the least bit of sense. Her last message to him is still unopened, and she sighs.

She looks again at the photo of the plaque in the tiny church and then at the flyer pinned in Lark's bedroom and at Fox's sketch, the three iterations of the child with the outstretched arms, and she thinks of Madame Web's words last night and she thinks, *It's there*, in Barton Wallop. The truth, it's in that image. It's in that village. It has to be. But where?

They can see the cathedral spire from the attic bedroom of their tiny apartment in the ancient city of Lincoln. The bells chime on the hour and each time they sound, it sends a rumble of awe and pleasure through Polly. The sound of cathedral bells aligns with her imaginings of what an adult life might look like, what it might sound like. Their flat is small, but it has character and high ceilings and beams and plush carpets and a cute kitchen with metro tiles. But most importantly, it is not a caravan.

They have moved to Lincoln for Arthur, for his degree course. His lectures start today. He is spruced and tidy and glowing with nerves. Finally, at the ripe old age of thirty, Arthur has begun his higher education. The course is called Physics with Quantum Mechanics. The University of Lincoln almost bit his hand off to offer him a place when they saw the breadth of what he'd been working on for the past two years. Polly got Arthur a grant to help with living expenses by applying to an entrepreneurial education program she found online, so not only can Arthur study, but he has his own money to live on too.

Polly goes to the front door to see him off. She straightens the collar of his shirt and smooths down his hair. He has grown into his looks, her boyfriend. She no longer looks at him sometimes and thinks, Who are you? She no longer sees the beaky lanky boy in the cheap trousers running a shoe shop in Portsmouth when she looks at him. She no longer only sees him as a way to Ophelia and her magic creams. She simply sees Arthur, her partner. And when she glimpses them together, side by side, she can see a correlation between them now; they make sense. They have grown together, almost like scar tissue, healing the bits of each other that were open wounds. It is fair to say that Arthur is the love of Polly's life, and she knows without a doubt that there will be no other. Apart from their natural compatibility, they have too many secrets. They are bound together by their mistakes.

Or *are* they in fact mistakes?

Maybe they are actually just stepping stones towards the future that Polly knows awaits them. And maybe there will have to be more mistakes to enable them to get there. And they're getting close, so close.

Her Perfect Peach persona now has nearly half a million followers on Instagram, and eighty thousand subscribers on YouTube. Arthur is going to university. They even have passports. They are normal.

Well, almost normal . . .

Because there is only so normal you can be when there are pints of blood in your in-laws' kitchen and dead bodies buried in woodland everywhere they have lived, and there's only so normal you can be when you were complicit in some of those deaths, when you waited outside your father-in-law's front door with a carrier bag for vials of blood and serum taken from his victims so that you could make expensive face cream to sell on the internet. There's only so normal you can be when your boyfriend was made to bring kids home from school for his father to torture and steal blood from, and there's only so normal you can be when your boyfriend's mother is immortal and his father drank his wife's blood every day in an attempt to keep himself alive because it's full of the innate magic that has kept her alive for a full 221 years.

They should make a film about them, Polly often thinks, a dark comedy: *Welcome to the Warshaws*.

But here, for now, in this tiny apartment with its views, her boyfriend handsome and shy in the doorway, money in the bank, dogs napping nearby, a career, followers, influence, a plan—she feels normal as dammit. She really does.

Polly closes the door behind him, feeling vicarious nerves on his behalf. Then she picks up her phone and makes a new post telling her followers that her boyfriend's gone back to school and she's feeling proud. Her followers lap it up, tell "Peach" to have a good day, they wish him luck as if he is their very best friend. They all care so much about her. In fact, they love her. And she, in her own way, loves them too.

She wants the very best for all of them. She wants every one of them to *fly*.

The dopamine pings through her system with every comment that appears under her post. Her heart fills with it. And then a comment appears that says:

> PLS PLS PLS DO A MEET AND GREET PLS!!
> I WANT TO MEET YOU IT WOULD MAKE MY
> LIFE COMPLETE PLEEEEEESSEEEEE!!

Someone replies to it a moment later, saying:

> YES! I'LL COME ANYWHERE!

And Polly feels a hot glow all the way through her. She pictures women on trains and coaches, in cars and on planes. She pictures them standing in clusters, dressed up to the nines, phones aloft, listening to her speak, queuing for selfies, leaving afterwards on a buzzy high for cocktails in town.

But then she has to delete the images from her mind's eye because that can never happen, her face will always have to be a secret because of Clara. She will have to be anonymous for the rest of her life.

It kills her, but she has no choice.

Thirty-Three

At lunchtime Jessica heads out to Soho to drop the pot of face cream with Julius and his boyfriend. They invite her to stay, but she's eager to keep working her case.

"What's the background on this?" asks Frank, Julius's boyfriend, staring down at the mint-green container in his hand. "What am I looking for?"

Jessica shrugs apologetically. "I truly don't know. I just think that there is somehow a connection between what's in this pot, the deaths of some homeless men in Harlem in the 1980s, and an anonymous beauty influencer running an Instagram account in the UK. I know that sounds nuts, but then this whole case is nuts."

Frank raises an eyebrow, skeptically. "Okey dokey," he says. "I'll see what I can do."

"How long do you think it might take?"

"Totally depends on how busy the techs are. And also, what they find. But I can try and get you some results by the end of the day? Tomorrow morning maybe?"

"Great, thank you so much. Can I give you some money? Or . . ."

"Bottle of wine would be fab," he says with a quick smile. "Or better still, champagne?"

* * *

It's just after one p.m. as she heads toward the subway, and she thinks of Malcolm leaving school soon. She checks her phone and sees that he has still not opened her message, which strikes her as odd, as he must surely have looked at his phone at points between classes. But she bats the discomforting thought away—she's sure there's a reason for Malcolm's radio silence. Maybe he had his phone confiscated? Maybe he ran out of charge?—and heads uptown.

The twins' school is in a wide beaux-arts building on East Eighty-Ninth Street, with creamy stone steps leading serenely from a busy sidewalk to handsome bronze-framed doors. It's just after lunchtime. A few students drift around the front entrance, but there is still the contained kinetic energy of a school in process. She waits for a group of students to leave and slips through the open door behind them into a clean, manicured, and inviting interior, nothing like the public schools she has visited before.

"Hi," she says, hitting the young man sitting behind the

reception desk with her best smile. "Jessica Jones. I'm a private investigator working on a child abduction case, and I have some questions for your principal, Mr."—her eye finds the name plaque on the door behind the desk—"Henri. It's about two of your students. Would you ask him if he could find the time to talk to me?"

The young man looks up at her with wide eyes, clearly keen to find out more about abducted children and private investigators. "Erm, sure, let me just see, I mean, do you have some form of ID?"

Jessica smiles tightly and pulls her plastic ID card from the pocket of her backpack.

The young man eyes it with one eyebrow slightly raised and his cheeks sucked in. "And who did you say you were working on behalf of?" he says, handing it back.

"I'm doing some investigations on behalf of the British police."

The eyebrow rises again, and she can see a small pulse of excitement popping at his temples. "Let me see what I can do." He gets up and knocks gently on the nearby door, and Jessica hears murmuring for a moment before the young man reappears and says in a very reverent tone of voice, "Mr. Henri has exactly twelve minutes."

Jessica echoes his reverence by lowering her head and saying, "Thank you so much." The young man buzzes her through into the lobby and leads her toward the office.

In his office, Mr. Henri sits to the right of a large vase of fresh pink roses, a half-eaten cake in a cardboard box behind him.

"It's my birthday today," he says with a soft French accent. "Lots of fuss. You know how it is."

Jessica doesn't know how it is, but nods and smiles. "Happy birthday," she says.

Mr. Henri nods, almost apologetically, and then says, "What can I do for you, Miss Jones?"

"Well, sir, I was hired by Amber Randall some weeks ago. She was worried about her twins, and I know that you called her in recently to talk about some concerns of your own, so I wanted to touch base as part of an investigation I'm doing with some other interested parties, including the British police."

"Wow," says Mr. Henri, stroking the edges of his tie and leaning back into his chair. "Wow, this seems bigger than I would've thought . . ."

"Maybe yes, maybe no. So tell me, I know you were concerned about them, about some kind of a *cult*? And I know that your investigation didn't uncover anything, but I wondered if you could share with me a little bit about what was happening here at that time? What sort of behaviors you were seeing?"

"Well, yes, it was very bizarre. It built up quite slowly. Last semester the twins, they were quite, I suppose you might say, average students. Well liked, but not popular. Good grades but not exceptional. And then when they returned from the summer vacation there was this kind of, I don't know how you'd say, a *rock star* aura about them. They looked very polished, very glossy. They became very, very popular, and then, well, it seemed that those who were not inculcated into this new hot clique were very put out, and I had a lot of complaints and suggestions of strange things happening."

"What kind of strange things?"

"A kind of trance state that some of the children were in, an obsession with songs and movies from the eighties, there was a song they all kept singing, it was called 'Perfect Skin,' I think. These children became more and more, well, obnoxious, I must say. Less and less engaged with school life, with the rough and tumble, just walked around staring blankly at the world, issuing this word . . ."

"Miranda?"

"Yes!" He looks at her in surprise. "Miranda. But then, it all seemed to stop."

"How long ago did it stop?"

"I'd say around the same time that Mrs. Randall came in to talk to me. Everything went back to normal after her visit. And I did wonder if maybe I'd imagined it? Or if it was one of those, what do they call them? A social contagion? Or in French we would say *folie à plusieurs*. But"—he claps his hands together softly—"now the children are just children again. They are listening to their terrible rap music and staring at their phones, and they are spotty, and they are plain, and they are bad at math." He sighs, sadly, but then he breaks into a broad smile. "And I am so happy to have them back to normal. Is there anything I can help you with, for your investigation?"

LISA JEWELL

"No," says Jessica. "But thank you. I'm so grateful for your time and your insight."

"It's my pleasure. And here . . ." He turns to the cake in its box behind him and cuts off a slice, wraps it in a paper napkin decorated with brightly colored birthday graphics, and hands it to her. "It's gluten free, but it's pretty good."

She takes the cake from his hand and smiles. "Great," she says. "Thanks. And enjoy the rest of your day."

"Fifty-two," he says with a sad smile. "I never thought I'd be this old."

Thirty-Four

Jessica doesn't leave the school immediately. With eyes on the cameras angled from nearly every corner of the building, she cuts a crisscross path through the corridors of the school, pretending to be looking for a bathroom. It's a small school, especially compared to the sprawling high school in Queens she attended, but still big enough for her not to draw attention to herself. A few students eye her curiously as she passes, and she wonders which of them were under the influence of the twins, and how. Or was it, as Mr. Henri suggested, a case of social contagion? Of the other children seeing the impact that Fox and Lark were having on the school population and simply imitating them?

She peers through windows as she goes, until she sees Lark sliding her books into her bag as her lesson draws to a close.

Jessica stands back from the door and waits for her to emerge and then follows her discreetly at a distance until she turns a corner toward the lockers and then she picks up her stride.

"Lark."

"Oh!" The girl jumps. "Er, hi." She looks around herself. "What are you doing here?"

"I was just talking to your principal about a few things."

"Right. I mean, how come?"

"I'm just trying to get a handle on things, you know, the Belle situation."

"Oh." She nods. "Right."

"Could I have a word with you, do you have a minute?"

"Yeah. I guess. I have a study period now, but the teacher never minds if I show up late." She gestures at a glass door open to a small, manicured garden area, where a couple is making out in the shadows of a conifer. They move apart as Jessica and Lark enter, giggling together nervously.

Lark sits on a bench and starts picking at her fingernails.

"So," says Jessica, "listen. I picked up on a strange vibe this morning, from your brother. Is everything okay there? I mean—is there anything you'd like to tell me? About Belle? About the summer?"

Lark's eyes darken. "Not that I know of."

"Not that you know of?"

"I mean, yeah. There were kind of . . . *things*."

"Things. What kind of things?"

"I don't know. It's just like . . ." Her gaze goes to the glass doors and around the garden and she lowers her voice. "It

320

feels like a blur now? All of it. The summer. I can't really remember most of it. But it did feel like there was something wrong. You know?"

"Can you remember the first time you felt like something was wrong?"

"Not really. I mean, at first it was just so great, Belle was so fun, and Debra was so sweet, and it was just nice to have something to do, somewhere to go, and then one day, I guess about a week in, maybe more, this guy showed up."

"Guy?"

"Yes, and he had this, like, RV? Like in *Breaking Bad*, and he pulled it up out front, and Debra definitely knew him, the dogs knew him too. And we went into this RV with Belle, and we were all playing with our phones and then—I can't remember much after that. I just know that everything felt great. And that we had the best summer ever. And then we got back to New York, and everything still felt great, but slowly that feeling faded, and the other day I realized I felt normal again, and the weird thing was that I liked it. I liked feeling normal again."

"But Fox . . . ?"

She twitches slightly. "Yeah, Fox doesn't like it. He's kinda pissy about it. He wants to . . ."

Lark pauses, watches some kids moving past a window.

"He wants to what?"

"I don't really know. I just think he's . . ."

Jessica holds her breath, waiting for Lark to finish.

"He keeps making phone calls. I don't know. I feel like . . ." She gazes up at Jessica with watery eyes. "I feel like I'm losing him." A tear slides down the side of Lark's nose and she wipes it away with the sleeve of her sweater.

Jessica touches Lark's arm, gently. "Lark," she says. "I can help get him back for you. But I need you to tell me everything you know."

"But I don't know anything. Fox won't tell me what's going on. He's cutting me out. He keeps disappearing. He's got this new friend . . ."

"Who?" asks Jessica. "Who is this new friend?"

"Some guy named Sly. We met him at boxing class a couple of weeks back. He literally came from nowhere and now he and Fox are, like, best friends or whatever. And last night, when we were meant to be home we went to Five Guys, and we met Sly there and I came home but Fox and Sly went off somewhere."

Jessica's nerves jangle like a bag of dropped dimes. *"Somewhere?"*

"Yeah. I don't know where. I just came home. But they said they were meeting someone? I don't know."

"Where is he now?" she asks. "Where's Fox?"

"He's in class, I guess."

"Which class?"

"I don't know. We have different schedules. Listen. I should go now. I've already missed ten minutes of class."

"Yeah. Sure. Of course. But, Lark"—Jessica pulls a business card out of her jacket pocket and passes it to the girl, who eyes it blankly—"please just call if you're worried about anything. Anything at all."

Lark nods and slides the card into her jacket pocket. "Okay," she says. "I will."

Jessica watches her leave then, her books tucked under her arm, her teeth chewing hard at the inside of her cheek.

* * *

Just as Jessica is leaving, she sees a familiar face. Jefferson. The boy at the birthday dinner at the Bleeding Heart, Fox's best friend.

She approaches him. "Jefferson?"

He looks at her quizzically. "Er, yeah?"

She flashes her ID card at him. "Jessica Jones. I'm a private investigator. I'm working on a case involving your friend Fox Randall. Do you happen to know where he is right now?"

"Er, yeah. I think he went home right before lunch. Said he was feeling nauseous?"

Jessica looks at the time on a clock on the wall. It's nearly two. "Are you sure he was going home?"

Jefferson shrugs. "I mean, I guess? That's what he told me, anyway."

"Jefferson—" she begins.

"Wait. How did you know my name?"

"Fox's mother told me about you."

"But how did you know what I looked like?"

She tuts and sighs. "She showed me a photo. Okay? But listen, I'm trying to find a boy named Sly. Do you have any idea where he might be?"

She sees a muscle twitch in Jefferson's cheek. "That dude,

I mean, I don't even know who he is. He just started showing up everywhere."

"Yes, but do you know where he might be right now?"

"No. I have no idea. But, like, half his stories didn't check out. He said his dad was some kind of, like, sports agent? And that he went to this public school? But Fox checked it all out, turns out he was lying. Fox was really pissed."

A chill surges through Jessica. "Really pissed when?"

"Last night. Said he was meeting up with him, was going to call him out on it."

Jessica points at the phone in Jefferson's hand. "Call him," she says. "Call Fox right now. Find out where he is."

"Wait," says Jefferson. "I mean, you don't really think he's done something?"

"I don't know if he's done something. So call him. Please."

"Okay. Okay."

Jessica watches as Jefferson brings Fox's number up and presses call.

The call goes straight to voicemail and Jefferson shrugs. "Do you think Sly's in danger?"

"Yeah. I think he might be."

"From Fox?"

She shrugs. "Yeah. Maybe."

Jefferson gulps slightly. "You know, that wouldn't surprise me. He's been acting so weird recently."

"So I hear," says Jessica, turning to leave, "so I hear."

Three Years Ago
Lincoln, UK

Polly meets Arthur for tea in a trendy café on Steep Hill. It's early autumn, but the sun is still holding its summer warmth and she's wearing a pretty dress, just the sort that Arthur likes, floral sprigs and puffed sleeves. She's wearing her hair down, as he likes it, and not too much makeup.

Arthur looks up from his laptop and smiles. He closes the lid and gets to his feet. "What would you like?"

"Just tea, please. And maybe a slice of that coffee cake."

Arthur heads to the counter, and she observes him from behind. Her student boy, he really looks the part these days. He even has friends. Curtis and Jacob. They're mature students, like him, geeky boys, in their late twenties. They go to the pub sometimes, to talk about quantum mechanics. Polly finds this quite adorable. Wholesome even. Which is funny really, given who Arthur is behind closed doors. Curtis and Jacob would never believe it if they knew.

Arthur returns with the cake and the tea on a tray and

places the items in front of Polly, before taking the tray back to the counter.

She smiles at him, then she says, in a very low voice, "I've found some."

"Some what?"

"Some . . . girls."

Arthur's eyes dart around the café, but the acoustics are terrible, and nobody would be able to hear.

She slides her phone across the table and shows him. There are three of them. They're all fourteen. They call themselves her *Peach Babies*.

"What have you told them?"

"Nothing. I'm just, you know, getting a feel for them."

"Grooming them."

She recoils. "Ew, *gross*," she says. "That's a horrible way of putting it."

He slides the phone back to her. "Well, yes, but it's true. It's what you're doing."

She can hear the disapproval in his voice. She hates it. Her cheek twitches with the effort of holding her temper. "I am *not* grooming anybody. They're fans. They're followers. They're doing what they want to do."

"They're children."

"Well, yes, and you'd know all about that."

He flinches. "I'm sorry . . . what?"

But he knows what she means. She's talking about his childhood friend, the one he lured back to his parents' chalet when he was only eleven years old at his father's behest, the one who ended up buried in the woods behind Eastney Beach and whose body was only found again ten years later.

"I didn't groom him," he barks quietly. "My parents told me I was allowed to bring someone home for tea. How was I supposed to . . ."

She shushes him. "You knew what you were doing. All you ever wanted to do was please your parents."

"Yes, and now all I ever want to do is please you. I've spent my whole life pleasing people. But this, Pol, this is too much."

Polly inhales, tries to bring herself back to sweetness. "I just need you to promise me that it's nearly ready. Okay? I won't be able to keep these girls hanging on forever. Teenagers change so fast. We need to start testing ASAP."

"It's not nearly ready. I keep telling you. It's far from ready. And Pol, you know, it might never be ready. You have to remember that."

She tuts. "You have an IQ higher than ninety-nine point five percent of the population. If you can't do this, then literally nobody can."

"And that's exactly what I'm saying. It's possible that no one can."

She grips his knee under the table with her hand and looks up at him through her eyelashes. "Arthur. Please. There must be a way. There must be something. We've come so far . . ."

He drops his gaze down to the table and then lifts it back to her. "There might be something," he says. "Something my dad once told me about. A kind of light."

"What kind of light?"

"I don't know. Someone showed it to him once, when he was traveling in Latveria."

"Whereabouts in Latveria?"

"I really don't know. He just said that it had something to do with blood and that it was meant to give people extra powers."

"What sort of powers?"

"He didn't say. But he spent years out there trying to find it and never could. They called it the blood light."

Polly gasps. "The blood light," she repeats in an awed whisper. She picks up her phone and immediately googles it. All she finds are links to a type of special effects makeup. She adds *Latveria* to her search. This brings up only one search result, a painting hanging in a gallery in Doomstadt.

"I can't find it," she says.

"Well, yes, that's because it probably doesn't exist. If my father couldn't find it, then it's safe to say it's just a fairy tale, a myth."

But Polly needs to know what this "blood light" does.

And Polly is going to find some, if it's the last thing she does.

Thirty-Five

Jessica calls Malcolm again on the street outside the school. His phone rings seven times before, finally, the call is answered.

"Malcolm!" she begins, feeling a huge pulse of relief. "Thank—"

"Oh, Jessica! I'm afraid Malcolm isn't here right now. This is Brenda, his mother."

Jessica closes her eyes. "Oh, hi, Mrs. Powder. Brenda. Do you happen to know where Malcolm is?"

"Malcolm is at school, Jessica."

"But you have his phone?"

"Yes," Brenda replies, slightly uncertain. "It's strange. He left it here this morning. Didn't take it to school. I didn't realize until just now. I just got back from work and when I walked past his room, I saw it flashing with your call."

"He left his phone at home?"

She laughs. "Yes. I think maybe for the first time ever. Teenagers. He always has his phone with him. You know what they're like!"

Jessica concurs. She does know what teenagers are like. More particularly she knows what Malcolm is like.

"Do you have any idea why he might have left it?"

"No! I have no idea! Unless maybe he has another phone that I don't know about."

"Is that possible?"

"Well, yes. It's possible. These children, the bad ones, they have multiple phones, yes? They have the, what do they call them . . . ?"

"Burners?"

"Yes, they have the burners. I don't know. He's a good boy, but he has some bad friends."

"When did you last see Malcolm?"

"Oh, last night."

"What time?"

"Around—" She stops. "Actually, no, it was yesterday morning. By the time he got home last night I was asleep."

"Did you hear him come in?"

"Yes. I mean, I think so. But he's always so quiet when he gets in. And I am a deep sleeper."

"Is his bed slept in?"

Mrs. Powder laughs softly. "How would I know? It's never

made. Sunup, sundown, Malcolm's bed always looks the same."

"Well, listen, Mrs. Powder, Brenda, if you hear from him, please will you ask him to call me, as soon as possible?"

"Jessica. Are you worried about him?"

"Oh. Gosh, no. I'm sure he's fine. I just got back from the UK and wanted a, er, debrief, that's all. Get him to call me."

"Of course, Jessica. Of course I will. And you? Are you okay?"

"Yeah. I'm okay."

"Malcolm told me about the woman in England, the one who took you hostage."

Jessica chooses not to correct Mrs. Powder's misinterpretation of the events, preferring it in many ways to the more accurate description of what happened to her. "Yeah, that was bad. Malcolm got me out of a rough spot. He's a great boy."

"Yes. He really is a great boy. I'm so very blessed to have a boy like him. Not all mothers are as lucky."

Jessica feels her stomach flip and churn at the sweetness of Malcolm's mother's pride, followed by a rush of nausea at the possibility that something bad has already happened to Malcolm.

But she has a feeling she knows where Fox might have taken him.

Thirty-Six

Jessica pulls on her beanie as she exits the subway and heads toward the Upside Down bar. Outside, she cups her hands to the windows and peers through a gap in the sheets of old newspaper taped to the glass. Nothing. An empty room with the usual debris of an abandoned space in the city. She scootches around the back of the building and tries to lift the window, but it's been locked from the inside. Beneath her feet is a manhole cover. She turns to check that nobody is looking, then lifts it off as easily as a milk jug cap and puts it to one side. She shines the light of her phone flashlight down the hole but sees nothing, just a damp tunnel leading into Manhattan's sewage system. She replaces the lid, then stands straight, rubbing grime from the knees of her jeans.

She begins weighing up her options. Should she smash a

window? Smash a wall? But no, it's clear that Malcolm is not here. And then she realizes that she is close to Luke's street, in fact only a few blocks away. It's nearly three p.m. Would he be home? She hasn't spoken to him for days. She still feels shy about Luke, what with not having told him about being pregnant with his child and all. But she could do with a debrief, a breather, a couch to sit on, a glass of water, a friendly face, a moment to take stock, away from the clamor and havoc of the Manhattan rush hour. And she really, really needs to use the bathroom. She thinks of the last time she turned up unannounced and the red-hot humiliation of finding Luke with another woman, and she sends him a message:

I'm close by and need to use your can. You home?

He replies immediately.

Here and waiting.

* * *

"Shit, Jessica, you look like hell."

"Why, thank you."

"No. Seriously. Are you okay?"

"Well, no, not really. I'm jet-lagged, my body thinks it's bedtime. And I've just walked"—she glances at the app on her phone—"twelve thousand steps since I woke up. My assistant has gone missing. My case is imploding. I've had my head messed with by some kind of super-powered witch. And all I've had to eat today is healthy food and decaf coffee. *Oh*, and according to Cassandra Webb, if I can't get to the bottom of this case, it's possible that a lot of teenagers could be injured. Or worse."

She places her hand on the inside of his door frame, falls against it at an angle, lets her head drop, and sighs. "I have had better days."

Luke smiles and leads her into his living room. He's halfway through a meal, some kind of meat with some kind of starchy carb that Jessica would kill for right now. "Sorry, I didn't mean to interrupt your—I dunno, what even is this—a *dunch*?"

"It's fine. Seriously. I'd offer you some, but this was the end of yesterday's leftovers. Can I get you anything else? I have chips and dips. I have beer?"

Jessica gazes at him, her gut churning with affection, with fear. "Chips and dips would be amazing. Thank you. And some very cold water."

"Coming right up."

She watches him across his kitchen counter. He pulls three different bags of chips from a cupboard and waves them at her. She points at one and he tips them into a bowl for her, spoons salsa into another bowl, drops ice cubes into her water. She wants to watch Luke Cage get her snacks for the rest of her life.

"This is the best thing that's happened to me all day. Actually, maybe my whole life."

She slides off her boots and massages her sore feet. She necks down the cold water and crunches the shards of ice.

"Shelves are still up," she observes, looking at the walls.

"Yup. You did a great job with the spirit level. Straightest shelves in Harlem."

He's put some books up. She didn't know he read books. There are two plants. And some photos in frames. His father in an NYPD uniform, his hat tucked under his arm, his mother holding him on her lap as an apple-cheeked toddler.

"Get you with your nice stuff."

"Well, you know, you gotta act like an adult if you wanna be an adult."

"You might be onto something there. You know, Malcolm cleaned out my fridge while I was away. He scraped mold off of it. Sprayed it. It was surprisingly profound to put food into a clean fridge."

Luke nods and gives her his fist to bump. "And you're how old, Jessica Jones?"

"Yup. But I'm growing. Slowly. I am. I just need . . ."

Her phone buzzes suddenly and alarmingly, reminding her that there is a world outside Luke's nice apartment and his bowls of chips. It's Frank, Julius's boyfriend. She mouths an apology to Luke and answers.

"Hey, Jessica?"

"Hey, Frank. Thanks for calling. Any news?"

"Yes. Just got the test results back. Are you ready for this?"

"Er, yeah. I guess."

"So, the technologist found traces of human adrenochrome in that sample. And wait for it . . . neuronal cells."

"Neuron—?"

"Neuronal cells, they're also known as nerve cells, specialized projections known as axons—"

"Literally, explain it like I'm five."

She hears Frank sighing. "Whoever created this concoction used elements of a living human brain."

Two Years Ago
Saffron Walden, Essex, UK

They're perfect. She knew they would be.

As they approach her car, Polly is a little concerned about the fact that they are all wearing the same navy uniform, it might make this meeting a little conspicuous. She hadn't thought of that. But she chose this corner of town deliberately after detailed research. No cameras, no people. It only takes one, after all, to blow the whole thing.

She throws open the passenger door and then turns in her seat to throw open the back door too. She's in her shiny gray C5, freshly valeted so it smells like a summer meadow. They look uncertain, but then they see Polly in her oversized sunglasses, her carefully applied makeup, her Dyson Airwrapped hair, and she hits them with her biggest, loveliest smile.

"Oh my God, girls! It's so good to meet you! Get in. Get in. Wow!"

They do as they're told, as Polly knew they would. She has spent over a year getting them to trust her, after all.

Polly takes all the back roads, to avoid cameras, and an hour later they arrive at the house. The girls are chatty and breathless. Polly can almost smell the adrenaline on them. They are excited and terrified in equal measure, and they are right to be.

When they pull up in front of the house, Polly can see that they are disappointed. It's not what they were expecting, but there hasn't been time to renovate and when they get indoors, Polly will show the girls the plans "Peach" has for the house that will replace this one, the house that will be 80 percent glass with a two-level indoor pool and waterfall, a home cinema, six en suite bedrooms, a circular kitchen that's eighty feet across.

The girls squeal when they see Debra's dogs and fall to their knees to greet them. The dogs jump and lick and wag, and Polly says, "They'll be your friends forever!" but does not tell them that with one small command, those six dogs would rip them all limb from limb.

One of the girls looks up at Polly. "Where is she?" she asks, brightly.

Polly gives her a quizzical look.

"Peach. Is she here?"

Polly smiles. "Not at the moment. No. But she should be here soon. In the meantime, you girls must be hungry."

She looks up at Ophelia, who is watching the girls with a sad glint in her eye.

"This is Debra," she says. "Debra is the custodian of the house. She's here to look after you all, feed you, keep you safe and cozy. Debra, this is Grace, Audrey, and Amina."

LISA JEWELL

Ophelia fixes a welcoming smile onto her face as the three girls turn to look at her. "Hello, girls," she says. "You must be hungry. Anyone want some spaghetti? I've made a Bolognese sauce. But I have pesto too, if any of you are vegetarian."

The girls get to their feet and cluster around Ophelia, drawn to her by her maternal warmth, the warmth that Polly does not exude and does not possess. Ophelia pours them drinks and tells them where to put their things, and Polly sits at the kitchen table and watches them carefully, checks for signs of nerves or regrets, checks that none of them will think better of their decision and try to persuade the others to leave.

But the girls look happy and relaxed. They join her at the table and Ophelia gives them cheese puffs in a bowl. They chatter about their lives. They talk about how much they hate school, and they talk about how much they love Peach.

One of the girls, Amina, takes her phone out of her pocket and looks at it, absentmindedly. Then she narrows her eyes and looks up at Polly and says, "Is there a Wi-Fi code?"

Polly smiles. "Sorry. We haven't had the Wi-Fi installed yet."

Amina's face falls slightly. "Oh," she says. "But there's no 4G here."

"No, we're a bit technologically challenged here."

"But how does Peach do her social media?"

"She goes into town." Polly smiles tightly, wanting to move the conversation on.

"Is that where she is now? In town?"

"Maybe," says Polly. "Probably."

Amina nods, but Polly can feel a wave of discomfort passing through the girls. She jumps to her feet. "Hey, girls," she says. "Want to try out some new samples?"

She grabs the tote bag hanging from the door handle and reaches into it, pulls out small pots of the creams that she and Ophelia made especially for today. They decanted the cream into her old Beauty X packaging; these girls are too young to remember when she was selling her brand online. She passes the pots around and says, "Go on, try these. I swear this is the most amazing serum I have ever used. Just look . . ." She turns her face towards them so that they can see the poreless finish of her complexion. "I'm thirty, you know."

She lets this sit with the girls and waits for the inevitable responses of "No way" and "I thought you were twenty" to erupt, which they do, immediately, and then she unscrews the lids of the pots and hands them around. The girls use the front cameras on their phones to apply the creams and Polly watches them, her mouth hard, praying that this stuff does what Ophelia promised her it would do.

And there it is, a few moments later, the energy in the room has changed, the girls are dreamy. Polly sees the edges of their worlds start to soften and fray. They look wide-eyed, slightly confused. The cream will make their skin look good, but it will also make them compliant and biddable. It will warp their perception of time and place. They will know that there is another life they once lived, but they won't be able to get a grip on what exactly it was. They will start to form thoughts that unravel as quickly as they begin. They will do as they're told and be happy all the time.

And whatever Ophelia engineered into this cream—and truly, Polly has no idea what's in it—it will make them feel perfect. So perfect that they will never want to leave. Not even when the bad things start happening to them.

Thirty-Seven

Jessica steps into Luke's hallway to take the rest of Frank's call, ignoring Luke's wide-eyed beseeching gaze as she goes.

"We can't even begin to establish what processes or procedures were used to make this product," Frank continues. "We've never seen anything like it before. It's complex and it's unique. And also, totally *freaking sick.*"

"Holy crap," says Jessica, leaning heavily against the wall.

"Holy crap indeed. You do know I will have to report this to the authorities. I really don't think I would have offered to let my techs bring this into the lab if I'd known, Jessica. I mean, this is shocking. The implications here are horrific, on par with cannibalism or—or *eugenics*. Where did you say this sample came from?"

"Well, I kind of *confiscated* it from a kid's bedroom. But

I'm currently investigating the possibility that the woman who made it is somehow connected to a serial killer. Google the Harlem Vampire."

"The Harlem Vampire. Wait. Why have I heard of that? Was that on Netflix?"

"No. Not yet. But I'm going to say it's only a matter of time."

"So you think this vampire guy killed people to make a face cream?"

"Yes, Frank. As wild as it sounds, I do."

Luke eyes Jessica questioningly when she walks back into his living room a moment later. He turns his hands out to her, palms up.

Jessica runs her hands down her face and groans. "Crazy case. Like I said."

"And this vampire guy you were just talking about? He was here? In Harlem?"

"Yeah. That's why I'm in your neighborhood. He worked at a bar on Old Broadway in the 1980s called the Upside Down. I was just there looking for Malcolm. But the whole thing's been bricked up or something, I don't know. I could not see a way down to the basement. And I really tried."

"You tried?"

"Yeah. I tried."

"Like, how hard did you try?"

"I mean, yeah, I looked."

"Did you try and knock down any walls?"

She shrugs, wipes nacho-cheese powder from her finger-tips. "Not really."

"How come?"

"I dunno. I just didn't feel up to it."

Luke throws her a questioning look.

She could say, *Listen, I'm just trying to protect our unborn child.* Or she could just not say that and pretend like it's not happening for a little longer. She decides to go with the second option.

"Guess I'm just a little wuss," she says, which makes him laugh. "Wanna help me find Malcolm?"

"You want me to help with your case?"

"Uh-huh."

"Seriously?"

"Yeah, why not?"

Luke shrugs. "Okay then, but I need to be up early tomorrow."

"I promise you you'll be in bed by ten."

"With you?"

"Probably not."

Luke's eyes go to his bedroom. For a moment Jessica thinks he's making a proposition. But then he goes in and emerges a moment later with a flashlight and a tool kit.

"These are the things you keep in your bedroom?" Jessica asks.

"Sure. Yeah. Why, what do you keep in yours?"

She throws him a wry smile and says, "Wouldn't you like

to know?" But then, before they can take this clumsy sexual flirtation any further, Jessica hears her phone buzz and glances at the message:

START MAKING YOUR WAY TOWARD CENTRAL PARK! . . .
THE COUNTDOWN HAS BEGUN! . . .
It's time to Meet Miranda

She shows the message to Luke.

"Cool," he says. "Let's go knock some walls down, find Malcolm, meet this Miranda chick, and save the world. You in?"

Jessica nods and smiles. "I'm in."

One Year Ago
Barton Wallop, Essex, UK

The research and development phase is going well. Arthur says he's made huge progress. He says he might have a product ready to take to the world by this time next year. It's time for Polly to start thinking about branding. And if there's one thing she's sure of, it's that Perfect Peach is not the right name for a major, world-changing, game-changing, era-defining technological development. Her product needs a mighty moniker, something immediate, something that will look imposing on billboards all over the globe. It needs to be a word that has multiple meanings, that works internationally, that trips off the tongue, something unforgettable, strong yet feminine, something that evokes an emotion, a sense of awe and aspiration.

It's all she thinks about these days. Her head, which is never a quiet place, which has been buzzing and humming with ideas and plans since the day she was born, is now deafening her in its determination to find the right name. She sees words everywhere she goes, they scroll through her mind's eye like subtitles, they hit her from left field, they repeat and repeat under her voice, as she cleans the kitchen, as she walks the dogs, until they sound like nonsense to her.

And then, one cold October afternoon, she finds it in the unlikeliest of places.

She doesn't know what sends her up the cobbled pathway that day, but she feels it might be kismet, fate, the same sort of kismet and fate that led her to Arthur and his family all those years ago. She still stares into the palm of her hand sometimes, creases and uncreases her fate line, the line that Ophelia told her only a few people have, the one that means she is special, that her life is predetermined, that she will be somebody. She is on a journey, a great, great journey, and now her destination is in sight. And there it is, the last piece of the puzzle, on the wall of the local church.

She gasps when she sees it.

It's a plaque commemorating the deaths of the children who were buried under a mud slurry in the 1400s, the children whose energy still lives on in the soil, the earth, the roots of the trees that have grown in the centuries since they passed, the children whose death imbued the land with the blood light that will one day make her product work. Their screams, their pain, their slow release of life force as they sucked in and breathed out their last, excruciating breaths are forever imprinted into the earth, the same way that the DNA of an unborn baby remains in its mother's body, in her blood and tissue, for eternity.

Finding this spot was her greatest triumph and now

poetically, perfectly, the source of the energy that is about to change the world has also given her her branding.

Engraved on the commemorative plaque is a simple etching of a child with arms outstretched to the sun. And in the inscription is the Latin word *admiranda*, which according to Google Translate means "wonder."

She closes her eyes, and she can see it. It's so simple. It's so perfect.

Her product will be called MIRANDA.

Thirty-Eight

Outside Luke's apartment, Jessica sees a group of young girls heading toward the subway. One of them has the *Miranda* flyer in her hand.

"Hey! Where did you get that?"

The girl eyes Jessica with suspicion. "Er, like in the girls' bathrooms at my school?"

"Any idea what it is?"

"It's like a pop-up meet with this influencer, I think." She shrugs.

Jessica feigns interest. "Oh yeah? Who's the influencer?"

"It's this, like, beauty reviewer girl?"

"Oh, right. Miranda?"

"Yes.

"Who is she? Who is Miranda?"

The girl shrugs. "I don't know."

"You don't know who she is?"

"Well, yeah, I mean I know who she is. But I don't know, like, exactly *who* she is."

Jessica frowns. "You know that makes no sense?"

The girl sighs. "She's just someone that everyone knows. Everyone talks about. That's all."

"And what do they say about her?"

"They say she does these treatments with, like, some kind of creams? And like, a laser? And she's launching the laser tonight. Here. World exclusive."

"A laser, huh?"

"Yeah. In your phone."

Jessica inhales sharply. "I'm sorry? A what in your phone?"

"I mean, I don't know. That's what I've heard."

The girl walks away.

Jessica looks at Luke, then pulls her phone from her pocket and switches it on. She feels that pulse of heat again and turns it off. She can't worry about this right now. She needs to find Malcolm.

* * *

After a few moments they turn the corner into Old Broadway and there's the bar, plain-faced, dark, quiet.

"This it?" asks Luke.

"Mm-hmm."

She leads him to the window around the back. Luke takes it out with his elbow and they climb through.

Luke uses his powerful flashlight to light up the interior.

"Whoa," he says, spotlighting an empty beer bottle lying on its side in a corner, the dusty bottles behind the bar, a plastic box of wine glasses. "This place has character. It's like, I dunno, like the *Titanic*. Like everyone was halfway through their drinks and then just left."

Luke is using his feet to bang at the floorboards, searching for echoes, then his fists to knock at the walls, feeling for hollows. Then he reaches into his backpack and pulls out a hand drill and starts drilling holes into the wall. After a few moments he turns to Jessica and smiles.

"There it is," he says, nodding at a section of the wall about ten feet to the right of the bar. "It's behind there." He takes up his fists, turns to bestow upon her a broad smile, and then proceeds to smash the wall into smithereens as easily as if he were smashing an avocado.

As the dust settles, she can see the outline of a doorway, and the rubble-strewn shape of a deep staircase descending.

"You ready?" says Luke.

"Uh-huh."

She follows him down the dark steps, down one level, and then down again. Jessica feels a swell of claustrophobia tighten her chest but ignores it and keeps heading down. At the bottom of the second flight of stairs is an arched entrance leading into a room twice the size of the bar upstairs. At one end are four circular tables framed by horseshoe banquettes facing toward a checkerboard dance floor. A bar runs all down one side, and there is a huge glitter ball hanging overhead that catches the rays of Luke's flashlight and sheds them down onto the dark, dusty floor, festooned with old police ribbon.

"Whoa," says Luke, sweeping his flashlight around the room. "So this isn't creepy as hell or anything. Where'd you say they found the dead bodies?"

"Under the dance floor."

Luke smiles wryly. "Of course," he says. "Where else?"

He bends down and lifts the colored tiles, revealing a short run of wooden steps into a dark crawl space. A terrible smell emanates, dark and meaty, damp and putrid. Jessica claps her hand to her mouth.

"My God," she says, under her breath, as Luke descends. "Please tell me there's nothing down there?"

Jessica stands over the hole in the ground, her mind filling with images of the young men who went missing in this room, wondering what thoughts were going through their heads in their last moments, when they realized they'd walked into a terrible trap, that they were going to die down here. She imagines people dancing overhead, under flashing lights, covered in glitter-ball sparkles, heads tossed back with joy, blissfully unaware of the suffering beneath their feet.

Then she imagines Malcolm: Malcolm following Fox down there.

She imagines calling Mrs. Powder, explaining that her one and only son is dead, and buried under a dance floor in an abandoned nightclub in Harlem, and at this thought she feels a rush of black to her head, the edges of the room start to fold in around her, her breath catches, panic envelops her. She falls to her haunches and holds her head in her hands.

"Luke!" she calls down.

"There's nothing down there," Luke replies as he ascends the steps a moment later.

Jessica breathes a sigh of relief. "Are you sure?"

"I'm very sure." He looks at her, curiously. "You okay?"

"Yeah," she says. "I'm good."

He climbs all the way out and lets the tiled floor shut again.

"You know, I'd really like to get out of here now," says Jessica, her eyes weaving around the room until the black energy in her head dies, settles like white ashes after an explosion, her breathing starts to calm, the panic subsides. And as she puts her psyche back together, she remembers another moment, not that long ago, when she felt that same black energy, that darkness, that fear.

It was in Sebastian Randall's cellar.

One Year Ago
Barton Wallop, Essex, UK

Polly pulls on her Hunters and her pink quilted Barbour and says goodbye to Ophelia, who is making breakfast for the girls.

"Where are you going?"

"To Barton Manor."

Ophelia throws her a look of disquiet. "Why?"

"You know why."

"It's too dangerous, Polly."

"I know what I'm doing. And I don't exactly have a choice."

She grabs her bag and leaves the house, walks the quarter mile to the main gates, and then waits a moment to ensure that nobody is coming down the public lane before walking out.

* * *

Barton Manor sits just at the head of the village. It's Jacobean, all leaded windows and gargoyles, with a decorative moat and a drawbridge through an arched walkway towards a huge double door framed with tumbling green ivy.

She presses a button by a side gate and a man's voice responds.

"Hello," she says. "My name is Rebecca Brown. I'm an interior designer. I wondered if I might be able to leave you my card?"

"Oh, yes, of course. There's a mail slot, just to your left."

Polly pauses. "I mean, I wondered if I might be able to hand it to you? And tell you a little about myself?"

There's a pause and then the voice returns. "Of course. Yes. Just give me a minute."

She waits, her eyes casting up and down the lane. And then there is a buzz and click, and she heads through the gate and onto the driveway, gravel crunching beneath her feet. The owner greets her on the drawbridge, a smallish man with a broad forehead, in jeans, a T-shirt, a plaid shirt open over it, paint-spattered trainers.

"Sebastian Randall," he says, holding out a hand. "Nice to meet you. Rebecca?"

"Brown. Yes." She takes his hand in hers. "Lovely to meet you too."

He appears to have no intention of inviting her in, so she peers fondly at the front door and begins the spiel she's practiced. "I'm sorry to drop in on you like this, but full transparency, I'm a Jacobean geek, it's my favorite period of architecture and I was driving past the other day and I saw your house and I could not stop thinking about it. How long have you been here, if you don't mind me asking?"

He looks at her thoughtfully and she can see that he wants to show it to her, his new toy. "Oh, just a couple of months. Starting to wonder if I've bitten off more than I can chew." He cocks his head and says, "Want a tour?"

She gasps. "Oh, my goodness, yes please. If you're sure?"

"Yes. It would be a pleasure. And it would be fantastic to hear your ideas. I'm just trying to stop it falling down right now, but at some point I'm hoping to make it look pretty too."

"Well, that I can definitely help you with."

He peers at her business card. "Do you have a website or something?"

"Not yet. Just setting it up. I only just graduated."

"Oh, what were you doing before?"

"Beauty," she says. "I still do beauty. But now I have two skill sets."

He regards her with admiration. "Good for you," he says. "Good for you."

And as he says it, she feels it, strongly, his attraction to her, and she puts this realization away for safekeeping.

He shows her the house, and she can feel how proud he is. According to her research he's a divorcé, father of two, has tried and failed to launch half a dozen careers while waiting for a huge inheritance from his parents. And he is apparently very much single.

But she is not meant to know any of this, so she smiles and says, "Do you have family here?"

"No, sadly not. My ex-wife lives with my children in New York. I don't get to see enough of them."

"Oh, that's a shame. I didn't see much of my father growing up either, he moved away with a new wife, new kids. It's tough."

They are in the kitchen now and Sebastian is talking through his plans for opening it up, installing a modern range to replace the old Aga, putting in an island, maybe some banquette seating, and she feigns fascination, makes all the right noises, but she's not really listening and she finally cuts into his monologue by pointing at a staircase through an arched doorway and saying, "What's down there?"

"Oh." He shudders slightly. "That's the cellar. I haven't been down there."

"Why not?"

"It gives me the heebie-jeebies. I think it might be haunted."

She smiles at him playfully. "Really?"

"Yes. In fact I know it is. And also: spiders. I have a terrible phobia." He shrugs and smiles again.

"May I?"

"Be my guest! You're a braver woman than me!"

She turns on the torch on her phone and heads down the narrow spiral stairs and as her feet touch the floor, she feels it: thick, black, intoxicating, just like she knew it would be.

It's there. She knows it's there. Tons of it. It chills her, but it also excites her.

"Apparently," Sebastian calls down, "this house was built

on cursed ground. Something to do with a tragedy over five hundred years ago."

"Really," she responds, disingenuously. "How fascinating. I'm surprised that didn't put you off."

"Ha! Well, I only found out about it *after* I'd paid nearly three million quid for the place."

She swings her phone light around the space. It's completely empty. But it feels full. She crouches and lays her hand against the dirt floor. She is sure she can feel it pulsing, rising and falling, like a slumbering child.

"There are no spiders down here, by the way," she calls up. "Not even any cobwebs."

"I don't believe you," he replies playfully.

"I swear!"

She takes one last look around the space, runs her hands down some piping, feels it glow beneath her hand, then ascends back to the kitchen, where Sebastian is waiting for her.

"Did you feel it?" he says.

"Feel what?"

"The ghosts. The *curse*?"

She beams at him, showing him her perfect white teeth. "No!" She laughs. "I didn't feel a thing!"

Thirty-Nine

Jessica walks to the window in her office and stares out for a moment across the street. The day is beginning to grow dark; the streetlights will come on soon, it's dry and still, a perfect night for teenagers to leave their cozy homes and cross town. Jessica can feel the dark energy building. The wrongness and the badness, the incipient chaos. But she can't figure out how to stop it. She scoots to her desk and opens her laptop and looks for updated news from the UK.

WHERE ARE OUR GIRLS? screams a headline from a paper called the *Sun*. Beneath are pictures of Amina and Audrey, who are still missing despite extensive searches of the Phipps property and grounds.

There are still no photos of "Debra Phipps" accompanying any of the news reports, but on Twitter, a woman named

Clarissa Stowe claims to have sold Debra all six of her Belgian Malinois over the preceding eight years and described Debra Phipps as an unassuming elderly woman with no interest in anything other than dogs. "She hated people, liked living alone, I cannot imagine in a million years why an elderly misanthropist would suddenly want to, or be able to, kidnap three fifteen-year-old girls."

Jessica feels answers swirling chaotically though her head, they're up there, but she cannot grab hold of them. But after a time, her thoughts are disturbed by the buzz of her phone and she glances down at it to see that her home screen image has gone, and the screen is now entirely black apart from a moving line of words scrolling across the screen in white text.

Hi, this is Miranda . . .
Thank you so much for downloading my app . . .
I'm on my way!

She rejoins Luke, who is standing in front of her corkboard trying to find a connection between the cellar at the Upside Down bar and the cellar at Sebastian's house that might help them work out where Fox has taken Malcolm. She unpins the flyer she took from Lark's bedroom and shows it to Luke.

"Look at that," she says, pointing at the QR code.

"What?"

"Don't you think that's a strange-looking code?"

Luke peers at it more closely. "I guess?"

"You know, when I scanned it earlier it made my phone burn hot in my hand."

Luke grimaces. "Seriously?"

"Yeah. And now apparently there is an app on my phone, but I can't find it anywhere. And those girls outside your place earlier, talking about a laser, in your phone?"

Luke stares down at her phone and then back up at her. "Know any geeks?"

"Well, yuh. Malcolm." She sighs. "Shit."

She picks up her phone and she calls Amber.

This Year
Barton Wallop, Essex, UK

Sebastian Randall is in love with Becky. He hasn't said it, but Polly knows it. He's beguiled and besotted by her. It's only a matter of time before he announces his feelings. Polly hasn't decided how she'll react when he does, but for now she's enjoying the attentions of a trust fund millionaire with a seven-bedroom house and a performance sports car on his driveway.

He's waiting in his doorway when Polly arrives that morning. It's a crisp January day, white clouds scudding across an acid-blue sky. His face lights up at the sight of her and he greets her with kisses to both of her cheeks.

She lets him hold her a little longer than is strictly just friendly and can feel him surreptitiously sniffing her hair.

"How are you?" he says warmly.

"Oh, I'm good. I'm fine. How was your Christmas?"

"Oh, you know. It was okay. Spent a couple of days in New York with the kids. A few days in Spain with the old folk. Nice to be back here." He gestures towards the manor house. "How was yours?"

"It was great! Thank you."

"Where did you go?"

"Oh, just stayed at home."

"Alone?"

"Yes, just me and the dogs."

Sebastian gives her that sad look that he always gives her when she mentions her tragic singleton existence.

"Oh, Becky. A girl like you shouldn't be spending Christmas Day alone. It's not right."

She gives him a wide-eyed smile. "I'm used to it, Seb. Please don't feel sorry for me. And I enjoy my own company."

Of course, it's not true that she spent Christmas Day alone with her dogs. She spent Christmas Day with the dogs and Arthur at the flat in Lincoln. They had turkey and Christmas crackers and expensive chocolates and champagne.

"You know," says Sebastian, leading her into the house, "I could have sworn I saw you going into the house up the lane the other day."

"Oh, which house?"

"The Old Farmhouse? The one with the big rusty gates?"

"Oh! Yes, you might well have. I'm doing some designs for the lady who lives there, Debra."

"Oh." His face brightens. "Good for you! Another client! That's fantastic news."

In the house he makes her a cup of tea and she shows him the mood boards she's put together for his children's bedrooms. They're visiting for the summer and Sebastian wants their rooms to be perfect. Polly, who has never designed a room in her life, has had fun over the Christmas break researching interior design on the internet and putting together mood boards that look pretty professional in her opinion.

She flicks to pages that show her ideas for their en suite bathroom and after Sebastian has made all the right noises about how wonderful it looks and how much the twins will love it, Polly says, "We'll need to check the water pressure. There's no point putting in an amazing rainfall shower if there's not enough pressure to get it up there. I have a plumber I use all the time. I saw him on the way over. He's actually in the village right now, working on another job. He could pop over now if that's okay?"

"Oh, of course. I mean, I do have my own plumber, but he always seems to be very difficult to get hold of. So yes, by all means. Give him a call."

Polly beams at Sebastian and makes the call. "Hi, it's Becky. I'm here with Sebastian Randall at Barton Manor now if you're free? Great! See you in a minute!"

* * *

Polly has to resist the temptation to laugh when Arthur appears on the doorstep a few minutes later looking very cute in work overalls and a baseball cap. He avoids her gaze and keeps a straight face as Sebastian walks him through the house. Arthur knows very little about plumbing, but then, Polly suspects, so does Sebastian.

Sebastian shows Arthur where the boilers live, in a room just behind the back door, and another one in the attic to serve the top floor.

"I'm going to need to access the cellar," says Arthur, on cue. "I think some of your pipes feed through there, I'll need to take some readings."

"Sure, yes absolutely, be my guest." Sebastian shows him to the staircase.

"I'll come down with you," says Polly. "Show you how the lights work."

At the bottom of the steps, they turn and look at each other. Polly lifts up on her tiptoes and kisses Arthur hard on the mouth.

"Brilliant," she whispers. "You are brilliant." Then she guides him across the room by the hand and says, "Can you feel it?"

He nods, nervously. "Yes," he whispers.

"Isn't it thrilling?"

He nods again and she can sense the adrenaline coursing through him.

"Here," she says, pulling a piece of chalk from her bag and drawing a circle onto the dirt floor. "It's right here. Touch it."

Arthur crouches and puts his hand to the ground. He snatches it back immediately and looks at Polly with wide eyes. He nods.

A few moments later they go back up to the kitchen.

Arthur says, "Might need to do a bit of work down there. Put in a new pump. Nothing major. Shouldn't take more than a few days."

"And that will give the kids' bathroom decent water pressure?"

"Oh yes, certainly. I can put an estimate together for you, get it over tomorrow?"

Sebastian nods and smiles. "Fantastic," he says, shaking Arthur's hand. "Thank you so much for helping to make this place great for the kids."

He looks back and forth at Polly and Arthur, completely oblivious to the irony of what he's just said.

Forty

Amber picks up Jessica's call on the third ring.

"Jessica, if you don't have news on Fox for me I'm going to the police."

Jessica inhales sharply. "You don't think it's a bit soon? He's only been missing four hours. He's sixteen years old. I'm not sure they'll be taking it that seriously."

"Well, I have to do *something*. I can't just sit here like this. I feel so helpless! And I'm sorry, Jessica, but I am paying you *quite* a lot of money and I can't help feeling there's more you could be doing, quite frankly."

Most investigations get to this point, Jessica knows, where the action isn't fast enough for the client, who has paid their money and expects results. Jessica sighs loudly. "Yup. Agreed. And I have people on the ground who are aware that we're looking for him. But short of traipsing the streets of Manhattan hoping for a glimpse of him, I'm not sure what you think I could be doing right now. Is there anything, Amber, anything you can give me that might help? Places he might be? People he might have been talking to?"

"No! Nothing! He's just been . . . *normal*. Going to school. Going boxing. Seeing his friends."

Boxing. Jessica blinks. *Boxing*. "Can I have the address, Amber, for the boxing club?"

"Yeah, er, sure, hold on, I have it just here. There . . ." She reads it out to Jessica. "You think he might be there?"

"I have no idea. But it's somewhere to start."

"Okay, well, keep me posted."

"And Amber? Have you heard anything from Sebastian? Since this all blew up?"

"Er, yeah. I have. He's feeling terrible."

"Terrible for what?"

"For letting the kids spend all their time at that farmhouse, with that Debra woman, and not checking it out. I mean, the thought of what might have happened. Those awful people. And he was saying that his 'girlfriend'"—she imbues the word with mild poison—"had done some work for the woman who lived there."

The mention of Sebastian's girlfriend sends Jessica's thoughts hurtling back to that strange feeling in Sebastian's cellar, the feeling that was mirrored just now in the cellar at the Upside Down. She thinks of Sebastian telling her about the water pump that his girlfriend "insisted on installing," to give his water system more pressure. But where *was* that water pump? There was nothing down there. Smooth floors. Pipes on the walls. Holes drilled to control the damp. But no water pump.

"Amber," she says. "I need Sebastian's number. I need it right now."

"Oh wait, I can't give you that."

"Why not?"

"Because then he'll know that I hired you to investigate him. He'll never forgive me."

"Amber, Sebastian has a girlfriend he didn't tell you about. I think that makes you even, yes?"

She hears Amber sigh. "I suppose. But please, don't mention it was me that gave you his number. Tell him it was the police or something, okay?"

"Yeah. Sure. Whatever."

She takes Sebastian's number, then checks the time in the UK. It's late over there, pushing ten o'clock, but she doesn't have time for politeness.

Sebastian picks up on the fourth ring. "Hello?"

"Sebastian, this is Jessica Jones, I met you last week at your house under the name Jessica Allan?"

"Ah yes, Jessica! Hello! I've been thinking about you."

"You have?"

"Yes. The timing of your visit to the UK, the mentions in the press of a private investigator from New York being involved with the arrests at the Old Farmhouse. Et cetera, et cetera. I had a feeling that might have been you."

He sounds slightly put out, almost hurt.

Jessica sighs. "Yeah. I'm sorry about that. I didn't mean to take advantage of your hospitality. And it was very kind of you to show me around your home."

"Well, yes. You did it with the purest of intentions, it seems."

"Yeah. But listen, there was something that was bugging me, after looking at your house. When I was down in the cellar, you told me that your girlfriend had a water pump installed down there for the upstairs showers?"

"That's right."

"But I didn't see a water pump down there. There was nothing down there at all."

"No, I can assure you that there is. It's *underground*."

"Underground?"

"Yes. They dug up the cellar floor and attached it underground."

"Why?"

There's a brief pause, and then Sebastian says, crisply, "I don't really know. I'm not a plumbing expert. Are you?"

"No. I'm not. But I do know that it seems a bit excessive to bury a water pump under a load of cement. Listen, your girlfriend, what else can you tell me about her?"

"Why?"

"Well, where is she now, for example?"

"She's away. On business."

"What sort of business?"

"Interior design business . . . I suppose?"

"I'd love to speak to her, if possible. Could you give me a number for her?"

"What for?"

"I have questions about the water pump?"

"The water . . ." He stops, and she hears him hissing through his teeth. "Are you serious?"

"Yeah, deadly serious. Your children, Sebastian," she continues, going in for the kill in an attempt to hit home with him just how messed up this situation is, "were given a key to a bar in Harlem when they were in the UK this summer. In that bar, twenty-six years ago, construction workers found the remains of three dead bodies buried under the dance floor in the cellar. They had been tortured and murdered and used for their blood."

"I'm sorry, what?"

"And I have been told that your girlfriend was doing some work at the Old Farmhouse."

"Who told you that?"

"I'm a private investigator, Sebastian. I ask people questions and people tell me things. That's how it works. So please. Let me have her number."

He breathes in long and hard and then says, "Fine."

She takes it down and says, "Name?"

"Becky," he says. "Rebecca Brown."

"Thank you." She scrawls it down. "And, Sebastian. What was she doing at the farmhouse? Did she tell you?"

"Like you said, doing some work for them."

"How long ago was this?"

"Beginning of the year, January?"

"Well, I've been in that house, and I can tell you for certain that nobody has laid a brush on that place in decades. So whatever she was doing there, it certainly wasn't interiors." Jessica pauses. "What do you know about her, Sebastian? What do you know about Rebecca Brown?"

There's a brief silence and then Sebastian says, "Very little, to be entirely honest with you. Very little indeed."

As she ends the call she looks up at Luke. She almost forgot he is here.

He looks down at her. "You okay?"

"Yeah," she says. "I'm okay."

The time is 4:52. She hauls him off the couch and slings on her jacket.

"Where are we going?" he asks.

"We're going to the Hit 'n' Fit."

"The what now?"

"You'll see."

This Year
Barton Wallop, Essex, UK

Amina and Audrey look nonplussed as they climb into the back of Arthur's van.

"Where are we going?"

"Just heading into the village," says Polly.

Amina's face lights up. "Are we going to meet Peach?"

"Not yet. No. But soon."

Amina nods, disappointed, her hands clasped tightly together in her lap.

"What's in those?" asks Audrey, pointing at the gigantic suitcases that Polly ordered specially from Amazon last week.

"Nothing you need to worry about. Now, when we get there, girls, I need you to stay really quiet. Just talk in your indoor voices and don't do anything until I tell you to. Okay?"

The girls nod and Polly shuts the back doors of the van and climbs into the passenger seat up front with Arthur.

Arthur looks grim-faced and slightly nauseous. Polly

punches him lightly on his leg and says, "Cheer up! It's finally happening! Aren't you excited?"

"No," says Arthur. "I mean, I'm happy that you're happy. But I'm not happy about those girls. Their poor parents . . ."

"Their *poor parents* sent them to bloody boarding school, Arthur. They clearly don't give a shit about them. At least they've been shown some true love and affection the last year. They've had home-cooked food and been tucked up in bed every night by someone who actually cares about them."

It's not really Polly's thing, but she has to admit it's been a little sweet watching how attached Ophelia has become to the girls over the past year and a half, how much she has loved the role of caring for them all. And they in turn have become truly attached to her. It was tough getting her to let go of these two today. Polly has never seen Ophelia cry before. But at least she still has Belle.

Now they wait at the gates of the grounds until there is nothing coming and then pull out onto the lane. The atmosphere in the van is dark and overwhelming and for the first time since she started planning for today, Polly feels a small wave of nervousness. What if it doesn't work? She can't go back to being a stay-at-home beauty influencer operating from behind a filter, she can't go back to being *normal*. Because Polly was not put on this planet to be normal. She was put here to change things, and everything that has happened since she entered Ophelia's booth on Portsmouth pier has been leading up to this moment. It was all predestined, all of it. She has brought focus and purpose to the lives of Arthur and his parents—what *were* they before? Just grifters and losers, going from caravan park to caravan park, staying under radars, keeping their incredible secrets and incredible talents hidden away instead of using them for the greater good. Whatever happens, she thinks, at least they will have done *something*.

Polly pictures glass boxes on California hillsides, full of the most brilliant minds in the world trying to work towards the place that she, Arthur, Ophelia, and John have reached in a small scruffy corner of England, and still not getting there.

But her little family has done it.

And not just that, but they're leagues ahead.

While the rest of the world is chattering about AI and the death of people's jobs and livelihoods, she and Arthur have harnessed it and taken it to the next level. Thanks to the untapped power of the blood light, the ethereal essence that lives all over the earth, living and breathing just under its surface but unknown to anyone but the most bloodthirsty, they have crashed through the boundaries of what modern technology is capable of and brought it to the next level—and beyond. Thanks to Arthur's super-boosted brain, Ophelia's magic powers, John's obsession with blood, and Polly's ruthless pursuit of perfection, they have made a product that will bring about the death of the beauty, cosmetic surgery, and fitness industries, not to mention life coaching and therapy. It will bring about total and utter freedom from the shackles of impossible beauty standards, the shackles of *inadequacy*. Imagine a world where everyone *feels good*. Where nobody feels inadequate.

Just imagine, she thinks, just imagine.

Her nerves settle as they approach Sebastian's driveway. He's out of town and has given her keys to the house so that she can oversee the work on the twins' bedrooms in his absence. There's nobody around, the village still sleeping. They park the van around the side of the house, out of sight of prying eyes, and Polly unlocks the back doors.

"We're here, girls."

"Why isn't Grace here?" asks Audrey.

"We need her at home, just for now."

"I miss her."

It's not surprising. These three girls have not spent a moment apart for more than a year.

"You'll see her soon. But before we go in, you need to sanitize your hands."

It's their daily ritual. The girls upturn their hands and Polly squirts the gel onto their palms, then they rub them together. Soon they become less inquisitive, ask fewer questions. By the time they are standing in Sebastian's kitchen, they don't know or care where they are.

"Okay then, girls, let's go." She guides them through the passageway towards the head of the spiral staircase. "This way."

Arthur throws Polly a terrible, beseeching look, a look that says *We don't have to do this*. A look that says *We can stop this right now, just say the word*.

But Polly has no intention of stopping right now.

She has only just begun.

Forty-One

The boxing club is in a basement on East 106th, below a piano shop. It has a flashing blue neon sign attached to the wall, a man wearing a boxing glove moving back and forth toward a punching bag. Underneath it says HIT 'N' FIT.

Luke follows Jessica down the steps and through the door.

Inside is hot, airless. A wiry white guy in a Hit 'n' Fit T-shirt comes toward them. He eyes Luke curiously, probably clocks him as a professional boxer, probably wonders what a guy like him is doing in a glorified fitness club like this. He pulls a clipboard from a counter by the door and says, "Hey, how can I help you guys?"

"Not here to hit and fit, sadly," says Jessica, showing him her ID card. "Jessica Jones. This is my associate, Luke Cage. We're looking for a club member, Fox Randall?"

"Oh yeah. Foxy!"

Foxy? Jessica lets it pass.

"Yeah," she begins. "He left school early today and hasn't been seen since. I just wondered if you had seen him or had any idea about where he might be. It's possible he was with this guy?" She shows him a photo of Malcolm on her phone. "He's been here a couple of times, hung out with Fox?"

"Yeah. I recognize this dude too. Can't remember his name."

"Sly. Sly McNeil is his name."

The guy nods. "Yeah. Right. I mean, they were in last week, Friday, but I haven't seen either of them since."

"And you can't think of anything that either of them might have said or done, anything you overheard? Places they might go? People they might be meeting?"

The Hit 'n' Fit T-shirt guy shrugs. "I mean, no, not really. You know, we don't talk much here. It's pretty much focused on the activity. And even if they were talking, I gotta be honest with you, I probably wouldn't be listening. I mean, teenagers, you know, they talk a ton of shit."

A young guy is standing a little away from them, and it's clear to Jessica that he has been listening to their conversation. As the Hit 'n' Fit guy heads away, he approaches them.

"Hey," he says, "were you asking about Fox and Sly?"

Jessica nods. "Yeah. You know something?"

"Yeah," he says. "Kinda. They were in on Friday, and I heard them saying something about a girl named Miranda."

"Uh-huh. What did they say exactly?"

"That they were going to meet her—*no*—that 'she is coming.'"

"Coming where?"

"Coming here? To New York? And that Fox was going to go to her place."

Jessica feels the terrible twin pangs of progress and danger familiar to this kind of case. "Her place?" she parrots.

"Yeah, I think it sounded like an Airbnb? He said something about how he had the code to get in. He asked Sly if he could come with him on Sunday night. Sly said yes."

"Good, good. And what else? Did he say anything else?"

"No, not really. Just that. Oh, and he said not to tell his sister. I mean, I just thought it was some girl shit. Or even drugs, or some such. But you think it's something bad?"

"Yeah. It might be." She passes the boy her card. "Let me know if you hear or see or remember anything. Anything at all, okay?"

"Yes. I will." He stares at the card in awe. "I'm really sorry," he says. "I wish I'd paid more attention. I wish I could tell you more."

"Seriously, you did good. Thank you."

* * *

Out on the street, Jessica calls Amber, who picks up in just under a single ringtone. Jessica puts the call on speaker so that Luke can listen in.

"Did you find him?" Amber begins.

"No. No I didn't. But I know that he was arranging to go

to an Airbnb with Malcolm last night to meet someone named Miranda."

"What!"

"Uh-huh. And I can only assume that that is where he currently is. But New York is a city of a thousand Airbnbs and I have no clue where to begin looking. But maybe Lark does? Is she there?"

"Yes. She's here. Lark! Hold on, I'm going to put this on speaker." Then a moment later she says, "Lark, what do you know about an Airbnb and a woman named Miranda?"

"What?" says Lark.

Amber sighs. "Apparently Fox is at an Airbnb, with someone named Miranda. I know you know someone named Miranda, Lark. I've heard you talking to her in your room."

"I have not."

"Yes, honey, you have. Why would I make something like that up? And you have that flyer in your room. The one that says MEET MIRANDA. So come on, just tell me. Who the hell is Miranda and why would Fox have gone to her Airbnb?"

"I literally don't know, okay. I just know that she's a beauty influencer, from England. And that she's over here launching some kind of new product. And that Fox is helping. But that's all I know."

"Fox is helping. But why?"

"Because of Belle."

"Belle—the girl in England? The one he liked?"

"Yes. That one."

"But she's not even named Belle, remember, she's named

Grace. And she's been rescued. She's in the hospital, being taken care of. He doesn't need to help her anymore."

"Yeah, well, I know that, and you know that, but he doesn't seem to care. He seems to think that Belle is really the girl he thought she was and that that Jessica woman had her abducted by the police against her will—*I dunno*, it's like he's turned into some kind of conspiracy theorist. It's because he's in love with her."

"With who? With Miranda?"

"No! He's in love with Belle! He can't accept that she might not be who he thought she was when he fell in love with her. And I don't know anything else."

"So you don't know where this Airbnb might be?"

"I have no idea. But why don't you look on his laptop?"

Jessica exchanges a look with Luke and then says to Amber, "Fox has a laptop at home?"

"Yeah, I think so."

"Just wait there, Amber. We're coming straight over."

* * *

As she and Luke stride down Lexington toward the Randalls' building, Jessica notices more and more young people in the area, staring at their phones, looking lost and out of place. A few clutch MEET MIRANDA flyers in their hands. She glances at the time on her own phone and sees that it is coming up to six p.m. She feels a small shiver of panic as the day starts unraveling into night and she is still no closer to finding

Malcolm, let alone stopping whatever the hell it is that Madame Web told her she needs to stop.

She starts to walk faster and Luke steps up his pace to keep up with her.

"Slow it down, Jessica, you're gonna run someone down."

In Amber's apartment, she directs them to Fox's bedroom, where Lark has taken Fox's laptop from a drawer under his desk and opened it up. Jessica stands over the desk and waits while Lark inputs his password.

"You know his password?"

"Of course," she says. "We're twins."

The screen comes to life and Lark goes to Fox's browser and selects his browsing history.

She scrolls down and Jessica sees at least a dozen searches along the lines of *Sly McNeil* and *Sly McNeil father*, and *Sly McNeil Robert F. Kennedy School*. And then finally, *Sly McNeil Jessica Jones*.

"Shit," says Jessica. "He was really onto Malcolm, huh?"

"Yup," says Lark, scrolling down further. "Looks like it." She glances up at Jessica. "Who is Sly, then? Really?"

"He's just . . ." Jessica and Luke exchange a look. "He's just a dude I know. A kid. A good kid."

"So why was he lying about his identity?"

"He was helping me."

"Helping you what?"

"Helping me find out what happened to you guys in the UK."

"Right." She nods distractedly, seemingly satisfied with

this response. "Anyway, there's nothing in his browsing history about Airbnbs. So"—she switches screens—"let's take a look at his online banking."

"How are you going to get into that?"

"I told you. We're twins."

She tries two or three passwords before she finds the one that works.

She moves out of the way so that Jessica can view the screen fully.

"There," Jessica says. "He bought something from a bodega on Amsterdam Avenue, just under half an hour ago. Let's see where that is." She switches tabs and searches the area on Maps.

"There," she says again, pointing at the screen. "There it is."

And then: "Hold on. Can you just zoom it out a little? And over to the left."

Jessica waits as Lark follows her instruction, and then points and says, "Look! That's Old Broadway. Just there. He's right near the Upside Down. Can you do a search for Airbnbs in that area?"

"Sure. Give me a second." She brings up the Airbnb website and types in the area and scrolls down the results. There are six in the vicinity. When she types in the day's date, three of them show as being booked up.

Lark clicks on the pages of each of the three booked-out properties. "Recognize any of these?" Jessica asks Luke.

He peers at the screen, then moves into Lark's seat so that he can examine the photos himself. "Yeah," he says, "I know where this place is. It's just by the church on Convent. And this one, yeah, this one looks like it's in one of the apartment blocks on West 129th. And this one is a street up from there, I think."

"Would you recognize them if we went there on foot?"

Luke shrugs. "Yeah. I bet."

"Right. Let's go."

Lark grabs her arm. "Can I come with you?"

Jessica looks at Amber.

"No, Lark," says Amber. "It's not safe. We need to stay here and wait for Fox in case he's coming back."

"But I can help," Lark says. "You know what we're like. How we can sense each other. I can help find him . . ."

"No. You're staying here."

"But, Mom. He's more likely to talk if I'm there. Less likely to run. I can persuade him to come home. Please. Just let me try."

Amber sighs. "Fine," she says. "But stick with Jessica and Luke and do everything they tell you. Okay?"

Lark nods. "Okay."

Three months ago
Barton Wallop, Essex, UK

From her hidden office at the back of the farmhouse, Polly hears the dogs barking. She swivels in her chair so that she can see the monitor that correlates with the camera by the front gates, and there they are, Sebastian's twins, waiting in the lane with their bicycles, looking around uncertainly.

She hears Ophelia greeting them over the intercom and then she hears the girl replying, "Hi. My name's Lark. I'm with my brother, Fox. We just arrived here for the summer and our dad's friend told us that there was a girl here named Belle?"

"Yes. That's right. Did you want to speak to her?"

"Er, yeah, sure. If that's okay?"

"Of course it's okay! Come in, come in. Follow the driveway around to the right, it's about a quarter of a mile. And ignore the dogs, I'll get them to back off."

Through the speaker, Polly hears the dogs start to settle. Then the lock clicks and the gates separate and the twins pass

384

through with their bikes. She swallows down a sharp breath of nerves. They're here. This is it. The final hurdle. She has four weeks before Fox and Lark head home to New York. Four weeks to be certain that the app really does work. And what better people to test it on than two gorgeous American teenagers who will take Miranda four thousand miles away. If it still works in NYC, then it will work everywhere.

She turns to face the monitors that display views of the kitchen and the hallway. A few minutes later, she sees the twins walk in and Belle get up from where she was sitting at the kitchen table.

"Hi," says the girl twin. "I'm Lark."

"Hi," says the boy twin. "Fox Randall. Happy to meet you."

"Hi," says Grace. "I'm Belle."

"And I'm Debra," says Ophelia. "Belle's family live abroad, so I take care of the house and of Belle during the holidays. Sit down, you two, let me get you something cold to drink, it's so incredibly hot out today. What would you like? I have Cokes, Sprites, juice, fizzy water?"

Polly stares into the faces of the twins on her screen, looking for physical responses to the setup they've walked into, but she can tell they're simply beguiled: beguiled by the cutesy *old-world* charms of the farmhouse, beguiled by the beauty of Belle, the warmth and kindness of Debra, the herd of handsome dogs panting at their feet looking for ear scratches.

Ophelia hands them all ice-cold Cokes and they chat for a

while before Ophelia says, "Why don't you take the twins outside to show them your new quad bike, Belle?"

Polly waits until she sees the three children leaving the kitchen on her monitor before sliding back the fake wall that separates her quarters from the back of the house and heading towards the kitchen.

Ophelia glances at her coolly as she walks in. "Well," she says. "They came. Now what?"

"Now we just wait and see."

Ophelia shrugs. "I don't like this."

"No," says Polly. "I know you don't."

"They'll talk, Polly. They're bound to. And people will ask questions. As far as the village is concerned, Debra Phipps lives here alone."

"They're not going to talk to anyone in the village."

"You don't know that."

"I do know that. Sebastian is totally antisocial, and so are the kids. But anyway, you can control what they remember, you can control what they say. You have the power."

"Well, I only wish that were true. I wish I could make you do what I want you to do."

"You could overpower me if you could be bothered."

"I don't have the strength, Polly. Not anymore. I'm too old and you're too strong."

Polly sighs and looks at Ophelia affectionately. "Ophelia, I'm just a girl. A mortal. How can I ever be stronger than you?" She sighs again. "I can't believe you're the same girl John told me about in that bar in Harlem all those years ago. That sexy, powerful girl who excited him so much, who turned his world upside down. And now you're happy to get old, to shuffle off, to leave this world the same way you found it when you go."

"Don't you see, Polly, don't you see? I have Arthur. That's my super-power now. It's in him, all of me is *in him*. I wanted more than immortality, more than youth, more than power. I wanted a child, Polly, even if it cost me everything. But you don't understand that, and I don't expect you to."

"No, Ophelia, I really don't understand it. If I'd been born with your gifts, your powers, I'd have turned the world upside down with them. I mean, you only managed two hundred years? I'd have been going strong at a thousand and still wanting more."

Ophelia shakes her head. "You have no idea," she says, "no idea what it's like to see everyone you love die. To never grow up. To see the same shiny twenty-year-old face staring at you from a mirror every single day of your life. To never feel the visceral skittishness of time passing too fast, the fairground ride of life zooming by. We were not designed to be here forever. This world is not designed to trap souls for infinity, like butterflies behind glass. This world was designed for a good time, not for a long time. Its pleasures fade after a while, and they are meant to. We are meant to leave this world wanting more of it. But . . ." She sighs. "No, Polly, I don't expect you to understand. You and I are very different creatures."

"We are, Ophelia. We really are." Polly tips her head at her, sympathetically. "I can't believe what you gave away."

"No, what you don't understand is what I got in return."

LISA JEWELL

"I don't need a child. Miranda is my child. Miranda is my *baby*."

"And you're taking *my baby* down with you to achieve your goals. And all those other babies. I should kill you, that's what I should do."

Polly feels a thrill of adrenaline pulse through her at these words. "You really should, Ophelia. Why don't you? You could do it right now. You've still got enough power left. Do it." She holds her breath, her eyes flashing, her arms folded tight across her chest.

She sees Ophelia deflate, as she knew she would.

Because Polly holds all the cards.

Polly has Ophelia's secrets, and Polly has her son.

Forty-Two

As they head back up to Harlem in an Uber, Lark is compulsively chewing the inside of her cheek and picking at the skin around her nails.

"You know," says Jessica softly as she observes these nervous tics, "you didn't do that before. When I first saw you. Can you remember that? Being so still and calm all the time?"

Lark shakes her head vaguely. "Kinda. I mean, yeah. I remember what it felt like then, feeling so happy all the time, feeling so chill. But I don't remember anything else. All the, like, detail. I mean, it's hard to explain."

"It certainly is," she says, throwing Lark a knowing look.

Lark says, "Wait. Did it happen to you too?"

Jessica nods. "Yup."

"So how did you shake it off, so quickly?"

"I, er . . ." She glances at Luke, but he's staring at his phone, doesn't seem to be listening. "I've had experience before of that kind of thing. My system was kind of ready for it, I guess. Knew what to do."

Lark nods. "What happened to you? Before?"

Jessica clamps her mouth shut. She doesn't want to say any more and she's grateful when her phone starts buzzing alongside Lark's. They both pull their phones from their pockets and stare at their screens.

Your one-hour countdown has begun . . .
Get ready to . . .
Meet Miranda . . .

Jessica looks at Lark. "So, you scanned the code?"

"Yeah."

"And? What is it?"

"I don't know," says Lark. "I swear, I have no idea. I can't even remember doing it. Not really."

"Who made the flyers? Was it Fox?"

"I don't know. I mean, it might have been. He's really good at drawing."

"Can you remember who gave them to you?"

"No. I don't. It's just, like, we were getting ready to leave the UK and I was packing my bag and they were in there, and I just kind of accepted that they were in there. And I just sort of knew I was meant to spread them around."

They get out of the Uber on Convent, next to the church,

and head toward the block that Luke recognizes from the Airbnb photos. On the panel outside there are twelve buzzers. Jessica looks at Luke and Lark, shrugs, and presses a button at random. "Er, hi," she says to the person who responds. "*Police*. I'm looking for an Airbnb on this block, do you happen to know which number it is?"

"No clue."

The resident ends the call and Jessica presses another bell.

It takes a full ten minutes of pressing buttons and talking to residents to establish that the Airbnb is apartment number 12 and that whoever has booked it has been living there for three months and has two small children and a dog.

Jessica sighs and leads them all to the next address. As they approach, Lark stops and stares up the building. "He's here," she says. "He's definitely here."

This building has closer to forty buttons on the panel outside, and Jessica looks at Lark and says, "Which one should I press first, then?"

Lark rolls her eyes. "I'm a twin," she says, "not a Find My Phone app."

As she says this someone exits the building and the three of them slip inside before the door shuts again.

Jessica and Luke follow behind Lark as they work their way through the halls, looking for a door that correlates with the door in the photos.

"Any spooky twin feelings?" Jessica asks Lark, but Lark just shrugs, apologetically.

Then a door opens suddenly farther down the hall and an

old woman appears, holding a Yorkshire terrier close against her chest. "What are you doing?" she asks accusingly, eyeing up the three of them with barely disguised distaste.

"We're looking for the Airbnb," says Jessica, pretending to be looking for something on her phone. "The owner seems to have given us the wrong details. He said it was on this floor, but . . ."

"That'll be the place at the very end. Number 356. Please though, tell me you're not planning a party up there."

Jessica smiles, reassuringly. "Oh no," she says. "No. We're just having some family time. We'll be super quiet."

"Good," says the old woman. "They ought to arrest the owner. Rentals like that are *illegal*. You get all sorts renting them out. All sorts. No respect for their neighbors . . ."

But Jessica is already walking away from the woman, calling out her thanks as she goes, heading toward the doors at the end of the hall.

Number 356 is the middle of three doors and bears an undecipherable tag in purple spray paint. Lark nods, eyes wide. "He's definitely in there," she says. "I can feel him."

Jessica steps forward and knocks. There is no response. She looks at Lark. "You sure?" she asks.

Lark nods, then knocks herself. "Fox. It's me. Let me in." She puts her finger to her lips and steps back. Then a moment later the door opens, just a crack.

"What the hell, Lark?" It's Fox's voice. "What the hell are you doing here?"

"What the hell are *you* doing here?"

"I'm just . . ." Fox peters off. "Nothing."

"Can you let me in, please?"

"No. I can't."

"Why not?"

"I just can't, okay?"

Lark turns and looks at Jessica and Luke and then stands back.

Jessica backs away from the door, then hurls herself at it. It splinters apart and she tumbles into the tiny apartment, followed by Luke and Lark.

"What the hell!" yells Fox, backing away from them and toward a small desk in the window, where a man sitting in front of two computer screens stares at them in horror.

"*Where's Malcolm?*" Jessica yells.

"Who the hell is Malcolm?" says Fox, cowering away from her.

"*Sly,*" says Jessica. "Where's *Sly*?"

She sees fear pass across Fox's face and feels her stomach dip and plunge into icy terror.

"What have you done to him, Fox? Where is he?!"

Then she sees his eyes go to a door to his right and she flings open the door and there's Malcolm, tied to a bed frame, gagged and bound and staring at her with bugged-out eyes. He wriggles and tries to call something out and Jessica rips the gag from his mouth, pulls open his wrist ties and leg ties, and in a voice filled with a frankly surprising level of emotion she says, "Are you okay?"

He nods, his brown eyes wide, his crazy bleached hair on

end, and she feels relief subsume her from the top of her head to the soles of her feet, and then a wave of something else that she has a horrible feeling might be maternal affection. She shakes it off and makes herself hard.

"Call your mom," she says brusquely, handing him her phone. "Tell her you're okay."

Malcolm takes the phone from her, his eyes still wide, and she leaves him there to make the call.

She walks back into the living room to find Luke strong-arming the guy who'd been sitting at the desk.

"Who are you?" she asks.

"I'm nobody," the guy replies, breathlessly.

His accent is English. He has brown hair, a slightly beaky face, very thick-lensed glasses, a pallid complexion.

"Nobody who?" asks Jessica.

"Literally nobody. I promise."

She glances at the screens on his desk, and then her eyes take in more details of the apartment. A small dining table covered with cell phones all plugged into a weird black box, three computer monitors and two laptops. There are piles of paper and empty paper coffee cups. A pizza box containing crusts frilled with bite marks sits open on the floor. The room smells dark and putrid, like the ass end of a dirty-hot summer's day.

In the kitchenette area is a sink full of plates, a trash can overflowing with garbage, more cell phones plugged into the wall; a plug from the wall connects to another big black box on the floor, which has a cluster of red charging cables hanging out of it. She touches the big black box and recoils slightly at the heat of it against her skin, the fizz of black energy it sends through her nervous system. Then she looks at the two screens on the man's desk and sees that one of them is divided into four windows, three of which display what looks like a view of Central Park. The other screen is dark.

"Malcolm," Jessica calls out. "Get out here."

He appears, sheepishly, and hands Jessica back her phone.

"Right," says Jessica, looking at Fox. "Are you going to tell me what the hell is going on here?"

"Nothing."

Jessica growls. "Nothing! Nobody! Geez." She turns and looks at Malcolm. "Please," she says. "Tell me something that makes sense."

"Shit, Jessica. I mean. I've literally been tied up in there for twenty-four hours. I wish I knew what the hell was going on."

"Okay, well, I need you to take that big brain of yours, sit your butt down here, and tell me what you can see on these screens."

The beaky guy struggles against Luke and Luke slaps him onto a chair and ties him down with some zip ties from a pile near the chargers.

"Don't touch those screens!" the guy yells out. "Don't touch anything!"

"Who is this?" Jessica asks Malcolm.

"I swear I don't know. He was just here when Fox brought me here yesterday. There weren't exactly any introductions."

"Lark," she says. "Find this dweeb's passport." Then she

turns back to the guy tied to the chair and says, "Who's Miranda?"

"I've never heard of her."

Jessica pulls the flyer from her jacket pocket, unfolds it, and shows it to him.

"See, I scanned this stupid code earlier today and ever since I've been getting weird messages from someone named Miranda telling me to come and meet them tonight. In Central Park. And for some reason you have a ton of cameras up in Central Park. So. Let's try again. Who are you? And who is Miranda?"

Lark steps toward Jessica then and hands her a passport. It's a British one. Jessica turns to the back page and sees a photo of the dweeb guy.

His place of birth is Portsmouth.

His date of birth is July 1990.

His name is Arthur Maximillian Simms.

"Fox," says Lark, turning to her brother, who has been standing with his back pressed against the wall since they burst in, looking dazed and shell-shocked. "Talk to me. Please. What the hell is going on here?"

He lowers his eyes and shakes his head. "Go away," he says softly. "Please just all go away."

Lark steps toward him and lays a hand on his arm. "Please. Fox. Whatever this is, it isn't good. Surely you can see that?"

"It *is* good," he says. "It is good. It's going to help everyone. So please, don't try to stop it." His voice cracks as he speaks, and he sounds on the verge of tears.

Then everyone falls silent at the sound of a ringtone coming from one of the phones on the dining table. Jessica puts a finger to her lips and crosses the room to press answer. The name *Pol* is on the screen, alongside a photograph of a heavily made-up, very pretty young woman with blond hair and her face pressed up against that of a beardy dog. Jessica presses speakerphone and indicates to the man named Arthur Simms that he should reply.

"Hi!"

"Arthur? Are you okay? You sound weird?"

"I'm fine. I'm good. You okay?"

"Yes. All good. I'm on my way into the park. I just wanted to check in."

"Yes. All good."

"Why am I on speaker?"

"Just, er . . . Can I call you back, in a minute?"

"Yes. Sure. Speak to you soon. Love you."

"Love you too."

The call ends and Jessica looks at Lark, who is staring at Arthur's phone in shock.

"That's her," Lark says, pointing at Arthur's phone. "That woman who just called. It's Becky, my dad's girlfriend."

Jessica looks from the phone to Arthur and then back again.

"Wait. Are you sure?"

"I'm totally sure. I recognized her voice as well. It's her."

Jessica throws a hard stare at Fox. "That true?"

Fox shrugs. "I didn't see," he says, sulkily.

Jessica hits the screen to bring "Pol's" contact details up and shows it to Fox.

He shrugs again. "Yeah," he says, "I guess."

"What the . . . ?" Her head spins with it all. "Hey," she calls over to Arthur. "What's going on? Why are you telling Sebastian Randall's girlfriend that you love her?"

"Because she's *my* girlfriend." He sounds almost proud; there's a triumphant tip to his chin.

"You know your girlfriend is sleeping with their father, right?" She nods in the direction of the twins and sees Arthur flinch, his Adam's apple bobbing dryly up and down his long neck.

She shudders, trying to assemble the broken parts into one complete piece. Sebastian's girlfriend is also Arthur's girlfriend. She, using the name Rebecca Brown, put the water pump in Sebastian's cellar. She told the twins to go to the Old Farmhouse to meet Belle. And now she is in NYC telling some random dweeb that she loves him and heading into Central Park, where . . . "Wait a minute," she says, as an unwieldy thought explodes through her skull. "Is this Pol, Becky, whatever her name is—is she *Miranda*?"

The Adam's apple bobs again. She turns to Malcolm. "Find me something on these screens. Find me *anything*."

Malcolm turns his attention to the screens and then he stops as an image appears in the dark window. "Er . . ." He looks back at Jessica and then to the screen again. "What the hell . . . ?"

Jessica moves closer to the screen. Her eyes try to make

sense of what she's seeing but her head tells her it can't be true.

It's a CCTV view of a dark space. At first it looks like an unlit, empty room. But as she stares at the image, she sees something, the same thing that Malcolm has seen.

Two pairs of wide, staring eyes.

Forty-Three

Jessica snatches the mouse from Malcolm's hand and uses it to move through the images on the screen. There are more shots from inside the weird dark space. One of them shows the outline of two people held inside what looks like some kind of canister. Another shows wires and tubes attached to the canister.

"What the hell?" Jessica turns to Arthur.

He hangs his head, and then suddenly and dramatically and quite shockingly, he begins to sob. "It wasn't me!" he says, in a shrill, girlish tone. "None of it was me! It was . . ." He stops and draws in his breath noisily.

"Polly?" asks Jessica.

He nods, and sniffs noisily.

"What is Polly doing, Arthur? And who are those people?"

"I can't tell you!"

"Arthur. Seriously. Whatever hold it is that Polly has over you, I need you to put that to one side right now and tell me what's happening. What is she doing in Central Park?"

"She's launching Miranda."

"But what the hell *is* Miranda? I thought she was a person."

"No, it's not a person. It's an app. All those people heading to the park? It's already on their phones. They downloaded it when they scanned the QR code on the flyer."

"But what does it do?"

"It's . . ." Arthur sighs. "It's meant to put a filter on you in the real world. It's meant to make you perfect."

Jessica feels a chill as she remembers her hours in the Old Farmhouse. "But how? How does it work?"

Arthur inhales deeply. "Do you know anything about quantum physics?"

"Do I *look* like I know anything about quantum physics?"

Arthur considers her for a moment and then shakes his head. "What about AI?"

"Again, no. Please just tell me in the most basic language you possess."

He casts his gaze around the room for a moment, and then snaps his fingers. "Dorian Gray."

"Dorian . . . ?"

"He's that dude in the book who had his portrait in the attic?" says Luke. "Right? Stopped him from aging?"

Jessica throws Luke a look, then thinks back to all those

books she saw on the new shelves in his apartment and gives a small nod of respect.

"Yes. Exactly. The portrait in the attic absorbed Dorian Gray's defects. It sucked them away. The Miranda app, it changes the light on the flash when you take a selfie with the front camera. The light, it's called blood light, it's existed on the earth for thousands of years, ever since human beings first started to experience grief and pain, it permeates your neurons, it infiltrates them, then expels your defects, every single thing that you don't like about yourself, and hurls them across the universe into a receptacle."

"A receptacle?"

"Yes. A . . . repository."

"What kind of repository?"

"Well, that's the thing." He licks his lips, and she sees that bony Adam's apple bobbing up and down again.

"The thing, Arthur? What the hell do you mean by '*the thing*'?"

"I mean, that's the bad thing. Because we tried making this work with inanimate objects. But it didn't. And we tried making it work with animals. And it didn't. And then we tried making it work on a human being. And it did. It worked!"

He looks animated for a moment, excited almost. But then his demeanor changes and he sighs. "But not for very long because the human being we used was old. She couldn't absorb that many defects. Her body gave up. And then we realized we needed young bodies. I mean, young people. That they were more . . . absorbent?"

"Oh my God," Jessica growls. "You're talking about people here, not freaking paper towels. And this"—she points at the screen, the two pairs of staring eyes—"these are the young bodies?"

Arthur gulps dryly and nods.

"So that's . . . ?" Jessica shakes up her thoughts, tries to get them to sit in a straight line. And then it hits her, hard, like a donkey kick to her gut, and she pulls out her phone and she calls the female police officer in England, her heart racing as she waits for her to pick up the call. "Pick up, pick up. Shit. *Pick up!*" But the call rings out to voicemail and she ends the call with a guttural yell. "Shit!" she says, looking at the two pairs of eyes staring into the darkness on the monitor.

She calls Sebastian. The call rings out. It's late in the UK. It's so late. Nobody's answering their calls. She scrolls through her contacts and then hits the number for Elliot. It rings twice before he answers.

"Oh thank God, Elliot. It's me, Jessica. I need you to do something for me, I need you to call 911, or whatever you have over there, and get them out to Barton Manor. And I need you to go over there right now and wake up Sebastian and tell him that he needs to get into the cellar and find a way to dig up his water pump. Whatever it takes. Right now."

"Is this a joke?"

"No, Elliot, it is not a joke. Seriously. Please do it now. There are lives at stake."

"Okay, well, I currently have my pajamas on, so I'm going to have to get dressed."

Jessica groans. "Just *go in your pajamas*. Just run, Elliot. *Run!* And call the cops while you're on your way."

She ends the call and looks at Arthur. "How can we stop this?"

"We can't. Polly has the controls now. The only person who can stop it is her."

Jessica looks at the time on her phone. It's twelve minutes to seven. The park is at least an hour from here on foot. Twenty minutes in a cab, probably longer at this time of night. She closes her eyes slowly and sighs. There is a way for her to get there in under five minutes, but she hasn't done it for a long time, and she doesn't even know if she can, or equally if she should. But then she thinks of Amina and Audrey, buried under cement in Sebastian's cellar, kept alive by God knows what dark, godforsaken magic, and she sees her daughter's face in her dreams, that serious tilt of her head, that firm set of her chin, her arms folded across her chest saying, *You need to get out of here. You have a job to do, lady*, and she zips up her jacket, tucks her phone deep inside her pocket, ties back her hair, and heads out into the night.

Now
SummerStage, Central Park, NYC

Polly stands in the shadows in her mask and dark glasses, watching as the children arrive. It's a perfect October evening: mild and dry, the sky just turned dark, the streetlights on gold-dipped trees making a fairy tale of the city. She is completely anonymous here, a small woman in black, tucked out of sight. Nobody would give her a second glance. Nobody would know that she is about to become the most powerful and influential woman in the world. After years hiding away in caravans and secret rooms, behind filters and pseudonyms, she is finally going to show herself to the world. She will step on that stage and rip off this mask, take off these glasses, and be Polly Devereux. At last.

She tries to do a rough head count, but every time she thinks she knows how many people are here, another hundred or more arrive, and at ten to seven she gives up trying. Arthur had sounded weird on the phone just now, she wants to call him back, but it's getting close now, she needs to pay attention and her blood is full of adrenaline, her heart is thumping with excitement, she needs to focus, fully.

This is it, she thinks to herself, this is what her whole life has been leading up to, since she was a young girl. She is about to become the greatest beauty influencer of all time, the greatest businesswoman in history. And not only that, but she is about to change the world forever. It won't take long until every single kid in the Western world signs up for Miranda. It won't be long until everyone in the world is perfect.

And being perfect is so much more than looking good. Being perfect gives people the chance to focus on other things, not just their imperfections. So now the kid struggling to master the A chord on the guitar his dad bought him for Christmas—he gets it, he moves on to the next chord, he gets that. He'll be playing like Jimi Hendrix within a month. The girl who currently sets her alarm at five a.m. to give herself time to contour and blend and stick on false eyelashes, she'll be free to sleep an extra hour or use the time to do something meaningful instead. All the time that is wasted every minute of every day in the pursuit of perfection, of self-improvement, of trying to live up to other people's natural-born genetic advantages, all that time could be used for good. It's the dawning of the age of wonder. Imagine that: everyone free of the shackles of inadequacy, a whole generation free to be philosophers or storytellers or cooks or nurturers . . .

So who'll clean the toilets?

That's what people always ask when utopia is on the table as a theoretical option.

Who'll clean the toilets?
Who'll take away the rubbish?
Who'll look after the ill?

And that's the thing, if everyone is good at something, if they look in the mirror and love what they see, if they lift the lid of a piano and play beautiful music, if they look into the sky and see nothing but beauty and wonder and joy, then that will feed into the jobs that they do. There will be no resentment in the world of Miranda.

Obviously, every brave new world has to find its feet, there'll be teething pains, cracks in the walls. It's not quite perfect yet, Polly knows that. But this is it now, Miranda is here, and by the end of the night it will be as ubiquitous a word as Apple, as Google, as Netflix. It will be, if it is not already, the most important development the world has ever seen.

Polly thinks of the girls in the cellars as heroines, not victims. What a chance they have been given, what a role they are playing, their parents should be proud, their parents *will* be proud.

She goes to the app on her phone, and she presses Launch Miranda. The Miranda logo appears huge on the screen, the crowd goes silent.

It's happening.

Forty-Four

Manhattan looks like abstract art at this speed, random streaks of red, gold, white, amber, people's faces stretched and contorted into snapshots of shock and awe, snatched fragments of voices—"Hey, lady," "What the . . . ?" "Holy shit"—as she passes, her legs white hot, her chest burning, her nostrils stinging with the ferocity of the air being inhaled and exhaled, her throat tight and hard as she yells out to people in her path, "Move it," "Move!" "Out of my way!" Her eyes stream and her nose runs. Her blood feels viscous, her breath feels acidic. All of her hurts, all of her stings—

And then there is the park in front of her, and a snatched glimpse of a clock on a building tells her it is 6:53, she has a mile and a half to go, she picks up her speed, makes her body work harder, harder than it's ever worked, she's never run this far before, and she's never run with another human being buried inside her soft, gentle spaces and she talks to her daughter as she goes. *I'm doing this for you*, she says, *I'm doing this for you*.

She sees the swell of a small crowd ahead of her, sees it growing bigger, ribbons of people heading in from all sides of the park and she knows that she is only just in time and as she nears the summer stage, as she finally slows and feels her engorged heart throbbing under her ribs, her pitiful lungs heaving as they slow, she looks and sees a screen and on that screen she sees a woman's face and it is the most beautiful face she has ever seen. She is captivated for a second, until the woman on the screen opens her mouth and says the words:

"Hands up—who wants to be perfect?!"

A thousand hands with cell phones in them go up, and then from the left side of the stage a small figure appears, and the crowd goes berserk. She's wearing a mask and a hat. She has long blond hair and is wearing fitted leather boots to her knees, tight trousers, and a voluminous pink puffer coat.

"Good evening, Manhattan!" says the tiny woman. "My name is Polly, and for the last ten years, I have been working to create something that would change this world for the better. Something that would give back to the world, something extraordinary. There has been blood, sweat, and tears over the last ten years. There have been sacrifices along the way . . . a lot of sacrifices . . . But isn't that always the way with anything that changes the world? . . . And this is up there with penicillin, with the internet, with air travel, with anesthesia . . . In fact, it's not just *up there*, it's more than all of them put together . . .

An app that turns a human being into an ideal version of themselves . . . and you want to know the best thing about it, everyone? You already have it in your phones! Yes, the app you downloaded when you scanned the QR code for this event has automatically upgraded your devices and given you access to a world of beauty and wonder. Belle and Miranda. So, enough talk. Tell me again—who wants to be perfect?!"

The crowd yells, a sea of open faces beaming into the light of the oversized screen, where the huge face of a woman named Miranda smiles beatifically.

Jessica is stultified for a moment, some still-damaged neuron in her brain somewhere remembering the sound of those words in her ears a week ago, and now she remembers that it was not Debra's voice she heard that night as she tried to take Belle away, but it was *this* voice. It was Polly's voice. It was *her* touch against her skin, Polly who turned a phone to face them both and said (the unearthed memory hits her like a freight train) "Let's take a selfie," and it was she who pressed the button to create that flash, that bloodred burn in her eyes, that whoosh of darkness and dread before all fell quiet, before she became a perfect, pointless simulacrum of a human being, a mannequin, a blob.

It wasn't Debra, it was Polly. The second woman that Cassandra Webb said she saw in her memories. The young woman. And Polly is Miranda. And Polly has a thousand young souls in her thrall here tonight and Jessica cannot allow herself to be one of them, she cannot. She forces her way through this crowd, using too much strength, hurting people as she goes, but she can't let this happen. She storms the stage where Polly stands in the beam of a single light and she rips away Polly's mask, snatches away her dark glasses.

She sees the shocked flicker of recognition in Polly's eyes and then a flash of excitement.

"Ha," says Polly. "It's you!" She turns to face her audience, theatrically. "Ladies and gentlemen," she says. "Look who it is. It's Jessica Jones, your local super hero, who has come here tonight to . . . ?"

"If you use this app," Jessica says to the crowds, "people are going to *die*."

Polly laughs uproariously. "Yeah," she says. "Right."

"Do not use this app. Reset your phones. Get this app off your phones. Do not use this app. Please. Just don't listen to this woman. She's a psychopath. She's—"

But as she says this, Polly lifts her own phone to her face, turns it to the front camera, takes a selfie, and then moves the phone away.

Jessica looks at her and gasps. Polly's face has changed. She is taller, leaner; she looks exactly like the woman on the screen behind her.

She has turned herself into Miranda.

The crowd gasps too.

"Do you see that? *Do you see that?*" Polly yells. "Look," she says, turning her face this way and that. "Look what this app can do. This isn't a trick. This isn't a scam. This is real. You've seen it now, with your own eyes. And it's on your phones. You have it. All you have to do is take a selfie. It's that simple. Take a selfie and you will look like you always wanted to look. But wait!" She pauses, eyes the crowd playfully. "Beauty comes at a cost. If you like the results, and you want more, you will need to download the newest version of Miranda. For $24.99, you get . . ."

The crowd is already starting to use their phones. Jessica screams *"STOP!"* but the crowd ignores her. While Jessica yells, a thousand other people are holding up their phones and smiling into them, a resounding shutter click reverberates through the park, a thousand faces on a thousand screens, pouts, puckers, thumbs-up, horn signs, protruding tongues, winks, awkward grimaces, and gangster poses.

Click.

Flash.

It is done.

And even as the first thousand take their selfies, there are still more and more kids coming into Central Park, by the hundred, each holding a phone aloft.

More flashes.

More clicks.

Jessica falls to her knees.

She was too late. She couldn't stop it. It's happened.

She gazes around at a thousand young people all staring at one another's faces in awe. It works. The app works. They all look the same: perfect generic plastic faces. A girl's hair that was a glorious orange color a few seconds ago is now a creamy blond. Another young man who was small in stature is tall and broad. They all have the same full lips, wide-apart eyes, dewy skin.

And if all these children are now perfect, then what is happening under Sebastian Randall's house right now, to those two poor girls? To Amina and Audrey?

As she thinks this, the sky fills with spinning blue lights, the screech of tires against tarmac, the boom of an NYPD officer with a loud-hailer shouting, "This gathering is in direct violation of code 7-4.2 of New York State Law. Please dissolve this gathering in an orderly manner. There are officers available to lead you to a safe exit. Please follow their instructions. Please move slowly. Please do not push. I repeat. *Please follow instructions*."

Jessica watches as the thousands of children do as they are told. The frenetic energy of a few minutes ago has dissipated. Polly stands proud on the stage even as she is approached by a dozen uniformed cops.

And as Polly is marched away, her arms firmly held behind her back, Jessica sees a look of total and utter triumph on her face.

"Miranda loves you!" she calls out as she is removed. "Miranda loves you!"

* * *

Jessica calls Malcolm as she walks away from the park, blending in as best she can with the freakish-looking crowds. She jumps at the sight of a young girl who has somehow developed a unicorn horn, another who now has legs so long that her jeans sit halfway up her calves. A young boy sports improbably bulging biceps that strain at his clothes and a girl who looks like she is only about eight years old has a full set of fluorescent white teeth that glow like tombstones under the streetlights.

Is this what Polly had in mind? she wonders. Is that what she has striven for all her life? For young girls to be able to grow unicorn horns? For young boys to look like steroid-busting gym-worn bodybuilders? Did she not realize that most people's idea of "perfect" is completely wrong? Did she have any idea in fact about what her market wants?

"Malcolm," she yells into her phone when he picks up. "I got here too late. It happened. The app has launched. What's happening with the girls in the cellar? Can you still see them?"

"Yeah," Malcolm calls back. "I see them."

"How do they look?"

"Hard to tell. Just get back here, will you?"

"I'm on my way. And tell Arthur—they've got his girl. They've got Polly. She's been taken by the cops. So whatever hold he thinks she's got over him, it's done. It's finished."

She jumps into a cab and heads back to the Airbnb. It's all as she left it. Lark and Fox are huddled together on the sofa. Arthur is tied to the chair, with Luke standing over him, his arms folded across his chest, and Malcolm sits in front of the monitors, his upended bleached hair glowing like a beacon in the middle of the room.

"Look," he says, moving aside a little so that Jessica can see what he's looking at. It takes a moment for her to work it out; it's some kind of CCTV footage of another, different dark room, but suddenly the room is brightly lit and she sees that the camera has changed and it's Sebastian's cellar, and, there, is—is it?—yes, it's Elliot from the pharmacy wearing pajamas and a big puffer coat, and standing gingerly behind him is Sebastian in boxers and a T-shirt, swinging a flashlight around, looking absolutely terrified.

"Where's this taken from?" she asks.

"Hidden camera in the cellar," says Malcolm, nodding toward Arthur. "I managed to gain access to it."

"What are they doing with her?" Arthur beseeches in a reedy voice. "What are they doing with Polly?"

"They've arrested her for a public misdemeanor. I'm sure she thinks her plan is foolproof, that she'll get off with a fine and consider it part of a 'marketing campaign.' But once the cops know what I know, they'll keep her, and it's only a matter of time before she cracks and tells them all about you."

She turns her attention back to the screen, just as Elliot turns to the camera behind him and says into his phone, "What should I do now, Malcolm?"

"There's a code, apparently," Malcolm replies. "It's on the wall, that panel, just there, behind that dude."

"What panel?" says Sebastian in a pinched voice via speakerphone, his eyes wide and staring. And then his flashlight hits it: a small glass plaque attached to the wall by the foot of the steps.

Jessica hisses at herself under her breath. How did she miss that?

"Touch it," says Malcolm.

Elliot touches it and the panel lights up, revealing a keypad.

"Now type in this code: 6-0-8-6-star."

Elliot punches in the numbers, his fingers fumbling slightly. "Shit," he says, as he makes an error. "Say that again."

Malcolm reads the numbers out to Elliot again and this time the panel beeps, and Elliot turns to Sebastian and says, "Whoa. Look."

Jessica squints to see what it is they're both looking at. It's the spot on the floor where she saw the drilled-out holes, and now there is light shining up through those holes, and a metal rod has appeared, which Elliot grabs hold of and tugs at before calling over his shoulder to Sebastian, "Help me."

Sebastian rests the flashlight on the floor and grabs hold of the metal rod and Jessica holds in her breath as they both tug and tug and then the concrete surface slowly lifts and bright light floods the entire room. Sebastian and Elliot cover their eyes with their arms and recoil for a moment before peering into the cavity together, their faces uplit and eerie on the monitor.

"Oh my God," she hears Elliot say.

"What the hell?" she hears Sebastian say.

"What do I do now!" Elliot yells into his phone at Malcolm. "What do I do now!"

Malcolm turns to Arthur. "What do they do now, Cuck Boy? Tell me."

"Stop calling me that," says Arthur.

"Well, stop being one," says Malcolm.

Jessica raises a wry eyebrow at the firm tone of Malcolm's voice. It's like he's grown ten years in the hour that she's been gone.

"I can't," says Arthur. "Polly will . . ."

"Polly will spend less time in jail if those girls get out of there alive. And so will you. So tell me how to get those girls out of there. Now."

Jessica raises an eyebrow again. Go Malcolm, she thinks. Go you.

Arthur begins to struggle against his restraints. "No," he yells. "I can't. Let me go. For God's sake. Just let me go. I need to see Polly!"

"Polly Schmolly," says Luke, shoving Arthur's shoulders back hard against the wall, making him wince. "You know what happens at the end of Dorian Gray, right? He thinks he can get rid of all the shit by destroying the portrait. But it doesn't work out like that, does it? Huh? Dude ends up dead and the *portrait* ends up perfect. Dude takes all his gross shit with him to the grave. And that's what's going to happen to you both anyway, so you may as well let those girls go before it gets any worse for you. You hear what I'm saying?"

Arthur nods, rapidly, his eyes wide and watering. "Okay . . ." he says. "Okay."

Luke loosens his grip on Arthur's shoulders and Arthur gulps and says, "There are two wires, a green one, a red one. And there's a tube. Just disconnect them all."

Malcolm nods and swivels back on the chair toward the screen. "Did you hear that?" he says to Elliot.

Elliot nods. "A red one, a green one, and a tube. Got it."

The room falls silent then and they all watch the screen as Elliot gets to work.

Jessica stares at the image on the second monitor, at the two pairs of open staring eyes. They don't move. They don't blink. Are they dead? Are they alive? What are they feeling right now? she wonders. And what, she thinks with a sickening sense of dread, will they be like once they're free?

"Okay," says Elliot. "I've done that. Now what?"

Arthur wriggles in his seat. "See those big black things? Turn them all the way, counterclockwise."

The room is silent again as Elliot turns and turns, his slight body rigid with the effort, and then he grunts and groans and falls back, something clutched inside his hand, and he leans down very slowly, peers inside the cavity, and says, "Bloody hell. Bloody hell! Sebastian"—he turns to the older man—"help me. Shit. Help me."

Sebastian finally peels himself away from the wall of the room, where he's been observing in horror.

"Shit," they hear him say, as he too peers down into the cavity. "Shit."

Both men lie flat on their stomachs, their arms in the cavity. They tug and they haul and there, a moment later, is a girl. A moment later a second girl. They lie floppy, prone, wet, like sea creatures being pulled from the ocean floor.

"Are they alive?!" yells Jessica.

Elliot and Sebastian feel them for pulses, for heartbeats, for breath. Nobody in the apartment makes a sound. And then Elliot turns to the camera, his eyes bright, his face flushed with shock and awe, and he says, "Yes. They're alive. Yes."

Forty-Five

Dozens of cops arrive at the Airbnb just after eight o'clock. There are four cars on the street outside, and two more pulling up at the building. One FBI agent interviews Jessica and Luke while the others box up evidence. Fox, Lark, and Arthur have been taken in for questioning. More officers are on their way to Amber Randall's apartment. Malcolm is on his way home.

It's nearly eleven by the time she and Luke are free to go, and Jessica feels raw and filthy.

As if reading her thoughts, Luke touches her hand and says, "Wanna stay at mine?"

Jessica thinks of his clean bed linen and fridge full of good things, the fat towels that hang in neat lines from a warm rail. "Yeah," she says. "Please. But not—"

"Yeah," says Luke. "I know."

It's nearly midnight by the time they get back to his apartment. Jessica's body clock screams at her that it is five in the morning and that she should be thinking about breakfast, but she overrides the circadian confusion and takes a long, hot shower, puts on Luke's T-shirt, and uses the brand-new toothbrush he offers her.

In bed she pulls the covers up high, nestles her head against the fat, crisp pillows, and turns on her phone.

"Turn that off," Luke says gently.

"Yeah, but I want to see what's happening in England. It's morning there, there'll be new headlines."

"The headlines will still be there tomorrow. It's out of your hands now. Other people are doing their jobs. Tomorrow, I'll take you out for breakfast and you can spend the whole time looking at your phone, but now you need to sleep."

"I'm too wired to sleep."

"You want some rainstorm sounds?"

"Excuse me?"

He picks up his own phone from his nightstand. "You can have rainstorms, fans, nature sounds, waterfall? Or maybe some *plinky-plonky* music? What do you think?"

Jessica places her phone on the nightstand. "Hit me with some nature."

She closes her eyes and pushes the soles of her feet against the warm flesh of Luke's calves. She should tell him now about the baby, she thinks, right now, while they are both encased in this bond of shared experience, of exhaustion, of partnership. But she cannot find the words and she cannot find the strength and her head is filled with too much black noise right now. So instead, she lets the white noise into her consciousness, lets it swish through her head and chase away the shadows.

Five minutes later she is asleep.

Forty-Six

The doctor looms over Jessica with a small magnifying glass and a light.

"If I could just ask you to stare straight into the center of the light, please, Jessica."

She follows the doctor's instructions, and then a moment later the doctor turns off the light and sits back in her chair. "Well," she says, "any laser-induced retinal injury usually takes a long time to heal, but yours is five days old and what is very interesting is that it appears to have healed almost entirely."

"Ah, right, yes," says Jessica. "I have an, er . . . well, my body heals quicker than most people's bodies. I'm . . . you know. I have . . . certain powers."

"Oh," says the doctor, her eyes widening. "Right. I see. By what sort of time factor would you say? Roughly?"

"I dunno. I've never calculated it. But what is it?" asks Jessica. "What is the injury?"

"Like I say, it's a kind of laser burn."

"But does it penetrate any deeper than the cornea? I mean, is there anything else in me?"

"Not that I can see."

"So there's no lasting damage?"

"There's a little light scarring. But it's nearly healed. We'll have you back in a week's time for another examination, but if you're feeling okay in yourself . . . ?"

"Yeah."

"Well, then I think you're good."

The doctor smiles brightly at her and then says, "It's amazing what you've done. I mean, just incredible. It's been an honor to treat you."

Jessica grimaces slightly. "Yeah, well, I'm not so sure I feel that way."

Jessica leaves the hospital a short while later and walks slowly back to her apartment. She feels beat-up and broken. All of her aches. She wants nothing more than to walk into a bar, pull out a stool, sit on it, and order shot after shot until she's comatose. But she still has work to do. The case is not over yet.

* * *

Malcolm arrives shortly after she gets back to her office. He looks a little shell-shocked, his skin slightly sallow beneath the peroxide hair that gleams too white.

"Malcolm," she says, "how are you?"

"I'm okay." He looks drained and punished.

"What can I do for you?"

"Well, I mainly came to get paid."

"Wow. Blunt. But yeah. Sure. What did we say?"

"We didn't. But I'm happy with a couple hundred."

She nods. He helped save her life and the lives of Grace, Amina, and Audrey. It seems like a good deal. "Sure," she says. "I can PayPal it to you?"

"Yeah, cash would be better. My mom's got my phone until this is all sorted out. So, yeah."

Jessica sighs again. "I'm really sorry, Malcolm. I shouldn't have let you get involved in this. It was a bad idea. I put you in too much danger and I'm telling you, here and now, that I won't be employing your services again. Not because you're not good, but because you need to stay safe and get yourself to college. So consider yourself retired from private investigations."

"Yeah, I don't think my mom would have let me come back anyway. But it's been, genuinely, the most incredible experience of my life."

Jessica raises an eyebrow. "Seriously?"

"Yeah. Seriously. And I wanna thank you for allowing me to be a part of it. I've learned so much. Including, yeah"—he smiles wryly—"my limitations, I guess. I really thought I had Fox Randall wrapped around my finger, y'know, but turns out that I'm not as good at subterfuge as I thought I was. So . . ."

Jessica looks at him, fondly. "That's not true," she says.

"Please don't take anything bad away from this. You need to keep hold of your self-assuredness. It'll take you a long way."

Malcolm smiles again. "That's praise indeed, coming from you." He drops his gaze to the desk and then back up to Jessica. His eyes are soft and a flush rises through his cheeks. "You are the greatest human being I have ever known. It has been an honor and a privilege to work alongside you." He holds out his hand to her. "Thank you, Jessica."

Jessica blinks. "Oh," she says, "sure." Then she takes his hand and shakes it. "Now get outta here," she says teasingly.

Malcolm gives her a small bow and leaves.

Forty-Seven

Every screen that Jessica passes over the next few days has rolling news coverage of the Miranda app story. Talking heads and technology experts fill the screens with more questions about what sort of science and technology was involved, how did it happen, what does it mean for the future of the smartphone, for the future of the world? Should children be allowed to have smartphones? Should *anyone* be allowed to have smartphones? Should they be banned?

The children themselves are fine. From the moment that Amina and Audrey were released from stasis in the canister in Sebastian's cellar, the effects of the app were stopped and reversed. But questions are now being asked about the meaning of happiness, about the pressures that young people exist under these days, the unattainable images they are bombarded with every second of every day—and now even their own images when used under a filter in an app—imagine, said commentators, living under the pressure of being able to see what you would look like if you were perfect.

Away from the mainstream media, social media and its cousins are fixated on the dark underbelly of the story: the freaky family comprised of a serial killer, a witch, and a genius savant using quantum physics to turn two innocent girls into modern-day portraits of Dorian Gray, all juxtaposed against the glossy visage of Polly Devereux in a turned-up collar and oversized sunglasses, looking like a Real Housewife of somewhere or other. Reddit is overrun with threads about the so-called Freaky Family, and the stories keep coming about homeless people who went missing, playdates that resulted in memory loss, sightings of strange paraphernalia, weird interludes, creepy vibes, a sense that something was off.

And then the rest of the story breaks.

Jessica is lying on her couch eating oatmeal when it happens. She sits bolt upright, puts down the oatmeal, and grips her phone with both hands as she scrolls through the news reports.

Two sets of human remains were alongside Amina and Audrey in the underground cell beneath Sebastian's house. One set has just been identified as belonging to Debra Phipps, the *real* Debra Phipps, the eighty-four-year-old owner of the Old Farmhouse, who lived there alone for nearly fifty years before her home was taken over by Polly and her family. Her cause of death has not yet been established, but Jessica remembers what Arthur Simms told them about vessels and receptacles and how an "old" receptacle had not been powerful enough to contain the force they were attempting to absorb.

The second set of remains has been identified as being those of John Warshaw, the Harlem Vampire himself, who, it appears, died of natural causes. But the most startling revelation of all is that he appears to have been dead for at least five years, drained of all of his blood and kept in a state of mummification. The woman claiming to be Debra Phipps is still being held, refusing to speak, and Grace Partridge is still unable to cooperate. The other girls, Amina and Audrey, are both in intensive care.

For the first time since the morning in early October when she nearly let Speckles the cat escape, when Hell's Kitchen was rolling blackly with thunder and the rain came down like bullets, when she felt bad things in the air and saw the girl in the silver coat, for the first time since then, Jessica feels her head still. It's like the sensation when a background hum that you haven't noticed stops and the sudden peace that follows has a curious empty feel to it, like something's missing. It's gone. All that's left is a sense of surprise that you didn't notice the noise all along.

She has only one thing left to do.

One last loose end.

Once that's done, she will take a holiday. Amber's payment went through the day before: twenty thousand dollars.

She will use some of that and head out to one of those places that women go to in the movies when they want some space: Cape Cod, maybe, or Madison, or Providence? Windswept beaches and ramshackle clapboard seafood restaurants. Handsome weather-beaten men, and rustic cabins with open fires. She will take her unborn child, her tired and ridiculous body, and her existential crisis and she will lie with them for a while until she comes to terms with all of it. And then, when she comes back, she has to find a way to tell Luke.

But first she calls the number on her phone that says Avengers Mansion. It's answered a moment later by someone whose voice she doesn't recognize, and she says, "Hi, this is Jessica Jones. Is there anyone there I could talk to about OB-GYN stuff, for, you know, women like me?"

* * *

The screen fills with oscillating patches of black and white as the doctor swooshes the transducer around her belly. It could be the bottom of a garden pond for all Jessica can see until, suddenly, there it is.

"There," says the doctor. "There's your baby. Looking very snug in there."

"Which way is it sitting?"

"Well, look, there's the top of the head and that there"— she swooshes down again and presses hard into the flesh of Jessica's abdomen—"is a pair of adorable tiny feet."

"Oh!" says Jessica as the image starts to come together for her. "Yes! Look at that. That's . . ."

"It's amazing, isn't it?"

Jessica nods, numbly.

Then she says, "You know, and this is gonna sound crazy, but a few times after I first thought I might be pregnant, I saw her."

"Her?"

"Yeah. Her. She's a girl."

"Oh, right." The doctor moves the transducer around the image of her baby again. She does so for a full minute before saying, "It's a little early to ascertain the baby's sex and I'm not seeing anything clearly enough at this point."

"No, I already saw her. That's what I'm saying. But she wasn't a baby. She was about five years old. At first, I thought I was going nuts, you know? Losing my mind. But every time I saw her, she was so real. I could, like, see a thread hanging off her coat. And I just wondered, in your experience of treating women like me, with, you know . . ."

"Super-powers?"

"Yeah, with super-powers. Have you ever known someone to have an unborn child that could already express its powers?"

"No . . ." says the doctor, pulling off her latex gloves and dropping them in a trash can. "No, I haven't. But I could see that it might be possible in the case of a child with heightened powers. For example, if both parents had powers?" She hitches an eyebrow and Jessica feels herself flush slightly.

"Yeah," she says. "That would be the case here."

The doctor nods and for a minute Jessica thinks maybe she

knows about Luke. But then she remembers that she has a reputation, that Luke is not the only guy with super-powers she has shared a bed with in her messy life, and that the doctor is probably just wondering which one it might be.

"Well," she says, "that's kind of exciting. What was she like? When you saw her?"

"She was—well, she was spectacular, you know? I mean obviously!" Jessica laughs, nervously.

"Obviously!" the doctor returns.

"And very strong. Kinda fearless. She talked me through a rough patch over in the UK. She's kickass and beautiful and I . . ." She suddenly finds herself tearing up slightly. "I don't know if I'm going to be good enough for her."

"Oh my goodness." The doctor steps across the room and takes Jessica's hand in hers. "Jessica. No, don't ever say that. You are an incredible woman. Look what you just did in this city. Look how many people you helped and saved. How fearless you were. You are going to be more than enough for this baby—and then some. You already are!"

Jessica sniffs and nods. But she doesn't believe the doctor, and she knows she has a lot more work to do before she will be ready to accept that she can be a good enough mother, especially to a child like this who is already better than her in a hundred different ways.

"Sure," she sniffs. "Yes. Thank you."

The doctor gives her a selection of printouts from the scan, which Jessica slides inside her jacket pocket before heading out into the pale darkness of the November dusk.

Forty-Eight

"Jessica, hi, how are you?"

Jessica looks at Amber Randall on the screen of her phone. She's moving through a busy street somewhere, her face framed by the fur of a raccoon-trim hood.

"I'm good. You're back in town?"

"Yeah. We got back last night."

"Me too."

"You went away?"

"Yeah. Just a few days down by the sea."

"Good," says Amber. "That's good. And listen. I wanted to check in with you. See how you're doing?"

"I'm okay." Jessica glances around her empty office as she says this, feels the rumble of hunger in her belly from her missed breakfast, sees the unzipped backpack she still hasn't unpacked from her trip sitting in the doorway to her bedroom. "Yeah. I'm good. How are the twins?"

"Getting back to normal. I'm taking them to see a hypnotherapist, every day. It's intense. But we're getting there."

"Great," says Jessica. "That's great."

"So I have had a cancelation, for this afternoon. Three thirty. Would you be able to get over to my place? I'd love to do that session with you that I promised."

"Oh." Jessica sits up straight. This she has not been expecting. But yeah, she thinks. Yes. Only a few weeks ago, she was a hard no on the subject of therapy. Now she is a soft, tentative yes. "Right," she says, "yeah. I guess. I'll see you there. Do I need to bring anything?"

She sees Amber smile. "No, just your good self. And an open mind."

* * *

Amber is wearing a sweater with a gigantic turtleneck that looks like it's swallowing her whole, when she greets Jessica from the elevator. She peers at Jessica through oversized reading glasses and smiles warmly.

"Come through," she says, leading her across the vast lobby and into a small office set into the corner of the apartment. It has a solid plate-glass window overlooking the back of the building, and a sliding door onto a tiny terrace filled with potted plants. The room is lined with wood paneling and lit with small halogens in the ceiling.

"Do sit." She gestures at a leather sofa. "Coffee? Soda?"

"Water, thank you."

Amber pours her water from a bottle in the fridge hidden inside the cabinetry and passes it to Jessica. There is a tiny, suspended silence as Amber observes Jessica and forms a smile. Then her expression cracks and she says, "I am so, so, so sorry."

"What for?"

"For what happened to you over there. But, you know, it feels to me like there was something else, something triggering? The way you were on the phone, when you wanted me to get you back to the US. You sounded so desperate. So close to breaking. What was that, Jessica? What was it that you found so triggering about your experience over there?"

And then Jessica tells her. She has nothing left to lose now. Her mind has softened to the concept of sharing her darkest secret with people who care about her. She tells Amber about the man named Kilgrave who kept her prisoner in his apartment for six months, who exerted mind control over her and made her behave heinously, used her as a puppet to perform depraved acts of violence, brutality, and control against innocent people.

Amber shakes her head disbelievingly when she finishes. "After what you've already been through, for it to happen to you again . . . I feel so bad. And please tell me, this Kilgrave, this 'Purple Man,' he's in prison, right?"

Bam.

It's still there. Anytime Jessica hears that name, anytime she sees a flash of purple, anytime her travels take her to the neighborhood where she was imprisoned by him for all those months, her heart rate goes up, her breath catches, fight-or-flight instincts engage to a sickening degree.

"I'm sorry," says Amber. "I can see that even the mention of his name is enough to retraumatize you. Is there a name you'd prefer me to use when I refer to him?"

"Yeah. How about *it*?"

Amber nods. "Okay. So, how long ago was it that you escaped *it*?"

"Couple of years."

"And during those years, what have you done to try to heal from the injuries it inflicted on you?"

"Drink."

"Drink?"

"Yeah. I have drunk my way through it. But now . . ."

"You can't?"

"No. I can't. I still want to. But I can't."

"So what are you using as a coping mechanism now?"

"Nothing. I have nothing. Tried to get into healthy eating, but that didn't stick."

"Exercise?"

Jessica makes a scoffing noise.

"So your crutch is no longer available to you, and you haven't found a replacement crutch?"

"Correct."

"Okay. So listen, I know this is painful, but can you tell me a little about what it was like, when you were under the control of *it*? What did it feel like?"

Jessica closes her eyes and casts her mind back to a place she usually tries so hard to avoid. "It was . . . disgusting."

"Disgusting?"

"Yes. It was the most disgusting thing. He was disgusting. The things he made me do were disgusting. The things he made me watch *him* do. Doing those things to those girls he made me pick up for him. The way he made me feel. And the smell . . ." She rocks backward into the sofa and emits a low groan. She can feel bile rising from the pit of her gut. "He had this smell. I think it was a cologne. But it was mixed in with his raw . . . urgh . . . his essence, his filthy, putrid essence, turned it to a stench, and that stench was all over me, always, without him even touching me. My skin smelled of him, my hair. I couldn't get rid of that stench for so long. So many months. I showered twice a day, I got rid of all my clothes. I had a haircut, to like, here." She gestures to her jawline with her hand. "And to be someone so strong. Someone built to do good in this world. Doing such, such bad things. Like being a poet forced to write Nazi propaganda. Or a singer forced to scream. The looks on people's faces when they saw the things I did. Those girls, when they realized I had betrayed them. I just . . ."

She stops, abruptly, lets her head collapse. "I'm sorry," she says. "I'm not sure I want to talk about this."

"No. That's fine. Of course not. But I want you to know now that you smell really good." She smiles. "Your trauma, I can see it. It's crystal clear. But him—it?—that's gone."

"I'm not so sure."

"No. I promise you. You are clean."

"Hmm." Jessica wants to believe her. But she can't.

"And now you are home to somebody else." She glances down at Jessica's belly. "How is that going? All okay?"

"Yeah. I had a scan. Healthy baby living inside there doing all the things it's supposed to do."

Amber smiles warmly. "That's great news, Jessica! And I'm so relieved to hear it." She places her hand against her heart. "I still can't believe I sent you over to England in your condition and put you both in the path of so much danger. I feel a personal responsibility for you to have a healthy pregnancy. I really do. And the father . . . Have you told him yet?"

"No. No, not yet. He's out of town, visiting family down south. And I feel like I'm gonna wait, you know, until the twelve-week mark. Because . . ."

"Yeah. I get it. You don't want to hurl a hand grenade into your relationship until you know for sure."

"Exactly."

"How do you think he's going to take it?"

Jessica exhales. "No clue. He says he wouldn't want to bring kids into this world. But that was a theoretical opinion, and this isn't a theoretical kid. So." She shrugs. "I really don't know. But I do know I want to keep it. Her. I want to keep her. With or without . . . him."

The realization hit her after her scan. She and this kid, they've already bonded. She is coming, regardless of Jessica's personal circumstances.

"Good," says Amber. "That's great. And tell me. What happened in the UK, what that woman did to you . . . How are you feeling now about that?"

"Disgusted."

Amber nods. "Right," she says. "The same way the other person made you feel."

"Yeah." Jessica's eyes widen with dreadful clarity; the parallels are almost sickening. "I mean, there was no trauma involved. I wasn't abused. If anything, it was amazing to feel that way, to feel all that wonder and awe, so at peace with myself, the world around me, the way I looked. It was quite magical. But to be in that same place again, like I was before, to be used to further another person's sick fantasies, their twisted ideals, to be used like a puppet, like a pawn, like I had no . . ." She feels hard for the word and then she finds it and grabs it. *"Agency."*

Amber nods encouragingly. "Right," she says. "Exactly."

"And the feeling of that woman's dirty fingers inside my head, using *my head*. For her goals. Making me believe that something good had happened to me, something sweet, something wholesome, when in fact it was so, so bad. Making me watch those cutesy movies with her, eating popcorn together. Urgh." She growls, feels nausea rising through her just thinking of it. "It's sickening, and I still feel waves of that when I think of what I experienced. I still find myself in that beat-up old kitchen, the smell of roast lamb, dog's breath, that kind of damp old house smell. I get that a lot. And then her . . . Ophelia."

"Tell me about her? What was it like finding out that she had these powers?"

Jessica sighs. "Kinda unsurprising. Explained a lot of stuff about her, about the vibe. About *all* of it. But also, I'm kinda angry with myself for not realizing it in the moment. For going in unprepared, leaving myself open. I feel like such an idiot to *let that happen to me again*. Like I can't trust myself. Like maybe I need to just lock myself away from the world. Stay home. Become . . . I don't know. Smaller."

Amber puts her hand hard against her heart and says, "No. Please don't ever, ever do that. The world *needs* you to be big. As big as you can be. The world needs you to show us how to be better, how to be strong, how to be *women*. I mean, look at you."

Jessica wriggles a little, throws Amber a questioning look.

"You're awesome, Jessica. I would kill to be you. You're gorgeous. You're clever. You're cool. You're loving. You're scary. You are so, so strong. What those people did to you, it doesn't make you weaker, it makes you stronger. You just need to believe that. And you need to open your heart to yourself. Break through the dark. Find the light. Do you see?"

Jessica nods, just twice, feels a solitary tear fall from the corner of her eye and roll down the side of her nose.

Amber passes her a tissue from a box and smiles at her. "And tell me, what's next for you? Are you working another case?"

"No. Not yet. I'm thinking . . ."

Amber eyes her questioningly.

"Yeah. Get to twelve weeks with this"—she pats her stomach—"then I'll tell the baby's father. Then I'm gonna slow down. And yeah . . . a new chapter."

"What does that look like to you?"

"It looks like . . . well, I will definitely still wanna work. I'm thinking maybe journalism?"

"Oh! Right, of course. I can see the crossover. Did you study? Go to college?"

"No. Nothing like that. But I have connections. I know people. And I can, you know, string a pretty good sentence together, believe it or not. I just think, being a mother, I need something more stable, less dangerous. But I will need something more than motherhood. I know that much about myself."

Amber nods. "That makes me happy," she says.

"Yeah," says Jessica, a warm plume of realization building in her gut. "Yeah. Me too."

Amber's eyes go to a clock on the wall. "So, Jessica, we have another forty minutes. I'd really love to use that time to do some work with you around this idea of disgust. Of uncleanliness. This idea that other people's dirty fingerprints are still in there"—she taps her temple with her fingertip—"in your psyche. But it will mean doing some deep digging. How do you feel about that? Are you ready?"

Jessica breathes in hard, thinks of the little girl sitting tight inside her right now, thinks of the sort of mother she wants that little girl to have, and she nods. "Sure," she says, feeling ready for this, at last. "Let's go."

Forty-Nine

"Hey." Jessica slides across the stone steps, making room for Luke as he approaches his apartment building holding two coffee cups.

"Decaf?" he says, passing one to her. "You sure?"

"Yeah," she says. "I already had my two hundred milligrams of caffeine today."

"They have a limit on that?"

"Yeah. They have a limit on that. But not for everybody."

"Then who for?"

She smiles. Not yet. Not yet.

"Thanks for coming," says Luke. "I've been missing you."

"You have?"

"Yeah. I really have. And I want to say that I should tell ya that over the last couple of months I seem to . . . I seem to be

441

thinking about you a lot. More than I was admitting to myself, you know what I mean?"

Jessica nods, her breath held.

"And I know you and me, we are just how *we are* with each other . . . I just wanted to tell you that I'm here. And I'm, well, *I'm here*. If you . . . I don't know. I just think about you, a lot."

Jessica laughs dryly. "You *like* me?"

Luke laughs too, and nods. "Yeah," he says.

"*Like me* like me?"

"We in high school now?" He throws her a playful sideways look.

Jessica takes in a hard breath and then lets it out again. "I'm pregnant."

Luke doesn't respond.

"It's yours," she says. "And that's . . . that's what I came here to tell you. And that's . . . yeah."

Luke still doesn't respond, and Jessica's heart races sickeningly with the thought of her unborn child being rejected by the man that she loves.

Finally he glances up at her. "Do you want it?"

She sighs. "Very very very much."

And then Luke's face opens, a smile subsumes every part of it, his eyes sparkle.

"All right, then," he says, taking her hands in his. "All right, then. New chapter."

ONE YEAR LATER
THE PULSE
Staff Writer: Jessica Jones

Three weeks ago, at the Old Bailey in London, UK, Polly Devereux, 32, was sentenced to thirty-eight years in prison without parole for the murders of Debra Phipps, 84, of the Old Farmhouse in Barton Wallop, and the abduction, false imprisonment, and attempted murders of Grace Partridge, Amina Sultanov, and Audrey Hill-Lock, all now 17. A year ago, I was working as an undercover private investigator on a case involving two New York teenagers who'd returned from their summer in the UK acting and looking like different people.

At first I thought I was looking at nothing more than a *Summer I Turned Pretty*-style glow-up, but soon it became clear that something very strange was afoot, when I heard Fox Randall's skin cracking and him intoning the name *Miranda* into the empty spaces of an uptown dinery in Manhattan. I immediately agreed to take on the investigation.

My time in the UK led me to a rambling farmhouse in the

Essex countryside, the house where Sebastian Randall, father to the Randall twins, told me his children had spent nearly all their time that summer. Randall was an unassuming man, a little bit of a dreamer, scared of spiders and ghosts, often talking about a secret girlfriend, who was also helping him to renovate his house. Little did I know that on that very first meeting with Randall I had already been given nearly all the answers to the mystery I was being paid to solve. For there, even as my hands caressed the newly laid concrete floor of his cellar and I wondered at the holes drilled there, even as I listened to Sebastian Randall tell me about the super-powered water pump this secret girlfriend had gotten installed for him down there, just below my feet two young girls were trapped in a kind of hell that even the most ardent horror movie fan could barely envisage: wired up, drugged up, engineered into human receptacles for darkness and misery.

At that point, as I stood in Sebastian Randall's cellar assuring him that there were no spiders down there, Amina and Audrey, the so-called Dorian Gray Girls, were absorbing the imperfections of a handful of early adopters of Devereux's as yet unlaunched app. But this was just the very beginning of the journey. Devereux used Fox Randall's love for Grace Partridge (who he knew only as "Belle") as a way to control him, sending him emails purporting to be from "Belle," beseeching him to do everything she asked him to do, including spreading the word about the Miranda app and making sure flyers were posted in nearly every school bathroom in the city. Within weeks of the Randall twins' return to New York,

Devereux and her partner in crime, Arthur Simms, were themselves on their way to America, and Amina and Audrey were hours away from being entirely subsumed, their consciousnesses and physical forms about to be overwhelmed by the insecurities and perceived "defects" of two thousand or more children in Central Park.

As it is, the girls are still a long way from recovering from their yearslong ordeal, and who knows if they ever will entirely. But as Devereux commences her sentence (Arthur Simms is due to be sentenced next month), we are only just beginning to understand the processes that underpinned the events of last year. In order to do so, we need to go right back in time to the summer of 1986, when a beautiful young British woman named Ophelia Simms entered a bar in a Harlem backstreet and started making small talk with the bartender, a soft-spoken man named John Warshaw, who had a fondness for blood.

I spoke to Ophelia in a Zoom call last week from the prison in Essex, where she has been held for the past year. She looked old, much older than the smooth-skinned woman I remembered from my time in Barton Wallop.

"This is what I look like without the cream," she says, referring to the special unguents and serums that she and Warshaw used to cook up together to keep her looking less than her two hundred plus years. "It's fine. I only wanted to look good for *him*. Once he was gone, I didn't really care anymore."

I ask how it worked, the cream. She tells me she doesn't

know. She never knew. John Warshaw was the only one who knew how the creams really worked, and now he was dead.

I ask her about the eighties thing: Why did people under the influence of her creams and unguents became obsessed with the era's music and movies? Why did I want to watch *Pretty in Pink* and sing The The songs? What was that all about?

She smiles, a small, secret smile. "That was John," she says. "He put that in there. He had developed a way of extracting the essence of a human being from their blood, and he used *my essence* to make the creams and serums that drugged those girls, my super-powers, my mind control, my timelessness, but also, just . . . *me*. He loved me so much, you know? He wanted to leave a bit of me in everyone, like a—What do they call it? Like an *Easter egg*. So he left that in the serums: my passions, my peccadilloes, my preferences."

I ask her about that meeting, in Harlem, what it was that led her from Portsmouth to New York all those years ago.

"His face. I saw his face, in a music paper. I never even used to buy that paper, but something made me pick it up that day, when I passed a paper shop. I didn't know how he was going to change my life, I just knew he would. I had this power back then, long since faded, along with all of my other powers, but back then I could read people across oceans, I could access their inner selves, just by seeing a picture of them. When I saw his face, I knew that he would be able to fix me."

"Fix you?"

"Yes, cure me of my immortality. Give me a normal life. Change my life. Finally."

And boy did Warshaw change her life. Using his ill-gotten knowledge about blood, gleaned from years of playing with it obsessively, he was able to somehow recalibrate her DNA, excise her immortality, make her, as she calls it, *normal*. It was what she'd wanted for so long: to live like everyone else, to be rid of the immortality that had, for whatever reason, kept her from bearing children.

"Why was he so obsessed with blood?" I ask.

And as is so often the way with fetishes, with murderous obsessions, it began with the smallest thing. "He was driving with his family down a freeway, the traffic was backed up, cars were slowing down to see what was causing it, there was a road accident; John was about seven years old and he said he looked out the window and he saw a kid, his age, spread out on the tarmac, and all around him was this thick puddle of blood, the sun shone down and turned the black blood to maroon, made it gleam, made it shine, he said it looked like rubies, like something precious and beautiful. He wanted, in that moment, to run his fingers through it to know what it felt like, all that blood, glistening and alive, while the child lay dead in the center of it. He said it struck him as a living entity, a thing with its own life force, its own . . . personality."

The results of Warshaw's work on Ophelia's blood didn't happen overnight. It took years and years for Ophelia to see the first signs emerge of aging. A solitary white hair, she tells me, along her part. She plucked it out with awe, and, she says, she cried. She was pregnant not too long after that, and then followed twenty years of relative normality. Well, apart from her husband's horrible hobby, of course.

"I sometimes wished he'd stop, of course I did. I'm no killer. I love children. I hated it really. But what could I do? I loved him, he'd given me the gift of mortality, which gave me the gift of my son. He'd made me a mother. So I left him to it. All men have their hobbies. This was his."

No doubt the family could have gotten to the end of their years like this, just another slightly weird family—every street has one—minding their own business. They could have taken their secret with them to their graves.

But then, thirteen years ago, something seismic and uncontrollable happened to the tight-knit trio in the improbable form of a caramel-blond, five-foot-three living nightmare named Polly Devereux.

Ophelia sighs when I mention her name.

"I knew from the very first moment I set eyes on her that she'd been sent by the universe to destroy me. I knew it. And from that moment on I was waiting for her to return. And she did. But what I hadn't expected"—Ophelia's eyes loom large from the screen of my laptop—"was that she'd have my son in her grips. When I saw the way he looked at her, I knew I'd lost him. I was middle-aged by then, and with every year that I aged my powers waned accordingly. I tried to control her, but I couldn't. She was so much younger than me, so much more powerful. And not in the way that I had been powerful. She didn't have super-powers. She had a more earthly power.

Polly Devereux is a psychopath. Pure and simple. And psychopathy is kind of a super-power in many ways. To not care about the effect on other people of your actions. To decide what's important and use innocent people to achieve your goals at any cost. Bend people to your will. Polly had that crazed blind ambition. I'd never had ambition, not in any of my two hundred years. I was a dreamer all my life. All I ever wanted was love. So I let her in, and I gave her what she wanted, just to keep my son close."

I was newly pregnant when I met Ophelia in Barton Wallop last year. I was in a bad place; I had a drinking problem, a man problem, an everything problem. But the person growing inside me, my daughter, Danielle, she was already making me try harder to be a better person, and since she came into the world, I try every day to be the sort of mother, the sort of *human*, I think she deserves.

Ophelia seems to want to be understood, but I tell her I find it hard to empathize with her justification for her actions. She kept three young girls drugged and controlled for over a year just to stay close to her son. She watched as two of those girls were piled into the back of a van and driven off to be buried alive. She turned a blind eye to her husband's killing and was complicit in bringing about the terrible events of October last year when thousands of young people were put at risk of permanent damage or death. Thousands of *other people's* children.

I ask her about this. How, I ask her, does her love for her son give her the right to endanger other people's children? If motherhood has taught me anything, it is how precious all children are and how precarious and perilous parents' existences are, each and every day. Your child is your heart taken out of your body. To harm another person's child is to harm that person ten times over.

She sighs. "What did *you* give up to become a mother?" she asks.

I want to say I gave up drinking, but I know that's not what she means.

"I gave up everything," she says. "Literally, everything. Immortality! Do you know what that feels like? And my other powers. I gave them all up, to be a mother. And I would do anything it took to make it worth the sacrifice. *Anything*."

There are so many other questions I want to ask Ophelia, but a prison official tells us our time is up. Still, I shoot in one more, just before the clock ticks down.

"Tell me about Mr. Smith," I say.

The old woman stares at me. "My cat?"

"Yeah."

Mr. Smith is Ophelia's familiar. She has owned him since he was a kitten—back in 1811. Mr. Smith is still alive. The people who rescued Debra Phipps's dogs rescued him too.

"Someone will adopt him, I assume?" says Ophelia.

"I assume."

"And they will wonder why he doesn't die?" She laughs wryly.

"Yes. They will wonder why he doesn't die." I pause. "But you will die?"

"Yes. Thank God. I will die. And it will be soon. And I will be glad."

Our session ends. I press a red button that says leave and I am staring at a black screen. I don't know what I have learned from my talk with Ophelia, but I know that I feel sad. I feel sad for the lonely girl who walked alone through life for almost two hundred years, and I feel sad for the lonely mother whose son found someone he loved better than her after only twenty years.

Three days after I spoke to Ophelia, she passed away. Prison guards said that she was smiling.

A bit after that I spoke to Grace Partridge from Barcelona, where she now lives with her parents near the boutique hotel that they own and run there. Since the events of last summer, Grace has become one of the most followed people on social media. At the time of writing she has eighteen million followers on Instagram and the number goes up another ten every few minutes. She posts as Not Perfect, Just Grace, and her message is loud and clear:

Don't be perfect. Be real.

She was recently listed as one of *Time* magazine's Twenty Most Influential Under Twenty and tours schools and colleges talking to children about the toxic and negative effects of social media and advising big corporations on how to mitigate the inherent malignancy. I ask Grace how she feels about Ophelia's death, and she is, strangely, but also maybe understandably, sad.

"She really loved me," she says, "weird as it sounds, and I know it does. But she really did. She loved all three of us."

"And what about Amina and Audrey, or the Dorian Gray Girls, as they are now widely known? Do you still see them? Are you still friends?"

"That's hard," she says. "It's been . . ." She sighs. "We were so close, before. We were everything to each other. We all lived and breathed the same air, had the same obsessions. And we were so excited to be part of Peach's plans, to help her with this huge project. I mean, what idiots we were, in retrospect. What total idiots. And then one day they were taken away and I was left behind."

"Why do you think you were left behind?"

"I had to be on the other side of the process. They had to test it on someone. And they chose me."

"Why you?"

She sighs. "I don't know why me. But I think . . . I think it was Debra's choice. Ophelia. Because as mad as it sounds, she really loved me. I was her favorite. And that's what caused this rift. Because what happened to me was bad, but Amina and Audrey, they have experienced something that no human being should ever have to experience. Their physical and mental trauma is too immense to even begin to comprehend. Locked away down there for months, their beautiful bodies, their beautiful faces, their beautiful minds being used as receptacles for other people's defects, other people's misery, sucking it all away, taking it in against their will." Grace shudders. "I hope one day they will be strong enough to find their places in the world again. But it's going to be a long, long journey."

"Is there anything you'd like to say to them, if they're reading?"

Grace glances away for a few seconds and I see her composing her thoughts into a message that she can share, not just with her former friends, but also with the wider world. She looks back up at me and I see how strongly she feels about what she is about to say. "We were perfect before Miranda, if only we'd all known it. Perfection isn't a goal. Perfection is a *scam*. You were perfect then and you're perfect now. We all are. Every single one of us. Trust me."

And now I look at my beautiful baby girl and I know that that is my single greatest job, as her mother. To let her know that she is already perfect. That perfect isn't in a bottle or on a screen or in a crazy black light made out of voodoo and high tech. Perfect is not defined by people who make money out of your insecurities, nor is it defined by a male gaze or the opinions of those who wish to demean you. Perfect is what you are when you are listening only to the beat of your own heart, the sound of your own feet on the road ahead of you, the one pure voice that exists inside you telling you that you are fine, just the way you are.

Marvel Crime continues with all-new novels
featuring your favorite Marvel characters,
written by your favorite authors!

LUKE CAGE
as written by S.A. Cosby

DAREDEVIL
as written by Alex Segura

Acknowledgments

My gratitude in the very first instance must go to the endlessly patient and caring Adam Wilson at Hyperion Avenue Books. Adam commissioned me to write this novel way back in January 2022 and might on occasion have rued the day, as I wrote and rewrote and missed deadlines and extended deadlines and kept him working right up to the wire to get this book out into the world. Thank you for taking a chance on me and giving me the opportunity to do something different and difficult and exciting and special. I was deeply honored to be asked and am still honored to be a part of this. Thank you for your faith and kindness.

Thanks also, of course, to Selina, my UK editor, who allowed me to take a break from my annual thriller-writing schedule to do this special project. I know it's made your life a little tricky, and I'm grateful to you for facilitating it and being such a huge and important part of it.

Thank you to the wonderful Dr. Will Brooker. Will is the professor of Film and Cultural Studies at Kingston University in South London who authored (amongst many other things!) *The Truth About Lisa Jewell*, a book about the writing of my twentieth novel, *The Family Remains*. He is also a Marvel aficionado and was kind enough to read my work in progress at a number of key junctures and was singlehandedly responsible for sending me back from the abyss of cray back in February 2023 by telling me that what I'd written was "total bobbins." Any bobbins that still remain are entirely of my own making.

Crucially, thank you so much to Javed Ghazi, my big-brained friend who came to the rescue when I was trying to work out how to pull together the closing chapters of this book by coming up with a perfect solution to a technical issue that had been tying me in knots.

And thank you to Sarah Singer from Marvel, who was amazingly helpful and supportive in guiding me through Marvel continuity and making sure my book was glitch-free and Marvel-approved!

Thank you to my family for putting up with me being stressed and grumpy for most of 2023—my husband said that this is the hardest he's ever seen me working in all the twenty-five years I've been at this job! And thank you to you, the reader, for picking this book up, for whatever reason—be it loyalty, curiosity, Marvel fandom, by accident, or just because you liked the look of it. I really hope you've enjoyed the journey, even if it wasn't quite what you were expecting!

And lastly, thank you so much to Jessica Jones herself. My God, I love her! She was absolutely the reason why I said yes to writing a full-length novel in a genre that I am unfamiliar with—who wouldn't want to spend a year with Jessica Jones?! She's absolutely my favorite person in the Marvel Universe, she was before I started writing this book, and she is even more so now. Jessica, I will miss you. Thank you for being so awesome.

And thank you, Brian Michael Bendis and Michael Gaydos, for your genius in bringing her into the world in the first place.